SLOP

The Wild Boar Nation

Keith T. Bishop

2013

SLOP – The Wild Boar Nation
Keith T. Bishop

Copyeditors: Charlotte Clebosky Kelley, Averyl Re, and Adept Word Management

Cover Design: Lauren Kelley

Published in the United States by 80 – 20 Productions
ISBN 978-0-9892063-0-3

SLOP – *The Wild Boar Nation* is dedicated to:

THE WORLD

For every living soul: regardless of nationality, political affiliation,
religious denomination, race, color, or creed
who rejects extremism and intolerance – everywhere.

While fictional and real characters are used in *SLOP – The Wild Boar
Nation,* all events in book are fictitious.

Enjoy!

Keith T. Bishop

About the Author

Born and raised in Dayton, Ohio, Keith graduated from Centerville High School before earning his BBA at the University of Cincinnati in 1983 with majors in finance and management. Upon graduation, Mr. Bishop moved to Chicago and acquired the science of trading options under the tutelage of one of Chicago's largest derivatives traders at that time and currently one of the most renowned card players in Las Vegas.

Later, Mr. Bishop had the honor of forging a trading partnership with one of Chicago's most prominent privately held derivative firms. Years later, the firm was sold to Goldman Sachs before the founder came within days of winning the 2004 Democratic nomination of Illinois for the U.S. Senate. It was this election that propelled a relatively unknown, Barack Hussein Obama, to win the senate seat. Four years later, he was elected President of the United States.

Mr. Bishop moved to London in 1994 and collaborated with another key partner in a London trading operation before returning to the U.S., where he entered the energy trading business.

After working on the energy trading desks for two major firms, Mr. Bishop joined a large software company. Seven years later he resigned to write *SLOP - The Wild Boar Nation.*

It was his three contemporaries, though, all different but with one thing in common—utilizing mathematics to quantify anything and everything—that encouraged Mr. Bishop to think beyond the first derivative. Without their mentorships over twenty years ago, *SLOP* would never have been written.

A proud father of three daughters and a son, Mr. Bishop seeks to obliterate the remaining political barriers to realize a true democracy, a democracy following the will of an educated and tolerant majority, not an intense and fervent minority.

Mr. Bishop's heroes are his deceased parents, Ralph T. Bishop and Rosemary Bishop, who not only encouraged individuality but also the responsibility of family, community, state, nation, and the world.

Dust

Amarillo, Texas; September 1936

Dust, wind, heat. The rancher surveyed the blighted landscape as he grudgingly sipped from his contaminated canteen.

"Be damned. Ain't nothin' no good no more," he thought.

The week's second cloud of dust spewed thousands of feet into the air and descended upon him like a blanket of death. Battered tumbleweeds collected along the fence lines, providing a netting to accumulate more dirt. The amassing topsoil left waves of earth where fences once jutted out from the landscape. Piles of dirt six, seven, eight feet high leaned against the west side of his home and barn. How much more could he take? Brown water, decimated crops, his barn on the verge of collapse, and fencing buried like an above-ground grave. The only thing fresh was the smoke from the bonfire fueled by dead brush from the previous night.

His two remaining cattle were feeble and disease-ridden while the hogs suffered from flystrike. The grotesque lesions and the maggots feeding in the swine's open wounds turned his stomach. Their only relief from the insufferable heat was wallowing in their own wastes. The cattle looked on in envy.

The healthy left long ago—California, Florida, anywhere but here. He, like the remaining ranchers, suffered the same plight. Weakness from lingering illness bound them to what had become a vast wasteland.

"When the hell's it gonna rain again, bless God? Give us a damned gullywasher? Fill up the cricks and the ponds again? Git me some sweet water back in my well? When the hell? Ain't there no God no more?" he wondered.

Abigail had mercifully died a few years earlier in this godforsaken drought. The thought of her trying to endure the foul-tasting water brought bitterness and despair. A buzzard that had made its presence known in the past week brought unease.

The sun hadn't even risen yet, and it was already hot. Slowly, the rancher parceled out a portion of feed that was only a fifth of that needed for healthy livestock. It was certainly more than he fed himself. The hogs skirmished over the last remnants of scraps; the few buckets of filthy water would be depleted soon after sunrise. Chickens scurried around him, pecking at illusions of feed.

As the farmer looked over his pasture, he squinted to see through the early morning dawn. The aging man shuffled closer to the field and through the gate, where he grimaced at the sight of what had transpired just hours earlier. His two remaining cattle, dead. Their carcasses nearly picked clean, fluids drained, leaving not a hint of their tainted juices. Coyotes—not the first time they had ravished his livestock.

Morning light. The landowner harnessed his beloved horse to the cart. As they trampled across the cracked earth, the wheels creaked, and the rancher felt as if he were riding on solid rock. He begged forgiveness for straining his already lame horse and prayed it would not be its last effort. Favoring his right front hoof, the horse haltingly approached the two dead cattle lying feet apart. No doubt the coyotes had surrounded them and had sunk their teeth into their frail legs while the pathetic animals offered little or no resistance. The rancher collected the remains, leaving nothing behind. The sight of the ever-present buzzard circling above the spoiled dirt haunted him.

Balance. The cattle's loss would be the hogs', horse's, and the human's gain. What little remained went to the survivors. It was the way. The rancher saved the best of the inedible meat for himself. The horse was offered slivers of flesh while the rest of the remains went to the swine. Every ounce, including bone, was ground up and mixed with a little wheat, corn, and water to create what he thought would be the best slop the pigs had had in months. Not equals, the chickens would die next.

The rancher wearily glanced at the damn buzzard perched in the tree just across the hog pen. The scavenger eyed the frail one's every move, patiently waiting. Knowing it was only a matter of time.

Dust. No one, no thing could escape it. Winds incessantly whipped across the lands, transforming daylight into dusk, smothering everything in its path with coat after coat of dust. Crevices overflowed. The constant taste of dirt reminded most living things that their lungs were quickly filling too, causing mass sickness as the environment spiraled out of control. The buzzard thrived.

Several days later. Although the dust provided relief from the blistering noon sun, its curse continued. Dust caked the rancher's nostrils, ears, and mouth. Suffering from dust pneumonia: fever and periodic coughs, producing yellowish-green mud-like mucus brought anguish with every breath. The well still provided water, but it was unbearable to see or smell, let alone drink. The heat, dust, and lack of rain had also taken its toll on the small abode, the barn, the gates.

The rancher deliriously stumbled around his tract, gasping as he stood amidst ruins.

He could feel the relentless scavenger. Like always, it was perched in the tree alongside the pen, waiting, knowing. Understanding the dire circumstances, the lifelong homesteader unlatched the pen's gate and turned away without looking back. He untied his horse and withdrew back to his home.

Staring out the dust-coated kitchen window, the rancher watched as the hogs began to wander, rooting for anything. The horse remained close. The chickens, long dead, were only an image in his mind. The buzzard stretched its wings.

The next morning, nothing moved on the property. The hog pen abandoned, the horse gone. A new veil of dust obscured any trace of their existence. No signs of life existed, except for the buzzard. The rancher, motionless in bed, collected his first layer of dust. The buzzard knew.

Vanished

Outskirts of Amarillo; May 2012

Nearly a hundred strong, the sounder roamed the Texas Panhandle with authority. The landscape proved ideal for the beasts and was home for hundreds of additional sounders. Blessed with a keen sense of smell and hearing, suitable vision, extraordinary physical characteristics, and remarkable intelligence unmatched by other animals, the boars' dominance over the region went unchallenged. Besides drought, their only threat had been the occasional coyote, owl, or bobcat poaching a piglet. However, that gradually changed when the first real risk to their existence emerged. Modern ranchers began converting more and more lands, renowned for their natural landscape and home to the wild pigs, to raise cattle, sheep, chickens, cotton, and wheat. Conflict was inevitable, the outcome uncertain.

Omnivores, wild boars located and rooted out the best available vegetation adeptly; they were well-equipped for such tasks. With a sense of smell five times greater than drug-sniffing dogs and the ability to run up to thirty miles per hour, the boars also easily preyed on small animals. But this group of hogs was of no ordinary stock. This sounder was larger, its members stronger and more merciless than the typical feral hog. And its habitat was slowly eroding in size and bounty.

Typically yielding two litters per year and four to five piglets per litter, the nation of wild boars multiplied rapidly. Splinter groups formed, traveling dozens of miles to establish new domains. Producing the most aggressive males, this line of sounders ran roughshod over the region and laid to waste anything in its path as it tore up the land, devouring both plants and animals alike. And as its size and strength evolved, so did its aggressiveness, appetite for blood, and relentless determination to preserve its terrain.

The sounders populating much of the country comprised a minority of pureblood Russian boars, descended from animals imported to the United States in the early 1900s for sport. The majority of the communities were made up of boars that had cross-mated with domesticated hogs that had escaped into the wild and mated with other feral hogs. Yet, the Russian blood dominated the packs until now, until this particular sounder.

Their hides were light brown or black in color with a cream or tan tint on the tips of their elongated bristles. Their ears, tails, and legs were darker than the rest of their coat. These boars had longer legs and snouts, larger heads, and shorter tails than the typical wild hog and periodically topped 500 pounds. Every physical feature was enhanced, including the calloused scar tissue on the skin which created a shield of armor. With upper and lower tusks averaging five to six inches in length, the sets complemented one another as the upper tusks served to sharpen the concave-shaped lower tusks.

One evening, soon after dark, while roaming the outskirts of their region, the sounder came upon a newly established herd of cattle. The pack's heightened temperament overcame the unruly beasts, and in an instant, the sounder of nearly a hundred boars charged from the edge of the thicket across a small buffer of native grasses before reaching the pasture.

They rapidly descended upon the weakest, while the bulk of the cattle clambered away. Working almost as one beast, the boars savagely rammed, gored, and maimed five calves. As the helpless creatures desperately attempted to regain their leg strength, additional boars joined the fray. Once down, the cattle's fate was determined. The boars were unyielding as their razor-sharp, piercing tusks repeatedly speared the calves. Their teeth and jaw bones locked onto the young animals' hindquarters, necks, and underbellies. The creatures' demises were as quick as they were gruesome.

Within moments of the attack, a few vultures hovered overhead. But there would be no reward for their promptness. True to their nature, the boars devoured in whole every sliver of their prey. They left nothing. Heads, tails, hooves, bones—gone. Even the dirt, soaked in blood and guts, was scoured clean. In a few brief moments, five calves had vanished from the face of the earth.

Full Moon

Perimeter of Sounder Territory; Texas Panhandle; August 2012

Between the drought and the continued expansion of lands being converted for man's needs, the wild hogs escalated their attacks on unsuspecting cattle and sheep to maintain their well-being. After a series of losses, ranchers became more vigilant in protecting their livestock. Banding together, landowners employed specially trained guard dogs to alert them. Many installed portable lighting to illuminate large areas near water troughs where livestock herded. Combined, the methods enabled the ranchers to kill and maim dozens of boars in a few months' time.

Consequently, the sounders began expanding their range westward in search of their staples: roots, nuts, grass, fruits, mushrooms, bugs, worms, rodents, rabbits, and even birds. But the new terrain was also filled with danger. The most abundant area discovered by the pigs abutted a nondescript housing plat plopped down amidst a diverse habitat of plant and animal life. The extensive neighborhood's unceasing activity at first alarmed the boars and prevented them from fully exploiting the wealth of available resources. For the boars to flourish, adaptation was critical.

And adapt they did.

Survival became a game of cat and mouse as the residential area became the favored target of the opportunistic omnivores. Pet dogs, cats, and caged animals became the next easiest prey for the bloodthirsty beasts. The boars quickly learned dogs secured to chains were the equivalent of boar-nation fast food. If the owners failed to hear the few squeals of the dog when the boars struck, the next morning they might find only partial threads of a collar lying on the ground, an empty chain, and a few splotches of blood.

Attacks on pets became habitual. Within a few months, dozens of dogs, cats, chickens, and even caged pet rabbits were ravaged. The boars brutally ransacked cages with their powerful snouts and incredible strength, destroying all shelters before consuming, in entirety, the live bodies of these domesticated animals. Facing little resistance, the boars grew fearless as their thirst for blood became unquenchable.

The community adapted as well. Pets normally left outside or subject to danger were no longer exposed. They were either housed indoors or in insurmountable shelters. Though a few homeowners successfully shot and killed several boars as they feasted on their beloved pets, nothing deterred the creatures. The turning point for the community, however, was just one incident away.

On the last day of August, during a full moon, the most aggressive sounder staged the unthinkable: an attack on a dog kennel on the edge of town. To date, it was the most devastating, disturbing, and disruptive wildlife attack in local history. The boars systematically attacked, killed, and ate three dozen dogs of various breeds quartered in outdoor kennels. The chain-link fencing encompassing the dogs proved no match for the highly aggressive, blood-seeking omnivores. Pens crumbled like matchsticks as they thrust their 400-pound bodies into the ordinarily reliable fencing. Protected by their rugged hide, the boars effortlessly deflected cuts, scrapes, and bruises from the steel-chain fencing to breach the pens and accomplish the massacre. The only things left were a few frayed collars and dog tags. Every shard of flesh and bone had been consumed, and the pools of blood were nearly licked dry.

The town was abuzz. The entire Panhandle contemplated a mass extermination of boars throughout the region. The boars had gone mad, and the community demanded action. Public debate ensued. No one could agree on how, when, or who would eradicate the boars. Weeks passed without further significant incidents, and the public's concern faded. Unbeknownst to man, three key factors—drought, dwindling lands, and an emerging brain disease—conspired at the same time to turn the wild boar into one of the most destructive wildlife species in modern history.

Meanwhile, intuitively the boars retreated, waiting.

So too, the vultures.

Four Boarsmen

Mid-Town; New York City, New York; Wednesday, October 31, 2012

Jimmy Richter sipped his Johnnie Walker Blue and surveyed the room to see which of the finest ladies at Club Felix was going to have the pleasure of his company and his bed that night. The bar rarely disappointed him in its choice of exotic women available for the taking. And the taking was never difficult. He possessed a lanky body with a precise, tapered haircut and spoke with a languid West Texas drawl, a drawl few women could place because New York bitches didn't know the difference between Amarillo, where he was born in 1980, and Atlanta. Dressed in his customary Anderson & Sheppard bespoke suit and custom-cobbled G.J. Cleverley & Co. shoes, Jimmy never went home alone any night he did not choose to.

He was the eldest of four brothers, which included twins David and Daniel and the youngest brother, Carl. He first perfected the art of baiting women while competing against his brothers back home. The siblings shared their triumphs over family dinners, and his father, James Richter Sr., kept a running tally of his sons' accomplishments, pitting them against each other in their libidinal rivalries. None of the boys, especially Jimmy, ever established, let alone appreciated, a committed relationship. It was a foreign concept, really. He knew enough about women to achieve what he wanted. Texas women wanted hearts and flowers before fucking; they expected politeness, chivalry, deference. New York ladies wanted men straight-forward and damn-near arrogant and in fact seemed to get more excited and infatuated the more egotistical a man became. He found the East Coast bitches, especially the ones from overseas, far less tedious.

Jimmy was a commodities trader who had successfully launched his own hedge fund. He saw the world as an amalgam of markets, just waiting to be conquered. He made no exceptions for Club Felix. He considered the women he eyed as merely commodities to be bought, sold, traded, bought again, sold short, taken delivery of, and even allowed to expire. Commodity option contracts, to be exact—his option to dine, to date, to vacation with, and of course to sleep with at his whim. And he relished pursuing multiple avenues. It amused him to evaluate and label each one as he looked them over. The blonde in the black mini was at market top, while the one in the power-red business suit, strutting four-inch, pointy-toed pumps was definitely stopped out. He gave the late-20s brunette 'AAA' status just on her firm body and attitude alone, but the redhead rated only a 'BBB'. If he considered her at all, possessing an abandonment option was mandatory. They were all fungible commodities, just of different grades; nothing more, nothing less. And certainly nothing to involve himself with on any kind of permanent basis. As his daddy always said, "Every man is born free and equal; if he gets married, it's his own damned fault." (Although this was more amusingly anecdotal than gospel on his dad's part since the senior Richter taught his sons that they were in fact without equal.) Jimmy did not consider his approach to women fraudulent. Any woman looking for something permanent in a bar was only deluding herself.

Jimmy knew of men who first scoped out the ladies he thought of as 'CCC' before going for higher-ranked women. The men considered the low-rated floozies a hedge: In case they bombed out at the higher levels, they still had something to take home and fuck. Jimmy never looked for a fallback position. He assumed every woman needed him more than he needed her. And by his choosing her, he conveyed to his woman-of-the-moment that he was a favor and a delight beyond anything she could attain elsewhere. So, no, he never needed to fall back.

Not that women didn't have their place in his life. They filled his hunger for the hunt, for competition. It's just that some made the chase too fucking pathetically easy, which was why he really liked the bitches who acted as if their pussies were only for the elite. The ones like Elaine, whom he had pursued for months and who was just on the verge of giving in. The ones to whom he had to prove he was equal to their status. The ones rivals didn't have the cojones to chase, thinking they were off limits, including his staff's better halves; halves his staff knew Jimmy considered fair game as well.

Finishing his second drink, Jimmy determined it was time to exercise his option on Ms. 'AAA'. He had already learned her name was Carol. Looking her over on previous occasions, he knew her confidence, her preference for Jimmy Choo stilettos, and her exquisite dress sense that perfectly enhanced her toned body. The trader realized that knowing about fashion and the names of all the bastards who made money at it was just part of mastering the game. A game like all others he was intent on winning.

In his quest to sway Carol, at calculated intervals over the past few weeks, he had sent her drinks with his business card and his compliments; drawing her in, but not yet making his move. She had acknowledged him and had given him her name, but, like the haughty princess she envisioned herself to be, did not encourage him. Just as well. Clearly she was worthy of the chase, but would never be his equal. He enjoyed the game.

He made eye contact with her now. She held his gaze then looked away, cool and serene.

Earlier, when he ordered his second Johnnie Walker Blue, he had also ordered the gimlet he knew Carol preferred. It was one of the things he found interesting about her. Most women seemed to order Grey Goose martinis with vulgar regularity; it was almost a tribal badge of New York's single women. Carol drank gimlets, clean with Bombay Sapphire and Rose's lime. He had given the waitress his card to deliver along with the gimlet. On the back, he had written "8:00 @ Per Se."

He knew the restaurant was a little bit of a cliché, but that was the point. Besides, he had already scored once that day, and it had put him in the mood to reel Carol in and score again.

Earlier during trading, after weeks of falling prices, he had been purchasing West Texas Intermediate Crude Oil at higher and higher prices. Traders had speculated the market would momentarily bounce and go back up to previous levels before selling off again. And it *had* rallied. With the market now churning in an area of resistance where it was widely expected to fail, Jimmy daringly placed an aggressive bid to purchase a large quantity of call options to precipitously drive up the price of crude oil.

On the phone with several brokers, Jimmy barked, "Where's the fuckin' offer on the December 90 call? Get me an offer for 10,000 contracts, all or none. I'll pay $0.47 right now! If you don't get me a market, you won't be doin' business with me . . . maybe ever! I need an offer right now, god dammit, before this thing explodes!"

The order spooked traders, causing the price of crude oil to breach a perceived area of resistance. The upside breakout brought a multitude of buy orders, all from weak hands, allowing Jimmy to sell every long contract and more, flipping his position from a bullish stance to a bearish outlook. The rally quickly lost momentum. Jimmy canceled his order to purchase the call options and furiously began selling more futures contracts, fueling a panic that took the price all the way back to the morning's lows. With no intent to buy, the bluff worked perfectly. Jimmy told himself not one trader in fifty had the cast-iron huevos to make that bold of a move, but he figured that's what separated the poseurs from the big dogs. And the market's whipsaw action set him up perfectly for the next time crude touched those highs. Then, he figured, while everyone believed the market would fail again at that level, he would quietly add to his long-term bullish position, fulfilling his belief crude oil would soon surpass its all-time highs of more than $145 per barrel.

Of course, creating undue volatility in the markets wasn't going to do any good to the bottom line for the end consumers, including the millions of fellow citizens driving the country's roadways, but that wasn't his concern. He certainly had no problem affording gas for his Ferrari 599 GTB Fiorano, or any problem affording the Fiorano itself, for that matter. Not that he gave a good god-damn about the soccer moms in their minivans anyway. He answered to his investors, and they were mighty pleased with how they believed he increased their portfolios.

Where he made his profits that day made it even sweeter. Being from Texas, crude oil and natural gas futures were two of his favorite commodities, and he relished the notoriety of conquering those products. The size and volatile nature of both markets enabled Jimmy to place big, brash bets, trades that left his cohorts in awe. All under the age of thirty-five, ego-driven, and full of testosterone, the fifteen traders Jimmy employed strived to one day be just like him. His colleagues had their own preferred markets as well, but rarely ventured outside their specialties. Jimmy, however, traded them all. He lived and breathed every market. It was his way of making sure everyone recognized that it was his firm. And that he was the king of all things traded, women included.

When others felt uncertain of a market's direction, Jimmy seemed to recognize discernible trends. It didn't matter which market it involved, whether the market was moving higher, lower, or trending nowhere. Jimmy appeared to have the innate ability to calculate the next potential move. Time after time, he initiated a trade in concert with his colleagues only to exit the trade moments or days later while his partners hung on just long enough to suffer significant losses. On the other hand, just as his fellow traders exited a position in fear of losses, Jimmy confidently rode the storm for a few minutes, hours, even days longer, and reaped the rewards; rewards he made sure all the others knew about. There was never a dispute about Jimmy's impeccable timing in everything he did.

In the middle of digits on screens flashing green and red as prices went higher or lower, amid the shouting and the fierce concentration as millions of dollars traded hands, Jimmy and the others bantered. In the office they cursed, taunted one another, and traded "fuck yous" as frequently as they traded wheat, soybeans, corn, cattle, pork bellies, gold, silver, currencies, stocks, bonds, oil, and natural gas. Jimmy valued and encouraged the creative tension. Along with his name at the head of the firm, Jimmy appropriated for himself the title of Smack-Talker Supreme. He always seemed to get the first, and often the last, demoralizing word in. He was gifted with the ability to think quickly, and his ingenious and frequent use of profanity trumped every New York, New Jersey, or Connecticut native.

As he approached Carol, he knew he was ready to twist that ingenuity to another purpose.

"Are you ready to go?" he asked her.

She looked at him coolly, ran one hand through her sleek dark hair, and studied him with blue eyes skillfully edged in black. "What makes you think I would go anywhere with you?"

"Because I know somethin' about you."

"Yeah? And what do you know?"

"That you are a beautiful, intelligent woman. And intelligent women know how to take advantage of opportunities that arise," he said as he smiled his best smile, where one corner of his mouth went up and accentuated his dimple. He knew the impact that dimple had on females. Coupled with his drawl, it was damn near irresistible. Too many women before Carol had said so.

"Oh? And what 'opportunity' do you perceive has 'arisen' in this case?" she asked him pointedly.

"Dinner with me at Per Se. Surely, dinner at one of Manhattan's finest restaurants beats the hell out of take-out. The offer only stands, by the way, until 7:30." At that moment, it was exactly 7:15.

"And what makes you think you're going to get a table at Per Se?"

"And what makes you think I can't?" he said, knowing that at least two days a week he had long-standing reservations.

"You sound like . . . that guy," Carol remarked, removing the straw from her drink and placing it between her lips.

"Tim McGraw?" Jimmy wondered, as he watched her gently bite the end of her straw.

"No . . . that Matthew guy. Matthew . . . McConaughey."

"Well, that could be. Seein' as how we both grew up in Texas. Do you think he's attractive?" he asked her.

She removed the straw from her lips and stirred her drink. "Maybe," she replied.

"Well then, darlin'. Perhaps it's high time someone confirm your opinion of Texas men."

And it was really that easy. Not because he said anything particularly clever, but because of the way he said it—knowing he was the best man she was likely to encounter on that, or any other night. And by 7:30, they were out the door, headed to Per Se.

Not especially a record, but still a respectable showing. Jimmy imagined to himself how he would relate this event if he were he still sharing conquests with his brothers and dad. He wondered what James Sr. would say about his progress so far with Carol. Of his three brothers, Jimmy was closest to the youngest, Carl; oftentimes the rivalry ended up Jimmy and Carl against the twins. Their father demanded from each of the boys proficiency in everything they tried. And then he made sure they tried just about everything.

Each of the Richter progeny was raised to be experts with firearms. Jimmy, with his dad's help, fired his first shot from a small pistol at age four. Training for the boys was as extensive as the family's cache of guns. There were at least five of every type of pistol, shotgun, and high-powered rifle: one for his dad and one for each of the four sons. The family kept well over a hundred guns under lock and key in the aptly named "Gun Room."

By the time Jimmy was fourteen, if he and his brothers weren't participating in target practice, they were shooting anything that moved. From squirrels to deer, snakes to antelope, all were fair game. But the one animal he especially had passion for hunting was wild boar. Considered vermin, the state allowed hogs to be hunted year-round, day or night, with no limits. Jimmy didn't need any further invitation to pursue his preferred pastime. And hunt he did.

Over his young lifetime, Jimmy and his brothers had slaughtered over three thousand wild hogs. It was not uncommon for them to ambush a sounder and, among the four of them, kill more than fifteen boars in a single attack. Using high-powered rifles (his favorite being the Nosler M48 TGR 2010 with a hand-lapped custom barrel—popular for hardcore big-game hunters) and coordinating their attack as precisely as a commando team, the brothers killed in volume. And since wild hogs were a major nuisance—destroying pastures, ravaging crops, and occasionally killing livestock—ranchers and private land owners gave the Richter family carte blanche to track and kill as many hogs as their hearts desired. The brothers' abilities to systematically wipe out almost an entire sounder in one strike earned them the title "The Four Boarsmen." Locals joked that if it weren't for the Richter family, the boar population would have grown tenfold instead of just tripling in the past several years.

Jimmy also excelled at sports, but he pursued one particular sport with the same passion he gave to hog hunting. Within an hour of Jimmy holding a gun for the first time, he was also swinging a nine iron. Being V.I.P. members of the most exclusive country club in the area gave the Richter scions access to year-round lessons and unlimited play. In addition, James Sr. brought one, if not all of the boys, along on a myriad of outings, often traveling by private plane to meet clients for golf excursions. The clients respected the fact that the senior Richter took such personal interest in the welfare of his sons and was preparing them for a life of unlimited success. And in the future, they too would bring their sons to carry on the family traditions. Not only did the Richter boys have the opportunity to master one of the key business gateways, golf, but the clients' loyalty became unwavering as they, too, espoused the importance of family. Of even greater significance, well before attending college the boys had established a diverse, powerful network from which to prosper.

As with firearms and golf, James Sr. introduced Jimmy to trading at an early age. Jimmy's dad was the most successful investment manager in the Southwest. He controlled the largest brokerage accounts in West Texas, Phoenix, and the nearby cities of Albuquerque and Oklahoma City. His contacts were extensive, powerful, and loyal. One of these associates enabled Jimmy to launch the hedge fund.

The business was based on the Richter family's guiding principles: "Just win, no matter how." Even the hedge fund's name, "At All Costs," implied that losing was not an option. The firm generally used the moniker AAC. When potential investors learned of the actual name, they usually made their decision whether or not to invest right then and there. Prospective investors either became alarmed and immediately terminated any investment considerations, or the prospect said, "Those are the type of people I want managing my money."

Jimmy liked it that way. As far as he was concerned, it immediately separated the winners from the losers. And he did not want to associate with the latter.

AAC controlled nearly $5 billion and aggressively sought more. Their returns had been extraordinary and, while Jimmy's greatest gains were captured in the gold and oil markets, he always considered his biggest coup to be in pork bellies. While the pork-belly market was relatively small compared to other commodities, whenever the opportunity to profit arose, Jimmy jumped in aggressively. And it was this assertiveness in the early phases of At All Costs that enabled him to nearly double the firm's assets in the first six months of operations. Soon after that, monies from Panhandle contacts and beyond began pouring in, increasing the firm's investment capital fourfold. Considering his passion for hog hunting, Jimmy always thought it was apropos pork bellies was his "go-to market" in trading and the cornerstone of his initial success.

At Per Se, Jimmy didn't feel the need to be overt in outlining his assets. Carol had ridden there in the Fiorano. And women like her knew very well how to match dollar signs to men's clothing and their cars. In addition, the familiarity with which they were greeted at Per Se spoke for him.

By the second course, he knew with certainty he would not go home alone.

The Swim

Amarillo; Thursday, November 1, 2012

The first day of November brought beautiful blue skies to Amarillo. It had been nearly seven weeks since the bloodletting attack on the dog kennel. Although the incident had not been forgotten, state officials, including Animal Control, the Texas Department of Parks and Wildlife, Texas Wildlife Services Program, and the county sheriff were unable to agree upon a solution: a remedy that would effectively eradicate a significant percentage of the wild hogs without compromising or endangering other wildlife or the environment. One resident, employed by Bell Helicopter, suggested that hunters destroy the vermin with automatic rifles from the air.

He argued, "If Governor Palin could hunt in Alaska from a chopper, why the hell can't Texans do the same?"

The entire council readily agreed. "Kill the damn irritants from the air!"

But when the number crunchers revealed the total expenditures, the votes were instantly null and void. The insurance cost alone would require more than the entire discretionary budget allocated for the next two years. There was no simple solution. Everyone merely hoped the problem would just cease to exist; nevertheless, all parties remained uneasy. The fact that a horde of wild boars could decimate a kennel, leaving fencing and poles in a tangled web and devour three dozen dogs of various sizes and breeds was unsettling to say the least. The graphic images of the onslaught still resonated throughout the community. A kennel in complete shambles, minute blood stains splattered over the entire complex and few, if any, remains to be found. And then . . .

Early that afternoon, a trio of boars ran wild through the urban streets of Amarillo. Initially, the scenario was as chaotic as a scene from the Keystone Cops. The first news team to arrive reported the chase involved both the Amarillo Police and Animal Control Departments. The reporter stated that two adult hogs and one piglet ran unfettered through neighborhoods, rummaging through yards, knocking over patio furniture, potted plants, and outdoor grills. She then detailed how the hogs couldn't resist rooting for potatoes and were almost cornered in a small garden in a resident's backyard. The police, however, were reluctant to fire upon the beasts in such a densely populated area, and in a matter of minutes the boars were off and running to their next random destination.

People were amused by the sight of three pigs darting through the parking lot of Buffalo Wild Wings and then down the busy thoroughfare before arriving at John S. Stiff Memorial Park, southwest of downtown Amarillo. The pigs ran by the playground, skateboard park, and picnic areas before leaping into the small lake and swimming to the other side. Fortunately for the pursuers, the swim across McDonald Lake provided them time to position themselves to safely destroy the trio. Unfortunately, dozens of people—all recognizing a prime photo opportunity when they saw it— ignored police orders and flocked to the area surrounding the lake. Until this time, the hogs had not displayed any aggression toward the spectators and had attempted to avoid any contact whatsoever. But that changed in an instant.

Unwilling to fire with so many people nearby, Animal Control snared the piglet as it emerged from the lake just seconds after the adult hogs. Its squeals alerted the two full-grown boars, who immediately wheeled around to see the two men struggling to restrain the piglet by its hind legs. In an instant, from no more than thirty yards away, both beasts were in full sprint toward the officers. It all happened so quickly that the men had barely let go of the piglet before the female boar, weighing nearly two hundred fifty pounds, struck the first officer full force, sending him sprawling and screaming in agony. The second officer barely avoided being pummeled, only to witness the largest hog that had just missed him turn on a dime and take aim at his colleague lying on his side withering in pain. The male boar slammed into the fallen assistant, sending its spike-like tusks into his midsection. The startled shrieks of the witnesses drowned out the cries of the victim. Just moments before, the onlookers had been entertained by the spectacle of police and Animal Control clumsily chasing two hogs and a piglet through the streets, residents' yards, and the park; then helplessly watching as the animals swam across the lake. Now the bystanders were terrified.

When the nearest police officer fired a shot into the air, the boars went on the run again. As they sprinted across two empty soccer fields, officers on foot gave chase while a squad car jumped the curb, quickly accelerated, and rumbled across the open field in fervent pursuit. The animals, in unfamiliar territory, found themselves cornered, unable to bypass the park's bordering fence. Determined to escape, they violently spun their massive bodies around and faced the oncoming vehicle. The officers immediately stopped their squad car, flung open their doors, and took dead aim at the agitated hogs. Less than twenty yards away, the two adult boars charged again. Without hesitation, the officers peppered the enraged animals with their .40 caliber Glock 22 handguns. The female hog collapsed on the third shot, but the male didn't succumb until the fifth bullet scored a direct hit to his neck. The hog fell just feet from the officers. The piglet trailing behind was destroyed seconds later by back-to-back shots.

Within minutes, a cadre of police, media, and witnesses swarmed the area. Sirens had quieted, but a multitude of flashing lights created a surreal setting. The wounded Animal Control officer was placed on a stretcher and put into one of the three ambulances that had arrived. A significant amount of blood trickled from his stomach wounds, but perhaps the most gruesome of his injuries was to his shin where the powerful boar had struck him in full stride just below the knee. The compound fracture exposing his protruding tibia bone was evidence of the strength and fury of the species. Those gathering around the scene pushed and shoved their way through the crowd in their attempts to get close-up shots of the dead animals, which immediately made their way online. Despite the officer's condition, most ignored his plight, except to take photographs with their cell phones of his battered body being loaded onto the gurney and into the ambulance. Instead, everyone was more interested in the boars. The media shouted out questions to any officer who looked their way.

"Where did the boars come from?"

"Were they exotic pets that escaped?"

"Weren't they in a garden less than a half-mile from here?"

"Why didn't the police shoot them earlier?"

"Did you *have* to shoot the piglet?"

Viral

Mid-Town; New York City; Thursday, November 1, 2012; 5:35 P.M.

"Jimmy, what the fuck is goin' on in Amariller? Holy friggin' shit, pigs gone wild? Not for nothin', but what in the hell type of friggin' town did you grow up in? It's the twenty friggin' first century, and you still have the Wild West there? And what is this shit about wild pigs destroyin' a kennel and eatin' a bunch of dogs a couple months ago? That's friggin' wicked wild. What kind of animals do you breed in Texas?"

Most of the time Mark spoke with the clipped, precise pronunciation of American newscaster English with only the faintest hint of the Boston "pahk-the-cah" non-rhotacisms. But when he was at play, and particularly when he was excited, he reverted to the dialect of the lower middle-class, triple-decker Southie from which he escaped only by the virtue of his brains and some hefty scholarships. Today, he was most definitely at play. Rarely did he have such an enticing opportunity to harass Jimmy and his obsessive pride of Texas. Mark would never allow such an opportunity to slide. His harangue was about as many words anyone had ever delivered to Jimmy without rebuttal, but he had caught his boss off-guard with his rapid-fire assault. Jimmy was trying to read the headlines on his monitor at the same time Mark's verbal shots were being lobbed one after another about his hometown and state. Mocking Amarillo, or anywhere in Texas for that matter, was an act of war to Jimmy. Mark and Jimmy both knew some form of retribution would follow, sooner rather than later.

"Just slow down the ten-gallon mouth there, asshole," Jimmy admonished Mark as he clicked on a link in the article and began watching a video. The story had gone viral. Numerous YouTube clips were circulating, depicting various scenes of the entire episode. Video captured the hogs in one backyard, knocking over a patio table and three chairs, then rooting in a flower bed prior to tipping over a grill. That was entertaining enough. A second video displayed two adult hogs galloping down a neighborhood street, darting, crisscrossing, and making their way from one YouTube moment to the next; all the while the piglet tried to keep up. That was downright hilarious. But wild boars in the middle of town? Then the pigs stopped for about ninety seconds to uproot potatoes in a small garden. All captured live! Another clip showed a number of kids chasing after the pigs as if they were trying to catch their runaway puppies. More video showed the pigs scurrying through the park, passing the playground and skateboard ramps. Watching police and Animal Control in futile pursuit brought more laughter and mocking of the officials. The looks on the faces of the Animal Control officers were priceless when the pigs ran straight into the lake and began swimming across.

Jimmy, Mark, and the handful of other traders who remained were hysterical. But the two videos that accounted for several million downloads in just hours were the brutal attack on the Animal Control officer and then the shooting of the three hogs. The men were engrossed and watched the epic episodes time and time again.

"Fucking hogs! Jesus Christ, those things are nasty! Look at the sinister-looking faces on those ugly-ass things! Are they always that vicious? Did you see how that thing clocked that guy? Knocked him right on his ass!

Nobody on the Jets can hit that hard. Then the other one fucking gored him. Right in the fucking gut!"

"Hell yeah!" Jimmy bellowed to Steve and the other awestruck traders. With their type "A" personalities, it took a lot to impress this crew. But the hogs' ferociousness certainly astounded them.

"Y'all know how many of those bastards I've killed?" Jimmy bragged. "Damn near a thousand, I'll bet. Me and my brothers hunt those big-ass pricks all the time! They're meaner than a skillet full of rattlesnakes. And we have more of 'em in Texas than you can shake a stick at. They damn near have taken over the place. I tell ya what, not only are they mean, they're fuckin' smart too. Smart motherfuckers. I'm serious as the business end of a .45. They don't surrender to anyone or anything except maybe mountain lions and wolves. Damn coyotes won't even fuck with 'em."

Elliot was shocked. "Are you kidding me? Wild pigs? Are they just in Texas or what?"

"Elliot, you dumbass, haven't you ever heard of Hogzilla?" Steve said trying to make up for his previous ignorance.

"They're everywhere," Jimmy assured him. "I'm headin' down there for Thanksgiving, and you can rest assured, I'll blast as many of those sons-abitches as possible. My twin brothers won't be able to make it, but my little brother Carl will be there, and we're gonna make up for lost time. I'm gonna get in three, four nights huntin' pigs. It's better than sex. And there's no limit, so we can blow away as many as we have bullets for. And I never run out of bullets! It's like fuckin' a new chick every few minutes."

"You can kill as many as you want?" asked Kevin.

"You betcha. Check this shit out!" Jimmy said as he clicked open a folder of photos on his computer. Quickly sorting through the pictures, Jimmy found the series he was looking for. Everyone crowded around his terminal to get a closer look.

"These are from last Christmas." Jimmy pulled up about a dozen photos of himself and his brothers hog hunting. The first photo showed Jimmy and his brothers standing on a heap of about fifteen dead hogs.

"We Santa Anna-ed this mess of hogs and killed all but three of 'em in about twenty seconds. They're called pigs for a reason; we just left that pile to rot! Gave those damn buzzards their own form of slop!" claimed Jimmy as he skimmed through the pictures. Finding a close-up photo, he zoomed in on a pig's head and snout to show off the animal's hideous features.

"They're disgusting!" commented Robert.

"Hell, I want to go!" Kevin declared. "Kill some fucking wild boars!"

Steve agreed, "Count me in. Hell yeah!"

"Come on. Bettah than sex?" Mark was skeptical. "Na-ah, I don't think so."

By the time the excitement peaked, Steve, Kevin, Mark, Elliot, and three others all wanted to hunt wild hogs. Hell, they were ready to leave right then. Jimmy, being Jimmy, egged on his cohorts, belittling them by telling them they weren't man enough to hunt the beasts. "Hell," he told them, "You motherfuckers'll pro'bly shit in your pants and scream like little girls the first time a boar comes at ya. I'd have to save your sissy asses. I'm gonna hunt, not play Boy Scout with a bunch of pansy-ass pissants."

The lively boasting of who was going to kill the first, the largest, and the most pigs continued. Jimmy had some decisions to make.

Jimmy loved a crowd, but he believed hunting with more than four people was inherently dangerous, and his brother was going to be there as well. Besides, markets never sleep. The meat of the office couldn't all be gone at the same time. Like everything Jimmy did, the final decision about who would go would be determined by reason. *His* reasons. Mark was Jimmy's best friend and, like himself, highly accomplished in most everything he did, including hunting. And considering that in his mind he had already chosen Steve, a complete novice at hunting, Jimmy knew he needed Mark to mentor Steve so he himself could focus on killing the first, the largest, and the most number of boars. Therefore, without question, Mark and Steve were in. Jimmy chose Steve because of his recent run of success trading energy products. He had earned large profits in both the oil and natural gas markets in the last month. Jimmy deemed these as two of the most lucrative markets going forward and wanted to reward Steve and encourage him to produce even more, to rival Mark.

On the other hand, Elliot didn't have the sense God gave a goose. He hadn't even heard of wild pigs and probably had never slept in a tent before. So he was out. Kevin was the final selection. While not an expert by any means, Kevin claimed to be a competent hunter who could fend for himself. Besides, he would wipe Jimmy's ass if asked to. Kevin was a preeminent gofer without being labeled as one. Jimmy liked that. But, more importantly, Jimmy wanted to evaluate Kevin outside the office. Kevin just wasn't making it, and Jimmy wanted to verify if it was time to cut bait with him or not. And there was nothing better than being in the thickets hunting wild boar to judge someone's intestinal fortitude.

The entourage consisted of five eager hunters, including Carl and himself. While not ideal, and by no means comparable to hunting with his three brothers, Jimmy considered it workable. It was set, the faction served a purpose. The group would fly out of New York early the Friday evening prior to Thanksgiving week. They would hunt Saturday, Sunday, and Monday before the gang flew back on Tuesday morning. Jimmy would remain in Amarillo to celebrate Thanksgiving with his father, Carl, and a host of friends and relatives. The rest of the office staff would have to settle for the frozen pork Jimmy promised to ship them after the holidays.

The Call

Waco, Texas; Friday, November 2, 2012; 10:18 A.M.

"Ted!" the gangly man answered the phone. He had bushy sideburns and a distinctive one-inch-wide graying strip of beard that ran from his lip to his lower chin.

"Hey, it's Derek! You hear about those fuckin' pigs in Amarillo?" his closest friend asked.

"Yep, sure did," Ted replied.

"Runnin' through the streets, gorin' people in the gut. We need to get up 'ere 'n hunt 'em sum bitches down! That's the type of crazy game I love. Can't wait to blow their fuckin' heads off!" exclaimed Derek.

"Damn straight!" Ted quickly replied before being cut off again.

"Let's leave t'night! Haven't shot a thing in a week! I'm gettin' an itchy trigger-finger."

"Pardner, love to, but can't right now," Ted explained, reluctant to pass up the opportunity to shoot or to blow things up, both activities he loved. "I have some shit to do this weekend. I'm tied up for nearly the next two weeks. I barely have time to hunt here at my own ranch. I might be able to go later that second week."

"Fuck! Ya cain't go any sooner?" Derek asked in desperation.

"Can't, cowboy."

Derek sighed on the other end of the line. "Damn! C'mon! Lock up a date, man! We need to rid the earth of those vermin just like that cockroach in the White House. His ass is out of there in just a few days. Clint's already sent the chair for Romney to sit in," the native Texan declared.

Ted, who lived on a sprawling ranch and hunted more than 300 days a year, thought about it and suggested, "Shit, how 'bout Thursday, the fifteenth? We'll leave early, 'bout five or so. We can be on the other side of Fort Worth before all those damn hippies and liberal fucks are awake, jammin' the roads as they sip their fancy coffee bullshit, or whatever the hell they drink. Half-milk, half-brew, that revoltin' mixed color. Should make it to Palo Duro b'fore noon."

"I'm in. And fuck Obama! Already voted for Romney. Cain't wait for that porch monkey to go back to Kenya," Derek bitterly rambled.

"I'll pick yer ass up at five. We're gonna bag us up the wildest of the wild boars, whole bunch of 'em. I'll bring a shitload of ammo," Ted promised.

"Hell yeah! We're gonna to put those pigs in their place. Damn vermin are just like the liberals, thinkin' everyone's equal," said Derek before both men hung up.

Duty

Jimmy's Penthouse; Upper East Side; New York City; Saturday, November 3, 2012; 3:15 P.M.

Jimmy fucked her. He fucked her some more. Then abruptly flipped her over onto her belly and entered her again. In, out, and back in again as he firmly cupped her breasts. He was rough with her, and she enjoyed the fine line between pleasure and pain. Elaine's moans bordered on screams of pleasure. In the course of an hour, she reached several highs she had never experienced before.

It was his duty.

Target Practice

Shooting Range; New York City; Tuesday, November 6, 2012; 6:15 P.M.

"You're all one of 'em," Jimmy chided his partners. He looked around at the crowd. "Right now, all these cocksuckers look like their mouths have overloaded their tails. These city boys are no hunters. Bunch of amateurs, I say. Steve, buddy, by the time I'm done teaching you, ya better be showing some damn potential. Kevin, I sure as hell hope you can shoot better than ya trade 'cause ya can't trade for shit."

"Come on, that last spike in natty was bullshit," Kevin protested, referring to the recent rise in natural gas prices. "We're going to frack the shit out of this land. Be so much gas forced out of the earth, be no place to store it," he argued further, trying to defend his bearish trading position.

"God dammit, Kevin, I swear to the good Lord above, you'd fuck up a two-car funeral," Jimmy told him, exasperated. "The only gas I'm smellin' is comin' from you. Steve killed it in the past month, abso-fuckin'-lutely. Damn near fifty million. The markets move in waves. They don't just go in one direction forever. Gas ain't goin' to zero, dammit! I told ya over and over, a position's like a two-dollar whore: useful for gettin' the job done, but don't get married to it. Steve scored in crude too. How much did he make last month in crude, about thirty, eighty million last month in energy? What the fuck have you done, besides screw up the nat-gas position, then piss away the move in gold because you wouldn't divorce that short bitch in gas? Ya gotta ride that position like ya ride a bull at the rodeo—know how and when to get on, know exactly how long to stay on, and know how and when to get off. Ya get off too soon, you're stuck with nothin'. Ya get off at the wrong time or in the wrong way, that son-abitch is gonna turn on ya and stomp ya all to hell. Gotta play the angles. See an openin', ya fuckin' take it! Ya take that bitch 'n ride it 'til ya find the next best wave. If it's not workin', ya get the fuck out. It's that simple. The market's a bitch. Our bitch. Just like what's happenin' in the White House t'night. There's *gotta* be some changes. Get that Muslim-loving socialist, liberal fuck out of there, so we can get our bitch in there. Why I ever let y'all, and I mean EVER, have offsettin' positions, even if it's just b'tween books is just fuckin' stupid. While you were so worried 'bout your short position in natural gas, we lost real opportunities to profit, and ya missed opportunities elsewhere. Remember the name of the firm! What is it? I'll tell ya what it is. It's At All Costs. That's its fuckin' name! AAC, At All Costs!"

Kevin was feeling the pressure, and he hated it. Not making money was bad. Losing money was insufferable. Jimmy was nothing less than brutal. But this was nothing new. The pressures in the office never ceased. The bantering and innuendos were as sharp and pointed as a boar's tusk. You either performed, or else. There was no room for mediocrity, let alone losers.

Kevin regretted not closing his short position in natural gas when he had a gain of nearly $25 million. Instead, he stayed short even as the market began to rise again, wiping out $10 million of the $25 million in profits he had booked. To make matters worse, he added to his short position, betting the price would decline just as Steve was madly buying natural gas. Before he knew it, the market went up another 4 percent, and he lost all of his profits and was now sitting on a loss of $7 million.

"Turning a $25 million profit into a $7 million loss in two weeks damn sure didn't earn me any street cred at the office," he thought to himself. Especially since his third quarter was anything but stellar.

Jimmy planned the night of target practice moments after he determined who was going to fly to Amarillo for the boar massacre. And again, like everything else, he implemented a regimented plan. Leave the office by five-thirty to be at the shooting range by six, ready to practice by six-thirty. The goal was to get a little practice in and to make sure Steve and Kevin were up-to-snuff handling high-powered rifles. Jimmy wanted to shoot a pistol as well. The group had decided to practice for an hour before heading out to dinner and a few drinks. Jimmy would have his customary Johnnie Walker scotch, but only a few. The team knew Jimmy was utterly intolerant of excessive drinking. Drunks or druggies were not allowed in his inner circle. The guys knew three drinks was the limit. Any amount beyond that was unacceptable and grounds for permanent exile. If the conversation continued beyond what was expected, water, tea, or a soft drink was ordered. As always, the objective was to be home by ten, so they could be in the office by six the next morning.

Jimmy believed, "You develop the plan, execute it, adjust as necessary, but always follow the integrity of the plan." It was uncustomary for him to deviate much.

But tonight, Jimmy strayed.

Making a phone call just before the first shot, Jimmy told everyone something had come up and he had to leave. "Mark, make sure these amateurs can handle a rifle. No faggots are allowed to hunt with me. Remember, they'll be usin' my Noslers. We have five of 'em. You can all use 'em if ya want. But make sure these guys are ready."

"Muthah a'Gawd. Yah friggin' kiddin' me, right?" Mark asked. "Whaddya, bookin' on me heah? Why not just ask me to cawna the wheat mahket next? Shit!"

"Quit bitchin'! If anyone can do it, it's you. Afterwards, go have dinner, enjoy yourselves, and determine some odds b'tween our wanna-be boar slayers on who gets the first, the largest, and the most boars. I'm takin' Steve straight up 'cross the board," Jimmy responded. The continued shots at Kevin were starting to be felt by all. And just like that, Jimmy left.

Within thirty minutes, Mark was already pissed. Steve was showing some ability, and his confidence was growing with every hit. But he was still a novice. Target practice is not the same as shooting outdoors: the lighting, the distractions, and knowing that a wild boar may charge—nostrils flaring, tusks positioned to gore the hell out of you. Those factors made hitting the target harder. A lot harder! But Kevin?

During the office discussion, Kevin stated that it had been a while, but that he used to shoot all the time and was pretty good. In actuality, he was no better than an advanced amateur. Basically, he sucked and grew worse throughout the practice, missing his target time and time again. By the end of the session, Steve's and Kevin's skills and confidence levels had crisscrossed like a damn pairs trade in the stock market.

In his mind, Mark pictured what the chart looked like. Steve's initial value resembled a penny-stock while Kevin's was priced like an unloved blue-chip equity. By mid-session their lines had crossed, and the trend never stopped. Steve's value surged and closed at a high; meanwhile, Kevin's price closed at session's lows. In the end, Steve had no profits yet, but there was a lot of potential revenue. Kevin was bankrupt. And Mark's imaginary chart of Steve's and Kevin's stock prices reflected that.

Over dinner Mark tried to minimize the collateral damage. He could see the tension and pressure crushing Kevin and tried to make light of the situation at the office as well as at the range. Exchanging past war stories, Mark made every attempt to artfully pump up Kevin. He realized the hunt was Jimmy's way of testing Kevin and that his boss's law of the land was simple. Weak people die. Or at least don't work for AAC.

While Mark delicately worked on Kevin, he couldn't help but notice Steve's growing confidence and ever-so-subtle jabs at Kevin. Mark sensed that Steve knew Kevin was ripe for the kill. And Kevin's demise would benefit Steve more than anyone. Steve was becoming Jimmy's new favorite. With Kevin out of the picture, the capital employed by him would be divvied up amongst the group. And Steve was confident the lion's share would go to him. Another law of the land, at AAC, it was "kill or be killed."

Kevin ordered a fourth, then a fifth Johnnie Walker Double Black. Mark joined him. Steve sipped the remnants of his third drink. Their conversation veered away from the markets and boars. Nothing was following script tonight. Mark asked Steve about his plans for the holiday after the hunt.

"I'll head back home to Connecticut. Spend some time with my parents and sister."

On Friday, his girlfriend would arrive to meet his parents for the first time, and he was confident they would love her. Mark had seen pictures of her and knew she was beautiful, elegant, and highly educated like Steve. Life couldn't be going better for him.

Mark reengaged Kevin; it was a rehashing of a few hours ago. The only thing positive for Kevin was that he and his wife were anxious to get their new standard poodle. Their old one had died last month. Mark couldn't block out the imaginary chart reoccurring in his head: two stocks, both in the same industry; one full of vigor, expectations, and moving higher. The other? In the middle of a death spiral.

It was ten forty-five before anyone arrived home.

Nip Then a Bite

Jimmy's Penthouse; Tuesday, November 6, 2012; 7:20 P.M.

Jimmy answered the knock at the door. They embraced well before the door closed. He immediately had one hand fondling her breast and the other squeezing and rubbing her ass.

Within minutes, both were naked in Jimmy's bed, passionately touching, kissing, and licking each other. Elaine playfully nibbled on Jimmy's earlobe. A nip on Jimmy's neck resulted in a tormenting bite on her breast. Again he played rough with her. She enjoyed it even more the second time, and she let him know it, feel it. Elaine could feel the moistness between her legs, and she craved that high again. She was willing to do anything to achieve it.

Jimmy didn't disappoint. For ninety minutes he stroked her, fondled her, pinned her while madly thrusting inside her. This time her moans turned to screams. And when she screamed, he squeezed her and pumped even harder, manhandling her in every way. It was what she wanted; it was his duty.

Elaine was light-headed and tried to catch her breath, somewhat surprised but not shocked Jimmy was able to take her to an even more intense high than just a few days ago. She lay in Jimmy's bed and tried to count how many times she had actually climaxed.

Jimmy got dressed and went into his office. His sole focus, Mitt Romney, the 45th president of the United States.

She was home by 9:45.

Carol

Jimmy's Penthouse; Wednesday, November 7, 2012; 8:30 P.M.

Jimmy fucked Carol.

Lambda in the Heart of Texas

Texas Panhandle; Thursday, November 8, 2012; Late Afternoon

Kenny and Lance made their way to the southern edge of the Texas Panhandle. It was early in the third month of their six-month charted road trip, and both of them found the new landscape captivating. They had enjoyed meandering through the Texas Hill Country, but this scenery exuded a greater sense of the expansive Old West. Their small, dated twenty-seven-foot motorhome suited them and provided perfect camouflage. They preferred to be discreet traveling from one private, state, or national park campground to the next. Even in the year 2012, there were just too many questions, odd looks, and negative reactions when they interacted with others. It was just easier to live and breathe without judgment. Neither had been in contact with relatives or friends back east since the second week of their excursion. Despite feeling confined by who they were physically and emotionally, the ability to inconspicuously explore and enjoy activities they mutually loved brought a feeling of contentment. They mountain biked and hiked through forests, hills, mountains, and beaches. They canoed, fished, and visited famous landmarks, rarely interacting with others. Traveling provided them a great sense of freedom.

Kenny and Lance were skilled mountain-bike enthusiasts and chose to visit the Panhandle in early November. The weather this time of year was ideal for biking. Highs typically reached the mid-sixties, and the lows dropped to an invigorating thirty-five, forty degrees. Both were eager to bike the Caprock and Palo Duro Canyons. After spending a week in Austin and the Hill Country, the Panhandle was the most logical route to their next desired destination, northern Arizona. They had no definitive timetable for how long they would stay in any one place, but they strategically plotted their current itinerary to accomplish two things: take in a mixture of the Southwest while visiting as many renowned mountain-biking spots as possible. The course they had chosen for this leg of the trip achieved just that. Arriving along the Gulf Coast via Houston, they made their way to Austin and the Hill Country before heading northwest to the Panhandle. The path took them straight through the heart of the largest contiguous state, providing them a diverse panorama of Texas. By the time they had arrived at the Panhandle, the couple's appreciation of the vastness and geographic diversity of the state had grown immeasurably. You could read about it, but until you have actually done it, it was almost impossible to fathom how large Texas is. Both Kenny and Lance were awestruck. The trip couldn't have been planned any better. And now they were eager to do what they loved most, mountain bike another of the country's incredible landscapes.

The couple lived modestly, yet their passion for mountain biking drove them to own matching gray high-end Diamondback Sortie 3.0 29Er mountain bikes which they had purchased just days before embarking on the trip. Of course, the motorhome was well-equipped with everything needed to properly maintain their most valued possessions: a custom bike rack, portable workbench, and a built-in storage case to house every spare part and tool essential to fine-tune their bikes. Their meticulous care for the machines bordered on neurotic. Lance in particular obsessed over his bike.

The only discernible difference between their two bikes was the Lambda sticker Kenny attached to his seat post. Kenny often reminded Lance that the sticker was further proof that his commitment to the relationship exceeded Lance's. Lance, on the other hand, often teased Kenny that he probably liked the other biker named Lance—Lance Armstrong—better.

Just before every ride, they scrutinized every aspect of their bikes. Checking, cross-checking, and testing every component. To set his mind at ease, when Lance had completed inspecting his own bike, he would then spot-check Kenny's. At first, the intrusion insulted Kenny, but in time he took comfort in Lance's concern and attentiveness. When their rides ended, they again inspected their bikes, verifying that they were in perfect working condition. Their interests perfectly intertwined, leaving little need for others.

After biking in the Hill Country, the two had looked forward to the unique terrain of the nearby canyons. They planned to peruse the Caprock Canyons the next three days before heading closer to Amarillo on Monday. They would then ride what many considered Texas's finest mountain-biking range, the Palo Duro Canyon, an immense natural wonder that appears out of nowhere. The bottom dramatically drops out of the earth. Over 800 feet deep and 120 miles long, the canyon was the second largest in the country, surpassed only by the Grand Canyon. The park possessed a number of natural features they hoped to explore, photograph, and embrace. Being in no particular hurry, they expected to remain at Palo Duro until Thursday: biking, hiking, and taking advantage of the beautiful, sunny, mild days and crisp nights before heading to Arizona.

Shed No Light

Mesquite Campground; Palo Duro Canyon State Park; Canyon, Texas
Monday, November 12, 2012; 11:45 A.M.

Kenny and Lance pulled into the Palo Duro Canyon State Park just before noon.

The three days spent at Caprock Canyons had exceeded their expectations. Not only was the landscape diverse and inspiring, but the abundance of wildlife made for a number of memorable moments. Lance was fascinated by coming within just a few feet of a nest of rattlesnakes basking in the warm sunshine, a rare sight this time of year. Being yin to yang, Kenny was petrified. Observing the park's famed bison herd, the two did agree that the enormity of the bison reminded them of their eternal drive across the heart of Texas. Until you've seen it or experienced it, you just couldn't appreciate it. The animals' mass was as astounding as the breadth of Texas. Numerous antelope, deer, roadrunners, and a Barbary sheep stole their attention. Seeing the rare sheep only intensified Kenny's desire to spot a bobcat, but that never came to pass. Nevertheless, the countless prairie dogs, lizards, birds, and insects kept them intrigued. The three-day outing had been an unforgettable experience.

Studying the Palo Duro Canyon map when they checked in to the state park, Kenny and Lance decided to camp at the Mesquite Campground located at the far end of the premises. The park ranger told them only one other camper was there, so they were welcome to choose any of the available slots.

As they pulled into the campground, they passed the lone visitor parked nearest the restroom and shower facilities. Kenny drove to the far end of the oval-shaped drive and selected the site farthest from the entrance. Not only was the location the most private, but it had the best views of the canyon. The two couldn't have been more pleased.

Once the motorhome was leveled and stabilized, their routine setting up camp never varied. Lance removed the bikes from their racks and set up the workbench while Kenny hooked up the water and electricity, and then rolled out the canopy on the passenger side. Together they unloaded the barbeque grill and a small blue table along with two matching folding chairs. Lance invariably centered the table and chairs perfectly under the canopy. This neurotic habit drove Kenny crazy, and watching it reminded him of a cat circling in one spot before finally curling up to nap.

Lance looked up at the seam in the center of the canopy then back down at the hole in the middle of the circular table before setting it in place. He carefully gauged the distances between the table and the motorhome versus the edge of the canopy. As if he were steadily focusing to line up a putt, he moved the table a few inches to the right before adjusting it an inch or so to the left. After observing this compulsive habit numerous times, Kenny suggested placing a small mark on the canopy to denote the exact center for future set-ups. But Lance would have none of that. He couldn't bear the thought of looking up and seeing even a tiny blemish on the fabric. The same ritual played out at every new campsite. In time, Kenny grew fond of the habit just as he had with Lance's insistence of rechecking his bike before every ride.

Most everything Kenny and Lance did was carefully planned and coordinated. It may have been a little odd that they scripted out much of their daily lives, completely unaware of just how much time they devoted to planning instead of the actual doing. They often set out with good intentions of accomplishing three or more activities in a day and never even completed the first goal. Neither wore a watch to track their day; they simply didn't care. There was always the next day. It was a huge component of what they deemed as their personal freedom, not having to be bound by time. They were always conscious about what day of the week it was, but specific days were irrelevant to them. A Tuesday was every bit as good as a Friday. Now more than four hours after their arrival, with their residence for the next few days established, and their bikes checked and rechecked, they eagerly began their initial ride in the canyon. Their only goal for that day was to view the sunset from the famed Lighthouse Rock Formation.

The mountain-bike trail system at Palo Duro was a simple network comprised of five interconnecting trails, offering various levels of difficulty: Givens, Spicer and Lowry (GSL), Capital Peak, Lighthouse, Cottonwood Flats, and Little Fox Canyon trails. Combined, there were more than thirty miles of world-class rugged trails. Being late in the day, the couple anxiously headed out of the Mesquite Campground at a pace that would provide them plenty of time to bike Palo Duro's signature Lighthouse Trail. Then they would hike the final steep climb to the Lighthouse Formation before sunset. They figured if they left there before dusk, they would still have enough light to ride their bikes at least halfway back down the trail before dark. Then with the assistance of their high-powered lights, they could walk the rest of the trail if necessary then ride back to camp on the main roadway. It was one of the few instances where "time" was actually dictating their schedule. However, neither were the least bit concerned about the imminent darkness. In past excursions, Kenny and Lance had often found themselves on a trail well after dark.

Riding in synch, they moved up the rugged terrain in spurts. They pedaled with great force one minute then suddenly came to an abrupt halt the next to take in an immense panoramic view or to spy an animal off in the distance. Their synergies and the ability to know what the other was thinking were truly extraordinary.

As they made their way up the path, both marveled at the scenery. The canyon was spectacular, stretching twenty miles wide at some points. The vibrant layers of red claystone and gypsum, spattered with green foliage and wind-weathered rocks, provided endless opportunities to stop and gaze, take pictures, and consume the wonder of it all. It was apparent to both why the Lighthouse Trail was the most popular route, as its indescribable beauty was breathtaking.

On their way up, Kenny and Lance encountered only a few other bikers and one lone hiker heading back down the trail. As always, they were cordial, yet kept moving. During peak season, there would have been far more visitors, but as it was a Monday in early November, few roamed the canyon. The conditions couldn't have been better for the blissful couple.

They reached the end of the bike trail about forty-five minutes before sunset. The base of the Lighthouse Rock Formation, however, was still about a third of a mile up a steep, winding slope. To access it, mountain bikers could lock their bicycles at the bike rack located to the left of the rugged incline. At the time, there were no other bikes there, enabling Kenny and Lance to clearly view how previous visitors had painted six of the ten vertical bars in red, white, and blue stripes. They parked their bikes in two of the three patriotic slots.

Glancing just to the right of the bike stand, Lance said, "Wow! Look at those arrows! That's really neat how someone arranged those rocks. That must be the way to the Lighthouse formation." He strolled toward the two indicators formed out of rocks: arrows that pointed toward a channel that curved to the right.

Kenny agreed, "That was so sweet of someone to do that. There are no park signs anywhere. Without the arrows, I would have taken the path over there by the picnic table."

"Hey, why don't we sit down there for a minute and catch our breaths before we head up to the base," Lance suggested referring to the table near the clearing's edge.

"OK, fine by me," Kenny agreed as they walked over to the table to rest and sip from their water bottles. Both in heaven, they flamboyantly continued discussing the "cuteness" of the bike rack and the makeshift arrows. Needing only a few minutes of rest, they were ready to proceed.

"Let's lock up our bikes and get up there before sunset," said Kenny.

To adequately secure their bikes, Kenny moved his to one end of the rack while Lance took the opposite side. Using the rack's end bars allowed them to secure the frame and both wheels of each bike. They had just unfastened their TiGr titanium long bow locks from the frames when three young men descended from the last few steps of the hiking trail. They had been lurking just around a bend close to the path's entrance, eavesdropping on Kenny and Lance's playful discussion about the bike rack and the arrows formed with rocks.

As they came closer, the tallest of the three greeted Kenny and Lance. Both smiled and said, hello. Impressed with the exquisite bikes, the second man complimented their fine cycles in a condescending tone. Questions about their durability, costs, and "Did they like them a lot?"

ensued. Kenny and Lance were pleasant but brief in their responses. The first man asked them where they were from, and again the two were vague.

"From the East Coast," Kenny answered. He and Lance were becoming a little uncomfortable with the intrusive interrogation.

Kenny and Lance finished locking up their bikes, curiously noting that the other men had not secured theirs, but instead had stashed them several feet away in the brush just beyond the metal table.

Kenny placed his helmet on top of his seat and began to walk away. "Kenny, I'm taking my helmet with me. Don't you think you should get yours?" advised Lance.

"Umm . . . sure . . . OK," Kenny responded as he turned to retrieve his helmet. The three men looked on.

Apprehensively, Kenny and Lance wished the men a good evening and then quickly proceeded up the boulder-strewn path that lead to the Lighthouse Rock Formation.

The climb was often steep and at times a little treacherous. Both, however, were in tremendous shape, and the rugged conditions proved to be of little challenge.

Once they reached the base of the tower, they marveled at the spectacular vast scenery. Few sights were as stunning and powerful as this interior view. Celebrating their achievement, the two embraced. Everything was perfect. The sun setting beyond the canyon created a spectrum of incredible colorations for them to appreciate. All around them, the power of the wind and rain was vividly displayed in the rock formations, crevices, and ruts throughout the massive gorge. Kenny picked up a piece of gypsum and gave it to Lance as a memento of their exhilarating experience.

Then the sun set.

"Fucking faggots! I'm telling you those two are gay as hell!" said the tallest of the three men as they watched Kenny and Lance disappear up the slope and around the bend.

"I think they are too. Did you hear the guy in the dark blue shirt say how cute those red, white, and blue stripes are on the bike stand?" The second man mocked them in a feminine voice. "He talked like a mouse. A fucking mouse! How the hell do they afford those bikes? Damn, look at them! I'm riding this piece of crap, and those faggots have those bikes?"

"How about when they started getting all giddy and shit over those damn arrows? Like a bunch of girls talking about shoes!" said the third.

"Those arrows were probably made by a couple of other faggots! Shit, look at that pink sticker on his seat post. That's a fucking gay symbol! Don't know what it's called, but I know it's some kind of gay pride sticker or something. Positive!" said the first man.

The third agreed, "I think it is too. Fuck 'em!" And before the first two could even respond, he picked up the largest rock from one of the arrows, lifted it over his head with both hands, and slammed it into the nearest bike.

The bike remained upright, firmly secured to the stand as its crank shaft and sprockets bore the brunt of the twenty-pound rock. Following suit, the other two were locked and loaded and positioned themselves to take direct aim at the second bike. Hooting and hollering, in a matter of moments, the men had trashed both bikes, leaving spokes jutting out, rims mangled, chains knocked off, and the lights smashed. The final insult occurred when the first man picked up a small, sharp stone and scratched the Lambda sticker off Kenny's bike. Without further delay, the three culprits were hightailing it down the trail, laughing, screaming, and mocking the two faggots, who in their minds got what they deserved.

With the sun cresting over the horizon, Kenny and Lance headed back down the trail toward the bike rack. As the lighting quickly diminished, they took caution on the steep slope where loose rock was sliding beneath their feet. It took more than ten minutes to reach their bikes. Or rather what was left of their prized possessions.

"Oh, my god!" screamed Kenny.

Lance froze, speechless; his heart racing, his stomach in knots.

Tears began to roll down Kenny's face. "Who? . . . Why would someone do this? . . . Why? . . . Oh, my god!" he screamed again, his voice resonating throughout the canyon.

"Those three guys we met just before going to the Lighthouse. That's who did it," Lance said solemnly. He trembled, not believing the mangled mess that stood before them.

Shock, horror, and outrage began to escalate in both of them. They stood next to their bikes, glaring at the wreckage. The rocks that once had formed the neatly arranged arrows now lay scattered around the bike rack.

Lance bent down and touched his prized asset. Both bikes were demolished. Everything but the frames and handlebars would have to be replaced. The spokes and rims were complete losses. The sprockets were bent, and the brake handles and cables were destroyed. The elite front and rear Shimano derailleurs were crushed, no longer even resembling a functional part.

It took nearly ten minutes to regain their composure. Lance reached out and put his arms around Kenny's shoulders. This time they held each other much differently than their tender embrace standing before the Lighthouse Rock Formation. They both looked up at the 300-foot tower that now loomed over them, shedding no light. A pair of vultures circled above them.

A Hateful World

Lighthouse Trail; Palo Duro Canyon State Park
Monday, November 12, 2012; Dusk

Distraught, Kenny and Lance could hardly look at their bikes. Every component on them was destroyed. The whole scene had both men scrambled. Lance began unlocking one of the bikes. Perplexed why Lance would take his bike, Kenny assumed he must have been mistaken and grabbed the second. Instantly, he realized he had Lance's because there was no Lambda sticker on the seat post. He asked to get a closer look at the bike Lance was trying to unlock, only to get an abrupt response.

"No, I don't have your bike!"

"But this one doesn't have my sticker on it," Kenny said.

"Neither does this one," Lance responded bitterly as the key failed to open the lock.

As they examined the bikes more carefully, Lance noticed a few gummy remnants left on the seat post. Even in the fading light, he could see the scratches. He did indeed have Kenny's bike, not his. When Kenny realized what had been done, he became even more distraught. It took Lance several minutes to console him.

Complete darkness had fallen, and it felt like the canyon was swallowing them whole. Clouds filled the sky, minimizing the moon and star's illumination of the canyon. With their bike lights in ruins and no flashlights, Kenny and Lance hoisted the remains of their bikes onto their shoulders and set off down the path toward camp.

They had hiked about a half-mile and were still two miles from the path's entrance, with another three miles along the park's scenic drive to reach the campground. Lance attempted to remain strong, but even *his* emotions surfaced now and then. Periodically he heard Kenny crying, but it was his whimpering that raised Lance's anxiety.

"I'd like to stop at the next shelter, Kenny. We can share my water bottle," Lance suggested, since Kenny's bottle had been so badly damaged that no water remained.

"OK," Kenny quietly agreed.

They gravely trudged on for a few more minutes before approaching one of the many shelters strategically located along the path. Constructed using the natural surroundings, four cedar trunks served as posts and supported another half-dozen or so smaller ones. The smaller trunks created a roof, shading a bench large enough to seat three to four people. The crudely made structures were highly effective, providing relief for visitors from the blistering summer sun while not taking away from the rugged aspect of the canyon.

The bench where Kenny and Lance sat was approximately forty feet off the main path. In daylight, this location presented a perfectly clear view of the Lighthouse Rock Formation. A few feet from the shelter was a sign displaying a photograph of the Lighthouse and Castle Peak formations. It also contained information regarding how the resistant sandstone beds, interlayered with the easily eroded shale, molded the canyon's sculptures.

The two disheartened souls wearily sat down on the bench and were talking quietly when they heard a rustling in the brush. They froze, intensely listening for any further noise. There was none.

"Think it's a coyote?" asked Kenny.

"Could be, not sure," responded Lance.

They both stood up to gain a better view. Just like the calm before a storm, the air was still and quiet. Neither of them saw anything, but they continued to stand motionless, breathing silently; only their eyes shifted around their surroundings. A half-minute later, the calm turned to horrific mayhem.

Bursting through the dense shrub, a pack of eight boars took dead aim at the two hikers, and before either of them could react, the wild beasts struck, upending both men. Kenny let out a bloodcurdling scream, rattling the canyon walls. The animals' tusks simultaneously punctured Lance in the front and back of his torso, wedging him between the ugly faces of the creatures. Within seconds, his kidneys were shredded, his right lung collapsed, and blood poured from his wounds.

Lying on his side, Kenny curled into a fetal position, arms folded over his face. He could not watch the slaughtering of his partner. The boars plowed into his back, hindquarters, and legs, effortlessly piercing the human flesh. With each penetration, the boars thrust their heads skyward, inflicting gaping wounds into the defenseless body. The fatal blow for Kenny came from a boar's tusk entering the back of his neck, severing his spinal cord. His body went limp as the boars began to devour him, ripping at his fleshy inner thighs and gut.

Lance died only seconds after Kenny had succumbed, but those seconds seemed like hours as the vermin's teeth gashed Lance's skin; their jaws clamping down on bone, mutilating the muscle and tendons of his body. The boars began consuming his flesh as he gasped for his last breath.

Skirmishing amongst themselves to savor the final remains, the wild hogs ingested everything, including the men's clothes and shoes to get to the flesh and bone of their victims' feet. They even slopped up the last pools of splattered blood that blended with the red claystone. The annihilation was now complete. Other than the battered bikes, the only things left were the two helmets Kenny and Lance had set on the bench beside them. And a small piece of gypsum.

Establishing their equal status at the top of the food chain, the pack stormed off, grunting and squealing—wanting to be heard, wanting to wreak havoc on anything in its path; unlike moments before when they had silently stalked the two anguished mountain bikers trying to make sense of a hateful world.

Once again, the trail was calm. A small cast of vultures silently settled to the ground, scrounging for any remaining fragments.

Later that night a brief, yet hard, rain, fell. It was the first in weeks. It pounded the parched earth so quickly flash floods ensued. By the next morning, the trail's red dirt bore new weather-related scars, but no signs of the brutal massacre that occurred just hours before.

Finders Keepers

Lighthouse Trail; Tuesday, November 13, 2012; Dawn

Nearly every weekday for the past year, Stuart and Gary drove into the canyon and ran both the Lighthouse and Capital Peak Trails. Being outdoor enthusiasts, their daily jaunts relieved their angst of perpetual unemployment. They always arrived well before dawn to minimize the number of mountain bikers they might encounter. Each loved to bike as well, but during their runs, nothing irritated them more than being brushed by an inconsiderate, out-of-control biker. Traveling the same course daily, they first ran the Lighthouse Trail, ascending nine hundred feet to the base of the tower, before heading back down the path and detouring onto the Capital Peak's loop trail. At the end of the loop, they finished the last leg of the Lighthouse Trail. The entire morning run was just shy of nine miles from the trailhead.

The desperately needed rain from the night before left the trail sloppy. In no time, the runners' legs were splattered with red mud. Running side-by-side and talking about the Monday Night Football game the previous night, they came upon a strange sight. Leaning against the shelter, just off the trail were two mountain bikes, both in shambles. They stopped to take a closer look and were puzzled.

Noticing the two helmets sitting on the bench, Gary walked over to further investigate. He picked up one of them and carefully examined it. "Damn, these are nice Bell helmets—the Sweep model. I'll bet they cost near two hundred apiece!" He approached Stuart, who was looking at the extensive damage to the bikes.

"What the hell do ya think happened?" asked Stuart.

"I have no idea, but it sure seems strange," responded Gary. They looked around and saw nothing but the two severely damaged mountain bikes and the two helmets sitting aimlessly on the bench next to a piece of gypsum.

"Damn, these bikes are expensive too! The derailleurs, brakes, crankshaft, wheels, everything's basically shot, but I'll bet these frames are worth at least a thousand each. I wonder why someone would leave 'em here," Gary pondered.

"Pro'bly just too damn lazy to carry 'em down the trail. They'll just buy new ones when they get home," Stuart retorted. Again, they both scoped the landscape. It was only a few minutes past dawn, and no one else had yet appeared on the trail.

"Shit, we should take 'em!" Gary proposed.

"I dunno, somethin's just not right. Look at these bikes. Looks like somebody purposely destroyed 'em for some reason. I sure don't wanna take the blame for that," replied Stuart.

"That's two thousand dollars in frames, dude! Plus the helmets! I think we should grab 'em now and just carry 'em out," Gary argued. "If we don't see anyone, we'll put 'em in the back of my truck and book it on outta here. If we come across someone and they ask, we'll just say we found 'em, and we're bringin' 'em back to the ranger station. Hell, I'm grabbin' one!" He grabbed a helmet and then picked up one of the bikes. "C'mon man, let's get this shit n' go!" Gary shouted. Hesitantly Stuart followed suit, and they hurried down the path.

As luck would have it, they made it back to the truck without directly encountering anyone. A lone hiker was outside his car putting on his hiking boots, but he paid scant attention to the two men carrying the demolished bikes.

Stuart and Gary briskly swung the bikes into the back of the pickup, carried the helmets into the truck cabin, and were on their way out of the park. It had been only about thirty minutes since finding the bikes.

With the mountain bikes and helmets now gone, other than the motorhome sitting vacant and paid for with the ranger station until two o'clock Thursday afternoon, there was not a trace of Kenny's or Lance's existence, or of their demise.

They Always Come Back

Jimmy's Penthouse; Tuesday, November 7, 2012; Late Evening

Jimmy fucked Anne with the same arrogance and aggressiveness as the last time he saw her six weeks ago. He knew she would come back. They usually did. But when they didn't, "Fuck 'em."

He could sense what she wanted, what she needed, the moment he met her, similar to his other bitches: the clenching, the muscling, the biting. Jimmy communicated those same desires equally as well as his prey. It was part of the mutual attraction, the chemistry between them.

While artfully participating in the initial small talk, Jimmy envisioned himself holding them down, fucking them at his will while still trying to create the illusion he cared about one thing they said. When he was confident that his charm, wits, money, and Texas drawl had secured his next lover, the only rap song he could ever relate to, "99 Problems"—but a bitch ain't one, played in his head. Women were his true release valve.

Although he portrayed that he controlled the markets, that the markets were his "bitch," he knew otherwise. He was cognizant of the fact that he had no extraordinary foresight, no intimate knowledge of where markets were going. Often, for every trade he made, there was an offsetting trade in another account. He went long crude oil in one account and sold an equal amount in another. One espoused a bullish position; the other bearish. You were always right, at least to half of the suckers. Whichever way the market moved, Jimmy would be set up to boastfully divulge his latest trading coup.

He was godlike to his brethren. To them, Jimmy fucked the markets like he treated his women. Predicting what the bid-ask spread was on every woman Jimmy would potentially fuck was the joke in the office. When the office calculated the bid was low—that Jimmy had little desire to sleep with a particular woman—the estimated offer was unanimously about the same as the bid, implying that the woman would do anything to please Jimmy. Interestingly enough, when the bid was high—that Jimmy wanted to bed someone—invariably the office pool's offer on whether she would gladly comply came in lower than the bid. The disciples believed Jimmy had the ability to sleep with anyone he wanted and that the hottest, most desirable women would throw themselves at him. Everyone in the office considered him the master, and they were his awestruck followers.

Anytime the opportunity presented itself, Jimmy used this aura to feed the beast. He subscribed to the theory of "perception is reality." He used this philosophy not only to create social capital amongst his comrades, but to generate much needed self-confidence as well.

In reality, Jimmy needed the endless pool of women more than they needed him. Despite his proficiency in every sport, game, and purported business deal, his insecurities were real. He knew how little control he had over his life. That he was, in actuality, just a pawn. And it was this unbearable realization that insidiously drove him on edge to be revered amongst his peers.

Sus scrofa

Earth; 2012

Scientific Name: Sus scrofa

Alternate Common Name: Feral Pig

Taxonomy:

Kingdom – Animalia

Phylum – Chordata

Subphylum - Verebrata

Class – Mammalia

Subclass – Theria

Infraclass - Eutheria

Order – Artiodactyla

Family – Suidae

Subfamily - Suinae

Genus – Sus

Species – Sus scrofa

Lifespan: 5 to 8 years

Weight: 150 to 900 pounds

Length: can exceed 5 feet

Cerebralization Index: 14

Chromosomes: 19

Winston Churchill

Animal Kingdom; 2012

> *"I am fond of pigs. Dogs look up to us.*
> *Cats look down on us. Pigs treat us as equals."*
> *Sir Winston Churchill*

The boars knew their place in the animal kingdom. Since the extinction or endangerment of many large cats and wolves in the Panhandle nearly seven decades ago, the boar had no equal beyond man. Their physical, mental, and social makeup surpassed every other creature except humans. In one critical aspect, however, the hogs actually exceeded man's capabilities: their ability and willingness to modify behaviors independently and collectively to enhance the sounder's sustainability.

During the Dust Bowl of the 1930s, the boars feebly accepted a rapidly deteriorating environment; however, in the second decade of the new millennium, unrest festered within the sounders when a confluence of perceived human events ravaged their habitat again.

Resentment brewed as the dominant hybrid males began questioning, "Are we not equal to man? Why do we, equals of man, continue to suffer at the hands of man? They take our lands and wreak havoc on the environment. When will the boar nation begin to punish the culprits crippling its lands?"

On Monday, November 12, 2012, shortly after seven p.m., unbeknownst to man, a faction of wild boars had unofficially given notice that justice would indeed be served.

With their stout shoulders tapering to their hindquarters, the boar was built to be compact, powerful, fast, and agile. Compared to domesticated pigs, their longer legs enabled them to reach top speeds rapidly with the ability to change direction on a dime. Incredibly athletic, boars could swim at a great pace and distance. Their pricked, highly sensitive ears enabled them to detect and localize sound to just four degrees, which allowed them to pinpoint noise better than any other creature in the animal kingdom. Multiple sensory receptors in their nasal disc at the end of their snout allowed the vermin to exploit an extraordinary sense of smell, detecting odors several miles away as well as several feet underground. They used their snouts as highly effective tools to manipulate objects and to dig deep into the soil. Over time through combat, their skin had toughened and hardened from cartilage and scar tissue, forming a shield over the most vulnerable parts of their bodies. A shield so tough it could repel bullets that would take down any other animal its size. Their ultra-sharp tusks could slice and penetrate almost anything except another boar's skin. The species' physical attributes created the perfect proportions in size, speed, agility, and toughness; characteristics not just to protect and to defend but to attack as well.

Both cunning and malicious, the boars' mental capabilities were unrivaled. Few animals had adapted their natural gifts to their existing environment better than the boar. If roots and nuts were accessible underground, they used their snouts and tusks to root them out. If small game and animals were abundant, they hunted them down using their tusks as lethal weapons.

Being opportunistic omnivores, the boars adjusted to conditions and ate almost anything. As their preferred wooded areas shrank, the boars learned to thrive in grasslands and a multitude of geographic ranges. The one aspect the boar had not altered over time was its fierceness, particularly when a piglet was in harm's way. If necessary, wild boars charged, attacked, and attempted to fatally wound any competitor, willing to fight to the death. They feared nothing when they, or one of their own, were under attack.

Socially, boars formed elaborate, all-inclusive groups consisting of between a half-dozen to as large as one hundred members or more. They communicated using more than twenty different vocalizations such as grunts, squeals, and growls, allowing constant communication with one another. Their social network was as sophisticated as any in the animal kingdom.

Whether greeting each other by touching snouts, snuggling in groups to stay warm, or grooming one another, the boars understood their superiority was not only in their physical prowess but their mental and social makeups as well.

Within the sounder, while females were nursing they shared maternal duties after the piglets were a couple of weeks old. Sows encouraged the piglets to play, frolic, chase, sprint, swim, and follow their instincts within the protection of the sounder.

Hygiene was another important aspect to the boars' well-being. The animals only excreted wastes far from their feeding and nesting areas.

With their individual and collective mind-sets structured to advance the species, the wild hogs were thriving. Open-minded, they willfully adopted and even enhanced relevant attributes of other carnivores and herbivores, as well as animals of solitude and of communal nature. Over generations, this meant the boars not only surpassed but widened their physical, mental, and social preeminence over any potential rivals. And as the environment began to rapidly change, so too did the boar. Whereas man had checks and balances to restrain fundamental change in unexpected times, the boars' social structure allowed for radical change as circumstances dictated. The boar nation realized they had become the most powerful, vibrant, calculating, and ruthless beast to roam the region in decades. Their time as a nation had arrived.

And boars, with high intelligence and lucid memories, had their own legends of which they as a nation were proud. They proclaimed to one another and to subsequent generations their history as a species: of ancestors who died at the hands of Mycenae warriors creating battle helmets of leather and boar tusks; of their kind, persecuted and slaughtered to extinction by medieval British proving their hunting prowess; of Asian ancestors who prevailed in battles with tigers. To these they added more modern tales of boars who fled for their lives, leaving mayhem and death behind. The fleeing boars told horrifying tales of infamous humans who used surprise and noise to devastate large numbers of their species. These humans killed, not to eat or for survival as boars have done. Indeed, boars admit those types of deaths, while mourned, are quite understandable. No, these humans acted entirely unprovoked and slaughtered members of the boar nation only to leave their bloody bodies to rot, often in heaps of innumerous carcasses. One even went so far as to collect pieces of the bodies to decorate himself, but not for any kind of needed protection. For vanity. Simply for vanity.

As more and more boars found themselves among those targeted for slaughter, the stories of these dishonorable humans grew until they identified six in particular—six especially evil because they not only slaughtered boars, they incited other humans to slaughter as well. These infamous six became identified as the Boars' Most Wanted, the ones they were determined to strike against and exact revenge. The ones they would destroy at all costs. The rumors of the six had circulated for years. Their descriptions were well-embedded in the minds of all boars.

In this way, the genus would continue to flourish as the boars sought out their greatest threat. Unlike man, they did not make war amongst themselves. Instead, a small faction determined to wage war against the one enemy they had left.

For now, they considered themselves equals of man. But the future *would* belong to them.

"X" Marks the Spot

Canyon's Edge; Outskirts of Happy, Texas
Wednesday, November 14, 2012; 10:29 P.M.

Standing next to Tom's black four-wheel-drive pickup, discreetly positioned near the edge of one of the canyon's thousands of crevices, they silently began undressing. Moments before leaving their homes, each had showered using perfume-free and odor-free soap. Instead of using toothpaste, the men brushed their teeth with baking soda. Removing their hunting gear from the ScentBlocker Dry Bags, they quickly dressed into their specially prepared clothing. The apparel had been washed that afternoon in scent-free detergent and then dried using a scent-killing dryer sheet before being stored in the special bags. Once fully dressed, the men took turns thoroughly spraying each other's clothes with Scent Killer Gold. With their scents carefully masked from headgear to boots, each grabbed a high-powered rifle and set off for the mile-plus hike.

The men parked in the same location as they had dozens of times over the past few years, southeast of the feeder amongst tall grasses, brush, and juniper trees, making the truck difficult to spot from the ground or air. The men then walked due north before heading west, so they always made their final approach coming from the northeast, which normally was downwind of the feeder. They considered this the finest of the thirty-plus locations they frequently monitored. Even though the process had become routine, years of experience taught them that no two evenings were ever the same and that every precaution had to be taken.

In spite of how many times they had executed the plan in the past, butterflies still fluttered in their stomachs. As they silently crept closer to their target, the anticipation of what they would find roaming in the open area elevated their heart rates. Killing is killing; the thrill never dissipated. It only grew. And hunting wild boar was the ultimate opportunity to fulfill those desires.

Shooting deer, aoudad sheep, and other big game for the men was physically challenging and psychologically rewarding. The animals required them to be experts at stalking and positioning themselves for the perfect moment to take aim, remain steady, and fire delivering the perfect shot. Tracking the typical big game animal, the hunter rarely got more than one shot to make his mark. Permits were usually required and limits strictly enforced.

Wild hogs, however, were a whole 'nother animal. They ran in packs of six, ten, twenty hogs. When feeders were used to lure them, more than a hundred hogs often circulated the feeding stations. Considered vermin, the state encouraged hunters to kill as many and as often as possible. For the men, it was the equivalence of having a harem. The ability to kill, and kill multiple times in one instance, excited them. In addition, knowing boars have violent instincts, lethal tusks, and would charge in an instant further fueled their adrenaline. Finally, wild-boar flesh paid cash, tax-free cash, and this stoked their desire to kill en masse.

As they approached the clearing, the men could hear the animals foraging. It was 11:16 p.m. They synchronized their watches and agreed that at exactly 11:20, they would fire the first shots. They would be about twenty yards from each other, and the four minutes allowed the men to strategically position themselves and select which hogs, meeting their ideal profile, could easily be targeted.

The hunters' eyes widened, and their hearts pounded more rapidly as they edged closer to gain visibility of the feeding area. The slop dispenser they maintained was placed in a small clearing of thicket and had drawn the largest pack of hogs they had ever seen in one spot. Surveying the scene, it appeared that well over a hundred fifty head wandered around the feeder.

The hogs seemed at ease, sensing no danger. Without the men's exhaustive efforts to mask their scent and their extreme efforts to remain quiet, the feral pigs, with their extraordinary sense of smell and hearing, would have bolted long before the hunters neared the area. Now in their final positions, the men studied the herd and determined the first, second, and third beasts each would target. They waited patiently for their watches to signal the silent countdown. Both had agreed that if the large horde became spooked prior to the prearranged time, firing would commence immediately.

When their watches displayed 11:19:55, the men took aim and silently counted to five. Perfectly in synch, the two gunmen unloaded three shots each before the boars could react. Out of the first six rounds, five boars went down immediately, hit in their most vulnerable spot, the lower front shoulder. Targeting this area pierced the heart or lungs, usually resulting in instantaneous death.

As expected, all hell broke loose. Although the men were prepared, they had never encountered a herd this large before. The majority of swine darted left, right, or straightaway from the shots. A half-dozen or so ran right between the shooters, denying the men an opportunity to fire at the risk of shooting each other. Two boars made a beeline toward Len, who sprayed them with multiple shots before they fell. It was the most chaotic scene the two of them had ever experienced since they began their operations.

Normally, when they had a clear shot, the men had eight to ten seconds to open fire, leaving only a few boars down after the initial three blasts. This time the animals panicked between the second and third dual shots, and the sheer volume of beasts that tried to escape was impeded by the congested feeding zone. For easily a dozen seconds, the men had ample opportunity to slay as many hogs as possible. And slay them they did.

It was the most bountiful night in their history. Seventeen boars lay dead. They were certain they had killed five of the six they initially targeted, and Tom was confident the boar he found fifty yards into the brush was the sixth. These boars had been targeted since they were the perfect size. Larger boars had tougher meat and more of a gamey flavor. The smaller ones lacked enough meat to make their efforts worthwhile. It was the mid-sized boars they favored, in the 150- to 175-pound range. And they got them. The men were ecstatic.

Meanwhile, from a distance, thirteen boars of another sounder who never fed from the manmade devices observed the massacre. There, they stood their ground, stirring, brewing, waiting.

Once the men congratulated each other and had a moment to come down from their exhilaration, the next phase of the operation commenced. The routine never varied and was designed to maximize the skills of both men. Len was taller, leaner, and three years younger than Tom. He was an excellent runner, so it was logical he retrieve the truck. Tom on the other hand weighed a rock-solid 220 pounds. His brute strength made his tasks for the next fifteen minutes just as reasonable. He dragged every boar and conveniently arranged them to be field dressed on the spot. When Len arrived with the truck, the final phase for the night would begin.

They had equipped the 2012 Dodge RAM 3500 Laramie Longhorn Limited Edition 4x4 Mega Cab specifically for their ventures. They had installed a water tank with a hose to wash off the hogs before field dressing them. Two huge portable coolers that could be locked into place consumed the remaining space. A tool chest built into the side contained an assortment of tools and butcher knives for their needs. With the modifications they had made, combined with the vehicle's accessories such as dual rear wheels, the truck was as beastly as the boars they hauled. The massive machine cost more than Tom's house and had always been sufficient for their needs. Tonight, however, their unparalleled success created a welcome dilemma.

They had never killed more than eleven boars at one time. And that yield taxed their capacity. Typically, they harvested six, seven boars. How the hell were they going to dress and properly store seventeen?

The men laughed in unison at their predicament. It was a good problem to have. With a pat on Tom's back, Len was on his way.

Tom's truck was parked about a mile away. Len believed he could make it there in record time. He could run a mile on a running track in just over six minutes, but this course was no running track. Plus it was nighttime, and he was wearing boots, not running shoes. Driving the truck from where it was to the feeding station took only a couple minutes. The round-trip to assist Tom never took more than sixteen, seventeen minutes, and that was after it had rained. Now that the ground was like cement, his pace should be quicker. The two-man team had it down to a science, and Tom expected his partner to be back in no time.

Having run the gauntlet so many times, Len knew every clearing of brush and thicket he needed to navigate to reach the vehicle path, a little more than a quarter-mile away. Whereas when the men were positioning themselves before the attack, they had to approach the feeding station from the thicket nearly a mile back to avert alerting the boars. If they had come from the path anywhere within a mile of the feeder, despite their elaborate attempts to dull their scent, the boars would have invariably sensed their presence and would have scattered well before he and Tom were positioned to strike.

The slaughter complete, all Len had to do was get to the trail as quickly as possible, which he normally did in a little over four minutes. From there, he would run the undeveloped road consisting of two tire tracks separated by withering native grasses that had been crudely cut by the undercarriages of occasional passing trucks. Depending on the amount of moonlight and the condition of the ground, it could possibly take another seven to eight minutes before he would reach the truck, and then another three minutes driving back to the killing zone.

Scaling the last few yards of the crevice, Len reached the tire tracks right on schedule. Feeling the drought-hardened ground under his feet, he was confident it would be a very fast run. Unfortunately, fast for him meant even faster for the boars. Because tonight, nothing was equal.

By the time Len made his way to the path, six boars were already stalking him. A little more than a few hundred yards behind him when they, too, reached the rudimentary road, the boars set off in fatal pursuit.

The hard earth made the track especially fast for the extremely athletic animals. Soon after their initial charge, the hogs reached top speeds of nearly thirty miles per hour and were upon Len in no time.

He hardly made it an eighth of a mile down the two-track path before the savage assault began. At the last second, his instincts slowed his pace. He stopped and turned completely around to see a pack of wild boars bearing down on him. With no rifle, the only things he had to defend himself were a buck knife and a small Smith and Wesson pistol—better suited for shooting rabbits, squirrels, and snakes; not 300- or 400-pound wild boars.

Before he could draw his pistol, the first boar struck him at full speed in the right thigh. The impact shattered his femoral shaft and knocked him off the track several feet to his left. Frantically, Len grabbed the tiny branches of a small scrub tree to pull himself deeper into the brush. Even if he could have staggered to his feet, he had no chance. Immediately, a second boar took aim and gored him in the left thigh and hip. A third deranged pig's tusk penetrated his upper ribcage just under his armpit. Wedged between the ribcage and right shoulder, the tusk shredded Len's subscapularis muscle and capsular ligaments. The wound to his right leg and his upper right shoulder left that entire side of his body paralyzed. A fourth boar clamped down on his left wrist and furiously shook its head, using all its strength to tug on the arm. Seconds later, the boar severed his wrist and quickly swallowed his entire hand. Two boars fought to gain position to consume Len's favored internal organs, while the boar that had leveled him gnawed on his limp right ankle. Soon, all six boars had gashed his body, ripped meat from his bones, and had eaten his flesh while their adversary remained alive. It took less than a dozen minutes for the boars to totally consume Len's corpse.

Much to the vultures' frustration, the hogs had eaten every last piece of meat. Like the native Indian who found use for every part of a kill, the boars had slopped up whatever bits of human tissues and pools of blood remained.

The area now completely cleansed, the pack confidently turned and trotted back toward the feeding site. The only signs of Len's being were his buck knife, a small handgun near the side of the road, and a strip of rubber from the sole of his boot lying in the brush, several feet off the track.

Meanwhile, Tom's efforts never ceased. In the twenty minutes Len had been gone, Tom had hauled in and prepared the seventeen boars for field dressing. He arranged the pigs to form an assembly line about fifteen to twenty feet from the feeder, each carcass placed on its back with its legs raised skyward.

A new moon left the sky pitch black. Until Len arrived with the truck's custom lights, only a dim glow from the floodlight attached to the feeding station provided minimal illumination to inspect the beasts. Yet, he could see well enough to marvel at their bounty. He figured they would collect $900 or more for the illegal meat, more than double any other night. He looked at his watch and smiled, knowing last month's mortgage would soon be paid.

It had been 22 minutes since Len had left. Tom glanced at the two rifles propped against the feeding station and thought that the makeshift tripod structures they had built to attract the hogs had never failed. "Those greedy bastards cain't help themselves. They always come back. And if they don't, fuck 'em. There's always another sounder. And people think pigs are so fucking smart." He laughed out loud. It had been a triumphant night.

The six boars regrouped with the remaining seven. Again thirteen strong, they surveyed the scene. Seventeen of their species lay dead before them, four more than their own band. The six boars that attacked and ate Len alive would now yield the meatier Tom to the remaining seven. Cautiously, step-by-step, the second group moved stealthily within striking distance of the self-anointed ruler of the animal kingdom.

Tom was growing antsy. It had now been twenty-seven minutes and counting since Len had left. He was beginning to worry. Where was he? Was the truck not starting? He checked his pockets to make sure he had given Len the keys to his truck. He had; his pockets were empty. Relieved, he walked over to the boar whose cloven hoofs stretched closest to the moon. He proudly stood next to it, then crouched down and admired its thick, six-inch tusks. Blood oozing from its mouth, the boar's head and face looked even more menacing. He thought he heard a snort. He sprang up and looked around, but saw nothing. Feeling a bit uneasy about the circumstances, he glanced again at the feeder less than twenty feet away. A touch of unexplained anxiety instinctively prompted him to move slowly toward the comfort of his precious rifle. He *would* touch the rifle again but not with his hands, as he who ruled by the rifle would die by the tusk.

On his first movement toward the tripod, the seven boars bolted in unison. Similar to Len, Tom never sensed their presence until it was too late. Within a second of his instinct to stop and turn around, he experienced a crushing blow that hurled him into one of the legs of the structure, knocking the rifles to the ground. The direct hit obliterated his knees and knocked the wind out of him as he hit the metal pole. He became disoriented and could barely make sense of the agitated animals approaching him, or the grunts and growls he heard as he desperately clung to the sturdy leg of the feeder. Dazed and unable to catch his breath, Tom collapsed on top of the fallen guns. After the initial strike, the boars immediately sensed that the strapping man was incapacitated. The first boar went straight for Tom's head. Tom tried to turn away, but in one crunching bite, the pig mutilated his nose and mouth, leaving little resemblance to a human face. Then the five-inch tusks of another boar gored Tom in the chest, and the boar wildly shook its head as it plowed deeper and deeper into the center of Tom's heart. He died almost instantly and was spared Len's misfortune of being eaten alive.

Again, within moments nothing remained but the feeding station and two rifles lying on the ground almost forming an 'x' as if marking the spot of the massacre. The six boars who had engulfed Len marched down to the feeding area. There the thirteen boars stepped through the carnage and sniffed their fallen peers that now lay on their backs, legs pointing to the sky, humiliated by man. The counterattack not equal, vengeance permeated amongst the rogue boars.

A kettle of vultures, having learned that nothing remained of Len, now circled above the feeding area waiting patiently for an opportunity to descend. Despite being denied again the delicacy of human flesh, the buzzards still reveled in man's ability to massacre in such abundance, an abundance that would feed scavengers for days.

The Drive

Waco; Thursday, November 15, 2012; 4:52 A.M.

Derek anxiously watched out his living room window and grinned when he saw headlights bouncing down the half-mile, part-gravel, part-dirt entrance to his property. No doubt his best friend was doing fifty miles per hour as he raced toward his expansive home. He could envision the dust clouds kicking up behind the speeding truck.

"That's Ted. When it comes to huntin', if he can't be on time, he'll be early." Eight minutes early to be exact—about what Derek expected.

Derek was fired up. They had been best friends since Ted decided to hang his hat in Texas a decade ago. Ted was an "outside the box" thinker like he was. Both were serious fans of hunting, Texas, and the Constitution.

Derek let the screen door swing closed behind him as he stepped out to meet his friend in the circle driveway just as Ted belted out, "Ya . . . hoo!"

They gripped each other around the shoulders and gave a firm hug.

"The next few days are gonna be all-out mayhem!" Ted announced.

"Hell, yeah! Pigs are gettin' nastier and meaner by the minute as this damn drought lingers. Damn things are overrunnin' the country! 'Bout as fuckin' bad as the 47-percent takers Obama breeds," insisted Derek.

"Derek, ya know how I feel. 'Obama, he's a piece of shit. I told him to suck on my machine gun.' 'Hey Hillary, you might want to ride one of these into the sunset, you worthless bitch,'" [1] Ted proudly reiterated an announcement he had made to his fans at a 2007 concert, sporting camouflage hunting gear and two machine guns.

With that, they tossed Derek's gear into the bed of the truck, and again Ted was hauling it down the driveway, dust flying.

The long-time buds exchanged pleasantries, checking up on the wives, kids, and grandchildren. Lots of catching up to do. Ted had fathered nine children in all from seven different women. Two were adopted out at birth and only recently came into his life, more than forty years later. Derek had six children: four boys with his first wife and two girls with his second. The two men had a great deal in common.

Topping speeds well above the speed limit, they arrived in Fort Worth a quarter past six a.m. Their pace slowed significantly on the next leg from Fort Worth to Wichita Falls. Route 287 passed through several small towns and was a well-known speed trap. Ted didn't worry too much. The troopers worshipped him.

Nearly ninety minutes had passed before discussion about the election results finally came up, possibly a record for either of them not bashing the president about something. Depression over Mitt Romney's loss was the root of the inordinate delay.

"How the hell did Romney lose? This country's bein' run by a fuckin' nigger, a damn foreigner. How the hell did this happen?" Derek asked.

"My comments the day after the election say it all when I tweeted, 'Pimps whores & welfare brats & their soulless supporters hav a president to destroy America.' [2] 'Goodluk America u just voted for economic & spiritual suicide.' Soulless fools," [3] Ted reminded Derek.

After passing through Wichita Falls, Ted again revved himself up full throttle as he continued his nonstop diatribes against the despised president. And it didn't end until they reached their destination, a private ranch adjacent to the Palo Duro Canyon, about eight miles south of the state park.

Drunk This Time of the Mornin'?

Canyon City Police Department; Canyon, Texas
Thursday, November 15, 2012; 7:11 A.M.

"Dispatch," answered the shift officer.

"My husband didn't come home last night. Have there been any accidents reported?" The voice on the other end of the line sounded concerned.

"May I have your name please?" asked Officer Frantz.

"Karen Harden. My husband's Tom Harden. He went huntin' last night with a friend, and he never came home. He's always back by now. He won't answer his cell phone, and I'm gettin' worried," her voice quivered.

"Who'd he go with? Do you know where they usually hunt?" inquired the officer.

"He went with Len . . . I think . . . or Ben? No, no . . . it was Len. Len Maloney? Heck, I dunno. He hunts every night. God, where is he?" She was beginning to panic.

"Have you tried calling Len?" questioned the officer.

"I don't have his number, and I've never spoken to his wife."

The officer tried to calm Karen, but unfortunately he had to ask her to come to the station and file a missing person's report. Once that was completed, he assured her they would begin to investigate. The officer hung up the phone and concluded his notes.

Detective Jim Dawson overheard the call and asked Frantz who was missing.

"Karen Harden called. She said her husband, Tom, went huntin' last night with a friend named Len Maloney, and he never returned home," his colleague told him.

"Let me know when she arrives. I'll take her statement and complete the report," responded the detective.

"No problem, Jim," Frantz replied.

Karen arrived at the police station promptly at 7:52 a.m. after dropping her daughter off at school. It had taken all of her strength to remain calm, not wanting to alarm her nine-year-old. She hurried into the station wearing jeans, a Dallas Cowboys number-nine jersey, and a matching Cowboys baseball cap with the famous star logo. Dawson greeted her and immediately escorted her to a cheap, metal desk. The detective recognized her and was confident he knew Tom and that Tom was friends with Len.

She looked about forty, a little heavy, but attractive in her tight jeans and fitted Cowboys jersey. He took her statement, filed the paperwork, and assured her the office would begin their preliminary investigation immediately.

"But what about the twenty-four-hour law? Don't cha have to wait twenty-four hours before ya begin searchin'?" she asked.

Dawson reassured her that was not the case. They could begin anytime. "Look," he said, "I know Len Mahoney. I think that's who you meant. Not Maloney. Len Mahoney is his name."

"That's it. Len Mahoney," Karen agreed.

Dawson continued, "I know where he lives. He isn't married. I'll drive out to his place as soon as you leave. I'll bet they're out there havin' a beer, smokin' a cigar, and celebratin' a big trophy," he said trying to reassure her.

"OK," she responded.

He began walking her to the door. "I'll let you know what I find. What number can I reach you at?"

Karen gave the detective her home number. She thanked him and, upon leaving, said, "That son-abitch is gettin' drunk again? All this time I'm worried sick about 'em. Drunk this time of the mornin'? God damn him!"

Dawson drove out to Len's shortly after Karen left the station. From the road, he could see Len's silver truck parked near the right front corner of the trailer. As Dawson pulled into the rutted dirt driveway, an American pit bull mix penned in a chain-link cage began barking incessantly, racing back and forth along the steel mesh.

The fifteen-year veteran promptly parked and got out of his patrol car. He had exceptional peripheral vision and consciously monitored every aspect of his surroundings, including the resident's truck parked just in front of his vehicle. Dawson slowly walked up to the door and knocked. He knocked again and loudly announced himself. There was no response. The detective backed down off the front steps, walked a few feet to his left, and glanced at the front window, which was nearly six feet off the ground. He then looked down the road at Len's neighbor, another trailer at least a hundred yards away. He did not see any vehicles parked in front of the dilapidated shack perched on cinder blocks. Dawson decided to explore further.

Passing the dog on the right-hand side of the trailer, Jim cautiously walked around to the back of the property, searching for anything out of the ordinary. Other than the dog's relentless yapping and aggressive behavior, everything was still and quiet. Noticing a hard plastic five-gallon bucket, he picked it up and carried it around to the front of the trailer. Jim set the bucket down and walked back up to the front door, knocking several more times while announcing himself. Again, there was no response. He gently twisted the doorknob to see if it was locked. It was. Dawson stepped down from the wooden platform, collected the bucket, and walked to the front window.

Approaching the trailer again, he rapped on the window several times and authoritatively yelled, "Len! Hey, Len! It's Jim! Jim Dawson. Detective Jim Dawson. You here? Are you OK?" All the detective could hear was the deflected barks of the agitated dog on the other side of the trailer.

Jim set the bucket upside down beneath the window, stepped up, cupped his hands to his face and pressed them against the glass. Shading his eyes from the glare, he looked inside the dust-coated window. A small kitchen sink full of dirty dishes sat on the other side. He could see a good part of the inside of the trailer and saw nothing of concern. The living area was clean but cluttered. Newspapers and magazines were scattered across a cheap coffee table, and a blanket was bundled up in the corner of the couch. An old blue recliner sat squarely in front of a modest TV. The two-person Formica kitchen table had a coffee mug sitting on one corner and a bath towel draped over one of the chairs.

The officer stepped off the bucket and carried it with him around the trailer to see if any other windows provided a peek inside. Unfortunately, the curtains on the second window in the front were closed. The bathroom window on the far side of the trailer had a vinyl window treatment that obscured the view. The one large and two small windows in back had bamboo shades rolled down. And the side closest to the dog pen was windowless. Dawson returned the bucket to its original spot and walked back around to the front.

As he passed the kennel, the dog stopped running back and forth and instead remained in the nearest corner of the pen, jumping against the gate, growling and barking madly. Jim surveyed the lot one last time then took out a business card and wrote on the back, asking Len to call him, noting his visit was due to Mrs. Harden's concern over her missing husband. He placed the card in the seam of the front door.

On his way back to his squad car, Dawson looked into the truck's cab and then checked both doors, which were locked. Still, all appeared normal including the bed of the truck, which was littered with multiple bags and coffee cups from McDonald's and about two dozen beer cans. Unconcerned, the detective got back into his car and drove off to a hunting site he and Len had visited over a year ago.

Plan B

Fire at Will Ranch; Palo Duro Canyon
Thursday, November 15, 2012; 11:15 A.M.

The ranch was stunning and one of Ted's favorite getaways. Since his relocation to Texas, he had become close friends with the owners and visited several times a year. In 2006, with Ted's financial backing, the owners refurbished the main lodge, more than doubling its original size from 4,000 square feet to 9,000 square feet. In addition, they built one three-bedroom and two two-bedroom cabins. The lodge and all three cabins were built near the rim, offering spectacular views of the canyon.

The spread was an oasis for the rugged outdoorsman. It encompassed 6,600 acres and had several direct inlets to the canyon, including dry riverbeds and active springs that lured wildlife onto the property. Native cactus dotted the landscape leading up to the lodge. Beautiful golden-colored native grasses with intermittent brushy thicket blanketed the scenic landscape. As visitors neared the canyon's rim, the grasses gave way, and the thicket became increasingly prevalent. This vegetation combined with surrounding winter wheat fields attracted a host of wildlife.

Game such as mule deer and white-tail deer as well as quail and dove inhabited the land, providing hunters plenty of options during hunting seasons. Barbary sheep, coyote, gray fox, bobcats, wild turkey, rabbits, roadrunners and, of course, wild boar were in abundance year-round for the avid hunter.

The greatest aspect of the lodge was its access into the canyon. Of the total, nearly 4,000 acres consisted of canyon, offering hunters adequate range and various levels to spot and stalk game in terrain that was as breathtaking as it was treacherous. Nothing pleasured Ted more than to move about the rugged trails that plunged several hundred feet into the earth in pursuit of his next kill.

Ted and Derek stood on the flagstone porch of their private three-bedroom cabin, taking in the views they had enjoyed numerous times over the years.

"Ya know, man, with Obamacare, we ain't gonna be able to enjoy this much longer. Healthcare's goin' to shit, and we ain't gonna be able to get decent care as we get older. Sum bitch gonna mess with our Medicare just as we begin to need it," Derek complained.

Trying to reassure him the hard right wing would regain power, Ted told Derek what he told the audience at an NRA convention in St. Louis in April 2012. "Varmints are sometimes clever, but they're really easy to outmaneuver. [4] And Nancy Pelosi? She's 'a sub-human scoundrel'." [5] Ted continued on before saying U.S. Representative and DNC Chair "Wasserman Schultz is such a brain-dead, soulless idiot." [6]

Unconvinced, Derek stated, "We need a *real* conservative like you to campaign, Ted. Texas folks love ya. Hell, all the conservatives love ya. With you, we could take back this country ONCE AND FOR ALL!"

Ted smiled and pondered the idea. "I dunno, pardner. This here's what I love doin': Stalkin' game, killin', blowin' up shit. I do know this; we

need to take back this faceless land Obama has created. Hopefully, God willin', we won't have to wait long."

"Amen!" Derek concluded before he went on his own crusade. "Ya know, Ted, Romney was all wrong 'bout the 47 percent. Damn Democrats created the first 47 percent. Now with Obama, it's become more like 52 percent. Fifty-two percent fuckin' takers. Hippies and whores and damn welfare takers never workin'. Yet, buyin' iPhones, boozin' it up, smokin' cheap cigars and crack all day, and drivin' around in cars with those fuckin' rims. Rims bigger than this canyon. Every time I see those damn things, I just want to fire out my truck window, take out both front and back tires, and see those rims grind and spark on down the highway. I say let 'em grind. Those lazy-ass bastards snatch up all these handouts while we, the job creators, work our asses off and just hand 'em more shit. Food stamps, apartments to live in, and free healthcare. Just so they can have more abortions when they get tired of droppin' babies one after another. Makes me fuckin' sick to my stomach. And now Obama's pilin' up all this debt, spendin' on wind farms, batteries, and bullshit. Not drillin' for oil. Costin' us jobs that the Chinese are stealing. How much do we owe those damn chinks anyway? Trillions? Shit, somethin' needs to be done way before 2016, or it's gonna be too fuckin' late. God save us," Derek prayed as the venom spewed from his lips.

Both continued to gaze out over the canyon. This place was a gift from God, a gift to exploit to their hearts' content.

"Let's grab a bite to eat and spend the next few hours up top here, so we can scout out where we wanna be tonight," Derek proposed.

Once again invigorated, Ted agreed, "Yeah, have ourselves a lil' quail, a Frenched rack of wild boar for lunch. God, I love this place!"

Lunch was as expected, succulent and filling. The rabbit and rattlesnake appetizers complemented the quail and wild boar entrées. Ted and Derek could never get enough wild game to eat. They were especially pleased with their meals when *they* had the pleasure of slaying the wildlife *themselves*. What could be more American than that? Vegetables and processed meats were for liberal-fuck pussies. During lunch they finalized their plans for the day.

They decided on a quick analysis of the reserve's grassland above the canyon rim. Using one of the eleven ATVs on the property, they began their quest through the grassy and brushy terrain, scoping it out for feeding and nesting areas.

About forty-five minutes into their expedition, the trackers found reeds in a grassy area that was evidently a boar's lair. Oddly enough, it was only one of two noticeable indications of wild hogs they saw all afternoon.

Ted and Derek grudgingly acknowledged that a wide swath of the nation's central zone was suffering from this God-induced drought. But even *they* were stunned that the ground was so damn hard, so unrelenting that not even three and four-hundred-pound beasts could leave imprints in the turf. They came upon a spot where boars had churned up a small patch of soil, rooting for insects, but other than the empty lair, that was it. Whereas, during earlier excursions, numerous rooting, wallows, tracks, and tree rubs were found.

After a few hours exploring the prairie atop the canyon, Ted and Derek returned to the compound and retired to their cabin for a much-needed late-afternoon nap. Neither mentioned the absence of the typical wildlife markings.

Dinner was served promptly at 7:30. Dusk had come and was long gone. The sliver of moon provided little light for the men to view the canyon in one direction or the vast prairieland in the other. The Great Room where they ate, however, provided all the eye candy a fervent hunter could wish for. The large room was a tribute to the animals tracked and hunted on the ranch over the years. Stuffed, full-bodied Barbary (aoudad) sheep and white-tail and mule deer adorned every corner while wild boar and coyotes guarded the three entrances. Mounted heads and stuffed bobcat, raccoon, grey fox, rattlesnakes, quail, dove, and tarantulas decorated the walls. The trophies sent chills up the men's spines. Anticipation of tonight's hunt was swelling with every bite of the locally harvested meat they savored.

"I haven't shot a thing in damn near three weeks," Derek complained.

"Yeah, I have no doubt the tension's buildin'. Easier to be without sex for that long," Ted figured.

"Gonna bag me up a big ol' boar t'night. Maybe two or three. Get the rust off my finger," Derek said.

Recalling the previous outing at the ranch, Ted said, "Remember the last time we were here? Twice, it took three d'rect shots to bring down those damn beasts. Tough sum-bitches. Perhaps the toughest hogs I ever killed. And now with this damn drought worsenin', they're gettin' meaner than ever, gettin' crazy, runnin' through the streets 'n' shit."

"I know. For every boar we slaughter, we should capture one and release it in the city to chase those gutless liberals bearin' no arms. Then maybe, just maybe, the truth'll be revealed to those losers. Stand up, be men! But no, we always have to run in and save their asses. And they say boars are considered vermin and a nuisance. To hell with those pussy liberals! They're the vermin; they're the nuisance, not the boars!" And with that, they both chuckled while the server, who had overheard Derek's comments about releasing the boars into the cities, howled with laughter.

Since it was a Thursday night, when none of the staff were present, Ted and Derek were the only ones in the room. Ted relished the tranquil setting but looked forward to the next day when a group of eight hunters was expected to arrive.

Mingling with the newcomers, pointing out which trophies in the room were his personal kills, telling tall tales, and out-and-out bullshitting with a bunch of other liked-minded, big game hunters thrilled Ted. He mentioned his excitement to Derek.

His friend understood. "It'll be great, Ted. Tomorrow, only noble people will be here. No liberal fucks would be allowed in this room, ever! Whores, drug-snortin' takers, and queers would be considered vermin if they overstepped this boundary."

Ted knew the eight arriving the next day were his kind of people; God-fearing, able-bodied job creators, conservatives who would never compromise any of their faith-driven beliefs to surrender to the characterless liberals polluting the nation. It was going to be a great long three-day weekend, shooting the shit with *real* Americans, practicing *real* American values.

Derek noticed Ted's dreamy state and asked, "Ya ready, madman? Let's go kill some boars!"

"Hell yeah, I'm ready!" Ted was pumped.

Typically, the ranch offered only guided hunting expeditions, especially while hunting wild boar at night. But with Ted being part owner, exceptions ruled. He could hunt alone whenever and wherever he so chose as long as he didn't interfere with paying visitors. The only drawback was, since the well-known guitarist had brought so much notoriety to the ranch, it created a catch-22. It sometimes put a stranglehold on exactly where he could hunt. On the other hand, both the original owners and Ted were quite pleased with the number of bookings the ranch brought in. Even with the drought, folks wanted to come to the Panhandle, crisscross the prairieland one day then negotiate the spectacular, rugged canyon the next. But to actually hunt in the canyon, clientele had to be resilient, possess great mental and physical endurance, and be prepared to withstand wide ranges of temperatures; attributes Ted admired and believed only hardcore conservatives possessed.

With no *real* Americans booked for the night, Ted and Derek had free reign of the grassy, brushy land above the canyon.

Eagerly, they walked back to the cabin and began their final preparations for the night's hunt.

Both rechecked their recently purchased Smith and Wesson M&P Performance Centered .223 caliber rifles. The semi-automatic, gas-operated rifles had a camouflage finish, held ten rounds per clip, and were equipped with the preferred barrel twist rate of 1:8—a key aspect to engage with Ted's favored ammunition for boar, the .223 70g Barnes TSX. The triple-shock (TSX) bullets' 100 percent copper bodies had multiple rings cut into their shanks. The bullets, blasted at a high velocity, did not fragment and, with the aid of four razor-sharp edges, penetrated 28 percent deeper than lead-core bullets.

With high-tech accuracy, the ammo was designed for quicker, absolute kills by inflicting significant damage to its target. If the bullet contacted bone, it drilled through it; as it ripped through flesh, the bullet rapidly expanded, resulting in a gaping hole. This enhanced technology, refined only in the last decade, now enabled hunters to use the smaller, more accurate caliber bullets to drop big game animals. Agreeably, it was the preferred setup for Ted and Derek to kill wild boar.

They followed the ardent hunters' protocol and showered, then dressed into their explicitly clean hunting gear. Once outside, they sprayed each other from head to toe with scent-killing spray. Using Ted's favorite ATV, the two set off for a night of mayhem with one goal in mind—to satisfy their desire to destroy as many boars as possible.

Twenty minutes into their journey, the men jumped off the ATV and began their hike to the lair they had spotted earlier that afternoon. They crept quietly through the grassland marked with brush and thicket. The earth beneath them was cracked and rock hard. Their heads barely swiveled while their well-trained eyes darted left, right, and left again. Ted inched closer to Derek, just a step behind on his right.

They sensed nothing as they neared the quiet nesting area. Apprehensively, they prowled forward only to find their instincts validated. There were neither boars nor any sign they had returned to the lair since the hunters' visit earlier in the day.

Disappointed and perplexed, they circled back in a snakelike fashion, attempting to scan as much ground as possible before reaching the ATV. The return journey took over an hour, and by the time they arrived back at the vehicle, both were uneasy. The boar population in Texas was exploding. Yet, why weren't they finding any tracks or evidence of wallows, rooting, or trampling of grasses and wheat?

The two soldiered on with the ATV bursting through open pockets of grassland and then slowing as they maneuvered their way around through thicket and brush. Neither spoke as they continued to scour the landscape, searching for any recent rooting activity. Another fifteen minutes went by before Ted spoke in frustration.

"Fuck it! Trackin'! Searchin'! Just not happenin' t'night!"

"Ted, I gotta kill somethin'! Tonight! I haven't shot a fuckin' thing in three weeks! My balls are burstin'!" Derek pleaded.

They both laughed. "All right, then it's plan B. We'll go to our favorite feeder. Ya ready to shoot some fuckin' pigs?" Ted responded.

"Hell yeah! Maybe we'll find some Obama supporters there, porkin' down on some slop, gorgin' themselves from the public trough!" Derek whooped and hollered.

Ted made a sharp right, and they were off to a spot normally reserved for paying hunters, where they almost always saw pigs. Looping back so they could be downwind of the wild swine, the men came within a half-mile of their destination before coming to a rest.

They gathered their rifles and a high-powered spotlight then began making their way to the canyon's rim. As they moved closer and closer, their instincts told them, "Smells like swine just ahead! O's takers must be close."

Crouched down and then on their stomachs, Ted and Derek peered down over the edge, and finally there was a sight to behold. Below them, twenty-five, thirty feral hogs of all sizes and colors were eating from the feeder that the ranch maintained to attract pigs.

The three-legged feeder was no ordinary corn and acorn machine. Every thirty minutes from 10 p.m. to 4 a.m. the contraption dispensed the ranch's specially fabricated blend of slop. Varied amounts of corn, Jell-O, acorns, potatoes, water, and table scraps from the kitchen each night made for a great stew. But what made the ranch's concoction so special was the moonshine brewed onsite and then blended into the mix. For this reason, for decades, the owners assumed the self-proclaimed title of having the "Best Slop in Texas." Knowing the pigs craved the slop fortified with moonshine only intensified Ted's desire to slaughter the commies of the animal world. "Damn pigs are like the Russians; it must taste like vodka or something," Ted would always say.

Ted and Derek patiently looked down upon the feral pigs as they rummaged through the remaining Texas slop from the previous dispensing.

At this juncture of the rim, there were no dramatic drop-offs into the canyon. They could vaguely see a series of slopes and elevations that led down to the feeder, which stood about fifty yards below the canyon rim among rock, brush, and shrub trees. The floodlight on top of the feeder provided just enough visibility for them to see the pigs while remaining hidden on the ledge. The spot was perfect for the strategic ambush.

After thorough consideration, the four largest swine had been identified. Ted would take the two on the left while Derek would concentrate on one in the center and another off to the extreme right. All others were fair game if the opportunity presented itself.

On the count of two, four rapid blasts echoed throughout the canyon. The herd instantaneously fled in the same direction, knowing their only escape was a single, narrow path further down into the canyon. Again, the men took aim and systematically fired three, four additional times. Within seconds the whole episode was over.

Ted and Derek looked down through the beam of the floodlight clouded by dust and took count. Three boars lay motionless. A fourth flailed, attempting to get up, and a fifth staggered down the path.

Ted took aim, fired, and missed as the wounded pig disappeared. Derek laughed, raised his rifle, and sunk two more bullets into the fourth beast that had regained its legs but had yet to locate the escape route.

After he set down his rifle, Derek grabbed the high-powered flashlight and zeroed in on the four dead swine. The mini-ambush satisfied both men's need to kill. Yet, they were pissed off that the fifth boar got away. Ted's philosophy was "kill pigs, any and all pigs." So to think one might have escaped and survived even one more day irritated the shit out of him.

They made their way down the trail to the feeding area where the four swine had met their fate. The men estimated their weight, the size of their tusks, and deemed them non-trophy kills. Not to spoil the feeding area, the hunters dragged the vermin to the ledge and shoved them over to fall forty-five feet onto the next plateau, where they would rot in the brush, to be devoured by a host of scavengers. Derek grinned at Ted and gloated, "I fuckin' love plan B!"

So, too, did the vultures.

Watch Out for Wild Hogs

Hardens' Residence; Canyon, Texas
Thursday, November 15, 2012; 6:24 P.M.

"Hello?" answered Karen Harden.

"Hello, Mrs. Harden. Detective Dawson, Canyon Police Department."

"Did you find 'em? Was he drunk?" she asked, talking over the detective.

"Um . . . no, ma'am. I drove out to Len's place. His truck was there, but I didn't see him or your husband. I looked all around the place, even peeked in the window. I saw nothin' unusual or suspicious."

"Did ya go out to their huntin' spot?" she quickly asked.

"Ma'am, I did drive out to a spot where Len and I hunted over a year ago. I didn't find anything. With the drought bein' so bad, it was almost impossible to see tire tracks or any other evidence that someone had been there recently. I'm sorry, but as of right now, I have no other information for you," he told her regretfully.

Panic overcame her. "Oh, my god! What am I gonna tell Emma? She'll be home in a few hours. What am I gonna do?"

"Mrs. Harden, can you think of anything . . . anything your husband may have said about where they were goin' huntin'? Anything at all?" asked the detective.

"No, I don't pay much attention. He hunts almost every night. Oh, my god! Where is he? I just don't know where he would've gone to!"

"Mrs. Harden, I have a complete description of his truck and license plate number. I'll notify the surrounding jurisdictions, including the Amarillo Police Department," Dawson explained. "If you hear anything or think of anything that might be of help, please give me a holler. I'll get back in touch with you later this evening. In the meantime, contact all your friends and let 'em know your husband didn't return home from huntin' last night. Is there anything I can do for you right now?"

"No, I already called several people I thought he could've been with, but nobody's seen him. Why hasn't he called me? His phone goes straight to voicemail. I hate it when he forgets to turn on his phone!" she said, veering from fear to anger.

"I'm sorry, Mrs. Harden. We'll keep searchin'. I'll call you before six. Hang in there, we'll find 'em. Goodbye," he replied.

Karen hung up the phone without saying anything else.

Over the course of the next few hours, Dawson notified the surrounding police departments and called a few of his hunting friends. He reasoned that someone may have heard where they were going or possibly knew of one of their favorite spots.

Dawson actually suspected they weren't even in Randall County. He figured they most likely traveled to nearby Motley or even Cottle County, a little farther southeast. Those two counties were renowned for an abundance of trophy wild hogs. The detective contemplated to himself, "Considering they were huntin' at night . . . they were huntin' for hogs, weren't they?"

Unfortunately, his inquiries provided no leads. As dusk fell, for the first time the detective started to become alarmed. Sitting at his desk reviewing a map, he began to reconsider his earlier notion that "Hell, men go hunting all the time, stay out late, get drunk, never give a rat's ass about anything or anyone. They come home a day or two late all the time, never once considering anyone else's concerns or worries."

Anxious, Jim knew he had to call Karen again with no new information. He decided it was best that he and Patrol Officer Williams drive to the Hardens' home and deliver the distressing news in person.

During the drive there, the men discussed the possibilities of the hunters' whereabouts. Williams agreed with the detective's initial theory. "They went to Cottle or Motley County. Damn counties are so overrun by pigs, they need to post *Watch Out for Wild Hogs* road signs."

When the officials pulled into the Hardens' short gravel driveway, Karen was already anxiously waiting for them on her front doorstep. Her trembling hands covered her nose and mouth as she took deep breaths, stricken with fear of the worst. The officers exited their vehicle and confidently walked up to meet her.

"Mrs. Harden, this is Patrol Officer Williams."

"Good evenin', ma'am," Williams calmly greeted her.

"We still have not located your husband or Len Mahoney," Dawson told her. "We've put out APBs to all the surrounding counties, including the Amarillo Police Department. There have been no reports or sightin's of them. I promise we'll expand our efforts first thing in the mornin' and begin searchin' several of the more popular huntin' areas. Officer Williams and I believe they most likely went to Cottle or Motley County. Do you know if they hunt there often?"

"I don't know," she said hesitantly. "I . . . well . . . I'm sure he does. He hunts the whole dern Panhandle and most of West Texas, I reckon."

98

The officers tried to reassure her that men extending a hunting excursion wasn't unusual. As the two walked away, Williams turned to Karen and said, "On my rounds later t'night, I'll go back out to Len's place and see if he's made it home. If I learn anything new, I promise to let you know."

Dawson then assured Karen, "I'll call you in the mornin', probably around 7:15 or so. Is that OK?"

Karen stood on the front porch quivering and wringing her hands. The men hesitated for a moment to make sure she was OK before turning toward their cruiser. As they began walking back down the sidewalk, they never heard her mumble, "Thank you."

Checkout

Mesquite Campground; Thursday, November 15, 2012; 3:15 P.M.

The park ranger slowly pulled up to campsite number ninety. It appeared that the modest-sized motorhome remained parked in the exact same position for the third straight day, facing the roadway. A canvas awning shielded a table and two chairs and abutted the campsite's fixed wooden structure which sheltered a metal picnic table.

Wilson proceeded to scope out the quiet, well-maintained area. He got out of his green ranger truck, walked directly to the door and knocked. He knocked again a little harder with no response. He sighed. To the left of the motorhome, he noticed a stainless-steel gas grill next to the picnic table and wondered if it had recently been used. Wilson waved his hand over the grill to check for warmth but felt nothing. Lifting the lid, he found the inside immaculate. He then walked up to the workbench situated directly behind the motorhome. It, too, was impeccable.

The campground had been quiet all week. Out of the twenty available sites, only the motorhome from New Jersey and two other campers had occupied the area. Wilson strolled back to his truck to review the reservation list; the paperwork confirmed the license plate number. With so few visitors that week, he distinctly remembered the two men. They had paid for Monday through Wednesday night. Normally, he didn't check in visitors, but he had been filling in for the assistant who was at lunch. He remembered telling them checkout was Thursday at 2:00 p.m. The driver of the motorhome asked if it would be OK if they decided to stay an additional night. The ranger assured him it was not a problem, but that they should confirm the extra night at the office prior to 9:00 a.m. on Thursday. He assumed the information was understood and chose not emphasize the point. This time of year, even the weekends were rarely filled with campers.

Seated in his truck, Wilson muttered to himself, "This won't be the first time, nor will it be the last, that a camper fails to notify us of their extended stay." As he rolled out of the campground, he continued to scan the area and decided he would stop back shortly before the end of his shift.

It was just before seven o'clock and now dark when Wilson returned to the undisturbed campsite. Still, all was quiet. It was apparent that no activity whatsoever had taken place since his visit earlier that afternoon. Regardless, the ranger walked up to the motorhome and knocked on the door. And again, there was no response. He walked over to check the grill. It was cool and had even collected a light layer of dust. Using his flashlight, he scanned the perimeter of the site and found nothing alarming.

A little perturbed, he headed back to the station. Entering the building, Wilson caught the park's assistant, who was just leaving. He updated her about site number ninety, which had not been paid for the night. The two of them made light of the situation and locked up before they left for the evening. The first shift would collect the $24 fee tomorrow.

Not Her Mark

Jimmy's Penthouse; Thursday, November 15, 2012; 7:40 P.M.

Going to his place on a Thursday night was risky, especially when she was supposed to be out with friends. It had been over a week since she last saw Jimmy, and the thought of him being gone for ten days drove her painfully insane. She tried to restrain her paranoia, but couldn't help but wonder about her husband. "Surely, he won't run into one of my friends I'm supposed to be with, will he?"

Knowing how many times she would intensely cum in the next hour filled her with exhilaration. But the lies were getting to her. Her husband was a respectful and faithful man. However, it made her shudder to think about having to fake a climax with him later that evening.

She reconciled her thoughts waiting for the elevator. If not now, it would be three weeks before she would be able to revel in the pleasures that only Jimmy could fulfill. Highs that could only be managed by reaching newer ones, and three weeks was just too long. She smiled as she thought, "I know I bring out those same intense feelings in him. Our lust and cravings for each other are equal." The elevator door opened, and she was on her way to the forty-fourth floor.

Just like her last visit, he hadn't even closed the door before they embraced, kissing passionately. Before she could even set her purse down, Jimmy slid his hands down her back and over her hips then began squeezing her buttocks. As she began to squirm, he let her slip from his grasp.

Elaine could feel his eyes lustfully following her as she pranced into the living room and sat down on the soft leather sofa. To take the edge off and calm her nerves, she asked Jimmy to make her a drink. "Vodka on the rocks, perhaps with a twist of lime?"

Jimmy glared at her and grudgingly walked up to the bar and fixed two modest drinks. She asked him what he preferred.

"Johnnie Walker," he replied.

"Nice, that's what my father drank. Which label?" she asked, knowing her scotches.

"Normally the Black, sometimes the Double Black. On special nights, I like to treat myself with Johnnie Walker Blue," he spoke bluntly.

"Are you going to have the Blue for me tonight?" she playfully asked.

Annoyed, he replied, "I said special nights. T'night, I'm havin' Black."

As Jimmy handed her the drink, she caught a glimpse of a barely noticeable mark on his neck. Her lustful desires exploded inside of her at the sight of it, recalling that night. She desperately tried to restrain her facial expressions as she curiously thought, "I can't believe it's still visible!"

Elaine began telling Jimmy how much she missed him. That she was so glad she could see him again without having to wait until he came home from his trip over the holidays. His response was indifferent.

They sipped their drinks, and she asked, "So what's your favorite TV show?"

"The markets, sports, a lot of politics," was his response, again with little enthusiasm.

103

Elaine stood up, drink in hand, and began studying the artwork, furnishings, and photos Jimmy had used to decorate the posh penthouse. When she commented on one of the statues resting on a solid oak pedestal, it only brought disdain to Jimmy. He loved the piece from Mexican artist Sergio Bustamante, *The Look,* but at this moment, he didn't give a shit about the statue or what she thought of the art, let alone her favorite TV show. He sat there watching her wander from the pedestal, to an end table, then to a desk and bookshelf.

He kept thinking, "What the fuck? Are you kidding me? You're not here for small talk! I don't have time for this shit! Why is it always the same? The third, fourth time, they all think the rules have changed. Like I give a shit about them! I have to entertain them? God damn it! Didn't I make it clear, you're not worthy of Johnnie Walker Blue?"

Elaine strolled through the kitchen and set her empty glass on the granite countertop. She then made her way into the adjacent living area and looked at a row of pictures sitting on a beautiful Theodore Alexander table in the hallway just outside Jimmy's bedroom. She was twirling her long, brown hair and asked Jimmy about one photo in particular. "Are these your brothers? Which one of you is the oldest?"

Jimmy came up behind her from across the room, ignoring her questions. Reaching from behind, he groped her breasts and began lightly kissing her neck. He let one hand drop just below her breasts and firmly pulled her closer to him. Then moving his hand down her body to her lower abdomen, he forced her buttocks to press up against his swollen groin. Her upper arms were pinned, leaving her hands just below her hips. As Elaine turned to lustfully kiss him, her hands were exactly where he wanted them. She could feel the pulsation of the bulge through his jeans and began stroking him.

"Oh Jimmy, you make me want you so badly. Do you want me too? What can I do for you?" she whispered seductively. Again, he ignored her questions.

Assertively, Jimmy guided her through his bedroom door and sat her on the edge of his bed. He pushed on her left shoulder, forcing her upper body to lie back while her feet remained on the floor. As she kicked off her shoes, he unzipped her pants and ripped off her rather expensive, tight jeans, damaging the zipper. While Jimmy turned to dim the lights, she sat up and removed her blouse, leaving on only her miniscule bright white panties.

Jimmy quickly undressed before he walked back to the side of the bed. Seeing her panties, he bent down and yanked them off. They would never be worn again.

Elaine welcomed his lean, muscular body standing before her as he forced his upper thighs and hips between her knees. For a moment, he paused to gaze at her voluptuous breasts, then lifted her legs so that her ankles rested on his shoulders. He probed her three, four times before he finally entered her. As Elaine felt his presence, she knew, it wasn't a matter of *if* she would climax, but how many times and how intense they would be. He implicitly understood this with all his lovers and considered it his duty to comply.

Jimmy had dimmed the lights exactly the same way he did for all of his sexual engagements; his ritual was the same with everyone. By his recollection, Elaine was his fourth different encounter since Sunday. But who was counting?

Although Jimmy halfheartedly tried making mental note of what turned each of his women on and their specific desires, it often became muddled. "Was it Anne or Carol who liked it harder?" They both begged for it rough, but he couldn't remember which one screamed and pleaded for more while the other just succumbed. Right now, he really didn't give a shit. He was fucking Elaine.

Knowing she was his most trusted colleague's wife, it aggravated him that it took over two years to sway her. He had scrutinized every part of her from the first time they met at the office. "Slender, tight ass, and perfectly shaped, firm breasts—36C. A tiger, no doubt."

Once inside Elaine, Jimmy's frustration of her prior rejections emerged. Their first two encounters could be described as animalistic as they uncontrollably pawed and nipped at one another. Tonight, Jimmy's clenching, restraining, and manhandling surpassed the two previous trysts. The forcefulness even shocked and somewhat disturbed Elaine, but wasn't that what she wanted as she stood outside the elevator doors downstairs, newer highs? Much to Jimmy's aggravation, her responses were tame, more affectionate, and wanting to be tenderly touched and made love to rather than savagely fucked.

Hoping to lure her into his sexual whims and intensify her cravings for him, he rolled over onto his back and briefly relented, letting Elaine crawl on top of him and feel close to him. He permitted her to do what she loved most, kiss his neck, nibble on his ear, and rub his bare chest.

As he turned his head to let her nip and draw on his other ear, Elaine noticed another mark on the lower left side of his neck; a larger, fresher mark—definitely not her mark.

Their lips met before she edged slightly lower and sucked hard on his neck, instantly bruising the flesh just above the new mark. Then with her cheek, she gently nudged his head to the left and cunningly took his right earlobe into her mouth, seductively licked it, and gently sucked on it before vengefully clamping down. Instinctively, Jimmy yanked his head away, her teeth partially ripping his earlobe, leaving it to ooze a few drops of his precious blood.

Jimmy angrily flung her off him, yelling, "Bitch!" and quickly reversed positions, putting himself on top of her. Gripping her arms just below her shoulders, Jimmy entered her again and refused to withdraw as she screamed. He continued to ravish her body, thrusting in and out as she tried to buck him off. He bent down and, with his lips and tongue, engulfed her large left nipple into his mouth and bit her so hard that the excruciating pain propelled her hips and lower body to violently recoil and push Jimmy out and off of her. He tried to regain his leverage, but she had already turned to her side. Jimmy firmly clutched her from behind, bruising her upper arms, but retreated when she began whimpering, then crying.

He stood up, stared down at her in contempt, and thought, "Why is it always the third or fourth time? Every damn woman gets so fucking emotional. What's their fucking problem?" Jimmy put on his jeans and retreated to his office, just like the two previous times.

Elaine went into the bathroom and tried to regain composure. Distraught, she stared into the mirror and questioned herself. "I thought we were equals. Who could rival me?"

She started to put on her panties when she realized the left-side string had snapped; the panties were un-wearable. Flustered, Elaine slipped on her jeans. She started to button them but was unable to raise the damaged zipper. The opening partially exposed the upper portion of her smoothly waxed pubic area. She put on her blouse, straightened her hair, and again tried to compose herself. Elaine reached down and picked up her panties. She fondled them, then, with a crafty smirk on her face, she walked back into the bedroom and devilishly slipped them under Jimmy's sheets. Five minutes later, she quietly let herself out.

When Jimmy finally heard the door shut, he muttered, "Fuckin' women, all the same! Equal? Equal with me? Fuckin' pigs! After a few visits, they all want to become soul mates. Don't they understand? Other than fuckin' them, I would much rather be with their husbands or boyfriends, huntin', tradin', anything but talkin' to them?"

Top of the Food Chain

Texas Panhandle; Thursday, November 15, 2012

The hogs were unaware of climate change or specific natural disasters and tumultuous weather events that had been transforming the earth. The animal kingdom had no way of knowing or understanding these circumstances. Trends such as rapidly melting polar ice caps and glaciers, rising seas, earthquakes, and devastating tsunamis across the globe were unknown to the boars. Nor could they be aware of what had transpired in the past decade in other areas on their continent: an unprecedented super storm, multiple hurricanes and tornados, flooding, and excessive snowfall. Most of those occurrences took place far from their immediate environment. What plagued the wild hogs residing in the Panhandle was drought, a drought that created excessive heat and dust similar to when man had altered the hogs' natural world decades ago, the Dust Bowl of the 1930s.

The drought began in October 2010 and dramatically intensified the following year. In 2011, numerous temperature records were set near Amarillo: an all-time high of 111 degrees set in June; fifty days that reached 100 degrees or higher; and fifty consecutive days of 90 degrees or higher.

July 2011 held the record for the hottest monthly average ever at 85.2 degrees Fahrenheit.

The extreme heat curtailed the region's tornado activity to a mere four compared to a historical average of twenty-one per year. The lack of storms minimized the rainfall, with the year yielding a scant seven inches where normally twenty inches were expected. Statistic after statistic proved 2011 to be one of the most taxing years for the environment in recorded times.

Every living organism labored to sustain its species. The rainfall in 2012 slightly improved the conditions, but it was still barely more than half the yearly average that fell from the skies. The entire continent averaged 55.3 degrees for the year, smashing the previous record by one degree, and 3.2 degrees higher than the twentieth century average.

Some areas tolerated the drought better than others, yet over 300 million trees died in Texas in 2011. Where plants had succumbed, the surrounding earth was virtually scorched, the turf barren and rock hard. The large expanses of native grasses and brush lost sapped an inordinate number of creatures that relied on it for food and shelter. Survival became dependent upon an organism's ability to garner essential nutrients more efficiently, and in non-customary fashions. For the boars, this meant they had to dramatically alter their dietary intake.

Normally, their nourishment was more than 90 percent vegetarian while worms, insects, eggs, rodents, small mammals, and even dead animals made up the balance. The boars recognized, with their natural predators long extinct, they sat at the top of the food chain—a disputed second only to man. With their intellectual and physical prowess, the transition from primarily vegetarian to carnivorous was skillful, as the boars, without fear, began inflicting their will on every moving creature except man, until now.

As conditions deteriorated, unrest amongst the many nations of boars grew. Their mindsets had evolved, and, unlike the last time man's activities had severely impacted the environment, the boars were no longer willing to remain passive. The belief, "It was time to confront and challenge man as equals," spread as quickly as the wildfires that had plagued their lands. They inherently understood in desperate times it was kill or be killed.

There is always a first mover, the first to change the ordinary. For the boars, that was a sounder that ruled the region in and around the Palo Duro Canyon, just outside Amarillo, Texas. The group's ancestors had formed the foundation over seven decades ago. Instituting authoritarian social principles, the sect enjoyed unprecedented dominance throughout the Panhandle.

To enhance the power and sustainability of the sounder, the ascendant males limited the size of the pack to approximately one hundred strong. When it expanded much beyond that, splinter groups formed. The new, far-smaller packs then migrated dozens of miles from their original herd. This pattern had been established several decades earlier and was strictly adhered to by a succession of pure Russian wild boars.

The Russian breed dictated mating relations and, to date, had no challengers. The splinter groups were always led by another Russian boar that was afforded several hybrids and at least two additional Russian females. But in the last several months, as the environment increasingly punished every plant and animal alike, a hybrid male with lineage to a domesticated stock threatened the supremacy of the dominant Russian boar. The cross-breed matched the Russian leader's size, strength, tenacity, and, most importantly, his intelligence. For the first time in the sounder's history, the genetically superior Russian variety's reign over the sounder was disputed.

The herd sensed upheaval, and the prospect of a hybrid hog leading the sounder for the first time generated great internal strife. The crux of the dissension centered on one issue; their relationship with man. The hybrids, who vastly outnumbered the Russian breed in nearly every sounder, argued; if equals, why did the boars allow man to rule the lands unequivocally and, in the process, destroy the environment and routinely commit mass genocide against their species without fear of retribution?

No Más, No Más

Ciudad Juárez, Mexico; September 2011
Oklahoma City, Oklahoma; Fall 2011-November 2012
Late Arrival Camping Area; Palo Duro Canyon State Park; Canyon, Texas
Thursday, November 15, 2012

In September 2011, the Vasquez family fled their hometown of Ciudad Juárez. In just a few years' time, the city had become one of the most dangerous places in the world. The turf war between the Mexican drug cartels increased the homicide rate tenfold to more than 3,000 murders in 2010. [7] Across the country, over 50,000 citizens had been assassinated over a five-year period as the drug lords battled to be the supply chain to the U.S. illicit drug markets. [8] The violence was startling. Gunmen invaded shops, businesses, and restaurants, slaying countless people at a time. The assassins left torsos in the streets after decapitating their victims and severing their extremities. America's thirty-year assault on drugs sparked a war on their own border as deadly and economically devastating as the wars they waged overseas.

The violence in Ciudad Juárez exploded in 2007 and continued after President Felipe Calderón sent 10,000 troops to maintain order in the beleaguered city. Prior to the crisis, 1.3 million people had made it their home. In only a few years, nearly 230,000 people, about 20 percent of the population, had fled. [9] As people departed in droves, crime surged.

Justo and Claudia Vasquez desperately wanted to remain and raise their boys, Carlos and Juan, in their native country. They themselves had been born and raised in Juárez and had established a successful business selling produce, fruits, nuts, and flowers. Their business allowed them to live well beyond the average household and to support extended family.

Then one evening, three different buildings near their business were burned to the ground. The next week, in broad daylight, several neighbors were horrifically slaughtered outside their homes. Their bullet-riddled bodies were left lying in the street as a gang of four men fired at the windows of anyone staring out. The faith of the Vasquez family was shattered. Justo and Claudia decided that night to be counted among those who had deserted Ciudad Juárez, not among those who had been senselessly murdered there.

It took them a month to arrange safe passage across the border into El Paso, Texas. Once the plan was finalized and the monies paid, they departed the next day, leaving everything behind. Upon crossing the border, they met their contact at a popular Mexican restaurant. The arrangements provided the family a used minivan with current plates, registration, a full tank of gas, and a map of the United States in the glove box. Justo and Claudia were handed fraudulent identification and green cards that would expire in fifteen months. The tools for their new life had cost them nearly their entire life savings.

The Vasquezes felt no shame or sense of debt to America for illegally entering the country. They knew the extreme violence in Mexico was directly related to a couple of issues: America's limitless demand for a plethora of drugs as well as ineffective and outdated drug policies. Like many of their fellow citizens, the Vasquezes realized the market for illegal substances was never going to subside and that it was the corrupt legislative system that enabled the failed policies to remain in place. With over 1.3 million drug-possession arrests per year—nearly half being offenses for small amounts of marijuana—a number of parties desperately sought to keep strict enforcement in place. [10] Police unions, representing scores of law-enforcement agencies trying to maintain federal grants to balance their budgets, and private prison companies, trying to maximize profits, would continue to lobby extensively to maintain the harsh penalties. Joining the hardliners, companies in the alcohol, cigarette, and pharmaceutical industries also worked vigorously to stifle any efforts to legalize marijuana or relax fines and jail terms, their purpose being to ward off future competition. Until the unjust, hypocritical, and counterproductive system was overturned, Justo and Claudia saw little hope for their homeland.

The Vasquez family was not alone. All of their acquaintances in Ciudad Juárez agreed and believed these were the critical factors that turned their homeland from one with hope and incremental progress to one of despair and unimaginable social denigration. The majority also believed Americans living along the boundary recognized the significance of the problem, but the rest of America was apathetic. For the vast majority of Americans not living near the periphery, the death and destruction in Mexico might as well have been on another planet, not a country sharing a nearly 2,000-mile border with the U.S. Realizing this, thousands of decent, law-abiding families remained in Mexico strictly out of pride. So when the Vasquezes abandoned everything they had, everything they knew, they did so out of necessity, not because they sought greener pastures in the United States. Yet, they felt little resentment. How could they condone the actions of their fellow citizens? Christians killing Christians, all on the account of American-bred selfishness and greed.

Upon their arrival, they sought no special privileges or entitlements. The proud parents just wanted to work and raise their children in a safe environment, to educate Carlos and Juan so they, too, would be able to raise their own families and be productive citizens.

In the fifteen months they had been in America, neither parent had abandoned their dream of returning to Ciudad Juárez to reestablish the life that was natural for them. Every day, their dream drove them to save money, to exude optimism to their children, and to wait patiently until peace returned to the country they loved. Whenever that peaceful day arrived, Justo wanted to return on his terms, and not before. He knew if that was to be the case, he needed to wisely navigate their lives while in America and not act or think like other illegal aliens.

His first key decision before entering the U.S. was choosing Oklahoma City to start their new life. Justo thought the town was the perfect distance from Mexico, large enough to support a diverse population, yet small enough not to overwhelm his family. More importantly, what illegal immigrant would purposely move to Oklahoma when just a few years earlier its legislature had passed bill 1804, considered the nation's toughest anti-immigration law? He knew there were numerous reports of thousands of employees and school children vanishing overnight, leaving shortages across a number of industries days after the historic bill passed.

He rightly reasoned, "Employee shortages mean higher wages for me." When employers would ask him why he moved to Oklahoma City, Justo could respond cogently, if not truthfully, "Because there are employee shortages, and I'm legal." Besides, he told himself, he considered the statement not untruthful, considering how much he had paid for his legitimacy.

Fraudulent or not, the Vasquezes' green cards would expire November 30, 2012. He had already made arrangements in El Paso to secure new cards that would be valid for another three years.

Like his predecessors in late 2007, Justo and his family one day suddenly vanished from the state of Oklahoma. When he walked out of work that last day, never to return, he voided all of his efforts and the goodwill he had generated being a model employee. Justo had told his employer his new green card would arrive any day, which was true, except it would be under a different name and birthdate. Not wanting to risk being identified if he remained in Oklahoma City, Justo and Claudia decided to relocate to Albuquerque where they had numerous friends and associates who had also fled Ciudad Juárez.

The move contradicted his earlier philosophies of thinking independently of other Mexican nationals, but the loneliness of Oklahoma City had taken its toll on the family. In his heart, Justo knew his children and, particularly, Claudia needed the presence of a larger and more tight-knit Hispanic community. In Albuquerque, they would renew longstanding customs, proudly celebrate their culture, and commiserate with others who shared similar life experiences. Oklahoma City had served its purpose; the family had learned to meld with the gringo culture. Justo and Claudia concluded now was the time to take what they had absorbed about American business and American values and implement those concepts in Albuquerque, where a larger Latino community existed. In a matter of a few hours, the Vasquezes quietly loaded everything they owned into the minivan and a seven-foot-tall cargo trailer he had purchased earlier at an estate sale, and left without a word.

They departed Oklahoma City with little regrets. While they actually had never heard negative comments, they believed many of the locals viewed them with mistrust and indignation. The state that only a few years ago passed a law that drove many of their countrymen out had accepted them mainly for one reason: small businesses could hire Claudia and Justo at a significant discount over their gringo brethren.

Following his unorthodox patterns, the family left late afternoon in the middle of the month, foregoing two weeks' rent. By design, they would arrive at a campground under the cover of darkness and quietly be on their way to New Mexico the next morning; a state whose name Justo had always considered ironic. He hoped the terminology would someday be applied to his own country, when Mexico was renewed, ridding itself of corruption and heinous crime. Once in Albuquerque, he would apply all that he had learned and act as if America was his native country until he could return to his own someday. That was their dream, their plan, and Albuquerque was the next logical step.

Their new home was about 550 miles from Oklahoma City, a solid nine-hour drive. Justo wanted to arrive in Albuquerque during the middle of the day, so there would be time to settle in with the Segovias, their friends who were going to house them for a few weeks.

He planned for the family to stay overnight in Amarillo, Texas, which was halfway between the two cities. They would awaken the following day and have a modest drive to their final destination. Wishing to remain inconspicuous, Justo planned to stay overnight in a private campground where the family could pitch a tent for the night. He had located one south of Amarillo near the beautiful Palo Duro Canyon State Park. The couple had decided they would be ready to go at first light, so they could spend a few hours touring the park before leaving for Albuquerque later that morning.

Even the best of plans experience unforeseen difficulties. The family arrived at the private campground around 8:45 p.m. Located on Texas Route 217 just off the highway, Justo and Claudia were shocked to learn that there were no available sites. The owner explained that, since losing their homes in the economic recession, permanent residents living in campers and trailers occupied every spot.

Claudia looked at her husband, a tight smile on her face, and asked, "You did not think to call, Justo, to make sure they had spaces available?"

"Claudia, how was I to know?" he answered her, returning the small, tight smile.

"Perhaps by using a telephone, heh?" she said. Although her tone was even and low-key, Justo could tell she was irritated with him. "You could have done that, Justo . . ."

"But I thought, this time of year . . . ," he said, interrupting her.

"But you didn't . . . ," she said, speaking over him.

All of this had been in Spanish, calmly and quietly, to hide from the campground owner that they were having a disagreement because Claudia knew Justo would not appreciate her making him look foolish in front of the gringo.

At this point, the owner interrupted both of them. "Uh, folks."

After such a long day, they were hot, tired, and easily irritated. Claudia's Spanish would soon be rapid-fire. The smiles disappeared, and the couple's voices rose ever so slightly with each exchange.

"And where am I to sleep, me with my two young hijos? Tell me that, my brave husband!" Claudia demanded. "We are tired, and we have come so far, and still have so far to go."

"Hey, folks, hey now!" the owner said, raising his voice to be heard over their own. The Spanish ended abruptly, and the couple glared at each other before turning their attention to the campground owner.

"There's another place not far from here," he said. "I'm sure there are available campsites."

Justo's and Claudia's smiles returned to their faces, and Justo nodded to the gentleman, confirming he understood.

"Oh, that is very kind of you, señor. Very kind," Claudia said in English. "Could you tell us please about this place?"

The owner instructed the family to drive straight down Route 217, approximately eleven miles to the state park's entrance. He explained that the gate would be locked, so they would not be able to access the state campgrounds, but that there was a legal spot to camp for the night down the gravel road just off to the right side of the park's headquarters.

"You can't miss it. There's a sign on the gate that says, *Late Arrival Camping Area*, with an arrow that points to the overnight campground. Just remember, no fires. You can't have an open flame there, OK?" he told the couple.

Claudia and Justo were skeptical, but the man appeared to be so nice and sincere that their gut feelings trusted him.

"Good luck! Make sure you visit the canyon tomorrow," he said as he waited for them to accept his recommendation. The couple looked at each other, then back at the helpful man.

"Gracias. Thank you so much for the information," said Justo. "We will head that way now."

Considering he knew no other viable alternatives, and that Claudia and the boys were likely to become more irritable after such an eventful day, he turned to his wife and asked, "Is it OK with you, Claudia?"

"Well, we will have to make the best of this," she sighed, then said a little more cheerfully, "And besides, we will be right at the canyon when we wake up."

Pulling out of the overcrowded campground, Justo told himself to trust the owner's advice. "I am legal; why should I be worried?"

After a few miles down the dark and desolate state road, Justo decided, "If the entrance and signs match what the man described, I will follow his suggestion and set up camp. Then at first light, we will pack the tent, register at the entrance, and drive through the canyon as planned."

As they approached the park, Claudia tried to distract her sons because she knew they were tired and hungry when they began to whine a little. She talked about how excited she was to visit the canyon. The boys asked, "What does the canyon look like?"

"Kind of like a giant hole in the ground," answered their father.

"Oh, Justo, it is more than just a giant hole in the ground, I am sure!" she chided him. "Still, it has been practically flat the entire drive here, and now we're only a few miles away. It is amazing that a giant canyon is just ahead!"

With anticipation, Carlos and Juan watched out the side windows, looking for signs of this "giant hole in the ground." They squabbled over whether or not it was going to be bigger than the swimming pool they went to last summer.

Moments later, the family pulled up to the park's entrance. Surrounded by neatly arranged rocks, a large wooden sign stood before them with the words in bright yellow letters, *Welcome to Palo Duro Canyon State Park, Texas Parks and Wildlife Department*. As they slowly drove past the sign, the boys yelled in excitement, "Ciervo! Ciervo! I see a deer!"

Justo came to a complete stop, so the boys could watch three deer only twenty feet off the side of the paved road. After letting the boys admire the graceful animals for a few minutes, he began to proceed, anxiously searching for the "Late Arrival" sign that the owner of the private campground had mentioned.

The next wooden sign Justo saw was also painted brown with bright yellow words. The sign had two panels. The top panel stated, *Hours of Operation*. The larger panel on the bottom had two lines. The first read, *Sun-Thu 8:00 a.m.-6:00 p.m.,* and just beneath, it stated, *Fri-Sat 8:00 a.m.-8:00 p.m.*

121

Traveling another fifteen yards around a slight curve in the road, the minivan's headlights exposed the building at the park's entrance where visitors could get maps and pay to enter. Adjacent to the building, a long, nearly five-foot-high steel gate blocked their way. It had two vertical and two horizontal bars that created nine separate, equally sized frames twenty inches tall and sixty inches wide. To the couple's delight, in the center of the top of the gate was the standard Texas Parks and Wildlife Department's wooden sign with bright yellow letters carved into it. The sign read exactly as the man had told them, *Late Arrival Camping Area*, with an arrow pointing to a gravel road off to their right. Just below the sign, covering the middle frame of the gate, was a large diamond-shaped, thin sheet of steel painted bright red to alert night visitors that the road leading into the park was blocked. Relieved, Justo maneuvered the minivan and trailer to the right, entering the rock-strewn road. They slowly made their way down the dark trail and into the primitive campground.

Towing the moving trailer, the older-model Plymouth minivan crept along, leading deeper into the brush and grassland. Justo reached a tight oval allowing him to go right or left. He steered right, slowly circled the entire loop once before deciding to camp at one of about a half-dozen unmarked but well-defined spots. The site was near a modest slope that eventually led to the canyon walls and had a fairly large barrier of grass and brushy area. Trying to best align the vehicle and trailer so he could use the van's headlights to pitch the tent, Justo inadvertently ran over low-lying brush that bordered the makeshift campsite. Once he positioned the vehicle just right, he and Claudia exited the van and opened the sliding back door to let the boys out.

Juan and Carlos ran in circles chasing one another, letting off nearly five hours of pent-up energy. Justo was amazed at their exuberance since he felt exhausted and stiff from loading the trailer and then making the long drive. Within a few minutes, both boys shyly mentioned they had to go to the bathroom. Justo hurried the two along and let them relieve themselves several yards down the road. Taking a hint from Claudia, he kept the boys busy for a few minutes, so she could do the same. When the father and sons got back to the van, Justo said it was time to set up camp. He asked the boys if they would like to help. Eagerly they yelled, "Yes!"

Leaving his headlights on to light up the area, Justo, Juan, and Carlos began unpacking the tent just yards from the vehicle, and within ten minutes the process was complete. Justo positioned the tent before he attempted to properly secure it with stakes. Driving the first stake in the front corner proved fruitless, as the unrelenting ground was as hard as rock; it only chipped the ground and failed to lodge firmly into the soil. He tried the opposite corner with the same results. Realizing his efforts were useless, he placed the stakes and hammer in the back of the van. Then he and Claudia carried the sleeping bags, pillows, a small cooler, a duffle bag, and the boys' stuffed tigers into the tent. After everything was organized, all four of them stood outside, proudly admiring their magnificent hut, illuminated by the van's headlights.

Because he did not want to drain the battery, Justo asked Claudia and the boys to get inside the tent while he went to the driver's side to grab the flashlight and turn off the headlights. The cheap plastic flashlight barely pierced the night, leaving the family in near darkness. Claudia admonished him to hurry; Juan and Carlos didn't like the dark. He quickly responded, "Just a minute. I want to lock all the doors."

He walked around the front of the van to check the passenger side then looked down only to discover the rear tire was losing air and would soon become flat. A sense of dread fell upon him. He knelt down with his flashlight to get a closer look but couldn't find any noticeable damage. Disheartened, Justo walked back to the tent and delivered the bad news. He asked if he should wait until morning when he would have light. After a brief discussion with Claudia, they concluded that every minute of daylight was precious, and, since he was very proficient with cars, it would only take a few more minutes to change the tire in the dark.

The boys protested. They didn't want to be left in the darkness. "Can we watch, Papa? Please can we watch you?" Claudia sighed.

Both parents knew the boys were restless and would be scared in the tent without their papa. So they agreed the boys could watch him repair the flat tire. The boys jumped for joy. Claudia grudgingly joined them outside while Justo promptly unhitched the trailer from the van.

From the moment the boys got out of the tent, they frolicked but never strayed more than a few feet from their parents. Despite the late hour, it was apparent that as the night air became cooler, their liveliness only increased. Time and time again, as they took brief moments to rest, Juan and Carlos asked question after question while eyeing the stars.

"Where did the stars come from? Did God make them? Can we visit one someday? How long would it take to get there?"

While Claudia tried to answer their questions as best she could, Justo loosened the lug nuts on the wheel, put the jack in place, and began to lift the rear passenger side of the van.

"Papa, Juan's taller than me! He can see the stars better than me! Can you lift me up?" asked Carlos.

Their papa laughed. The boys, five and six, insisted they would be able to see the stars so much better if they could lie on the roof of the trailer. Then they could see the stars equally as well.

Claudia told them, "Do not bother your papa while he is working. You can see the stars just fine on the ground. It would not be safe to put you up so high on the top of the trailer!"

Justo, however, laid his tools aside and picked up Juan, stood on the sturdy fender, and lifted him onto the trailer's roof.

"Now stay right in the middle of the roof. Do not move around," Justo told his son, "and keep an eye on your brother. I do not want either of you to fall, OK?"

Juan nodded and said, "Yes, Papa, I will. I promise not to let Carlos fall." Justo then gently lifted Carlos and reiterated to his youngest son to stay right next to Juan in the middle of the roof, and to be careful not to fall. They immediately lay down and gazed in wonder at the star-filled sky.

Walking back to his work, Justo looked into his wife's eyes and saw her apprehension; she was annoyed with him for putting her babies in danger. "They will be just fine, Claudia," he assured her, "and they will stay free of my work while they are up there."

It was a clear night, and the crisp air had the boys huddled together to stay warm. To comfort them, their mother went to the tent and brought back their sleeping bags and stuffed tigers. Unable to clearly see them on top of the trailer, she moved several feet away to the edge of the brushy area to keep a watchful eye on the pair. She sipped a Coke as the two giggled and pointed to the sky, telling her all that they saw: a dragon, a cat, and tigers just like theirs. Even a large, scary bird.

The boys' joy and unconcern for their current plight brought great comfort to Justo and Claudia. Finding sparkly patterns in the star-laced sky not only entertained the boys, but their parents as well.

Justo listened to their comments and laughter as he removed the damaged tire and placed it a few feet away from the vehicle. Working with the small flashlight slowed his pace, but he knew the boys were content and that Claudia would wait patiently, knowing he was doing all he could. He thought to himself: He was a blessed man with his beautiful wife and his two fine sons. For that he thanked his Lord, Jesus Christ.

Excerpt from the Declaration of Independence, July 4, 1776
"We hold these truths to be self-evident, that all men are created equal,
that they are endowed by their Creator with certain unalienable Rights
that among these are Life, Liberty, and the pursuit of Happiness."

Equal was in the mind of the beholder. The Vasquezes considered themselves equals but never felt as equals during their time in America—or when they resided in their beloved country of Mexico. It was impossible to look across the border, past the tens of thousands of shanties with tin roofs and no plumbing, and feel as though anyone on their side of the dying river was an equal of anyone living on the hallowed side. In fact, during their lifetime in Juárez, Justo and Claudia felt the gap had only widened, as the effects of the drug war and drought extorted an even greater toll on their already impoverished nation.

While the violence would kill a soul in a heartbeat, the drought equaled a slow insidious death. In less than two decades, the Rio Grande River's depth in El Paso had fallen from over fourteen feet to barely three feet. The lack of rain in the Midwest, throughout Texas, and into Mexico drove food prices dramatically higher across the continent. Commodities, including cattle, which were once consumed in their homeland where they were desperately needed, were now exported in record volumes north of the border where consumers could afford to pay higher prices. Free enterprise was the explanation, the law of supply and demand. To the Vasquezes and many of their countrymen all men were created equal in the eyes of God, but in real life they understood they would never be equals. Like the hogs, their fate often rested on the will and actions of men who professed the concept of equal opportunities for all. A concept misguided from inception when, more often than not, those men didn't truly believe all men were equal anyway. So why give equal opportunities for all? As for the pigs being equals? They were pigs, not man, and surely not equals.

Being illegal immigrants, not U.S. citizens, Justo and Claudia were not given the opportunity to pursue their unalienable rights as declared by the U.S. Declaration of Independence: Life, Liberty, and the pursuit of Happiness. Even if they had been legal U.S. citizens, tonight it wouldn't have mattered. The boars didn't know their nationality. To the boars, they were humans: humans who didn't consider their species equals; humans who would die as the boar nation sought their own equality.

Justo had just placed the spare tire onto the wheel studs and was reaching for a lug nut when he heard the most horrific sound of snapping bones. The spine-tingling vibration of a 350-pound hybrid hog smashing into the back of Claudia's legs, sending her up and over the boar's massive body, then hearing her land with a thud on the rock-solid ground, sent waves of panic throughout Justo's body. He did not witness the boar's crushing blow, but when he looked up, he saw a second creature had descended upon her as she screamed in terror.

Justo leapt to his feet and turned toward her, only to be broadsided by a third boar that drove him to the ground, writhing in pain. The jolt was so violent he never even felt the deep gash to his left thigh from the six-inch razor-sharp tusks.

Startled, the boys got onto their hands and knees and crawled to the edge of the trailer's roof. As they looked down, they saw a creature strike their father, plunging a tusk into his shoulder area, wildly shaking its head. Juan grabbed his brother, scooted back to the center of the roof, and squeezed Carlos's trembling body. The boys listened as two boars, fighting to get at the fallen man, slammed into the van, knocking it off its jack. The loud crash was the only thing that interrupted the constant grunts, growls, and high-pitched squeals. Petrified, Carlos cried for help; Juan squeezed him harder while cupping his mouth, whispering, "¡Silencio! ¡Por favor, silencio!"—"Be quiet! Please, be quiet!" Claudia would have been proud of her oldest son remembering the more polite "silencio," rather than "cállate"—"shut up."

But Claudia was beyond noticing niceties as five boars quickly encircled her. Immediately, a boar bit her right arm and, in one rip, stripped away most of her bicep. Another boar gored her just below her left hip and then clamped down on her left thigh, thrashed its head back and forth, and took a large chunk of flesh from her leg. Claudia's screams continued as five boars now tore at her body, none inflicting a fatal wound. Separate boars gnawed on each extremity while a fifth desperately tried to devour her lean stomach. Unable to latch onto her midsection, the last boar plunged its tusks into her belly and applied all of its weight against her body to drill down deep inside the desired organs. It was at this point, Claudia's screams turned first to breathless whimpers, then silence.

Justo never had time to scream as four additional pigs latched onto him the instant he was down. The first boar wildly ripped and pulled on one ankle, dragging his body several feet, almost severing his foot while the savage beast violently twisted its neck. Two boars continued to clash as they vied to sink their teeth into his belly section. A fourth boar delivered a quick fatal blow, gripping Justo's throat, slicing the first and second carotid arteries. Justo immediately lost consciousness. Blood poured out of his neck, covering the boar's snout and face with the bodily fluids. Things quieted while the nine boars proceeded to feast on the parents' unresponsive bodies.

Their eyes slammed shut, the boys covered their ears, trying to block out the sounds of grunts, growls, and high-pitched squeals that erupted again as the boars skirmished over the last scraps of flesh, bone, and blood.

What seemed like hours were only moments before the nine beasts had completely devoured the mother and father of the two beautiful boys. The boars wanted more blood, so they circled the trailer, knowing that two quivering, succulent bodies lay just above them. They could smell them, hear their shakes, and sense their fear. They continued to grunt and growl, pacing around the trailer. The boys clutched one another, never opening their eyes or letting go of each other. Carlos's sobbing only agitated the flesh-eating creatures even more. The boars finally retreated and, for nearly two hours, the pack waited quietly in the brush, anticipating the boys would jump down to an equal plane.

Over the next fourteen hours, the boys never even looked over the edge. They remained where their papa had told them to, right in the middle of the roof. Neither of them slept, remaining glued to each other, slowly rocking in unison the entire time as Juan repeatedly whispered, "No más, no más!"

Madder'n a Wet Hen

Canyon City Police Department; Friday, November 16, 2012; 7:41 A.M.

The phone hadn't finished the first ring when Karen anxiously picked up the receiver. Her parents and younger sister stood next to her. They had arrived the previous evening shortly after the detective and officer had left.

"Hel . . . hello," she stammered.

"Good morning, Mrs. Harden. Detective Dawson. I assume you haven't heard from your husband?" he asked, even though he was confident he knew the answer.

"No, I haven't," she responded meekly.

"OK, Officer Williams went by Len's trailer last night, and no one was there. I had another officer check the property at sunrise this morning with no luck. Mrs. Harden, I contacted the appropriate officials of every county in the Panhandle as far east as Childress and south to Lubbock. Does he hunt outside of Texas as well?" he asked.

"Well, he's talked about huntin' in New Mexico, but I'm sure he stayed here. He told me he would be home Wednesday night," she responded, relieved the detective was being so thorough.

130

"Good, good. We'll find him before long, I'm sure. But Mrs. Harden, do you understand, if we don't locate him by late this afternoon, we should alert the media of his disappearance? Are you OK with that?" he asked.

"Oh my, please do. I just go from a feelin' of panic one minute to being madder'n a wet hen the next. If he's on another three-day huntin' and drinkin' binge, I'm gonna be about as friendly as fire ants when he gets home. He's gonna wish he was injured. It'll serve him right to have all this public embarrassment. I just can't believe he's so insensitive. My momma and daddy and my sister are here with me right now, and they're fed up too. My daughter still doesn't quite understand what's goin' on. I haven't told her much of anything yet," she replied.

"Well, Mrs. Harden, you do realize once the media is notified that will no longer be possible. How old is she again?" asked the detective.

Thinking about her daughter, Emma, Karen became emotional again. "I know, I know. She's nine. She turns ten in a few weeks."

"OK, I'm glad your parents and sister are with you. Stay strong, Mrs. Harden, and give me a holler with even the slightest hint you may have regarding his whereabouts. I promise to keep in touch with you throughout the day," Dawson replied.

"Thank you, Detective," Karen said as she hung up the phone.

The Roof

Late Arrival Camping Area; Friday, November 16, 2012; 11:46 A.M.

Since daylight, less than two dozen vehicles had entered the park. No one had any reason that time of day to take the side road which led to the Late Arrival Campground. Later that morning, George Becker, a retired park volunteer, decided to check on the provisional area before heading to the nearest town of Canyon for lunch.

Driving a small Jeep Wrangler Moab soft top, he swept down the gravel path leading to the campground. The bulky tires kicked gravel outwards and into his wheel wells. The pebbles beating against his Jeep generated enough clatter to drown out the country music he favored.

As George approached the temporary sites, he slowed down to make the sharp right turn. Immediately, he spotted the blue minivan and cargo-moving trailer parked at the far end of the small loop. Coasting to a crawl and then to a complete stop, the volunteer sat and stared at the minivan and, in particular, the mass on the roof of the trailer. Only seconds passed before he watched in confusion as a little boy lifted his head up from under a blanket to get a glimpse of the vehicle that had just arrived and then ducked back down to hide. The brothers lay motionless, huddled together and plastered to the roof.

The older man gently put his Jeep in gear, rolled down the single-lane road, and came to a stop right behind the trailer. He climbed out from the cab and cautiously approached the scene. He called out, "Hello, hello, anybody here?" There was no response. George walked past the trailer to the back of the minivan. He could see that the rear passenger side was leaning. The trailer had been unhitched and was three to four feet from the van, allowing him enough space to walk between them. As he looked through the gap, he hesitated, then decided to first look in the driver's side window. He saw nothing of concern and walked around the front of the vehicle making his way to the passenger side. Again, the volunteer loudly announced himself. "Hello, hello, Park Service. Anyone here?"

His heart skipped a beat as he rounded the front end of the vehicle. Two buzzards that had been scavenging on the passenger side hissed at him and spread their wings in the horaltic pose, exposing their nearly six-foot wingspan. He knew they were harmless, but the sight of their ugly, red, bald heads with their yellowish hooked beaks alarmed him. Standing about six feet from the foragers, he was astounded by their enormous size. The birds hissed again then, one after another, took a few hops, laboriously flapped their massive wings, and launched themselves into the air. The two-tone dark brown and silver undersides of their wings were easily visible as they flew away. He stood there studying them for several seconds before he looked back at the van.

Moments before, his heart had only skipped a beat. But now it was racing as he fixed his eyes upon the car's rear axle resting on the ground, the tire and jack crushed underneath it, and what appeared to be splotches of dried blood where the buzzards had been. He anxiously called out to the child, asking where his parents were. And again, the boy stayed mute.

Becoming very concerned, the volunteer quickly retraced his steps to the driver's side of the van, looking for any signs of an adult. He found the door unlocked. He nervously opened it and climbed partially inside to have a look around, but found nothing unusual. He stepped back outside and again called for the boy to answer him. He squinted, attempting to further inspect his surroundings, desperately searching for an injured driver or some other explanation.

The retiree rushed over to the rectangular-shaped tent. It was a good-sized shelter, gray with yellow trim, over six feet tall in the center, and large enough to sleep six. While gently shaking one of the aluminum support poles, once again he shouted, "Hello, hello. Park Service. Hello, anyone in the there?" He shook the pole a little harder, rattling the entire frame. After no response, George bent down and unzipped the tent. The polyester panel folded over, and the volunteer crouched through the opening and found a small red cooler with a white lid just inside the door. There were two navy blue sleeping bags with cream colored pillows laying on the floor about six feet apart and two light blue pillows on the floor between them. A duffle bag sat at the front of the tent to the man's left, opposite the cooler. Everything seemed to be in order. He looked closely for any more blood stains but found nothing.

Still puzzled, he walked the short distance back to the trailer and climbed onto the fender, trying to get a closer look at the young boy who had been avoiding him. Standing above the dual wheels, the man held onto the top and slightly boosted himself up, peering over the edge. The moment the children's eyes met his, the youngest screamed. To his astonishment, there were actually two Hispanic boys huddled together on the roof, not one. They lay there with unzipped sleeping bags draped over their entire bodies, barely allowing their eyes to be seen.

"Are you OK? Let me help you down," George offered.

The boys cried and inched away from him, scooting closer to the opposite edge of the roof. He could now see their entire faces and again offered to help them. The boys muttered incoherently. They continued to lie there and stare back at the man with hollow gazes. In his seventy years, the old man had never seen such mesmerized looks. The fear on the boys' faces haunted him.

The volunteer gingerly squatted down, eased himself off the fender and back onto the ground. He frantically looked in the nearby brush on the passenger side but found nothing. The old man shuffled across the gravel road, searching for an injured adult among the grasses and shrubs in the center of the loop. There was no evidence of anyone.

As he stood about seventy-five feet from the trailer, George could see the two children on top of the roof. From the distance, he loudly called to them, pleading to let him help them down from the roof. As he began to approach the trailer, the boys' silence was broken.

The volunteer thought he heard "¡no más, no más!"

He quickly climbed back onto the fender, this time on the driver's side, and was now a little closer to the children. It was "¡no más, no más!" the man had heard as the oldest boy cried repeatedly.

"It's OK, it's OK, no más, no más. Please come to the edge of the trailer, so I can help you down," begged the volunteer, stretching out his arms to them. The boys remained glued to the roof and to each other, sobbing uncontrollably.

Their cries spoke volumes to the gravity of the situation. George knew that a terrible, terrible tragedy had occurred. Not nearly as carefully as the first time, he scurried off the fender and rushed to his Jeep, grabbed his cell phone from the passenger seat, and dialed the rangers' station.

"Palo Duro," answered Rachel, the rangers' assistant.

"Yes, this is George Becker, the volunteer from Ohio. I'm in the Late Arrival Camping Area, and I think there's been a horrible accident. There's a minivan and a cargo trailer parked in one of the spots, with two little boys on the roof of the trailer. They're very scared and won't budge. I can't find any adults around, but it looks like the van had a flat tire, and the jack collapsed while someone was changing it. I found what looks like dried blood next to the vehicle. I think whoever was repairing the tire was hurt, put the boys on top of the trailer, and walked off to find help. You'd better get out here fast!" the old man blurted, beginning to panic.

The assistant attempted to absorb all the information. "OK. Mr. Becker, correct?"

"Yes, George Becker," he replied.

"All right, let me see if I have this right. You're in the Late Arrival Campground. And you think a fallen jack may have injured someone tryin' to fix a flat, who then left two little boys on the trailer's roof?" Rachel verified.

"Yes, the Late Arrival Campground just a few hundred yards from the park's entrance. The little Hispanic boys keep crying, 'No más, no más!' They're probably in shock and will not get off the roof of the trailer," the distressed man conveyed. "They just remain huddled together, smack dab in the middle of the darn thing, and I can't get them down. I'm really afraid their father was seriously hurt. I don't see any signs of him anywhere."

"OK, Mr. Becker. I'll get a ranger out there immediately. Can you wait until he arrives?" asked the assistant.

"Yes, of course I'll wait. Please hurry. I have a bad feeling about this," pleaded the old man.

"I'm radioing them right now. I don't know where the two rangers are in the park, but one of them will be there shortly," Rachel replied.

"OK, I'll wait 'til they get here. Please hurry. I'm really worried," begged the man before he hung up.

Park Ranger Kent Irving was at the Visitor Center located on the crest of the canyon barely a mile away when he received the call about an accident with a cargo trailer and two little boys. The assistant was also able to reach the second ranger, Jack Wilson, who was on his way back to the park's headquarters from the Trading Post just a few miles further down at the base of the canyon.

Upon making a right onto the loop of the campground, Irving could see something on top of the cargo trailer, but couldn't make out what it was as his truck partially fishtailed on the loose stones. He regained control, quickly sped up, then skidded several feet before coming to a stop next to the volunteer's Jeep. The sudden noises frightened the young boys.

Irving hopped out of the truck and quickly introduced himself to Becker. The volunteer reiterated what he had discovered, pointing to the roof of the trailer where the two boys were.

"There has to have been an accident," Becker explained to the ranger. "I think the van fell off the jack and wounded the father. He must have wandered off searching for help. Come over here and look at the blood!" The old man hurried the ranger to the other side where the dried spots of blood remained and the rear axle rested on the hard ground.

Irving looked around and studied the scene. There were a few splotches of blood near the rear wheel, and a larger tainted area—where the boars had dragged Mr. Vasquez and torn him to pieces—about six feet from the vehicle. He, too, felt uneasy about the situation and called out to the children, "Boys, I'm climbing onto the trailer, OK?" He stepped onto the fender and placed his hands on top of the roof to steady himself, just as the volunteer had done earlier, then poked his head above the roof and saw the two boys completely buried under their sleeping bags. As he tried to talk to them, he noticed that Wilson had arrived. Seconds later, his partner was standing behind the trailer, looking up at him.

"What's going on, Kent?" Wilson asked.

"I'm not sure, Jack. Mr. Becker here and I have a very bad feeling about this. Look." Irving stepped down off the trailer and led the ranger over to the still-visible blood on the dirt.

"What do you think?" Irving asked, pointing to the blood, then the fallen jack.

"The boys won't say anything?" questioned Wilson.

"In the few minutes I've been here, besides crying, one of the boys keeps saying, 'No más, no más,'" stated Becker.

"And I suppose you don't speak Spanish, Mr. Becker?" asked Wilson.

"No, not a lick," responded the volunteer.

"Is Maria working today?" Wilson asked his partner.

"I don't think so, but let me radio headquarters. I'll see if anyone on duty speaks Spanish," Irving offered.

"Can't believe nobody here speaks Spanish. Those poor boys. We need to get them down," the retiree said compassionately.

Irving radioed headquarters and verified that Maria was off for the day. He asked the assistant if anyone else on staff spoke Spanish. Rachel told him she was confident that at least one of the maintenance crew did.

"Would you like for me to contact them?" she asked.

"Yes, please do. And send them over here right away," Irving requested.

The moment the ranger got off the phone, Becker continued, "Those boys experienced something really, really horrific. I can tell. I've never seen such terror on someone's face, ever. They looked at me as though they were seeing right through me. I'll never forget that look."

"Kent, I agree with you guys. Something just doesn't feel right. I think we need to be ultra-cautious about this. This could be a crime scene. Do you think that's possible?" asked Wilson.

"That, or an immigration issue. I just don't know, but something's definitely unusual. We should be careful not to disturb anything, including those boys. I think we need to have Canyon send out a few officers," suggested Irving.

"I agree," said Wilson.

"That's going to take another twenty minutes. We can't continue to leave those children up there," Becker protested.

"No, no. I think we better," replied Wilson.

"I'm going to keep talking to them. Try to console them even if they can't understand me. Coax them down the best I can," Becker said resentfully.

"That's fine. I'm OK with that. If they come down on their own, that's one thing. But we're not gonna go up there and physically take them off that roof, understood?" Wilson ordered.

"Those boys should be helped down immediately, given some water and a hug. We have no idea what they've gone through," replied the volunteer.

With that, Wilson called the Canyon Police Dispatch.

As they waited for the police, the three men heard the boys sniffling and their repeated cries of "No más, no más." Trying to soothe them, Becker took bottles of water from the cooler inside the tent, twisted off the caps, and placed them on the roof. After a few minutes, the boys tried to sip from the bottles, but they spilled more than they drank as their hands trembled uncontrollably. He could hardly watch as the children's incessant quivering shook him to the core.

Thirteen minutes later, two squad cars pulled up behind Wilson's truck. Becker climbed down from the trailer's wheel well and urgently waved them over. Officer Barron and Officer Tyson, apparently in no hurry, exited their vehicles and greeted the rangers, ignoring the volunteer. Wilson pointed to the roof of the trailer where the boys remained, unwilling to come down. The officers quickly scanned the site, taking note of the collapsed jack and the blood stains in the immediate area. The boys whimpering, "No más, no más," unnerved even the officers as they questioned the two rangers. After walking the periphery of the general location and checking the tent, Tyson went back to the trailer and stepped onto the fender, wanting get a look at the boys. As soon as they saw the officer, they turned their heads and looked the other way, tightly squeezing each other.

Tyson spoke to the children, trying to calm them. After moments of silence, the officer asked them, "Do you speak English?"

The boys only responded, "No más, no más."

The officer stepped down from the fender, then all five men re-examined the scene. Tyson, the park rangers, and Becker walked deeper into the brush while Barron thoroughly searched the minivan. He cursed as the combination lock prevented him from looking inside the trailer.

As Tyson headed back toward the van, he noticed an empty can of Coke lying on its side along the edge of the brush. He walked over to it and saw what he thought were probably more speckles of blood. He called for Barron to take a look. As the two examined the area near the can, they couldn't help but notice how the dirt had been disturbed, dug up.

The rangers and Becker joined the two officers. Wilson studied the dirt and gravel then construed, "It looks as if wild pigs have been rooting here. It doesn't look natural."

Wilson continued studying the area near the Coke can while the other four men walked back toward the collapsed minivan where the first signs of blood were found. Scouring the area, Irving noticed the ground nearest the van, where a small amount of dried blood existed, appeared normal. But when he looked closer at the ground six, seven feet away where the larger blood stain was, it was similar to the ground near the Coke can.

SLOP: The Wild Boar Nation

Despite being rock solid, it just wasn't quite right. Confounded, he turned toward the van. Just then, the sun's bright reflection off the van's chrome molding caught Irving's eye. As he approached, he noticed a few hairs lodged between the sheet metal and the trim around the wheel well. He pulled out one of the bristles and examined the color, felt the texture, then said to Barron, "I swear this hair is from a wild boar. Feel that."

The officer took the hair from the ranger, briefly looked at it, and then rubbed his thumb and forefinger together, flicking the preposterous evidence to the ground, mumbling to himself.

It appeared to the volunteer that Barron didn't understand the trauma the boys had been through. The two perched on the roof had grown quiet again, allowing him to think. The old man's mind began racing as he contemplated possible scenarios. "What? A wild boar knocked over the jack, injuring the man? Where are the father and mother? Why didn't he simply walk up to the park's headquarters just a few hundred yards away?"

Wilson joined the others near the van, and Irving pointed out the wheel well. "Jack, I swear these hairs lodged in the trim are from a wild boar."

Barron scoffed at the ranger, mocking him. "The spic probably needed help, so he asked some pigs for assistance. Hogs are supposed to be smart, right? Smarter than Mexicans at least."

Tyson was just as baffled as the two rangers and Becker. And after surveying the scene again, he announced to his partner, "Barron, I think we need to call police headquarters and alert Detective Dawson and Chief Thompson."

"Are you kiddin' me?" Barron responded. "I'll tell ya what's going on here. They're damn illegal wetbacks. They got a flat tire, were too stupid to fix it, got hurt, and left their two kids behind for the rest of us to raise and pay for their college. That's what's going on here."

141

The volunteer stared at the second officer, trying to gauge Tyson's reaction.

Barron continued, "What we need to do is climb up on that trailer, pull those two illegals down, and take 'em to headquarters so Immigration can figure out what to do with 'em. It's not our damn job. This is a perfect example of why we need to pass an immigration law like Arizona did. End this shit once and for all."

Barron then spit a large volume of saliva laced with chewing tobacco onto the ground near the blood-stained dirt. The officer's outburst prompted the two rangers to walk back toward the tent to talk privately.

"Y'all don't touch or move anything. I'm treating this as a crime scene until the chief and detective arrive," Tyson ordered. "Did y'all hear me?"

They all responded, "Yes."

Tyson quickly turned and made his way to his squad car. He instantly notified police headquarters of the situation, reporting the description of the vehicle, the license plate number, and the cargo trailer tags. Then he specifically requested that both Detective Dawson and Chief of Police Floyd Thompson be informed immediately. Within moments, the chief of police radioed Tyson, stating he would be at the scene in twenty minutes and that Dawson would arrive shortly thereafter.

Tyson walked back toward the trailer and continued to examine the scene. Becker realized it had been a while since the boys had made any noise whatsoever. Without informing anyone, he climbed onto the fender and continued to kindly reassure the two young brothers. As he spoke softly, Becker gazed out over the drought-stricken landscape. He then looked skyward, wondering if it would ever rain again. Out of the corner of his eye, he caught the two vultures gliding in circles above them.

Becker thought to himself, "Damn birds give me the creeps. I'll bet they know what happened. They always do."

Stay in the Middle

Late Arrival Camping Area; Friday, November 16, 2012; 12:54 P.M.

Chief of Police Floyd Thompson arrived, accompanied by Sergeant Ben Givens, and parked behind the second squad car. The rarely traveled road was now congested with a minivan, a trailer, the volunteer's Jeep, two rangers' trucks, two squad cars, and the chief of police's unmarked black Ford Crown Victoria.

Tyson quickly introduced the chief and sergeant to the rangers and the volunteer. The seven men stood next to the collapsed jack while Tyson spent the next few minutes briefing his superiors.

Privately laughing at his shift partner, Barron idly stood by, hoping his fellow officer would make a fool of himself mentioning anything about wild boars being involved. Becker sensed Barron's callousness, and his frustration grew as scant attention was being given to the two boys who remained silent atop the trailer.

Together they all walked over to the near-empty Coke can to inspect the blood there. Tyson pointed out that the ground surrounding the can appeared slightly disturbed, as if wild hogs had rooted the turf near the blood stains. The chief of police bent down and rubbed his hand across the dusty surface without comment. Barron's smirk at such a suggestion led the two rangers to make eye contact with each other.

"Sir, may I remind you that there are two petrified little boys on the top of that trailer?" Becker condescendingly commented to the chief. At this point, he didn't care if he sounded disrespectful to authority. They certainly had been severely apathetic about the physical and mental well-being of the two young children who had obviously been through something unfathomable, who knows how long ago.

Becker thought to himself, "Not only are they terrified, but they have to be hungry and thirsty as well. Not to mention that they don't even know where their parents are. And what about going to the bathroom?" He didn't even want to think about that.

"Are you going to get them down now, or not?" he demanded.

Thompson shot him a stern look and, without responding, walked back toward the minivan. Givens was right on his heels, followed by the officers, the rangers, and finally Becker. The chief and sergeant continued around to the driver's side while the others stayed behind. After a brief chat with Thompson, the sergeant called for Tyson and Barron to assist him in getting the boys down from the roof.

Barron responded immediately, rushed between the van and the trailer to the driver's side, and joined Sergeant Givens. He then eagerly hopped onto the fender, banging the metal side with his feet. Tyson remained on the passenger side and gently climbed onto the fender, trying not to rock the trailer or make any startling noises. Barron's head was the first to appear above the roof. The boys quickly turned to look the other way only to see Tyson appear on the other side. The two clung tightly to one another as if they were Siamese twins and blankly stared at the officer.

Barron took the opportunity to hoist himself onto the top of the trailer, then bear-crawled over to the children and flung the sleeping bags off them. In the process, both water bottles the boys had been nursing tipped over; streams of water ran down the side of the trailer. On his knees, Barron grabbed their tiny upper arms and squeezed so hard neither boy dared move. Juan and Carlos tried desperately to tighten their grip on the tigers that had been wedged between them, huddling as one under the sleeping bags.

Sadly, neither boy was able to maintain control. Carlos dropped his tiger first, as the overzealous officer had hold of the arm that was embracing the stuffed animal.

"Come on, let's go! You're getting off this trailer right now!" Barron barked as he stood up and dragged them toward Tyson, sending both water bottles spinning off the roof.

"You're OK, you're OK," Tyson tried to reassure them.

The eldest started kicking, then ceased when Barron compressed his left bicep even tighter. Tyson was close enough to grip Carlos's ankle and scoot him to the edge of the roof as Barron released his arm. Then the officer managed to turn him in order to get a strong hold of the boy's upper body and hugged him close. Looking the frightened child in the eyes, he gently bent down and handed him to Wilson.

Before Tyson turned around to help the oldest, Barron swatted the tiger out of Juan's hand. The toy flew out of his grasp and landed on the roof behind them. Juan looked back and stretched his free arm, trying to rescue his stuffed friend, but he couldn't reach it. The officer strengthened his grip, holding him right at the edge of the roof, impatiently waiting on his partner. Tyson steadied himself, then took Juan in the same manner as he had Carlos, and handed him to Irving. Once both boys were safely on the ground, Tyson jumped down and joined the two rangers who were carrying the wailing boys to the front of the minivan.

Barron stood on the roof and scowled at the sight of the two illegals being comforted by three enablers. Disgusted, he looked down and, with the outside of his right foot, flicked one of the tigers off the roof, sending it tumbling to the ground several feet behind the trailer. The second tiger was only a step away. But instead of alerting Tyson to catch it or even tossing it to the ground, he aligned his body just so and then booted the stuffed toy over the remaining sleeping bag. It sailed through the air, landing several feet beyond the first lifeless victim. Besides each other, the only comfort either boy had had since their parents' demise was now coated in red dust. Still not satisfied, Barron marched to the back of the roof. Again, with his right foot, he side-kicked the second sleeping bag, launching it over the edge. The comforter fell to the ground next to Juan's sleeping bag, which had slid off the roof when the officer had first snatched the boys. Barron stood proudly on the roof, knowing justice had been served. He looked down past the minivan and made eye contact with the chief, who was standing between the van and the tent. Just then the racket from pebbles pounding the underside of Dawson's car caught his attention. His grin turned to scorn as he eased himself down from the top of the trailer.

The procession of cars was piling up as, seconds after the detective arrived, two more park service trucks entered the loop. Due to the nine vehicles lined up behind the minivan and trailer, the last truck barely made the turn before stopping. The maintenance supervisor who spoke some Spanish was in the first truck, while three of his employees, two who were Mexican, were in the second vehicle.

Now twelve men and two little boys congregated next to the abandoned minivan leaning awkwardly from a missing tire. The chief of police briefed Dawson, excluding any reference to the disturbed dirt and the hair lodged between the minivan's sheet metal and chrome trim.

The chief did, however, feel obliged to offer information about what was obvious. "Whoever was changing the tire was injured and left the boys on the roof." Of course, it didn't take a sleuth to figure that out.

Thinking out loud, Dawson wondered, "If the father was hurt, why would he put them on the roof? Doesn't make sense. Wouldn't you put the boys in the van?"

He squatted next to the vehicle and inspected the hub lying on the ground. He saw no blood anywhere under the van. No stains on the axle, hub, spare tire, or even the jack. A small blemish of blood remained a few feet from the van, and an even larger blotch about six feet from there but nothing directly underneath. The detective found this a little profound, considering everyone assumed the minivan had fallen and injured the driver.

"You said you found the children on top of the roof with sleeping bags, Mr. Becker?" Dawson asked.

"Yes, that's correct. I found them on the roof hiding beneath the sleeping bags," the volunteer confirmed.

Barron shot Becker a piercing look.

"Where are the sleeping bags?" asked the detective.

"Probably still on the roof," Tyson said.

"They're on the ground behind the trailer," Barron interjected.

The detective approached the two boys and, in a fatherly manner, asked them if they were hurt. They just stared right through him, maintaining their silence. He closely examined their clothes, arms, necks, and faces, searching for scratches or traces of blood but found none. "Can someone get these boys some water?" he shouted out.

Trusting that someone would actually follow through with the simple request, he immediately walked behind the trailer, picked up the dusty sleeping bags one at a time, and closely studied each one. The rest of the men followed him; Tyson and Becker lagged a few steps behind, escorting the boys.

"I don't see any blood on the children, their sleeping bags, or the sides of the trailer. Was there any blood on the roof?" Dawson asked.

"No," Barron reported.

"If whoever was hurt helped them get on top of the trailer," Dawson wondered, "why wouldn't there be any traces of blood?"

"Quite possible someone else put the boys on the roof," the chief suggested.

"What are these?" Dawson asked, pointing to the stuffed tigers.

"Some stupid stuffed animals the boys had on the roof. They were holding onto them when I got them down," Barron replied.

The detective walked over to the nearest one, picked it up, and looked at it closely. There was no sign of blood on the cuddly plush, either. He walked over to the second one about ten feet away and found nothing. Holding them in his hands, Dawson began walking back to the group when Carlos let out a cry and pointed at him. The detective understood; he calmly walked up to the children, smiled, and slowly extended his hands, giving each boy their treasured toy. They inspected them closely to make sure each was hugging his personal tiger.

"So you've gotten no information from the boys yet?" asked Dawson.

The chief responded, "No. No one here can speak Spanish, and we'd just gotten 'em off the roof when you showed up."

The detective looked at the two Hispanic maintenance workers and asked if they spoke English. The shorter of the two, a man in his mid-30s said, "Yes, I speak pretty good English." The second worker only nodded yes but did not say anything.

"Will you ask the boys where their mother or father is? And when was the last time they saw them?" Dawson requested.

"Sí, yes, señor," the worker replied. He questioned the children in their native tongue.

The boys quivered, unable to speak, and just stared down at their feet. The man asked them again. Dawson thought he saw Carlos vaguely shake his head no.

Juan looked up and in broken English cried, "No más! No más! I not know. We watch stars. Mama scream. We hear noises. We look down and see scary, ugly animals. Papa say to stay in middle of roof. We stay like I promise. Mama, Papa, no más, no más!" Then he and Carlos broke out in tears.

"Scary animals? What's he talking about? What exactly does 'no more' mean?" asked the detective.

Tyson was quick to relay what the rangers had surmised about the ground around the blood stains and the hair caught in the minivan's chrome trim.

The detective's puzzled look pleased Barron. "What an idiot!" Barron thought to himself. "Wild boars in the campground? They're going to think you're a dumbass, Tyson."

Dawson walked back to the blood stains next to car and saw nothing unusual about the dirt.

"No, it's fine here, but look at the larger spot," Tyson elaborated, pointing to the area where they had seen the dried blood. "And there's more over where the Coke can is," he said, leading the detective.

By now, with so many people walking around the scene, the dirt mixed with gravel near the second blood stain looked similar to the rest of the campsite. Dawson shook his head then walked over to the Coke can. There the detective recognized inconsistencies in the ground and the misplaced gravel scattered in and about an eight-foot radius. Dawson thought to himself, "The ground is so damn dry, so damn hard, might as well be concrete." He could vaguely see some kind of long scrape marks, but couldn't determine if they were relevant to the case or if they were from the recent chaos at the scene.

He wandered several feet into the native grasses and brush and found nothing of concern, but there appeared to be some trampling of grasses indicating wildlife activity.

Meanwhile, the chief of police slithered back to his unmarked car and made a private call. The remaining men stood next to the van, chatting among themselves, speculating where the parents could have gone and what could've happened. Realizing Juan and Carlos were listening, Becker squatted down to their level and tried distracting the children, asking them if their tigers had names. Noticing that neither responded to the volunteer's question, the Mexican native translated the question in Spanish. Still, the boys remained silent, looking down at their shoes and gently rocking side-to-side while tightly hugging their tigers.

Dawson continued to scan the area as he walked back to the minivan and waited for Thompson to join them before he spoke. As soon as the chief arrived, the detective declared, "Chief, I believe we need to cordon off this entire area. Designate it a crime scene. We need to start checking all the local hospitals for any admittance of patients treated for injuries. Do we have any information back on the van?"

"Just got it," Barron replied. "The van was reported stolen sixteen months ago. Belonged to a Susan Welden from Houston. Originally, it was green. I'm tellin' ya, they just dumped those kids here and took off."

The volunteer listened closely with his arms tightly folded across his chest, clenching his upper arms. He glared at Barron, trying to hide his outrage.

"Jim, did you see the hairs in the chrome stripping?" Tyson asked the detective, confident he was offering pertinent information. Barron just scoffed and shook his head.

Dawson walked over to the van and plucked one of the remaining hairs. He examined it closely and wondered out loud, "Did they hit a wild animal which caused the flat, but left no visible damage to the vehicle?"

Chief Thompson agreed with the detective to barricade the area and ordered, "Gentlemen, tape this area off. The sergeant and I will take the boys back to the station and contact CPS. Rangers, please make sure no one enters this area after we leave. I want the road to this campground restricted to my personnel only. Jim, call Amarillo and get the Special Crimes Unit out here ASAP."

The detective immediately grabbed his phone and called the special unit. Sergeant Givens looked at the Mexican maintenance worker who spoke English. "Tell the boys everything is OK. That I'm taking them to get some food and a place to rest, so we can find their parents."

The maintenance worker followed the sergeant's request. Juan and Carlos began to tremble again, afraid to look at anyone except the man who spoke their native tongue. The chief simply glanced at the boys with little regard.

"Come on, let's go!" Thompson said to the sergeant, expecting him to round up the boys and escort them to the car.

The sergeant placed a hand on the back of the neck of each boy and started to gently lead them away from their van. Carlos resisted and started to whimper, so the maintenance worker compassionately reached out and touched him on the shoulder. Then out of nowhere, Carlos pulled away from the only one he trusted at this point, threw himself to the ground, and began wailing, "Mama! Papa! Please! I want Papa! Mama! No . . . !"

He curled up into a ball on the ground. Juan quickly dropped to his side, grabbed his little brother, and started sobbing. The Mexican was quickly at their side; he knelt down beside them and bowed his head, his eyes beginning to swell with tears.

Tyson and Barron had gone back to their squad cars to gather the yellow crime scene tape and a few stakes when they heard the commotion. Tyson looked up, panic-stricken. Barron shook his head and grumbled, "I don't know what's wrong with them boys. Hell, we're the ones who have to figure out what to do with 'em."

Tyson looked at Officer Barron, not believing what he had just heard. "My god, Barron! They're just little boys!"

"Whatever. Come on, Tyson, let's get this place taped up," his partner directed.

The rangers and volunteer froze in shock, at a loss of what they should do next. Becker, the one who well over an hour ago had found them hidden under sleeping bags on top of the abandoned trailer, stood there with a small tear rolling down his cheek. He would never forget this day.

Givens and the Mexican worker gently picked up the limp boys drenched with tears and coated with red dust and carried them to Thompson's Crown Victoria. The boys wearily lay in the backseat with their faces buried, quietly sobbing and occasionally calling out, "Papa . . . Mama . . ."

Carlos cried between breaths, "We . . . were . . . sup . . . posed . . . to . . . see . . . the . . . canyon . . . the big hole . . . in the . . . ground . . . and go . . . to . . . our . . . new home."

Givens heard Juan whimper, "It's no fair, Papa. Come back. It's no fair."

The boys' translator was left standing there with his co-worker, amazed at what had just taken place and nervous about what would be discovered in the park they maintained.

Seconds later, they all glared in disbelief at the chief of police. To avoid the log jam of cars, Thompson plowed right through the natural landscape inside the center of the loop while exiting the campground. Navigating around a few small trees and bushes as he drove across the native grasses, he flattened several narrowleaf yucca plants. He never even looked back as he passed the sign at the head of the loop, *Ground Fires Prohibited.*

As instructed, the officers began securing the area. Barron tried to drive a steel stake into the ground to attach the yellow tape, but the four-foot rod failed to lodge into the earth. "God dammit!" he yelled.

Disgusted with his partner, Tyson called out from brush area, "Barron, forget it. We'll wrap the tape around a few bushes and that scrub tree over there and then string it around the perimeter. We'll set a few rocks on the tape to keep it in place. No one's going to be coming back here anyway. The tape doesn't have to be elevated all the way around; it can just lie on the ground on the driver's side of the van."

The moment the chief of police's car was out of sight, the two rangers and Becker walked to their vehicles and agreed to meet at the park's headquarters. All three were utterly disgusted with how the investigation was conducted and the audacious attitudes of the chief of police and Officer Barron.

As if in a funeral procession, they solemnly drove away, one after the other. Each glanced back to their left as they crept along the opposite side of the grounds. The second ranger paused near the crushed plants inside the loop and surveyed the damage. His anger flared even more at the disregard of the park's natural environment. He looked back again at the restricted scene and noticed Barron following him with his eyes. The ranger gradually let his foot off the brake and slowly pulled away.

"This isn't a crime scene," he thought to himself. "Something much more disturbing happened here last night."

Perched in a nearby tree, a wake of vultures looked on.

Don't Tread on Me

Palo Duro Canyon State Park Headquarters; Friday
November 16, 2012; 1:45 P.M.

The two rangers, Jack Wilson and Kent Irving, and the volunteer, George Becker, sat in the small office at the park's headquarters. The men could hear visitors at the front desk checking into the tiny, yet charming, Cow Camp Cabins at the far end of the park's canyon floor. Before leaving, the couple asked the young lady who was helping them where the nearest bathroom and shower facilities were.

"Right across the street in the Mesquite Campground. Ya can't miss it," Rachel replied.

Wilson's stomach instantly tightened. The thought raced through his mind, "The Mesquite Campground, the two men in the motorhome! Are they back yet, or did they leave without paying?" He knew the park had their names and credit-card information, so he wasn't too worried about collecting the fee. But it had been so quiet there all week, and he couldn't remember seeing either of the men after they had checked in on Monday. When the rangers had made their rounds since then, there were no signs of any activity at all, including yesterday when he drove by. "Are they missing too?" he wondered.

156

Abruptly, Wilson looked at the volunteer and said, "Mr. Becker, we really appreciate all your help. You've been a great asset to the park."

"It's not a problem, I love it here! But please call me George," the man responded.

"Absolutely, George. Well, Kent and I have a little work to do. We have each other's numbers, so if you need to contact us, please feel free," Wilson said to the man he admired for being so conscientious of the boys.

"All right, I'll keep my eye out for anything unusual. I sure hope they find those boys' parents. I have a really bad feeling about them. I just figured the father was injured changing the tire. Do you really think an animal or boar attacked and injured them?" Becker asked.

Concerned that their conversation might be overheard, Wilson quietly stated, "I think it's a coincidence, just a coincidence," as he led Becker out of the office and past the counter to see him out. Back in the office, Wilson turned to Irving and said, "I think we need to take a little drive," putting his index finger to his lips.

Irving tilted his head curiously and responded, "Sure, we can do that."

As they were walking out of the office toward the counter, Rachel asked the rangers, "What's going on with those two little Hispanic boys being left in the Late Arrival Campground? Is it true they were abandoned on top of a trailer?"

"It appears that way, but we're not sure. The Canyon City Police are taking the lead now. Just to be cautious, they've taped off the area as a crime scene. No one really believes a crime was committed. Just some spots with blood were found. And like the call you took from Mr. Becker, we believe someone was fixing a flat tire when the jack collapsed. That's all," Wilson answered, skirting around her question.

"Wow! That's so crazy. I haven't seen that many cars go down that little old road since I started working here a few months ago," she commented.

"Yeah, it was pretty crowded over there. We'll see you later," Irving told her.

Kent lifted the hinged counter top, and he and Wilson walked to the other side. Before they left the building, Wilson asked the assistant if she knew if the two men in the motorhome at site number ninety in the Mesquite Campground had paid for yesterday or checked out.

"Not to my knowledge. It's a little frustrating when people don't let us know about extending their stay, even if we only have a few visitors. It happens all the time," Rachel complained.

"Well, I think it indicates how much people like it here. Thanks," he replied as they left, closing the door behind them.

Walking toward their vehicles parked side by side, Wilson offered to drive. No sooner did they get into the truck, Irving curiously asked, "What's up? You want to go check on that motorhome?"

"Yep, I think a drive down to the Mesquite Campground would be a good idea. They were supposed to check out yesterday. I'm wondering if they are there or if they've already left without paying," responded Wilson.
Realizing something didn't feel right, Irving replied, "Yeah, I agree. It's been awfully quiet down there. Can't say I've seen a trace of them all week."

"I know. As soon as I heard Rachel tell the visitors who were checking into the Cow Camp Cabins about the facilities being right across the street at the Mesquite Campground, I got this weird feeling inside. My stomach knotted up. This whole thing has a strange feeling about it," Wilson commented with uncertainty.

"Well, I suppose we'll find out in a few minutes," Irving paused, then said, "At least the campground is peaceful."

Driving down the steep, winding canyon road never grew old for the two rangers. There was always something new. Every day was different; the lighting, the colors, the time of day or year provided infinite ways to view the park.

They reached the bottom of the canyon, passing the first campground and the Trading Post. And as they approached the Hackberry Campground where George resided, the two began talking about what a jerk Officer Barron was and how cynical and insensitive he was toward the children, how he undermined his partner, and about his rudeness toward Becker. Their conversation was briefly interrupted when Irving spotted a flock of wild turkeys near the first river crossing. They continued their discussion as they drove toward the back of the park, passing through the second, third, fourth, and fifth crossings of the Prairie Dog Town Fork of the Red River. The four crossings in succession were within three-fourths of a mile from each other as the river zigzagged throughout the canyon.

After passing a Day Use Area and another campground, they drove by the Cow Camp Cabin entrance on the right and then pulled into the Mesquite Campground just a few yards farther down on their left.

Similar to all the other campgrounds, the entry road formed a loop. With the mesquite and cottonwood trees recently shedding their leaves, the small number of junipers and shrub cedar trees did little to obscure the campsites, allowing the rangers to immediately see the motorhome sitting by itself at the back of the loop. There was only one other visitor in the campground, a trailer parked in the third site on the left near the bathroom and shower facilities.

Wilson veered right and made his way to the far side of the loop. Although the campground was a little larger than the one atop the canyon, it still only took a few seconds to reach the motorhome. He parked the truck right in front of the site and got out. Everything looked exactly the same since the visitors' arrival on Monday.

Wilson walked up to the door of the motorhome and knocked. Irving eyed the canopy; the perfectly arranged table and chairs appeared undisturbed. As he was walking toward the grill, he could see that the workbench was spotless, with no tools or evidence it had been recently used. He checked the grill; the light coat of dust remained and the inside was still sparkling clean. In fact, the grill looked brand new to him.

He was surprised they had a gas grill because so few did. He thought about all the headaches rangers suffered when a burn ban was in effect, like the one implemented on November eighth, just over a week ago. The ban of ash-producing fires meant charcoal grills were prohibited. And since almost every visitor had a charcoal grill, there was always someone who violated the ordinance. When rangers would arrive to enforce the regulation, invariably tensions would flare. The park officials took the enforcement seriously and most always traveled in pairs. Too often, those who openly defied the law had been drinking as well.

Reflecting back, one particular episode came to mind. Shots were almost fired when he and Wilson had tried to enforce the policy; the camper got offended and became irate.

"This is fucking America!" the visitor screamed. "You have no right to stop me from having a fire! It's my constitutional right! Don't tread on me or my family! Do you hear me? Don't tread on me! Do you hear me, you fucking government whores? You put out my fire; I'll blow your fucking heads off! Why are you harassing me when you allow that grill over there?"

The inebriated camper had lost his balance when he swung around to point to an area with a gas grill burning four sites from his. He staggered a little then braced himself on the beam supporting the wooden shelter at his family's campsite. Irving had already called for backup as they tried to reason with the man and explain that gas grills didn't produce any ashes; the ban specifically addressed what was and wasn't allowed, and his charcoal grill was not. In the end, it didn't matter. It took four Canyon City police officers plus Wilson and himself to subdue and arrest the man, his wife, and their teenage daughter, whose belligerence exceeded her father's.

There was no response to Wilson's knocks on the door and announcing himself, so he retreated and met Irving at the grill.

"I'm going to leave my card in the door," Wilson stated.

"Huh? What did you say?" asked Irving, abruptly ending his flashback.

"I'm going to leave my card in the door with a note," Wilson reiterated.

"I think we should," agreed Irving.

Wilson took out a business card and a pen, then wrote on the back. "It's Friday, 2:15 p.m. Please contact the rangers' station." He stuck the card in the door frame next to the handle where it could easily be seen.

Before getting back into the truck, they took one more jaunt around the motorhome. Inspecting the bike rack, Wilson asked, "Do you remembering seeing any bikes all week? I don't; they definitely weren't here yesterday. Maybe they got into a really bad biking accident on one of the trails."

"I think we should immediately notify the Canyon City police that these guys haven't been seen since checking in on Monday, and that they have overstayed their visit going on two days now. At least give them a heads up that we're gonna file our own internal report," Irving suggested.

"I'm with you, pal," Wilson agreed. "Something's just not right here either. It's like they've just vanished, like the Hispanic parents at the top of the canyon. I just can't imagine where they could be. The park isn't that big. You would think someone would've stumbled upon these guys and the boys' parents if they were in the canyon somewhere. And if they did get into an accident, how could the other hikers and bikers not notice them?"

"Let's get back up there and inform the Canyon officers," Irving repeated. He quickly walked away, Wilson right behind him.

Wilson started the truck, drove around the loop, and stopped at the trailer parked near the entrance. Wanting to gather as much information as possible to include in their paperwork, the rangers got out of their truck and introduced themselves to an older couple in their late sixties, sitting at the picnic table under the shelter. They were the only other guests in the campground since the visitors nearest the facilities had left first thing Thursday morning.

"Good afternoon. Gorgeous day, isn't it?" Wilson greeted them.

"Yes, indeed it is," answered the gentleman. "How can we help you?"

"We're just curious. You've been here since Wednesday? Is that correct?" asked Wilson.

"Yes, we arrived midday Wednesday. Wonderful place! We're really enjoying it down here," the man replied.

"We were wondering if either of you have seen anyone or any activity, anything at all going on at the campsite on the other side of the loop here." He cocked his head, directing their eyes toward the abandoned motorhome. "Two men, I'd say . . . maybe in their early forties, checked in a couple of days before you folks and were supposed to check out Thursday, but we haven't seen any sign of them. We're just wanting to make sure everything's all right," Wilson informed the couple.

"No, sir. Can't say I've seen anybody over there. Have you, dear?" the man asked his wife.

"When we first walked around the campground, I saw they had Jersey license plates, but I haven't noticed anything over there either," the wife added. "They must really like it here though, coming from so far away. I hope they're OK."

"Thank you, we appreciate your time. You folks have a good day now," Irving responded calmly, not wanting to alarm the couple. They slowly walked back to the truck, pausing for a few seconds to quickly scan Kenny and Lance's site from a different perspective, hoping to see something they hadn't seen before. They didn't.

About fifteen minutes later, Wilson and Irving pulled back into the Late Arrival Campground. Tyson was assisting Dawson, combing the entire area, meticulously keeping an eye out for any other clues. They didn't want to leave even one rock unturned.

The rangers proceeded toward the scene. As they walked between the two cruisers parked side by side, the driver's door on the vehicle to their right swung open. It stopped them in their tracks as it blocked the five-foot-wide gap between the vehicles. A moment sooner, Wilson would have walked right smack into the door.

Barron casually got out of the cruiser, looked at the rangers, and condescendingly remarked as he closed the door, "Oh, didn't see ya comin' there."

He inched along ahead of them, still inconsiderately blocking their path while typing a text on his cell phone. He then turned and spit a huge wad of chewing tobacco to his right. The rangers bit their tongues and passed the officer on his left once they cleared the two cruisers.

As they approached the yellow tape, the detective called out for them to not cross over the boundary. The rangers stopped just before the tape, while Barron brushed past them, stepped over the plastic ribbon, and openly laughed, looking back at what he thought of as two second-rate officers.

Dawson walked up to the two gentlemen and explained, "I'm sorry, guys, but you have to stay outside the tape. Hope you understand, but until forensics gets here, I want to keep the area as pristine as possible. We've already disturbed the area enough today. You do understand, don't you?"

"Sure, no problem, Detective," replied Wilson.

"Not an issue at all," Irving added. "But there is something concerning us that we'd like to speak with you about."

"What's that?" asked the detective.

Just as Wilson was getting ready to explain, Barron brazenly interrupted the discussion. "A few spics get left behind in the state park, and now you guys have become Sherlock Holmes? You might want to stick to playing *Clue,* boys."

"Officer, I 'm not sure what's up your ass, but this is the state park," Irving curtly informed him. "We take all matters here very seriously. We're only trying to help."

Wilson looked at the detective, making sure he had regained his full attention then continued, "On Monday, two men in a motorhome checked into the park around noon. They had reserved and paid for three nights and were to check out yesterday by two p.m. Often campers do this, extend their stay without communicating with the park. But when we went by their site late Thursday afternoon to collect their fee and reregister them, neither of them were around. We went back after dinner a few hours later, and they still weren't there. The more Kent and I have thought about it, we haven't seen any activity at their site since the day they checked in. We stopped back again today once we left here, and the motorhome was still parked in the same place with no signs of any activity whatsoever. I left them a note to call the rangers' station. But we have a strong suspicion something's wrong. It just doesn't make sense."

Barron turned away and grumbled under his breath. "Dumbass park rangers. Every little problem, and ya have to call us to clean up the damn mess."

"I see. And you're sure you haven't seen any sign of them since they checked in?" asked the detective.

"Yeah, we're sure," Irving told him before adding, "What's really strange is they have a bike rack on the motorhome, but we don't remember ever seeing any bikes the whole week."

Dawson fretted. His mind began to race, and he contemplated, "In a matter of a day or so, we now have six people possibly missing. Every one of them just vanished?"

"Hmm . . . OK, hang out here for a few minutes. The forensic team should be here any time now. Once they arrive, you guys can take me down to the site. I'll leave Officers Tyson and Barron up here to monitor," the detective told the rangers.

"We can do that, sir," replied Wilson.

Mr. Lin

Canyon City Police Department; Friday, November 16, 2012; 2:30 P.M.

"Givens, has CPS been contacted yet? I'm not runnin' a damn daycare center here!" the chief of police snapped.

"Already called them, sir. They should be here within an hour. The boys are in my office. I had Stafford get them something from McDonald's," replied Givens.

Chief Thompson heard the response but purposely failed to acknowledge it. His rude mannerisms were widely argued about in the office. Some believed it was an intimidation and controlling tactic; others thought it was just another one of his personality quirks and he meant no harm. Regardless, whenever the chief wasn't treating the world with indifference, he was grumpy. The majority of the force preferred indifference.

The chief walked into his office, then closed the door when his cell phone rang. He knew the number but wouldn't answer it, at least not in the office. Policemen are leery; police chiefs, downright paranoid. The phone rang five times before it rolled over to voicemail; however, he knew the caller would not leave a message. Thompson got up, walked out of his office, down the hall and out the backdoor, then got into his unmarked car and drove off so he could return the phone call.

"Chief, I am very pleased you called back so promptly," Mr. Lin answered calmly.

"It took me a few minutes to get out of the station," Thompson replied.

"Where are you?" asked Lin.

"Usual spot when I need to make a private call," the chief confirmed. "Drove through McDonald's and am now sitting in my customary location where I can keep an eye on everything."

"Good, good, Mr. Thompson. So, I ask, where are my supplies? Why have I not heard from you?" the businessman wanted to know.

"I apologize. There's been some troublin' circumstances in the community that required my immediate attention," Thompson informed him.

"Excuse me? We had a deal, Mr. Thompson, thirty head per week. The last three months you have failed to deliver as promised. Last month you shorted me fifty-five?" Mr. Lin began to interrogate the chief. "How many have you delivered so far this month, eleven? Where are my supplies you were supposed to deliver yesterday, Mr. Thompson?"

"Well, sir, a little issue has come up with my team . . . ," Thompson tried to explain, but Mr. Lin abruptly cut him off.

"It is not your team, Mr. Thompson. It is my team. I own the fucking team. Do you understand? You work for *me*!"

"I, I . . . I do, yes, I understand," the chief stammered.

"How am I to get paid when you fail to deliver? Yet, I advanced you thousands of dollars to assemble my team! For what? Do you realize if you would organize your cowboys better, we could increase the pipeline fivefold, Mr. Thompson? Maybe more!" he yelled.

Thompson tried to respond, but Lin's ranting continued, "Every time you fail me, I have to make it up with certified product. Then where is my cost advantage? If you would just do your job, deliver what you have promised, you would be able to retire in a few years. Instead, you embarrass me, make me look unreliable, and you try my patience. You are a wild fucking pig, Mr. Thompson, a delicacy, like the business that we are in," Lin said.

"I understand you want to grow your market. I can do this. I need time to reshuffle my team. In the meantime, can't you ship from other states?" pleaded the chief.

The suggestion further infuriated Lin, "I need god-damn supplies from Texas! Those freaks over there noticed the last time I swapped Florida hogs for yours! Their palates know! I cannot sell Florida fucking hogs! There is a big premium for everything Texas! That is why I hired you! And do not tell me how I should run my business! I have fronted you thousands of dollars! I purchased a first-class truck for your operations! Will you, or will you not, provide me my quota, Mr. Thompson?"

"Yes, yes, I will," the chief promised.

"When, Mr. Thompson?" asked Lin.

"Soon, I promise," answered the chief.

"Mr. Thompson, do you know how much we make per hog liver?" Lin asked.

"Umm . . . ," the chief stuttered.

"Let me be clear, it is nowhere near the price I could get for a human liver. Understood?" Lin threatened.

Lin's comment sent chills up his spine. "I'll call you tomorrow," Thompson promised before he hung up the phone.

It's Just Speculation

Late Arrival Camping Area; Friday, November 16, 2012; 2:41 P.M.

Moments after the rangers had spoken with Dawson, the Special Crime Scenes Unit arrived. The team of four had already been briefed on the situation. Dawson again reviewed what they had found so far, including the strange remnants of hair caught between the van's sheet metal and chrome trim.

The officer told them that all the evidence found remained in place except for the two stuffed tigers he let the boys take with them to the police station. The team's leader frowned.

"I know, I know. I just didn't have the heart to tear those stuffed animals away from them. The terror in those boys' eyes. The tigers were the only thing that calmed them. Look, the two sleeping bags are right there," as he pointed to the hood of the van where the blankets had been set. "The boys were wrapped up, hiding underneath them the whole time," added the detective as Victor motioned to one of his team members to begin searching where the Coke can was found.

"Victor," Dawson sharply addressed the forensic leader to gain his attention again.

"Yes, detective?" he responded.

"Listen, I need to go check on something the rangers are concerned about. I'm not sure if it's connected or not. It's doubtful, but considering this and another case I'm working on, I just want to be sure. I'll be back in umm . . . ," the detective paused. He turned to the rangers about fifteen yards away. "How long does it take to get to the campsite? Ten, twenty minutes?" he asked.

"Fifteen or so," answered Wilson.

"I should be back within an hour, probably sooner," the detective told Victor.

"No problem, Jim. From what I know so far, any further clues would surely be welcome," replied Victor.

"Thanks," the detective said before turning toward the rangers. The three walked away and headed for their vehicles.

"I'm going to follow you guys. I need to make a few calls on the way," Dawson said.

"Detective, just so you know, once you get down into the canyon, few people ever get cell phone service," Irving replied.

"OK. But my radio should work, right?" he asked.

"Yes, I believe so," Irving responded.

"Do you have the motorhome description and license plate number?" asked the detective.

"I do; here it is." Looking at his paperwork, Wilson read off the details before the detective made his way beyond the rangers' truck to reach his car still parked near the loop's entrance. The detective took down the information and told the rangers he would call dispatch and run the plates.

"Sounds good. We can be there in less than fifteen minutes," replied Wilson.

Once in his vehicle, Dawson immediately called dispatch and asked for the plates to be run. He knew the descent into the canyon was only a mile away. He quickly called Karen and told her he had only a brief moment since he was descending into Palo Duro Canyon State Park and would lose cell phone service any moment. She had not heard from her husband.

Sounding somewhat confused, she asked, "Why would he be there? You can't legally hunt in the state park, can you?"

"Only at certain times of the year with a special permit, but I'm checking on a couple other things . . . ," was all he could say before the call disconnected.

Once at the bottom of the canyon, the rangers picked up the pace, and the three arrived at site number ninety in the Mesquite Campground in just over thirteen minutes.

The rangers parked a few feet beyond the motorhome, allowing the detective to pull up directly in front of the camper. They all stood at the entrance to Kenny and Lance's undisturbed campsite.

"You can see the grounds are impeccable. As far as we can tell, nothing has changed since they checked in on Monday. The awning's down, the table and chairs are in the exact same position. The gas grill is like new with no drippings of any kind. There is no way that grill has been used in the past two days. And look over here," Irving explained as they walked under the awning by the chairs to view the workbench behind the motorhome. "It doesn't look like this bench has been used all week. Look at the dust on top of it."

"And you've seen no sign of them at all since they checked in?" asked the detective.

"No, not one iota," answered Wilson as he moved toward the rack attached to the back of the motorhome. "They have the workbench and the bike rack, but we don't remember ever seeing any bikes all week."

"Have you checked with any of the other visitors?" the detective continued.

"The only other camper here is that trailer over there," Wilson said pointing to the older couple's site. "We talked to them just before we headed back up the canyon to see you, and they have not seen anyone or any activity whatsoever since they checked in on Wednesday afternoon."

"And the door and windows are locked?" the detective asked.

"We didn't try to enter the vehicle," answered Wilson again.

"Knock again and announce yourself loudly. If no one responds, check the door. If locked, see if you notice any indication of a security alarm on the dashboard, then check the sliding windows on the sides," the detective requested. He walked back to his car, opened the trunk, and removed a small tool from a leather case.

Wilson removed his business card from the crease in the door before he knocked and then waited a second before he loudly announced himself. He again received no response. As he suspected, the door was locked. With Irving's help, Wilson hopped up onto the driver's front tire and peered through the window looking for any flashing indicator of an alarm. He saw nothing. He and his partner then checked the sliding windows and confirmed they were locked before they met the detective on the passenger side.

"Did you notice any evidence of an alarm?" asked Dawson.

"Didn't see anything flashing, but I'm not sure. It could possibly be out-of-sight. Then again, it's an older motorhome; there may not even be one," replied Wilson.

"Well, if the alarm is on, rocking the motorhome should trigger it. Let's try that. If that doesn't set it off, I'm going to force the door open," the detective explained.

In unison, the three men exerted all their strength pushing three times against the passenger side, noticeably rocking the motorhome. Failing to trigger an alarm, Dawson walked up to the entrance of the motorhome and inserted the object into the rudimentary lock, jimmied it, and slipped his hand into the recessed notch to pull outward on the plastic door handle. Opening the door activated a step that extended from underneath the vehicle to assist people getting inside the coach.

The rangers observed his illegal entry but said nothing. The detective announced himself. When there was no response he stepped inside the home. He motioned for the rangers to follow him. It wasn't surprising to find the inside to be as tidy and orderly as the outside.

Dawson opened the glove box and found the vehicle registration, insurance card, and some miscellaneous papers. He quickly scribbled down all the information. The two rangers remained standing next to the small kitchen table across from the sink and had to partially crouch inside the table area over the bench seats to allow the detective to slide by them and access the rear section of the home.

Dawson peeked inside the tiny bathroom and found it to be sparkling clean as well. The small pantry just before the bedroom area was stocked with soup, spices, bread, and an assortment of condiments and Gatorade.

He reached the bedroom area where a queen-size bed stretched to the edges of the room, practically filling up the entire cramped space. The bed was centered between two very narrow built-in closets that were connected by overhead storage cabinets high above the mattress where the pillows rested. He had to crawl onto the mattress to access the narrow path along the right side of the bed. There, he looked directly at his reflection in the full-length mirror that served as a closet door. He opened the door and found several shirts on the left and blue jeans to the right. A single drawer at the bottom of the built-in unit stored underwear and socks. The detective climbed back across the bed to get to a much shorter closet on the other side of the confined room. The second closet door also served as a mirror,

173

although this one was cropped about chest high. Inside, the men had an assortment of t-shirts and riding gear arranged by color. Just below the closet, a tiny built-in nightstand sat adjacent to the bed. The table stood about six inches taller than the mattress, and two stacks of magazines were neatly arranged on top. The detective recognized issues of *GQ* in the first stack. He picked up the top copy of the second stack and flipped through a few pages before looking down and seeing that the next copy was a different issue of the same magazine, titled *Out*. He set the magazine down exactly as he found it. The detective nodded his head with the additional information about the men. He also noticed the layer of dust that had settled over every surface in the otherwise immaculate room. It appeared he was the first person who had disturbed the dust in days.

Without even seeing them, the detective could sense the rangers were becoming restless. He hesitated and decided not to open the two glass storage doors above the pillows. Through the glass, though, he could see a blanket and extra linens filled the rectangular cabinet.

He scooted himself down to the edge of the bed, stood up, and said, "I think we can leave now. I don't see anything of concern."

Relieved, the two rangers exited the motorhome ahead of the detective. As Dawson made his way down the narrow hallway, he opened the relatively large refrigerator and examined the milk's 'sell by' date. The gallon of skim milk was two-thirds full, and the date read, "Sell by 22/Nov/2012," still another six days away.

Taking one last glance around, the detective concluded with the rangers that there appeared to be no recent activity at all. Before he shut the door, he flipped the lever to lock it, stepped down off the sliding step, and closed the metal door behind him. As the step disappeared under the motorhome's carriage, the detective double-checked that the door was secure. Wilson again inserted his business card between the door and the frame near the door handle.

The detective looked at the rangers and said, "Gentlemen, I share your concerns. I don't think anyone has been here for days." He chose not to mention that two local men had also been missing for a day and a half now.

Trying to piece the puzzle together, Dawson reconciled what he knew. Len Mahoney was a loser, had always been a drunk, and would always be one; once a skunk, always a skunk. He was also as unreliable as they come and had been known to disappear for days at a time. The man had no ethics, manners, and not enough common sense to dunk his ass in a bucket of water if it was on fire. Why Tom Harden, married, with a daughter, would ever associate with the likes of Len Mahoney was beyond his comprehension. Flabbergasted, Dawson's thoughts then turned to Karen, Tom's wife.

"Why can't I meet someone like her?" He imagined holding her, massaging her buttocks as they embraced with her large breasts pressed firmly against his chest.

"I think we need to file missing persons' reports," suggested Wilson. The ranger's suggestion jarred the detective out of his trance.

"Um, yeah, I agree. First, let me radio the office to see if they have any information on the plates yet," the detective stuttered, trying to merge with reality again. The rangers shrugged at each other about the detective's odd behavior then followed him back to his car to radio dispatch.

Standing together next to the door while the detective sat sideways in the driver's seat with his legs hanging out of the car, the rangers could hear both sides of the communication exchange.

"Dispatch, Detective Dawson. Any feedback on that motorhome with Jersey plates that's parked in the canyon campground?" he requested.

"Yes sir. The vehicle is registered to a Kenneth X. McDonald, age 44, of Morristown, New Jersey." Dispatch provided the exact address that matched the vehicle's registration and insurance card. There were no warrants, outstanding tickets, or any other violations. The owner and the vehicle were clear.

"Thanks, Julie, out," the detective concluded.

"McDonald is the name they registered with; it's in the log file in my vehicle. I don't think the second man provided a name," Wilson informed the detective.

"Are you sure? Can you go check?" Dawson asked him.

Before Wilson could even turn toward his vehicle, the detective received an incoming radio call. "Dawson, Thompson here."

"Yes, Chief, what's up?" he responded.

"Where in the hell are you?" the chief asked impatiently. "I've been tryin' to reach you on your cell phone, damn it!"

"I'm down in the canyon at one of the campgrounds with the rangers," the detective responded. "We believe there might be two men from New Jersey missing as well. It's all very strange. Just doesn't feel right."

"What do ya mean 'you believe'? Your uncertain beliefs at this point are irrelevant! We know we have two men from our own backyard missin' for god-damn two days now!" the chief barked.

The detective, knowing the rangers could hear, quickly pulled his legs into the car and shut the door. "Chief, it appears there are now three different instances of people missing, up to six people in all, sir," the detective tried to reason with his boss.

"No, it doesn't appear that way. The only god-damn thing we know for sure is that Tom Harden and Len Mahoney are missin'! That is all we know, Detective! The rest is only absurd speculation. I strongly suggest you get your ass back to the station immediately! I want a detailed review of what we've done to find them. Our priorities here are Harden and Mahoney. They're our people. We're not gonna waste our time right now on two illegal immigrants and some city folks from New York with sticks up their asses who probably illegally hiked down the canyon outside the state park. Do you understand?" screamed the chief.

"Yes sir, they're from New Jersey, sir," replied the detective.

"I don't give a flyn' flip if they're from Mars! Report to the station, now! That's an order! Do you read me?"

"Yeah, I read you, Chief," and the radio went silent.

The rangers could tell a heated conversation had taken place. Wilson never even went to his truck to look for the name in the visitors' log. Dawson exited his vehicle, approached the rangers, and shook their hands. "Kent, Jack, thanks for your assistance. I've gotta head back to the station right now. Go ahead and file your internal reports," the detective told them.

"What? But you said just a moment ago you shared our concerns. Did we hear correctly that there are two men from Canyon who have been missing for a couple days now? There are six people missing in a matter of hours? What's going on here?" Irving asked.

"Not sure of anything right now. No new leads on the whereabouts of the Mexican parents. They could be anywhere. And these two guys here? It's just speculation they are missing, only an assumption," the detective stated with little conviction.

"Come on, Detective, you don't really believe that," Irving protested. "And what's up with Officer Barron? He's not just unprofessional, he's a jerk. How he can even be allowed on the force is beyond me. Is this the type of people we have serving Canyon? Is the chief the same way? I don't think he took the entire situation seriously. Did you see what little regard he had for those children?"

"Detective, I only hope the forensic team is more like you and Officer Tyson, and not anything like Barron. Your chief is questionable as well, and I'm being polite," Wilson added.

"Rangers, thanks for your cooperation. I have to go. Please file any internal reports you feel necessary," the detective told them before he headed back toward his car.

"Detective, don't you want me to see if I have the name of the second visitor?" asked Wilson.

"It's not necessary right now," Dawson said before he raced off in his police car.

Not My Liver!

Canyon City Police Department; Friday, November 16, 2012; 3:33 P.M.

Dawson hurriedly wove his way through the canyon and up the steep grade to the park's entrance. He passed through the exit gate, flattening the tire spikes guarding the exit way, and then made a sharp left. Pebbles were flying as he sped down the elongated S-turn into the Late Arrival Campground and onto the loop. As he was approaching the scene, he saw Barron standing next to his cruiser terminate a call on his cell phone.

Quickly exiting his vehicle, the detective then stepped over the crime scene tape and immediately sought the head of the Special Crimes Team. Victor was squatting next to the van examining every fine detail of the axle, hub, spare tire, jack, and the ground underneath. He had heard the vehicle swiftly approaching and assumed it was the detective.

Without turning to look, Victor spoke when he heard footsteps behind him. "Any significant findings with the rangers, Detective?"

"Possibly, but I'm not sure, Vic. Evidently, two men checked into the campground on Monday. They were supposed to check out Thursday afternoon, but didn't. The concern is that no one has seen any sign of them since their arrival, going on four days now," Dawson explained. "We ran their plates; everything is clean. No missing persons' reports have been filed. I don't know. Are they missing too? Just like Harden and Mahoney, the two local hunters. Now this? It's like five, maybe six people have just vanished."

Victor was intently listening to Dawson then informed his colleague, "You know, there are no signs of blood on the axle, hub, tire jack, or anywhere underneath the van."

"Yes, I know," replied the detective. "It's evident no one was injured from the jack collapsing. But even if we're wrong, why would someone put the boys on the roof of the trailer and not inside the van? They couldn't have climbed up there themselves."

"The three separate blood markings lead me to believe there is more than one victim," Victor reasoned. "I'm speculating these two near the car are from the same person; splotches at the edge of the brush by the Coke can are from a second victim."

"This probably sounds off the wall, but have you seen any evidence of wildlife, in particular wild boar?" Dawson asked.

"Yes, we have noticed areas that indicate the presence of wild hogs. We're trying to capture all of that as well. There's no doubt a number of boars have been in this area within the past twenty-four hours. I will keep you informed of our findings," responded the head of the special team.

"Vic, you realize what the boys said, don't you? That they saw ugly, scary animals," Dawson confirmed. "And when we asked about their parents, they kept repeating, 'No más, no más!'"

"Yeah, the boys' remarks imply they saw some kind of creatures," Vic responded.

"The most disturbing part is," the detective surmised, "it seems that it was after they saw the animals, their parents were no more."

The forensic expert paused and then hesitantly replied, "Jim, I understand. We're collecting everything we can and will not rule out anything. I really believe something eerie occurred, and I've seen more than my share of bizarre and gruesome crime scenes."

"I need to head over to the station now to meet up with the chief. Thanks, Vic. I appreciate your thoroughness. Please keep me informed, and let me know if you need anything," the detective said before he turned and made his way to his vehicle without acknowledging either officer.

The moment Detective Dawson turned onto Texas Route 217 headed back into Canyon, he called Karen.

"Hel-lo?" she answered. He could sense tension and fear in her voice

"Mrs. Harden, Detective Jim Dawson here," he responded.

"Oh, Detective, I was hopin' you'd call! Did ya find Tom or his truck?" Karen asked, praying he would say 'yes'.

"No, not as of yet, Mrs. Harden. I'm sorry," he replied.

"What are we gonna do? Where is he? I thought ya had a lead on his truck. Did ya think it was in the state park?" she asked.

"No, Karen, we haven't found his truck. But we will, I promise," the detective responded.

Her mind was filled with fear, and she didn't catch the slip. "My god! Where is he?" He could hear her sniffling and quietly whimpering.

"Mrs. Harden, I think it's time to alert the media with a complete description of your husband, Len Mahoney, and the truck. Are you OK with that?" he asked.

She tried to catch her breath. "Yes, yes, please do! I just want my husband home." Diverting her attention from fear to anger, she continued, "He's already behind on last month's mortgage, and my car needs some work done on it! Do ya know how much that damn truck cost? More than our house, more than what our house is worth! He always makes sure he pays that truck loan; he claims he needs it for business. I don't know what business he's talkin' about, 'cause he spends more time huntin' than he does with me or takin' care of business around here!" she ranted.

Feeling no guilt, Dawson welcomed the unhappiness in her marriage. "I understand, Mrs. Harden. I'm heading to the station now. I will go ahead and alert the news media. Think positive, OK?" Dawson told her before hanging up.

Again, Thompson impatiently called the detective, wondering where he was. "I'm here. Just pulled into the station," the detective told him. The phone went dead.

Dawson parked his vehicle in his customary spot, went straight to the chief's office, and knocked on the door. "Come in!" the chief hollered. The detective opened the door and stood facing his boss.

"Sit," the chief ordered.

Before Dawson was able to settle into the worn, stiff chair, Thompson pried him for details about the case on the two missing local men, Tom Harden and Len Mahoney. Step-by-step, the detective filled the chief in on the investigation. Then added that he had just spoken with Karen, and she agreed to alert the media.

"Wait another few hours," Thompson said.

"But, don't you want this to be on the six o'clock news?" Dawson questioned the chief. "If we wait much longer, it won't be reported until much later."

"The last thing I need is the community alarmed over two lowlifes who are most likely on a drunken binge," responded Thompson.

"Chief, I originally had my doubts as well, but now with the two separate disappearances at the campground, don't you think . . . ," was all the detective could say before his boss cut him off.

"More god-damn reason to think twice about panicking the public! I want this resolved quietly," the chief ordered. "I can see it now on the news.

'Two local men missin'! Never returned home from a hog-huntin' trip days ago; two illegal immigrants drivin' a stolen car with expired plates leave children behind, blood at the scene, parents nowhere to be found; two campers not seen in four days, local police clueless.' You think that's what I want leadin' t'night's news? A slew of missin' people along with incompetent police investigations? Is that what you want reflected on you, Detective?" the chief fired back.

"That's not true, Chief. The investigations have followed protocol. The reality is several people are missing. We've . . . ," Dawson tried to reason with his boss before the chief interrupted him again, refocusing on the local missing men.

"I want more details about Harden and Mahoney," the chief demanded, expecting that the detective's background information would verify his unfavorable suspicions about his two hired men.

"Well, both seem sketchy. Harden's wife is a really nice lady. They have a daughter about to turn ten. Sounds like they're havin' financial problems. According to her, he's done similar things in the past, gone on week-long hunting and drinking binges, but while he was gone, never went longer than two days without calling. Mahoney? He's a real winner. I met him a little over a year ago. We hunted together with another guy. When we met, I'm sure Mahoney had no idea I was a detective, or he would not have joined us. Since then I've learned a lot about him. He's always just out of harm's way, unreliable, a liar, and a known thief. Been in and out of drugs but never convicted. Surely not someone you can count on," explained the detective.

The chief sighed and thought to himself, "Shit! I was afraid of that. I hired two drunken idiots! And I'm going to lose my liver because of those morons."

"Find their damn truck! Get a chopper and search from the air!" Thompson demanded.

"It's nearly four-thirty! By the time we get in the air, we'll have, at the most, thirty, forty minutes of light," countered Dawson.

"I don't give a damn! Follow orders! Call Amarillo, now!" shouted Thompson.

Immediately, the detective went back to his desk, phoned his contact in Amarillo, and asked for an urgent air search of Motley and Cottle Counties for a black 2012 Dodge RAM 3500 Laramie Longhorn Limited Edition 4x4 Mega Cab truck. Dawson informed Kurt, of the search and rescue team, the license plate number and that the owner, Tom Harden, and his hunting partner Len Mahoney were last seen late Wednesday evening. He asked him to please search isolated roads known for hog hunting.

"Not a problem, Detective; it's on your dime. We can be in the air in ten minutes," Dawson was told.

"Do what you can while there's still light. Crisscross those two counties and report any potential sightings of a truck with that description," the detective respectfully ordered, then added, "a truck that certainly neither one of us can afford."

"No kidding. We're on it, Jim. I'll let you know when we're in the air and keep you up-to-date on anything we find," responded Kurt.

Excruciating Touch

Manhattan, New York; Tuesday - Friday; November 13-15, 2012

The planned hunting excursion could not have been more ill-timed. Jimmy's hedge fund, At All Costs, finished the week in total disarray. Notorious for outlandish conduct, twice Jimmy reacted in an unprecedented fashion in the days leading up to their hog-hunting trip. Elliot, Kevin, and Steve shrugged off Jimmy's business practices, tirades, and erratic behavior.

"Jimmy's just being Jimmy," Elliot told Robert Tuesday morning when their boss blatantly backed out of a trade, leaving a broker with a busted deal.

"I never gave you a firm bid to buy that shit, ya fuckin' moron! You became a broker 'cause ya couldn't hack it as a trader. Fuck you! They ain't mine! You're in the box, asshole! We're not doin' business with ya for at least a week! Ya hear me? At *least* a week, jerkoff!" Jimmy hollered before he turned off the volume for the spurned broker on the device that controlled direct lines to six different over-the-counter agents. "I don't want y'all doing business with Simpson or any other pricks there!" Jimmy yelled to no one in particular on the trading floor.

"Jimmy, what the fuck? Are you outta your mind? He's our most trusted broker! We need Simpson!" protested Mark.

185

"Shut the fuck up! Your friend sucks! He's not forcin' bullshit trades on me! He's in the fuckin' box 'til I say so!" Jimmy ordered before getting up and storming out of the room.

Mark stewed while everyone went about their business. He had seen Jimmy pull some pretty shady tactics before, but his refusing to confirm a buy for a huge number of February 2013 gold call option contracts damaged not only Jimmy's reputation, but Mark's as well.

Word traveled fast in the trading community. Reputations were earned, and anyone associated with a firm who reneged on a trade was deemed a scumbag, guilty by association. Mark understood this and was furious at Jimmy. The fact that the broker and Mark were friends and regularly attended New York Giants and Yankees games together only made matters worse.

Two days later, the atmosphere in the office became notably more uptight. Jimmy didn't show up until 10 a.m. Attempts to reach him on his cell phone and at home were unsuccessful. The stock market had been open for thirty minutes, and the over-the-counter markets had been trading for hours before he arrived. Jimmy's inexplicable absence had cast a gloom over the entire room. Mark kept his thoughts to himself, but the other traders bickered over what Jimmy would do.

"Should we buy gold put options?" Kevin asked.

"No, you dumbass! Jimmy was buying those before the election! Now that Obama's still president, the economy's going to tank, and gold is going to the moon. We should buy some gold call options," Steve lambasted his inept partner.

Moments later, Mark was stunned when he secretly turned on the volume for the direct link to Simpson, only to find the connection dead. Unbeknownst to AAC, the brokerage firm had cut the line Wednesday afternoon. Panicked, Mark walked out of the office, rode the elevator down thirty-four floors to the lobby, and privately called Bob Simpson.

"Bob, what the fuck's goin' on? Why is the direct line dead?" he asked his friend.

"Mark, what the fuck do you want me to do?" countered Bob. "I cut it yesterday afternoon. You know how expensive they are? I'm not paying for a direct line into a shop I'll never use again."

"Are you shittin' me? You have to be friggin' kiddin'!" Mark stuttered.

"Mark, it's all on tape. Dude, I about jumped out the window on Tuesday! That was a huge order! In a matter of minutes, I was sitting on two, three million in losses because of that asshole! The trader on the other side demanded the trade was good. I pleaded with him that it wasn't my mistake. That Jimmy, 100 percent, backed out of the trade. My whole firm, everything I built up in fifteen years, was gone in an instant because of that arrogant prick!" Bob explained, defending his actions.

"Who was it? Who was the trader?" Mark asked.

"I can't tell you. You'll eventually hear on your own. He was so pissed. I was freaking out. I literally ran back to the audio recorder in our I.T. room, replayed the entire episode, and recorded the conversations onto my phone. I didn't know how else to quickly prove what happened because the other trader refused to take my call after I told him the trade was a bust. He told me tough shit, I owned them; it was my problem to find another buyer. Mark, there wasn't another bid even close to that price. I was screwed, man!" Bob animatedly described his situation.

"Ah man, fuck! I think Jimmy was just tryin' to prop up his position, create an illusion there was demand out there, keep prices inflated," Mark offered as an excuse what Bob already knew.

"Yeah, no shit! His bluff almost cost me my business! I had to take a car over to the other firm and beg them to listen to the recording of me brokering the deal. The only thing that saved my ass was that his boss has known me for years. He intervened, and they agreed to listen to it. We sat in the conference room, scrutinized both conversations in real time, how I secured and verified both his trader's offer and Jimmy's bid. I even told Jimmy I had an offer that might have some room. Jimmy point blank told me to tell the son of a bitch to hit his bid. A split second later, I told Jimmy he owned them, and he just exploded on me. It's all on tape, Mark. The managing director agreed; I represented both parties fairly and had every reason to believe the quote was good. He let me out of the trade."

Bob continued, "But they're pissed at AAC, Jimmy in particular. The trader wanted to take it to arbitration. The managing director was a little more cool-headed, but he told me if I wanted to continue to broker any of their orders in any markets, I could never broker an order from Jimmy or AAC again. Ever! You know the business. Everyone talks. I had to cut the line. I had been thinking about it anyway. Fuck Jimmy! Tuesday took ten years off my life!"

Mark was silent on the other end of the line.

"How do you work for such a dirtbag?" Bob warned him, "You know word's getting around about him. He still hasn't paid his brokerage from August. He has over $100,000 outstanding. Do you know how hard it will be to collect that now that I cut the line? I didn't do this lightly. I had no choice. Another thing, rumor is a broker at another firm wants revenge because he just found out Jimmy fucked his girlfriend. Now you can't use that firm either because you know they'll fuck you."

"Fu . . . ck! Fuck, I understand," was all Mark could say before ending the call. Then dreadfully he took the elevator back to an office under siege.

When Jimmy finally arrived that morning, he didn't offer, and no one asked, where he had been. Yet it didn't take thirty seconds before he began boasting that he had been right again.

"Damn market's gonna be cut in half soon. Between Obamacare and the fiscal cliff, all hell's 'bout-ta break loose. The market's down over 700 points since the election, and it can't even give us a bounce to sell more? Dow's going to six thousand, game's over for the stupid public 401k plans."

In reality, it was the seventh consecutive day the markets had been relatively quiet, with little movement in any direction. As predicted by Jimmy, if Obama won, the stock market would instantly decline, and it did. But the bearish trend was tepid, less than 4 percent and stabilizing; not the precipitous decline of 15 percent or more that the hedge fund needed to profit from their option positions. Bonds declined as well, but only modestly, while the U.S. dollar, oil, and gold churned slightly higher. The actions in every market were the worst-case scenarios for AAC as they sought huge moves, not minor blips. What Mark had feared all along had come to fruition. The markets had been correctly forecasted and priced for an Obama win; there were no policy surprises, and, as such, they were dead in the water. While the markets churned nowhere, and the options quickly lost value, AAC piled up huge losses.

Well before Jimmy had purchased the first put options on gold near the third week of October, they had begun arguing about pre- and post-election strategies. The debates were often heated, but what enraged Jimmy was Mark's assertion that Obama had been the clear favorite for a while, and the odds of his winning were strengthening. Even when Mark, for arguments' sake, would simulate a Romney victory, his post-election market forecasts failed to mirror Jimmy's. He believed there was more risk to the economy and world stability under GOP stewardship than under Obama. Weeks prior to the election, they sparred over which candidate would create more jobs.

"Romney's created hundreds of thousands of jobs. What's that damn community organizer ever done besides support ACORN's prostitution and tax-avoidance schemes? Romney's a professional businessman. He knows how to create wealth the old-fashioned way, hard work. He did it himself. Obama? He's nothin' but a taker. Takes student loans, scholarships, and then redistributes the wealth from the job creators to those too lazy to earn it," scoffed Jimmy.

"Jimmy, that's bullshit! What does Obama have to do with ACORN?"

"He represented ACORN in the past when he was an attorney. Plus he helped train them on several illegal activities. That's how he won the god-damn election. This election, the sonabitch doesn't have ACORN to cast millions of illegal votes."

Frustrated, Mark tried to reason with Jimmy on the facts. "Obama worked, what? A couple of hours with ACORN in training sessions? When he represented them, he was on the same side of the lawsuit as the justice department. Jimmy, you keep distortin' reality."

"Reality? Reality is the financiers, the risk takers; they're the real job creators, not the government. If it weren't for the top 1 percent, unemployment would be at 20 percent right now. And if the god-damn Democrats continue to attack the wealthy, we *will* be at 20 percent. The top 1 percent don't make enough. That's why we have all these fuckin' losers who went to Harvard like Obama, stealin' from the masses. They have it too good. They just breeze through life, content livin' the good life while contributin' nothin' of significance. And don't even get me started about the middle class. Fuckin' ridiculous!"

"What the hell are you talkin' about?" Mark fired back. "Income is at its greatest disparity since the 1920s, just before the Depression. The problem is the middle class is gettin' squeezed. They don't have enough purchasing power to drive the economy. It's a thrivin' middle class that's the key to a strong economy; and they're livin' paycheck to paycheck. That's why jobs are not bein' created. What good is it to create a new product when no one can afford to buy it, especially the middle class?"

"Fuck the middle class. Before cities with shared services existed, it was every man for himself. Darwinism ruled. Once cities existed, you had a bunch of takers. For centuries now, 80 percent of the people don't do shit. Haven't ya ever heard of the 80-20 rule? It's a fact. Twenty percent of the people do 80 percent of the work," Jimmy claimed.

"Jimmy, there's always goin' to be takers. What about all the people who could be the 20 percent, but never get the opportunity? Growin' up in shitty, broken homes, attendin' crappy schools, just think about the violence they deal with every day. You know how many kids get free meals at school? Fuck, millions of kids don't even have basic healthcare. They never have a chance from day one. They get stuck in the perpetual cycle of poverty," Mark argued.

"Screw 'em! They need to rise above it. Hell, I didn't have a mom. I'm tired of all these fuckin' excuses. The problem is people have it too damn good. There isn't even a decent 20 percent anymore. There ain't enough inducement to be a risk taker. That's what's wrong with the economy today. Fuckin' Obama wants to punish the people who are great successes. We're sick of it, Mark. The top 1 percent creating all the jobs don't make enough. Obama is takin' away all our incentives. Everything we do trickles down to the masses. We're the innovators, the ones who give five-, ten-, twenty-fold back to society, makin' their lives better 'cause of our efforts, not theirs. They just sit back and let us do all the work. Then we offer scholarships for art and music? Fuckin' joke. While I work my ass off, most of the 20 percenters are jerkin' off on Facebook all day."

"You're outta your mind, Jimmy! Your views are why Romney's goin' to lose. It's an insult to all the hardworking people out there. You, Paul Ryan, and so many other Republicans espouse all these Ayn Rand philosophies when it suits you, but when it doesn't, you just change the facts. Seriously, Jimmy, you got a lot a . . . ," Mark started to say before he stopped.

"What, Mark, I got a lot of what? Instead of readin' all that liberal bullshit, you should read Ed Conard's book, *Unintended Consequences*. He used to work at Bain Capital and is one of Romney's biggest supporters. He's the only one with the guts to tell the truth. We need more inequality, not less. That's the only way to motivate all these art majors. Force 'em to get off their asses and work to their potential. So Mark, what is it, what the fuck do I have a lot of? What, god dammit?" Jimmy demanded to know.

"Nothin'," Mark answered while he thought to himself. "Jimmy grew up in the top 10 percent of the top 1 percent, the richest of the rich. Everything was handed to him. And what has he done for society? What innovation has he created that's trickled down to the masses? He's a friggin' hedge fund trader, no better than me."

"Yeah, nothin'. That's about what Obama's accomplished, nothin' but one failed policy after another," claimed Jimmy.

Wanting to end the heated dispute, Mark walked toward the door leading to the elevator bank then turned back toward the room for all to hear, and predicted, "We'll see, Jimmy. I bet the markets make new highs within months of Obama's reelection."

Like always, Jimmy had to get the last word in. "Obama's one and done. Nothin' more than a failed experiment based on hope and change. You're gonna look like a fool real soon," he boasted before Mark disappeared through the doors.

Jimmy considered Mark's views blasphemy and, as the election neared, became hell-bent on proving his colleague wrong. In a week's time, he bought thousands of options on stocks, bonds, the U.S. dollar, oil, and especially gold. He was steadfast about an imminent Romney victory and was convinced stocks would soar far beyond the most bullish outlooks, so he purchased a huge quantity of call option contracts on the December 2012 and March 2013 S&P 500 equity index futures. He believed bonds, no longer a deflationary hedge, would plummet as investors bet on an economic recovery similar to the one Reagan had fostered.

To profit, he bought thousands of put options on the U.S. 10-year Treasury Note March 2013 futures contract. Furthermore, he believed that the Romney-inspired economic miracle would spur growth around the globe, pushing up crude oil to record highs while the trust and respect the American currency deserved would be reestablished in weeks. To benefit, he purchased call options on both the West Texas Intermediate and Brent crude oil contracts and opened new positions on every major currency traded on the Chicago Mercantile Exchange. Finally, with Romney firmly in control, the world, overnight, would realize gold was near worthless; there was no need to purchase a metal in fear of a debt implosion and impending economic collapse.

Jimmy was convinced of this position more than any other and mocked opinions contrary to his. Hour after hour in the days prior to the election, Jimmy layered onto to his position and purchased more put options at a variety of strike prices on gold futures. His final short position in gold, betting the price would plummet, exceeded all of his other market positions combined.

"And if you're wrong?" Mark tried asking him several times. Jimmy rationalized that, if Obama somehow stole the election, they would initially lose money as the markets moved against them, but at the first opportunity, he would reverse all their positions. In the end, he believed if Obama did win, AAC would probably make more money faster anyway as the markets went nuclear. Yet Jimmy considered the odds of Obama winning inconceivable.

Mark would never forget Jimmy's words one day. "Mark, no president has ever been reelected with unemployment this high. The bastard single-handedly trashed the economy, drove unemployment to obscene levels, and tried to pick winners and losers. People see he's a socialist who's exploded the deficit. There's no way he'll win. Prayer can accomplish great things; maybe you should try it sometime."

No matter what angle Mark attempted, or logic he employed, nothing would change Jimmy's mind that Romney would win, and the markets would ignite. In the days leading up to aggregating the massive options positions, Jimmy and Mark's arguments over tactical positions intensified. The strategies each sought to employ were as polar opposite as their views on the coming election. The political animosity between the two reached a fever pitch Monday morning, the day before the election. From inception, Mark vehemently argued that a Romney victory was pure fantasy, and he stood his ground. "Jimmy, you're ignoring all of your analytical skills, your ability to reason! My god, Fox News, Romney's staff, and all of the conservative commentators can spin their internal polls all they want, it doesn't change the fact that the most credible, unbiased polls show Obama leading in almost every swing state; the odds of a Romney victory are slim. Obama is going to be reelected; you have to prepare for that!"

In front of the entire team, Jimmy brutally ridiculed Mark for his naïve analysis. Fixated on CNBC during trading hours, Jimmy cheered on Joe Kernen, Michele Caruso-Cabrera, and Larry Kudlow as they slammed Obama daily, segment by segment, guest by guest over the course of his term. The incessant bashing by the three correspondents primed Jimmy for the evenings when Bill O'Reilly and Sean Hannity of Fox News continued their extraordinary attacks against the president. When Donald Trump appeared on either show, the world stopped as Jimmy revered the real-estate tycoon.

He felt a connection with Trump when he learned one of Trump's ex-wives deemed *The Donald* the best lover she'd ever had.

Mark triggered Jimmy's complete meltdown that morning when he again mentioned prominent statistician Nate Silver's analysis showing the probability of an Obama victory. "Jimmy, look at the trend; the probabilities of an Obama win keep escalating. Over the past month, the probabilities have steadily increased from 65 to 70, 80, and now, the day before the election, a 90 percent certainty of an Obama victory."

Jimmy exploded, "If I hear that douche bag's name one more time, I'll fuckin' kill ya myself! Have ya ever seen that faggot on TV? He's another liberal tryin' to deflate the conservative message. He's been in O's pants from the beginnin'."

"Jimmy, he correctly called forty-nine of the fifty states in 2008," Mark shot back.

"2008 was an aberration, like Carter winnin' in '76, a one-off event," Jimmy defended. "Once Romney wins, you'll never hear Silver's name again. Another brilliant business decision by *The New York Times*, publishin' his blog. Fuck 'em, spreadin' their European socialist bullshit!"

"Jimmy, your analysis is flawed. The risks you're takin' are dangerous, but let's . . . ," Mark tried to rationalize with Jimmy but was unable to finish his thoughts.

"I'm wrong? Fuck you! Last I looked, I own this firm. Don't ever say that to me again, ya hear? Dangerous? Fuck you!" Jimmy screamed, slamming his fist on his desk.

"I just don't think the markets are going to move much if Obama wins. And for the one-in-ten chance Romney wins, you're long on the wrong side of all the options. The market will be spooked with a Romney victory, not an Obama victory. Buyin' all these options could crush us. You know how expensive everythin's priced. We could lose 10, 15 percent in days," pleaded Mark.

Jimmy flew out of his chair and began pointing his finger at Mark. "Ya fuckin' sayin' I'm wrong again? What'd I just say, god dammit! You're a fuckin' idiot, buyin' into that liberal media bias bullshit! Ya think I'm a fool, asshole? I live and breathe the markets and world news! Ya think Joe Kernen, Larry Kudlow, and Bill O'Reilly are wrong? They're behind the scenes. The real job creators like Trump ain't in the positions they're in by bein' wrong. The conservatives built this country. Not the liberals, and certainly not the damn unions. The liberals are just leeches, fuckin' parasites, bleedin' this country dry. It ends tomorrow when Romney stakes his claim to the White House." It was his last rant prior to the election.

The morning after the GOP debacle, the anger and bitterness in the office could not be measured. Making matters worse, Nate Silver had correctly called all fifty states, pending the final results of Florida, which he predicted at the final hours would go to Obama. No one dared mentioning this fact to Jimmy.

Obama's triumph devastated Jimmy, and gains in the senate by the Democrats only added to his resentment. From the moment he learned of Obama's decisive win late election night, his sole objective became crafting a strategy for the end of the free world. Instead of gold getting crushed, it would now double the hyperbolic gains it had already made in the past several years. From the moment the markets opened, Jimmy began selling all of his gold put options and immediately began purchasing just as many gold call options. He couldn't decide what to do in bonds. He knew the economy was going to tank, but the exploding debt was going to cause an inevitable crisis, sending interest rates skyrocketing.

One contradicted the other. So he hung onto his long put options in bonds and bought thousands of bond call options as well. He just knew bonds were in for an explosive move; he just didn't know which way. In the stock and crude oil markets, Jimmy furiously sold all his long call options, betting on massive price rises, and purchased equal amounts in put options in both markets to profit from the coming declines. He reversed all of his currency trades and now bet on a collapsing U.S. dollar. It took him several days to unwind his initial positions and establish trading positions for a world on the brink of economic calamity.

"Fuck it!" he thought. "As Obama destroys the free markets with government expansion, drowns his own people in irresponsible debt, and continues to pick the economic winners and losers, the 1 percent (the job creators) will retrench. They'll teach the middle class a lesson and show them who really runs this country. When unemployment finally surpasses Depression-era levels, I'll have already booked billions. Fuck the public, fuck the 47-percenters, and fuck Ohio. Ohio? Everyone's acting like Ohio determined the election. Fuck that worthless Yankee state! All of them are going to get what they deserve for electing that damn socialist!"

Only Mark understood the risks Jimmy was taking. The rest of the traders had only studied the nuances of options and were ignorant of the multitude of factors that influenced their price. By Thursday's close, only two days post-election, Jimmy had lost over $130 million. The losses they assumed on their original positions neared $60 million, but the losses on the new positions accumulated even faster. Virtually every trade that reversed the old position was a loss from inception. Stocks, bonds, currencies, gold, and crude oil were basically churning, creeping back and forth with no discernible direction. Volatilities, one of the key elements in determining an option's value, were in the early stages of getting crushed.

The strain between Mark and Jimmy only escalated. Mark argued against buying any options. He wanted to sell, believing all options, both calls and puts, would decline in value. He pleaded with his boss, "Jimmy, look at the charts. Everything's meanderin', goin' nowhere. Look at the VIX. I think it made double top yesterday. Look at all of the other volatility trends, they're all goin' down. There's no panic. We need to sell volatility, not buy it. Please, we need to close our long positions and then sell more; actually go short all the options, not long them."

Jimmy just stared at his screens as if he had heard nothing Mark said. When he tried again, "Jimmy, Jimmy! The markets aren't spooked Obama won. It was expected! The Republicans will have to compromise on the fiscal cliff. I'm tellin' you, the markets will be indifferent for weeks, maybe months!" Jimmy became enraged.

He leapt to his feet and pointed to the United States and Texas flags near the entrance of the office and screamed, "If the country's goin' down, I'm gonna damn sure profit from it! When the people rise up and throw that communist out, I'll close my positions! Fuck you! It's because of people like you that we're in this mess!" Over the course of the next several trading days, Jimmy continued to add to the massive long option positions.

Later that Thursday, the day before the hunting trip, Jimmy took a phone call just after lunch was delivered. While the rest of the team barely flinched, Mark was appalled over Jimmy's brazen attitude. The president of a second brokerage firm demanded to speak with Jimmy, despite Jimmy telling his assistant, Jan, he was unavailable and to hold all calls. She started to explain to Jimmy that he had called twice earlier in the morning before he snapped, "Put the fuckin' prick through!"

Jimmy picked up the line, "Jimmy Richter."

"Mr. Richter, Hank Moore, Worldwide Commodities and Asset Brokerage," said the voice at the other end of the line. Jimmy was listening to a quote of $14.55 at $14.85 on the March 1750.00 gold call option come across the speaker box and ignored Mr. Moore's introduction. "Mr. Richter?" the senior vice-president of the firm tried again to gain Jimmy's attention.

"What can I do for ya, Mr. Moore?" Jimmy tersely responded before he took a bite out of his sandwich.

"Mr. Richter, I'm calling concerning your account. Is everything satisfactory with our services? I've noticed your account is well beyond sixty days past due."

The man from the brokerage firm waited patiently as he listened to Jimmy smack his lips and sip from his iced tea before answering, "Satisfactory? Are ya fuckin' serious? Your firm is a fuckin' joke!"

"Excuse me?" Moore said.

"Your firm is a fuckin' joke!" Jimmy said and then yelled out to his team for the senior executive to hear. "Hey pardners, where does Worldwide rank among the brokers? Fifth, sixth? Are they even in the top ten?"

Kevin meekly replied, "Fifth maybe," as Jimmy glared at him.

"Ya see, Mr. Moore . . . that correct, Moore?" Jimmy asked.

"Yes, Hank Moore," he responded.

"Ya see, your firm sucks so badly my traders didn't even respond. I guess ya don't even crack the top ten of the dozen firms. Now, does that answer your question?"

"Mr. Richter, Worldwide Commodities and Asset Brokerage, for over two decades, has been one of the top three OTC brokers in the world," Moore calmly assured him.

"You're nothin' but Goldman Sach's and Citigroup's bitch. I don't give a fuck how big ya are! Ya asked if everything's satisfactory? My response is, no. Your brokers give us shit service. Quotes no one else even looks at. I'm still tryin' to understand why we even let ya in our shop!"

"Mr. Richter, in August we provided $65,000 in brokerage services for your firm. September $88,000 and October nearly $145,000; all of it is outstanding," Moore claimed.

"It's outstandin' for a reason. I ain't payin' it," Jimmy explained.

"Excuse me?" Moore asked.

"Ya heard me, asshole! I'm not payin' it! You go back to your brokers, ask 'em what kind of service they provide us. Then you'll realize my point. If ya improve your service, maybe I'll pay August. The rest of it you can fuckin' eat!" Jimmy threatened.

"Mr. Richter, not including November commissions to date, you owe Worldwide nearly $300,000 in brokerage fees. We expect to be paid in full," Moore replied.

"Hank?" Jimmy said.

"Yes, Mr. Richter?" he replied.

"One of your brokers, Mike Vinson? Ask him how his girlfriend is 'cause I fucked her. Several times, in fact; actually, just recently. But I haven't fucked her nearly as many times as your firm's fucked me in the last month." Jimmy waited a few seconds for a response. Moore said nothing before Jimmy hung up.

Jimmy looked around the room to make sure everyone got the message—he was in charge—before he declared, "I fucked that bitch three, four times last August." Then he laughed as he said, "Made up the part about fuckin' her recently though. Can't believe she still sees him."

"Way to make the brokers realize they're our bitches, Jimmy," laughed Kevin, still trying to suck up to Jimmy in any way possible.

Mark sensed an all-out train wreck. He sat there and thought, "I can't just walk out the door and potentially leave a $5 million or $6 million bonus on the table, can I?" He dreaded the thought of getting on a plane and spending three straight days with Jimmy. Mark consoled himself, "At least hunting, he'll have to keep his damn mouth shut most of the time."

The rest of the day was relatively uneventful except for the times Jimmy openly predicted that Kevin would get clocked by a boar or shoot himself in the foot, prompting Kevin to inflate his skills, "Oh yeah? You just wait! I'll kill the biggest boar of all!"

Departure day brought more dread. Modest openings across the board meant further declines in the options markets. By mid-morning, the implied volatility of every option had been trounced, causing option prices to continue to plummet. With Thanksgiving the following week, traders were unconcerned about any potential market moves before the holiday and were mercilessly extracting next week's time value. The brevity and sum of the losses didn't shock Mark as his worst fears were being realized. As of Thursday's close, losses topped $300 million since Jimmy went on his option-purchase spree, and Mark figured the losses would easily climb another $125 million by Monday morning. In little over a week since the election, AAC had lost nearly 9 percent of its capital. Mark knew investors didn't like surprises, and if they lost much more, they would begin to liquidate their investments. He had seen it before. Investors open their month-end account statements, realize a fund lost a large chunk of capital, and they immediately invoke their thirty-day redemption notice. It's like a game of musical chairs, and with the most recent scandals burning some of the most prominent names in investing, no one hesitated to protect their remaining capital. It was literally every man for himself. Even modest redemptions could result in a death spiral as the fund is forced to close positions to return investor capital. Jimmy knew this as well, yet continued to add to his position, this time in the stock market, minutes before he left for the day.

To catch their five forty-five flight from LaGuardia to Dallas and on to Amarillo, the gang had decided to leave the office by one-thirty p.m. Kevin and Steve would meet at Mark's house; then a car service would take them by Jimmy's on the way to the airport.

Twenty minutes before leaving for the day, Jimmy stared at his monitor and couldn't believe his eyes. "Look at how cheap this shit is! Boys, this is an opportunity of a lifetime! I'm loadin' up for wild boar," he bragged as he bought more S&P 500 Stock Index March futures put option contracts.

As usual, he had been leading the bantering all day, but now it backfired on him. From the entrance, Jimmy's desk was at the end of the row to the far right. When he had turned to brag to the team, Elliot, for the first time all day, got a close look at him and broke out in laughter. "What the fuck, dude! Fuck, I've got Evander Holyfield sitting next to me! What the fuck happened to your ear?"

"Bitch bit my ear last night! Hurt like hell! Felt like she took off my whole fuckin' lobe," Jimmy said as he gently touched just above his shredded ear lobe.

"What the fuck did you do?" Elliot asked in astonishment.

Before Jimmy could catch himself, he blurted, "Put that bitch on her back, pinned her down, rammed her so hard I thought I went right through her, and then I bit her left tit even harder. She yelled so loudly, neighbors in every fuckin' direction could probably hear. Tried to bite her right one too, but she bucked me off. First time some bitch ever bucked me off. She launched me like a fuckin' rocket ship."

The whole room was in an uproar. Several bent over in laughter as they crowded between desks to see Jimmy's mangled right ear. Robert was the first to pass Elliot's desk and stood right on top of Jimmy.

He looked down at Jimmy sitting at his desk and howled, "Fuck, it's not just Evander over here, it's Evander the vampire Holyfield! My god, look at that hickey on your neck! It's not the option premiums; it's the women that are sucking the life right out of you!"

Despite being the king of smack talk, for the next fifteen minutes Jimmy bore the brunt of endless ridicule. The jokes and insults followed him even as he walked out the door with his three fellow hunters. As he stopped to perform his daily ritual of caressing the Texas flag upon leaving for the day, Elliot yelled out to Jimmy, "Since you'll be gone for ten days, can you give me that bitch's name and number? I want to be her rocket ship too!" They all burst out laughing.

The car service was waiting for Jimmy and Mark when they exited the building. Kevin and Steve hopped into a cab for the short jaunt to the Union Square area where they lived. They planned to be at Mark's condo by three forty-five where the car service would pick them up, and then swing by to get Jimmy a few blocks away before heading to the airport.

Jimmy lived on 63rd and Mark lived on 66th Street, both in the fashionable Upper East Side near Central Park. Mark hoped the car ride home would provide him an opportunity to reason with Jimmy, persuade him to at least reduce his positions, if not flat-out close them.

He wasn't subtle, "Jimmy, we took a huge hit today. You have to stop the bleedin'."

"I can't believe how cheap this shit's gettin'," replied Jimmy.

"It's goin' to get cheaper. If the stock market rebounds at all, and it looks like it will, they will crush the premiums. You know that," Mark hypothesized.

"Ya still don't get it, do ya, Mark? We have a fuckin' socialist gonna start his second term. If he could ram the stimulus and Obamacare down our throats in his first term, what'll the Muslim do in his second term when he has nothin' to lose? Take over the banks once and for all? Institute central plannin'? He's already taken over healthcare; he's tryin' to centralize education. We own General fuckin' Motors; the god-damn government owns General Motors! How can that be? The corporation should've gone bankrupt like Romney said. That's how capitalism's supposed to work. He's too much of a pussy to do anything about Iran and North Korea. He allowed our embassy to be overrun by terrorists! On 9/11, no less. The markets are gonna come to this conclusion any day now. We need to keep buyin' options. It's the only way we'll get our money back and for you to collect your bonus. With the leverage, in days we could make forty, fifty percent!" Jimmy lectured Mark.

"But Jimmy, the markets are not behaving as you expected. You need to get out and start fresh," countered Mark.

"Why ya don't see how Obama's single-handedly destroying free enterprise is beyond me. It makes me sick. Fuckin' sick to my stomach ya voted for him. Born, raised, and a lifelong Republican, and now ya support that piece of shit? It's 'cause of people like you this country is where it is today. You should be fuckin' ashamed! The end for him will be when he comes for our guns. Ya know he will. He's a socialist; it's in his foreign blood. When he comes for our guns, the conservatives will rise up and put a stop to this travesty. This is what happens when ya elect a non-Christian!" Jimmy's voice boomed as he scolded Mark.

Dejected, Mark said nothing else before Jimmy was dropped off. Three blocks later Mark was home. In disgust, he shook his head when he made eye contact with the driver and said, "Thanks, Rudy, see you at three forty-five."

"See you then, Mr. Shannon," the driver said before heading off.

It had been a brutal week. Mark stood outside his building for a minute, marveling at the tranquility of the street and neighborhood in the heart of the city. He wanted to walk to the park, let the brilliant fall day clear his head before he rushed off to the airport, but he looked at his watch and knew there was not enough time. Needing a few minutes alone, he settled for the garden behind his building. Nearly an acre, it was one of the largest private gardens in the city and was meticulously maintained. He sat on one of the benches facing a large modern stainless-steel sculpture. The beautiful setting eased his mind to contemplate Jimmy's comments, historical perspective, and future outlook.

He wondered, "How can my perception of reality be so vastly different than his? Relative to everything that occurred in Obama's first four years?" He ran through a mental checklist of what had transpired since the historic 2008 election: the stock market up 50 percent since his inauguration in 2009; passage of a comprehensive stimulus package that stabilized an economy on the verge of collapse; saved the automobile companies and millions of jobs when complete shutdowns were eminent as the credit markets were frozen, negating any opportunity for the free markets to function as designed. On the president's watch, modernized financial, healthcare, and education reforms were passed. He increased Pell Grants and eliminated banks from acting as middlemen collecting billions in fees with no risks whatsoever in government-guaranteed student loans. As promised, he ended one war, declared the wind-down of a second, and still killed Osama bin Laden. "Don't Ask, Don't Tell" was repealed, the use of torture denounced and suspended; instead of acting unilaterally, he formed a consensus with key world leaders to place the most extensive sanctions ever agreed to against Iran. All achieved in one of the most trying economic times since the Great Depression. None of these accomplishments mattered? The country wasn't significantly better off today than the fall of 2008 when markets, economies, and whole societies were on the verge of cataclysm? My god, how could anyone forget the dire circumstances of just four years ago?"

The car ride home was the final straw; the breach between he and Jimmy had grown too wide. He decided, right then and there, he would resign before returning home to New York. He finally had given up trying to sway Jimmy in any manner. He questioned himself, "Am I capitulating on Jimmy and AAC, like investors invariably do when they routinely sell their stocks at cycle lows, foregoing possibly $5 million in bonus? Just when things would turn around? Six weeks until the end of the year when bonuses would be determined? Quitting right now is ludicrous." Then he thought otherwise, "If we have another week like the past one, it won't even matter. There'll be no bonus. And if I bail now, before the whole thing blows up, at least I'll preserve my dignity and respect among my peers."

It disturbed him; despite Jimmy's powerful persona, he was unable to reason with him to reduce their exposure. What bothered him even more was his inability to articulate to Jimmy, to get him to recognize, how his all-out hatred of Obama only blinded him; prevented him from seeing the opportunities that were presented each day. Instead, Jimmy only saw the unwinding of democracy and false scourge of socialism. Able to only see those two paradigms, Jimmy became more radical and intolerant of different viewpoints. The tunnel vision that Obama was the devil of a free society completely distorted his ability to rationally analyze and dissect every conceivable scenario that would affect a market. He often acted like a child pouting, taking the ball away, and effectively ending the game when he didn't get his way.

Mark had known for a while, but didn't want to admit it. Jimmy had become the poster child of a class of people he termed the CRWF—the Collateralized Right Wing Fringe—a group who had become so vigilant in their beliefs, unwilling to be receptive enough to cooperate or compromise in any fashion. He remembered back to his first semester in college when his political science professor discussed how 'An intense minority was far more powerful than an unorganized majority'. It frightened him that this almost occurred in 2010, the prime of his life.

Spurred on by angry, bitter, and radical television and radio talk show hosts, the CRWF nearly seized control of the entire political spectrum. Despite only being a fringe, their fervent beliefs captivated them to aggressively impose their will on the American people regardless if the majority disagreed with their philosophies. He had always believed the

206

majority of Americans were truly centrists, not center right as constantly reported. Studying polls to specific questions, he found the majority favored key elements of the president's Affordable Care Act, yet high numbers disliked the bill. He found similar discrepancies regarding the Dodd-Frank financial reform bill, the rescue of General Motors, and the president's reaction to the British Petroleum Gulf oil spill. It seemed the majority agreed with the president's proposals, but when they responded to the totality of the bills, often opposite tallies were recorded after the right wing successfully labeled every legislative effort as a government takeover. 'Obamacare' and 'Government Motors' became the catch phrases of the GOP to rally the masses and defeat what the Republicans deemed a liberal agenda.

Being a political junkie, early in 2009 Mark researched the history of job creation and deficits under different administrations. He thought, if the president was the quarterback who received the bulk of the praise or criticism for economic performance, it was fair to record how much of the deficit had been accumulated under Democratic presidents versus Republican leaders. Reviewing certified statistics by the U.S. Bureau of Labor Statistics, he was astounded by what he learned. The greatest deficits occurred during two periods. The first was the twelve years under Reagan and Bush administrations when Reagan espoused deficits didn't matter. When taking a closer look at the data, Mark came to the conclusion that the Reagan revolution was a fraud. During his presidency, the one known as *The Gipper* nearly tripled the country's deficit. Following Reagan, Bush 41 then increased the deficit another 40 percent in four years even though in the 1980 primaries he labeled Reagan's theory on deficits as *Voodoo Economics*.

Reading through the sixty years of data, Mark then noted Bush 43, with the backing of a Republican house and senate, more than doubled the deficit again. The Republicans, with bill after bill, swelled the total deficit to nearly $12 trillion at the end of fiscal year 2009, a year in which Obama had little control. Over the sixty years, Republican presidents were responsible for more than 80 percent of the deficit Obama inherited. Yet despite all the prior government spending, Obama inherited an economy in shambles with massive future deficits all but guaranteed. Mark thought, "And the Republicans are considered the economic conservatives. How could the public be so fooled?"

Mark's research led him to another incredible misconception, "Republicans are the party of job creation." Not according to his investigation. Again reviewing U.S. government data, Mark learned that over the past seven decades, under Democratic presidencies versus Republican leaderships, Democratic presidents created nearly two and a half times more jobs than Republicans. During this period, the Republicans held office thirty-six years compared to thirty-three for the Democrats.

Mark wondered again, "Why don't people know this? Why aren't the Democrats publicizing these long-term trends and statistics?" He was relieved when multiple reports by *The New York Times*, *Bloomberg,* and a university professor began publicizing the real facts about which party over the years created the most private-sector jobs.

On Election Day, the majority did speak and reelected Barack Obama. While he was always confident the president would be reassigned to office, he was relieved by the resounding victory. All of his research and diligence of maintaining a pulse on the American people paid off; Obama took every swing state, humiliating Romney 332 to 206 in the Electoral College, and winning the popular vote by over three million. The win validated what he had always believed: The majority favored the policies of the president, and not the radical right he referred to as the CRWF. The people wanted financial and healthcare reforms; an end to wars; environmental policies to protect the water, air, and food we eat; reduction in fossil fuels; a long-term solution to climate change; better education, especially for the poor; freedom of choice; and game-changing infrastructure projects. They understood government played a critical role in their lives, providing services and fulfilling projects no single company could finance, let alone complete.

Mark thought about a book he had read. It discussed four of the greatest projects in American history: the Manhattan Project, the Marshall Plan, NASA, and the Federal-Aid Highway Act of 1956. All transformed the country and propelled American prosperity to be the envy of the world. Yet, each endeavor was government-planned, financed, and executed. He thought it was ironic, "If that were the case, why did everyone always blame the government, demand for it to get out of the way?"

His mind whirring, Mark thought about another historic effort in the mountainous mosquito-infested jungles of Panama. "Wasn't it the French government who began construction of the Panama Canal before the United States government bought it? After twenty-three years of struggles, the U.S. government (our government) took over and completed in ten years the forty-eight-mile waterway that connected the Atlantic and Pacific Oceans. What private institution could have done that? Build an international waterway that cut 8,000 miles off circling the southern tip of South America, and guaranteed the safe passage of any ship even in war? My god, it is considered one of the Seven Wonders of the World!"

Mark could understand people's complaints about big government. He just wanted better government. A government that enacted laws and regulations that promoted free markets—free markets that could help monitor and guide other free markets. All within a framework of guidelines and standards designed to promote equal opportunities, not equal outcomes. Why couldn't Jimmy see this?

Mark opened the door and went straight to the kitchen where he heard his wife. He greeted her with a tender kiss.

She had just returned home after having lunch with friends she met every Friday. They made small talk before he calmly dropped the bombshell. "Honey, I have to go on this trip. I can't tell you how much I dread it, babe. It is goin' to be a miserable plane ride, and an even worse weekend. Jimmy's outta control, and I can't deal with it anymore. I can't reason with him about anything. Being associated with AAC, especially after what transpired this week, has tarnished my reputation. I plan on resigning before I get back on the plane headed home, Tuesday morning."

Elaine was shocked. Her facial expression and body language told him she was very uneasy about the news. "What are you going to do? Does Jimmy have a clue?" she asked, trying to keep her composure.

"I don't really know yet. But I'll figure it out," he shrugged. "Don't worry. It's for the best. Jimmy's always been pretty ruthless, but you always know where you stand. In the past few months though, he's become an irrational, impulsive monster. I don't even know what he's capable of anymore. Since the election, he's gone completely nuts. He talks as if the world is comin' to an end and as if it were up to him and his fellow conservatives to rise up and do somethin' about it. It's crazy! He truly believes Obama is a message from God of pending Armageddon. He told me that last week. It's insane!" He continued, "He keeps making reckless trades that appear to be out of desperation. Elaine, listen to me! He is no longer capable of using reason to assess the markets! Or his brain is demented. Hell, it could be both!"

"Mark, I . . . I . . . I'm shocked," she said. "Do you think you'll remain friends?"

"Seriously, Honey, the less I see of him, the better off we'll all be. He absolutely despises my political views. Thinks people like me are to blame for the world's problems." Mark stopped for a minute. "Come here," he said as he approached her and gave her a hug. He pulled her close to him, pressing her breasts firmly against his lower chest. She immediately squirmed, pushing her hands against his chest to relieve the pressure between their two bodies. His hands remained draped on her, and he massaged her upper back and lower neck without reciprocation.

"Are you upset? Are you OK, sweetheart?" he asked, slightly taken aback by her mannerisms.

"No, honey, I guess I'm just shocked you're resigning. Aren't you leaving Jimmy in a bad spot? He counts on you to mentor everyone," she replied.

Unsure how to interpret Elaine's answer, Mark tried to reassure his wife, "Sweetheart, trust me, in the short run, it is going to sting a bit. But in the long run, it's by far the best thing for us. I wish I'd resigned a month ago when I knew something wasn't right. I just couldn't put it all together. Now I have. It's time."

A sense of panic coursed through her body. "He's put it all together? Oh, my god! Does he suspect something?" Elaine began to fidget. She fought back tears and the desire to spill her guts right then and there, admit her sins. But her upbringing kept her in check.

Mark could tell she was disturbed, but still had no idea the extent. He thought it was all about money. She was accustomed to a certain way of life—had been since childhood—and didn't see any reason for that to change.

"Elaine, relax, babe. This will all work out. I promise. We'll be just fine," he assured her before he went into the bedroom to get ready for the hunting trip.

She kept herself busy in the study while he packed. She responded to a few emails, confirmed her charity ball meeting that was scheduled the

Tuesday prior to Thanksgiving, and then filled out her weekly NFL picks for the AAC office pool, a ritual she loved. Knowing Jimmy had to see her name every week when the picks were submitted and then again when the standings were updated aroused her. She was back in the kitchen on the phone with a friend when Kevin called Mark on his cell phone to let him know they were already seated in the limo outside. It was 3:40; Mark let them know he'd be out in a minute.

While she was on her cell phone, he sneakily walked up behind her and kissed the back of her neck then reached around her to squeeze her large, firm breasts. His right hand grasped her bosom a split second before his left hand reached its destination. His approach happened so fast, she was unable to prevent the excruciating touch. Upon the slightest brush against her left breast, she jerked around and pushed away from him. As she held her phone face down at her hips, he gazed into her eyes and saw her agony. He placed his hands on her shoulders, keeping a slight distance between their bodies; he noticed a bruise on her arm.

"You OK? Somethin' wrong?" he asked. "You look like you're in pain."

She whispered, "I'm fine. I'm just worried you're leaving Jimmy's firm at the worst possible moment."

"Everything will be all right. I love you, Sweetie. My plane arrives mid-day Tuesday. I'll see you then," he said before turning toward the door. Mark heard Elaine put the phone back up to her ear and say, "Carol, I'm sorry, I need to call you later." Without looking back, Mark subconsciously tugged twice on his right ear before tentatively opening the door to exit his high-rise apartment. In the elevator his mind raced, "Carol? Carol? One of Jimmy's lovers? The Growler?"

Rudy opened the back door for Mark. Somewhat dazed, Mark stood next to the car for several seconds before Rudy asked him if he was all right.

Without responding, Mark slowly took a seat on the passenger side, facing backwards. Rudy then grabbed his suitcase and put it in the trunk. Mark knew he had a meager three blocks to regain his composure. Kevin and Steve acted like excited little boys on Christmas. The trip was a huge deal to them, an opportunity to be with Jimmy, try to impress and befriend him for life. Sitting in the limo, his colleagues tried to engage Mark.

"We're going fucking boar hunting!" Steve hollered.

"Hell yeah! Gonna slay me some wild-ass boars," boasted Kevin.

They knew something was wrong; Mark blankly stared out the window, solemnly watching everything fade into the distance.

"It'll be interesting," he mumbled as they pressed him to respond.

He just sat there deep in thought, reflecting about his wife, her habits, and their discussion right before he left. She loved to kiss and nibble on his ear, but hadn't done it in weeks. The occasional hickey was a thing of the past. When he informed her he was resigning from AAC, she never once expressed concern about money or what he was going to do. Was it just his imagination? Everything revolved around Jimmy. Mark pulled on his earlobe a few more times, and then rubbed the left side of his chest in a firm circular motion. His heart sank, a bead of sweat formed on his forehead right below his hairline. "It couldn't be true. It had to be coincidence. Why was there a bruise on her arm? Was her breast sore?"

"You OK, man?" Steve interrupted his thoughts. "You're not having a heart attack, are you?"

Mark looked to his right at both of them, "I'm fine, little indigestion," he said as they pulled up to Jimmy's building.

The twenty-minute ride to LaGuardia was unbearable for Mark. Instead of being centered on how great a trader Jimmy was, how he mastered every market, the conversation turned to Jimmy's infamous hunting exploits.

"I remember the time me and my brothers were in Cottle County, 'bout fifty miles from our ranch. I killed two of the biggest boars I'd ever seen. Pissed my brothers off, I got both of 'em. They weighed nearly 500 pounds apiece. Tusks were six, seven inches long. That's what we call trophy hogs, my friends. Big fuckin' mean-ass sons-abitches. Mounted both of 'em. Wait 'til ya see how menacin' they look. There's nuttin' like holdin' one of their heads with your bare hands right after the kill when their bodies are still warm and limber," bragged Jimmy.

"Are we going to hunt that same area?" asked Steve.

"No, but not too far from there. My brother Carl has been home for a week. He's been stockin' a feeder a little closer to the canyon. You'll love Palo Duro. It's beautiful. Of course, ya know, all of Texas is God's country," replied Jimmy.

"It *is* the Lone Star state," added Kevin, trying to impress his boss.

Jimmy smiled before he falsely stated, "Only state in the union with the right to secede. That's why it's called the Lone Star state. God, I hope Governor Perry tells Obama to just shove it. Texas will be the model for all of the other god-fearin' states to follow. Perry could make that decision any day. Monday sounds good to me. Don't know what the fuck he's waitin' on. Course, I'd have to move back to Texas. Can ya imagine what'd happen to the markets if Texas decided to secede? What's Obama gonna do, send troops to Texas? Fuck him. He'll find several million Texans waitin' for him at the border, the national border of Texas."

Mark sat silently, amazed at Jimmy's ignorance, and Kevin and Steve's willingness to blindly accept such nonsense.

"I'll tell ya somethin' else. We have a governor who takes care of Texans like the NRA takes care of its own. Perry doesn't take any shit from Washington just like the NRA aggressively represents its members and tells all those liberals to go fuck themselves as they try to take away our constitutional rights. Man, I can't wait to be home," Jimmy gloated.

Considering the internal turmoil Mark was going through, he remained remarkably composed. The four routinely went through security and boarded the plane. Mark and Jimmy flew first class but were in separate rows. Kevin and Steve sat together in coach. The plane took off on time, and the group landed in Dallas forty minutes prior to their next flight. The three-hour, forty-minute flight from New York to Dallas provided Mark an opportunity to further reflect about work, his marriage, and his relationship with Jimmy.

As they hurried their way to another gate to catch a smaller regional aircraft for the hour-and-ten-minute flight to Amarillo, out of the blue Mark asked Jimmy, "Why didn't your father ever remarry? It must have been pretty hard to raise four boys alone."

The subject was one of the few Jimmy tried to avoid discussing. "I dunno. We were all young when she passed away. We never talked about it. For as long as I can remember, we had a live-in maid who was like our mother. She took care of us, cleaned the house, did our laundry, and cooked all the meals. Ya know all the things a mother does. She just didn't do anything *with* us. It was always my brothers and me with daddy. I think he liked it that way. He got to see plenty of women."

The flight from Dallas to Amarillo went like clockwork. Fifty minutes after landing, they arrived at the Richter Ranch.

James Sr. and Carl greeted them at the front door. While they all firmly shook hands, Mark commented to Carl about his hand-blocked cowboy hat with the unique band around it. When he asked about it, Carl took off the hat and showed it to them.

"Boar tusks," he proudly explained about what adorned the hat. "I cut 'em outta every trophy hog I kill. These are from some of my biggest kills." The large tusks gave a primitive, almost savage look to the sleek, dark hat.

James Sr. seemed to dismiss Carl and his hat as he led them to the stunning Grand Room. It didn't take them long to realize the origin of Jimmy's personality. Silently, they all agreed that apple didn't fall far from that tree. Nearly ten minutes into a rambling monologue about himself, James Sr. finally asked Jimmy, "Ya gonna return 35 percent or better this year?"

"We'll get there. If this option strategy we're tradin' right now works as expected, we may even double that," he told his father.

Those were the first words spoken by anyone other than James Sr.

"Excellent, excellent. That's my boy," the elder Richter boasted.

Carl asked Jimmy how he liked the city.

"It's certainly not Texas," was all he could say before James Sr. began another long-winded one-way conversation.

"Damn liberals are ruinin' this country. Obama better not ever visit Texas, that's all I gotta say. He'd best keep in mind 1963; I'm already on an exploratory committee for a Perry-Palin ticket in 2016."

Then he went on another five-minute diatribe against the Democrats and Obama in particular. It didn't take long for the three guests to understand the pecking order.

Jimmy finally interrupted his father, "Daddy, we had a long day. We're gettin' up early tomorrow for a few days of huntin'. If you will, please excuse us."

"That's all right. I hope y'all enjoy your stay. It's a mighty fine place here," James Sr. said before his two sons and three guests retired to their rooms.

Set on 175 acres, the 9,800-square-foot sprawling ranch-style home was as spectacular as Jimmy had described. The front entrance led to a grand room/combination kitchen with high vaulted ceilings, a well-stocked bar, and every amenity imaginable. The house curved to form a gentle "U" shape, wrapping around an exquisitely landscaped pool and spa area. A hallway off one side of the Grand Room led to five exclusive southwestern-style bedrooms; at the opposite side of the home were the gun room, master bedroom, and maid quarters. The wide hallway resembled a resort; it ran along the front section of the home leading to five guestrooms which provided striking views and individual patios accessing the pool area. Mark had never seen anything like it. His spacious bedroom and bath were elegantly decorated and had the finest linens. The extravagance reminded him of Elaine's parents' home back east. As he prepared for bed, he heard whispers in the hallway and then a bedroom door close. Though barely audible, moments later he suffered through the maddening sounds of Jimmy having sex. Her moans and periodic, "Oh Jimmy, Jimmy," drove him insane. The lustful affair lasted nearly an hour and a half before Mark heard a door open and two people walk by his room. Shortly after that, he heard Jimmy's footsteps pass by again, his door shut, and then silence. Mark didn't sleep a wink the entire night.

What the Hell is Goin' on Down There?

Len Mahoney's Residence; Canyon, Texas
Friday, November 16, 2012; 6:05 P.M.

Detective Dawson sat in the chief of police's office, defending his response to the missing local men.

"Look, nobody reported Len Mahoney missing. When Mrs. Harden called yesterday morning, he had been missing only a few hours. I filed a report, drove out to Len's trailer, checked out a site where I know he frequently hunts, and then sent out APBs to all the local agencies with details on both men and Tom's truck. There are no leads as of yet. It wasn't until this afternoon that Mrs. Harden decided to alert the media; you requested I not move forward with that until I got your approval. To complicate matters further, two little Mexican boys were discovered stranded on the roof of a trailer at the top of the canyon, their parents nowhere to be found. And then only a few hours later, the rangers at Palo Duro Canyon State Park inform me they are concerned about two male campers who've not been seen for four days. So, Chief, exactly where would you like for me to focus my efforts? The parents of two petrified little boys, two tourists believed to have vanished four days ago, or two lushes who are notorious for going hunting, drinking, and who knows what else for days at a time? We just dished out money for a chopper to look for those two deadbeat imbeciles. Don't you understand? Mahoney doesn't have a life. Only thing he *does* have is a vicious dog that probably goes unfed for days at a time."

"I want Harden and Mahoney found! That's what I want, dammit!" replied Thompson.

"If that's the case, then why are we waiting to alert the media?" the detective asked just before he answered his cell phone, "Detective Dawson."

"Jim, Kurt in Amarillo," said the head of the Amarillo Search and Rescue Unit.

"What did you find, Kurt?" the detective asked.

"Sorry, Jim. The search was suspended fifteen minutes ago. We didn't find anything. No sign of them or the truck," Kurt replied.

"OK, hang on," the detective requested, then informed his boss, "Amarillo found nothing. You want them back in the air first thing tomorrow morning?"

"You're god-damn right! Search everywhere! I want those two found, yesterday!" the agitated chief responded.

"I will notify them to also be looking for the two men from the campground and possibly two illegal immigrants as well," Dawson informed him.

"Whatever! Just find Harden and Mahoney!" the chief ordered.

"Kurt?" the detective spoke into his cell phone. "Please resume operations again first thing in the morning. How much area were you able to cover this evening?" Dawson asked.

"The northern half of Cottle and a small portion of Motley," Kurt replied.

"OK, start heading north, northwest. Concentrate on the terrains and remote areas between Caprock Canyon and Palo Duro. From there, move westward toward Buffalo Lake. Got all that?"

"Not a problem," Kurt said.

"Couple of more things," interjected the detective. "I have no reason to believe they're connected, and we don't even know for sure if anyone's missing. But early this afternoon, two young Mexican boys were discovered lying on the roof of a moving trailer at the Palo Duro Canyon campgrounds near the entrance to the park. We can't find their parents and think they're illegal immigrants. There is speculation one of them is injured. That's all we know at this time, so please notify your spotters to be looking for one, possibly two adult Latinos wandering, hitchhiking, or anything out of the ordinary. The other thing is the park service suspects that two Caucasian adult males are missing. One we know is Kenneth X. McDonald, age 44, of Morristown, New Jersey. We're not sure of the second man but believe he is approximately the same age. Their camper has been empty for several days now, and no one has seen either one of them since they checked in Monday. Make sure your unit is keeping an eye out for them as well. There is a good chance they're on mountain bikes," the detective directed Kurt.

"What the hell's goin' on down there?" the Amarillo officer asked.

"I wish I knew," Dawson responded before hanging up. "May I alert the media now, Chief?" he then asked Thompson.

"Brief Carla, and have her go through the proper channels," the chief of police directed.

Dawson went back to his office and immediately called Carla, who was in charge of all media correspondence. He provided her all the pertinent information concerning Harden and Mahoney, when they were last seen and the exact details of Tom's truck. As he hung up his phone, his thoughts turned to Karen.

Slowly walking back to the chief's office, he ducked his head in and told Thompson "I'm going to head on out to the Hardens' and talk with

Tom's wife again, see if anything clicks—anything at all." The police chief ignored him.

On his way to visit with Karen, he thought it was best to stop by Len's trailer first for another look. As he approached the lot, the darkness of the country road couldn't hide the blighted homestead. The moment his headlights shone on the bumpy dirt driveway, he could hear the pit bull's fury. He left his headlights on, grabbed his flashlight, and made his way toward the house resting on blocks. He first looked into Len's truck and tried to open the door, but it was still locked. The complete darkness made it apparent no one was there. He walked around the side of the trailer near the dog kennel and directed his flashlight onto the dog.

The animal, a reddish-brown color with white markings on his chest, barked and pounded against its cage, daring the detective to let him out. Dawson scanned the pen with his flashlight. The dog's water bowl was dry; no food appeared in the second filthy bowl. He then glanced over the area behind the trailer, pausing for a moment to illuminate a rusting washing machine and a pile of debris just twenty yards from the pen. The kennel, the trash, the entire grounds disgusted him. He walked towards the back of the trailer looking for any signs of a storage container for dog food but only found the bucket he had used the previous day to look inside the windows. Next to the bucket, a hose laid in a jumbled pile. It was attached to a faucet on a galvanized pipe that came out from the ground near the trailer.

"There's no way I'm opening that gate," he said out loud to himself.

He looked at the gray-colored bucket that once had held five gallons of paint, tipped it on its side, grabbed the free-swinging handle with his left hand then bent down and grabbed the end of the hose with his right. He walked toward the pen dragging the hose behind him, set the bucket upside down, and dropped the hose next to it. The entire time, the dog barked and raced from one corner of the pen nearest the trailer to the next. The pen shook violently each time the dog rammed into the steel mesh.

Irritated, Dawson went back to his vehicle, grabbed a half-eaten Big Mac and an extra-large bag of French fries, and grudgingly walked back to the cage. With no desire to be near the dog, the detective set his flashlight down, carefully stood on the bucket, reached up, and dropped the fries through the holes in the top of the cage. The dog, that just seconds earlier had been going ballistic on the other side of the fence, began devouring the fries. The detective then ripped in half what was left of his burger and smashed each part through the cage. The two pieces splattered as they hit the ground and were gone before the detective stepped down from the bucket.

He picked up his flashlight, walked over to the faucet, turned on the water, and made his way back to the cage. To prevent any chance of being bitten, he held the hose about eighteen inches from its nozzle. As he snaked the limp end of the hose through the fencing, the dog ripped at the rubber tubing and yanked the hose from the detective's hands. Water spewed everywhere before the fiend let loose and began lapping up the streams of water. Dawson regained control of the hose and, at a distance, directed the main stream of water into the dog's water bowl. With water spurting in every direction from the punctured hose, the dog's entire upper body was drenched as he vigorously began drinking from the bowl while was it was filling.

Muddy streams began spilling out from under the fence. By the time Dawson was able to shut off the hose, his shoes were caked with mud.

"Why would anyone—anyone but white trash and gangbangers want to own such a vicious animal?" he cursed.

He walked back to his car, opened his trunk, and pulled out a white towel to clean his shoes. The first swipe left the towel streaked with a thick, reddish-brown muck that emitted such a stench it caused him to pause and look at the towel, then at his shoes.

"Stupid-ass dog!" he roared.

He stormed back to the faucet, reeled the nozzle back toward him, and turned on the water again. Soaking the towel and then ringing it out, the detective began to wipe his shoes of the mud that had mixed with feces and urine. The process was nauseating; twice he had to wring out the towel to continue cleaning his shoes. Holding the hose between his knees with watering spraying everywhere from the shredded nozzle, Dawson, thoroughly rinsed his arms, wrists and hands. He flung the excess water droplets off his hands, turned off the facet and walked away, leaving the wretched towel and enraged dog behind.

Dawson's foul mood grew darker as he drove away wondering, "How could such a sweet, attractive woman be married to a man who hangs out with people with the likes of Len Mahoney? Is Tom just like him?" It angered him he that had never found someone so appealing, yet a despicable man like Tom Harden had.

His spirits lightened as he neared her home. "Maybe no one will ever find the bastard, and Karen would become mine." Pulling into her driveway, he dreamed of coming home as 'Jim,' not as 'Detective Dawson.'

Karen saw his car and was immediately standing nervously on the modest front porch. As he exited his vehicle, the detective suppressed a smile when he saw her. Even under the circumstances, the opportunity to see her brought butterflies to his stomach. His excitement dwindled when he saw her parents and sister in the doorway.

The detective promptly greeted her, "Good evening, Mrs. Harden," while nodding to her family.

Already in tears, Karen asked, "Oh, my god! You haven't found him?"

"I'm sorry, Mrs. Harden. We've found nothing so far. We had a chopper in the sky late this afternoon for about forty-five minutes before it got dark; we plan on resuming the search first thing in the morning. We also alerted the media, and we're doing all we can. I'm doing all I can, I promise you," reported the detective.

She began sobbing uncontrollably and turned to hug her mother; her father and sister wrapped their arms around them all.

"Mrs. Harden, you can't think of any special place he might be?" asked the detective.

He barely heard her say, "No."

With her back to him, the detective made eye contact with her father and said, "I just left Len's home again. He wasn't there, and I didn't see any signs that anyone had been there since I last checked. I promise to keep you updated. If you can think of anything or hear of anything at all, please call me immediately, OK?"

"Yes, we will. Thank you, detective," her father replied before Dawson turned and headed back to his car.

While the family solemnly went back inside, the detective sat in the driveway for a brief minute. He radioed dispatch to see if any additional information had come in to the station about the two men, the missing campers, or the parents of the little boys. To his dismay, all had been quiet.

Karen heard his car backing out of the gravel driveway and partially opened the curtains to watch him pull away. He had just started to drive off slowly when he saw the curtains move. Unable to resist, he stopped the car and made eye contact with her for several seconds, then tipped his hat before she closed the curtains.

He was entranced by her watching him and hesitated a little longer before he drove away and headed back to the main part of town.

The majority of his dinner having been fed to Mahoney's dog, he considered stopping at any number of fast-food joints besides McDonald's, but visions of the dog kennel, cleaning his shoes, and the smell of the muck-stained towel squelched any appetite he had. Anxiously he drove up and down the main strip several times before finally heading back to the office.

His first stop was the men's room to wash his hands. He stood there looking into the mirror, scrubbing his hands and lower arms up to his elbows and thought, "Possibly six people missing. Six! Is it truly possible a few wild boar hairs pinned between the chrome trim and the minivan's sheet metal is the most significant clue?" He shook his head in disbelief. "What did the boys mean about the scary animals, no mas, no mas?"

The Dinner

Great Room; Fire at Will Ranch; Friday, November 16, 2012; 6:45 P.M.

Ted was full-throated even before the appetizers were served. He and Derek had had an incredible morning stalking a Barbary sheep deep in the canyon. The magnificent creature had been spotted by them only a half dozen times during previous visits to the ranch.

Native to northern Africa, the Barbary were introduced to the southwestern United States in the 1950s. Weighing in excess of two hundred pounds, the powerful, athletic animals can leap over six-foot barriers from a standing position, walk along ridges barely wider than a tightrope and climb the most improbable slopes. They prefer arid, mountainous regions where they graze on grasses, bushes, and lichen. If necessary, all of the water they need comes from the grasses and wood they consume.

Ted loved the curled shape of their tough horns. But it was their noble beardlike hair that grew from their throat that truly excited him. The male's beard often extended down its neck and chest then draped down between its front legs covering its knees. The opportunity to see one, let alone stalk and hunt one, ranked high in the men's hunting achievements.

Thirty minutes into their hunt, using high-powered binoculars Derek spotted one less than a mile away. Perched on a steep slope facing the canyon, the sheep, with its sandy-brown coat, stood like a statue next to a juniper tree jutting out from the canyon wall. Ted and Derek spent the next thirty-five minutes inching their way forward and coming within two hundred yards of the animal. They waited patiently, taking aim but not firing until the perfect shot presented itself. Abruptly, the majestic animal bobbed its head before turning broadside, parallel to the canyon wall. Still not feeling threatened, the sheep confidently eyed the distant stalkers before it staggered tumbling twenty feet down the steep incline.

Ted's ammo, the .223 70g Barnes triple-shock (TSX), performed as advertised. The bullet pierced the sheep's hide and, upon impact, the bullet's head peeled back like a banana peel to form a wider, blunter flower-shaped head. Traveling through the flesh, it ripped a path through the animal's vital organs, killing it instantly. Derek was ecstatic with the expert shot.

After inspecting the fallen animal with the sheep-like horns and a goat-like beard, the two hurried back to the ranch and secured a couple of ATVs. With the assistance of one of the ranch hands, they set off to bring the prized animal home. They navigated the ATVs to within fifty yards of the beast. It was even more beautiful to the hunters the second time they saw it with its head slumped on a small boulder. Before the three of them picked up the 220-pound animal, Ted reached into his front pocket, pulled out a guitar pick, and placed it on the ground next to the boulder. It was a ritual Ted performed whenever he participated in what he considered a trophy kill. Even though he hadn't actually taken the shot, it was his ammo that brought the sheep down with one bullet. He was proud and wanted to mark the spot.

Derek cleaned the wound area to minimize any bacteria accumulating, and the three strapped the animal to the back of the ATV driven by the ranch hand and made their way back to the compound atop the canyon. There, the animal was immediately gutted, cleaned and skinned before being placed in cold storage, waiting to be taken to the taxidermist to be stuffed and propped for display. Ted and Derek relaxed the rest of the day, cleaned their guns, and absorbed themselves in the beauty of the canyon from the porch of their cabin.

As the minutes passed, their anticipation for dinner grew. The opportunity to spend a raucous evening with eight blue-blooded Americans centered on guns, more guns, hunting, the GOP, and how the fuck they could vaporize Obama and the Democrats invigorated them. Plus both knew the visitors would relish hearing about the morning's kill.

The party arrived just before sunset and had an opportunity to take in the beauty of the canyon before the sun disappeared beyond the horizon. The first question they asked Gilbert was if Ted had arrived, as he had promised the week before.

Gilbert confirmed, "Oh yeah, he's here and looking forward to meeting y'all for dinner."

This roused the gang to a fever pitch. Ted was their hero, and despite their own successes in business, any one of them would have traded their positions for Ted's iconic life.

The rocker, originally from Detroit, not only possessed their political and social views verbatim; he also had the public forum that allowed him to openly express them.

"Fuck Obama!" was their mantra.

They willingly expressed that to everyone they knew who espoused the same philosophy, but the men weren't ignorant. When doing business with others holding contrary opinions, they remained mum, only espousing their love of God.

Ted, however, generated millions of dollars spewing his self-professed God-driven principles. In fact, the more he ranted publically against the queers, whores, pimps, sluts, takers, foreigners, Muslims, and soulless liberals, the more he made.

The men were astonished he could make insinuations about killing the President of the United States and members of Congress and get away with it.

At an NRA convention during Obama's run for reelection, Ted told his ardent followers, "If Barack Obama becomes the president in November again, I will be either dead or in jail by this time next year." [11]

As for the rest of the Democrats, Ted suggested, "We need to ride onto the battlefield and chop their heads off in November," [12] while members brandished their rifles in the background.

The main rallying cry was Ted's statement, "It isn't the enemy that ruined America, it's good people who bent over and let the enemy in, if the coyotes in your living room pissing on your couch, it's not the coyotes fault it's your fault for not shooting him." [13]

The eight men couldn't get enough of Ted. A week before coming to Palo Duro, Alan had the slogan, "Suck on my machine gun!" superimposed on a picture of Ted on stage with his guitars and machine guns and emailed it to each of the men prior to their arrival. Several saved the image and used it as a screen saver while one used it as his wallpaper for his phone. All had drunk the Nugent Kool-Aid.

Five of the gregarious hunters travelled from four different states: two came from South Carolina, three from the impoverished southern states of Tennessee, Alabama, and Mississippi. The other three avid hunters resided in the host state of Texas: two from Houston and the third from Dallas. The three men from Texas and one man from Tennessee had graduated from the tradition-bound Texas A&M University, while the men from Alabama and Mississippi had bided their time at the University of Alabama. As for the two from South Carolina, Bryant graduated from the University of South Carolina and Tony from Clemson. Although only a few of the men had met prior to arriving at the ranch, all shared a common bond with Alan, who lived in Dallas and had organized the hunting trip.

As they left their rooms in the main lodge a little early for the reception dinner, Alan announced to his posse, "I assume Ted will be fashionably late. Most people in his position are, aren't they? We should be able to easily knock down three or four scotches before he arrives. Hopefully, they'll have Johnnie Walker."

They all had a good laugh. Everyone knew Ted did not partake in this great American pastime, and they wanted to respect his values while with him.

Much to their surprise, Ted and Derek were already in the Great Room concluding their discussion about whether the aoudad sheep Derek had shot that morning should replace the one Ted had pretentiously displayed in a corner of the room. There was no doubt; Derek's sheep was slightly larger than Ted's, had bigger horns, and a beard that extended an inch or more past its front legs. In the spirit of killing, Ted reluctantly agreed to the swap. Ted's submission, however, didn't dull his spirits or his confidence. He noticed the 'great eight' enter one of his favorite rooms in the world.

"Gentlemen, gentlemen, welcome to the ranch I humbly nicknamed 'Fire at Will.' This is God's country; none of you are liberal fucks, are you?" Ted boisterously asked his guests.

All erupted in laughter. The men were ecstatic meeting the legendary rocker, hunter, and gun advocate.

Bryant whispered to his business partner, "You know he has his own ammo supply line. The guy rocks."

Tony nodded; he was fully aware.

Ted commanded the room just like he did the stage, personally introducing himself to each of the men he considered brothers in arms.

As usual Derek had no problem taking a backseat to his best friend. This allowed him time to get to know the visitors and listen to them boast about their successes, money, and of course their allegiance to the only real American party, the GOP.

Despite the men arriving early, the staff was prepared. Iced teas, waters, and tantalizing hors d'oeuvres made of rattlesnake, quail, dove, rabbit, wild turkey, and venison were served including Ted's favorite game, wild boar. All agreed the boar liver pâté was to kill "each other" for.

As the men mingled, Ted, having already established that liberals were not welcome, directed the conversation to hunting, guns, and his personal line of ammunition.

Standing in the corner next to the stuffed aoudad sheep, Ted exclaimed, "It was incredible. We saw that fuckin' sheep from nearly a mile away. Since Derek noticed it, he got to shoot it. Amazing spot by him. Damn things are like a wax mummy; their colors blend perfectly with the rock, near impossible to see. But shit, watching them move! What incredible strength and agility they have roving the canyon. Ya know they can jump over six-foot hurdles. And look at the beard on that beast!" Ted bragged as he stroked the long hair dangling from its neck and chest. "Hell, the one Derek got this morning is slightly larger with bigger horns and has a longer, more prominent beard. Just before y'all got here, we agreed to replace mine here with his," he explained.

Alan, waiting to get a word in, complimented Ted. "Beautiful ranch you have here. I can't wait to shoot a sheep like this fella. Mighty nice of you to showcase Derek's kill."

"Man, he's a good friend. His kill certainly out-does mine. But he never would have gotten it if he hadn't been using my ammo. You're all going to use my ammo this weekend, right?" Ted asked.

"Of course we are," Alan assured him. "We already made arrangements with Gilbert. We've been looking forward to this since last week when he told me you would be at the ranch the weekend we were booked. Got pretty damn lucky, considering this has been planned for months."

"Yes . . ." Ted started to say before Derek cut him off, knowing his buddy was only getting warmed up.

"Ted, I never thought I would hear the day you would admit my kill topped yours," laughed Derek.

Ted allowed Derek his due then continued on, "Yeah, you are damn lucky I am here this weekend. Gilbert is a good partner. We decided on the spur of the moment to come up here and massacre as many of those wild fuckin' pigs as possible. Ya know what I do? 'I kill pigs. I am a pig killer. Big pigs, small pigs, fast pigs, slow pigs, momma pigs, daddy pigs, little baby pigs. Black pigs, brown pigs, yellow pigs, red pigs, tan pigs, calico pigs, striped pigs, swine of every imaginable description. I kill them all.' [14] I've killed big game all over the world. There's nothing like killing a wild boar. Brought here to be released and then hunted for sport. 'I do believe that wild pigs are to this day, and will more than likely forevermore remain my bowhunting quarry of choice. Pigs turn me on.'" [15]

Not finished Ted bellowed, "Every year I hunt and feast on the succulent beasts with my great friend Rick Perry. To think he's only governor and not president is sinful. At least Rick's governor of the greatest state ever created."

Gilbert, the main owner of the ranch, had overheard Ted's comment that he was a good partner and approached the circle of men. "Ted, a good partner? Considering I'm a native Texan, I'm a great partner, aren't I?" Gilbert asked.

232

Ted looked directly at Gilbert and said, "Hell yeah, you're a great partner, the best, Gilbert. Together, we have the greatest hunting ranch in the world."

Turning his attention back to his guests, Ted asked, "Fellow boar slayers, ya hear about those pigs straying outside the canyon a few weeks ago and running into Amarillo, wreaking havoc, chasing the few liberal fucks we have around here, and badly wounding the animal control officer before they were gunned downed in the park? Ya heard about that right?"

"I did," Alan responded. "We're going to hunt sheep in the morning then hog tomorrow night. Can't wait to hear their squeals."

Bryant jumped in, "Ted, what's the biggest hog you ever killed?"

"A lot bigger than those that rampaged Amarillo several days ago. I've killed ones nearly 500 pounds. Those in Amarillo were like 250 or so," answered Ted.

"Damn, that was crazy," Tony remarked.

"Yeah, last night Derek suggested that for every boar we kill, we should capture one and release it in the cities to terrorize all the liberal pussies destroying this country like fucking Obama, the cities' pimps, whores, druggies, and takers. We don't have many liberal fucks around in these parts. At least not ones that are brave enough to admit it. But the more I think about it, that animal control officer who was injured in the park must have been a liberal doing a conservative's job or he would've been smart enough and tough enough to get the hell out of the way of that pig, no matter how mean they are," Ted theorized.

They all laughed.

"Hey, Ted, why don't you run for office? This country needs more real Americans like you. That's the only way we can end this communistic regime once and for all," suggested Alan.

"Appreciate it, Al. Trust me, I've thought long and hard about it. You never know, I just might. But I just enjoy stalking, killing, and blowing things up so much. It's in my blood. Hell, if I had to be around all those traitors every day, listening to their placating the 47 percent, or as Derek claims is now 52 percent, my head would fuckin' explode," claimed Ted as everyone howled again.

"Perry – Nugent 2016 is what this country needs!" shouted Derek.

"Hell yeah. Ted, with Representative Steve Stockman's help, you could take all of Houston," one of the men from Houston yelled.

"Steve's a good man, a true conservative and great friend of mine. We're both true patriotic Americans who stand up for our rights. I'll tell you what, if I ever do run, this will be the symbol of my campaign," as he tapped the confederate flag on the T-shirt he wore.

The men roared with approval. "Ted, we need you! Run for office, so we can put the confederate flag where it belongs: back on top of the state capital of South Carolina," encouraged Bryant.

Just before the dinner bell rang, Ted added one more thing; he railed the Muslim community for proposing to build a new mosque near Ground Zero. "Let's call a spade a spade here. If Islam is the religion of peace, then I'm a malnourished, tofu-eating anti-hunter. Islam is no more a peaceful religion than Jim Jones was a Christian prophet. I know not all Muslims are religious whacks who deserve a bullet, but the statistics are alarming." [16]

On that note, the men all took their seats.

Dinner was served at a beautiful rustic table capable of seating sixteen. The setting couldn't have been better for Ted and his minions; a Great Room suitably adorned in trophies that once roamed the prairie beyond the window and the canyon below. The entire group was energized. Ted, being the leader of the fringe, relished the limelight while his flattering devotees would have stories, pictures, and autographs to crow about. The anti-Obama and liberal bashing never ran its course as the ten men tried to outdo each other's outrageous suggestions.

"Pot smokers should get life terms!" cried one.

"End welfare and abortion!" declared another.

"Prosecute the damn gays for sodomy; they are destroying the traditional family!" demanded Tony.

"Global warming is bullshit. Biggest hoax cast on the ignorant public in centuries!" claimed Alan.

"Build fucking dual electrified fences on the border and zap those wetbacks!" argued all five who resided in Texas.

"Just in case they do get past the fences, give any law-abiding citizen the right to shoot on sight. You know they have tunnels!" added Derek.

It was unanimous; Texas should secede.

Bryant declared he just may have to buy a home in Texas soon and try to declare residency even though his business was in Charleston. "Don't know if I can take that chance. If Texas does secede, I have to be a citizen from inception," he pledged, never mentioning South Carolina had a 7 percent income tax while Texas had none.

Around nine p.m., Ted and Derek retired to their cabin. The hunt, the relaxing day prepping their guns, and the dinner bonding with true Americans had been a great success. The privileged guests remained in the Great Room for another two hours expanding their stories as the drinks flowed. In all, they drained slightly more than three bottles of Johnnie Walker Black. With visions of semi-automatic rifles rattling the canyon's walls, the men baited one another as they returned to their rooms. Who would spot the first sheep and be awarded the opportunity to kill? How many hogs could each slay? They prayed that by mid-day tomorrow, the canyon would have sacrificed sheep with enormous horns and beards trailing down their necks, and that by night's end, menacing wild boar heads with protruding tusks to mount and hang on their office walls. They licked their chops, envisioning the feast of fresh liver and French racks of boar. What they couldn't eat would be processed on site and shipped to their homes as a testament to their skills. The men slept well.

Amarillo Special Crimes Unit

Wayside, Texas; Saturday, November 17, 2012; 9:18 A.M.

"Detective Dawson," he answered his cell phone.

"Jim, it's Kurt. We're confident we found the truck," the head of the Amarillo Search and Rescue Team relayed.

"Any sight of the men?" Dawson asked.

"No sir. We did a pretty extensive fly over. Spotted a hog feeder about a mile from the truck but didn't see anyone. And, Jim, they told me that there are fifteen to twenty dead boars scattered around the feeder. It appears they were being prepared to be field dressed because many of them are lined up and lying on their backs," Kurt told him.

The detective was relieved the truck was found and that the men weren't. He felt no guilt for his feelings.

He asked, "So the boars were just left to rot?"

"My understanding is that doesn't appear to be the intention. If they were left to rot on purpose, why would someone arrange them and turn them on their backs?" asked Kurt.

"I'll see and smell soon enough. Where is the truck?" the detective asked.

"It's parked in a small cluster of juniper trees in the canyon about five miles north of Wayside Road, State Route 285. Off 285, take the gravel road to McNeill Ranch Airport outside of Happy. You know where I'm talking about, right?" asked Kurt.

"Yes, I'm somewhat familiar with the area," responded Dawson.

"OK. When you get to the ranch, veer to the left then head north on the dirt road about a third of a mile west of the airport. When you come to the fork in the road, stay to your left, and drive along the ridgeline. The truck is about a mile down on your left. It gets pretty rough beyond that. It's basically two dirt tire tracks, so you better have a four-wheel drive truck. Just continue down the path until it ends to get to the feeder. It's maybe a third of a mile from where the tire tracks end. You might have to walk from there as you begin to descend into the canyon. Just follow the ridgeline. Got all that?"

"I'll get officers out there immediately," Dawson said and then thanked Kurt.

It had already been a long morning for the detective. He was still at home but had been on the phone at least a half-dozen times with the Palo Duro Canyon ranger station and his department. As expected, the motorhome remained vacant with no signs of either McDonald or his companion. Child Protective Services had placed the two boys in a foster home, but he had not heard if any additional clues had been discovered. Worse yet, Victor from Special Crimes Unit had no pertinent information besides what they already knew or suspected. The blood was human, and the hair stuck in the van's siding was from a wild boar and a few droppings nearby were from wild boar. Victor did say he was awaiting the results of one final report that could be vital, but it might be another twenty-four to forty-eight hours.

Exasperated, the detective wanted to scream. He was especially aggravated with the chief. During their last discussion Friday evening, Dawson had suggested notifying the next of kin of McDonald to determine if there had been any recent contact with family or friends, but the chief vetoed the idea.

"I don't want any god-damn panic! Get people all riled up over nothing. I want more evidence of foul-play or reason for concern. Damn Yankees come down here all the time and think the rules don't apply to them!" barked the chief.

Jim's thoughts turned to Karen. He hadn't talked to her yet and didn't want to until he had more details about the truck's location and condition. The thought of talking to her, possibly seeing her, excited him. And the fact that her husband hadn't been found excited him even more.

Dawson called the chief. "Amarillo spotted the truck."

"Well, it's about damn time! Where's Harden and Mahoney?" Thompson eagerly wanted to know.

"The chopper team saw no signs of them, sir. They did notice a hog feeder in the area. Oddly enough, they found fifteen to twenty dead boars that appear to have been prepared for field dressing," informed the detective.

"Hmmm . . . and where's the truck?" asked the chief.

"In the canyon, just north of the McNeill Ranch Airport in the town of Happy, off State Route 285. I'll call and get a few officers out there immediately. I'm going to ask Detective Mills to ride out with me as well. I need to stop by the station first to pick up an SUV. The road is pretty rough, and Amarillo told me I'd need a four-wheel drive vehicle to get to the feeder," the detective informed Chief Thompson.

"Get on it! I want those two found today!" the chief said before abruptly hanging up without asking anything about the two young boys' parents or the two men from the north.

The detective called dispatch and asked for two officers to head out that way and for them to coordinate with the Armstrong County Sheriff's office. He then called his friend and colleague, Detective Dan Mills.

"Dan, they found Harden's truck a few miles north of Wayside Road, Route 285," Jim informed his assistant. "I need you to take a ride out there with me in a few minutes."

"Sure, I'm at the station right now. Where are you?" Mills asked.

"I'm still at home," Dawson replied.

"You're on the way. I'll swing by and pick you up," suggested the junior detective.

"Great! Hey, we'll need a four-wheel drive vehicle. Swap one out, OK?" requested Dawson.

"Will do. See you in about ten minutes."

The forty-mile drive allowed the detectives to discuss details of all three cases. The only commonality was that in each instance, two people seemed to have just vanished. Dawson mentioned a possible second recurring clue.

"What's that?" asked Mills.

"Wild boars," responded Dawson.

"Really? And how's that?"

"Although we still can't explain the boar hairs stuck between the sheet metal and the chrome stripping on the minivan, Victor said there was plenty of evidence boars had been near that minivan only hours before the park volunteer discovered it and the trailer. The children had mentioned seeing scary creatures. And Kurt just informed me there are numerous dead boars around the feeder. They're propped up as if they were being prepared to be field dressed," explained Dawson.

"Unfortunately, we won't be able to interrogate any of the boars," joked Mills.

"No, we won't," Dawson barely chuckled.

There was a lull in the conversation, and then Dawson commented about his irritation with Chief Thompson, to which Mills responded, "No doubt, the man's strange. I don't know how someone like him ever made it to that rank. He has no communication skills. And lately, he's been so damn irritable; I just try to avoid him."

"Yeah, he's been about as friendly as a hornet lately. He's more worried about the public's perception and his reputation than doing the most responsible thing. It just doesn't make sense to me," Dawson pointed out.

It took nearly an hour before the detectives arrived at the location of the truck. Officers from the Canyon Police Department and deputies from the Armstrong County Sherriff's Office had arrived within moments of each other, a good fifteen minutes ahead of the detectives. Knowing they would be using their four-wheel drive SUV to reach the feeder, Mills drove around both vehicles and parked in front. As they exited the SUV, Dawson was confident the black truck hidden among the junipers was the missing vehicle. Upon closer examination of the truck, it proved to be Harden's. The description, plates, and vehicle's registration sticker all matched state records.

The detectives introduced themselves to the Armstrong County sheriff deputies.

"I assume the truck is locked," Dawson inquired.

"Yes, it is," replied Tyson.

Officer Williams couldn't contain himself, "Look at that monster! That's one hell of a truck!"

Even the deputies from Armstrong County were impressed by the truck's massive presence and pristine condition. Dawson and Mills searched all around the vehicle, looking for any signs of the men.

"The truck's pretty well hidden in this cluster of trees," Mills commented.

"Why'd they park the truck like this, hidden among trees in the middle of nowhere, if it was night time?" Dawson asked his partner.

"If they were shooting hogs, they weren't poaching, so I don't know," answered Mills.

Dawson grabbed the top of the tailgate and pulled himself up onto the truck's back bumper and carefully studied the truck's bed. "Dan, look at the coolers and the water tank," he pointed out.

Mills joined him on the bumper to take a look.

"They must be using the truck to transport hogs," Dawson said before he climbed over the tailgate and stood in the narrow path in the bed that ran along the passenger side of the truck. He opened the first cooler nearest the back of the truck then the second cooler closest to the cab. Both were a third full of icy water. The fifty-gallon water tank that abutted the truck's cab on the passenger side appeared to be full. He then climbed down off the truck and tried to open the custom-built tool case embedded in the side of the truck, but it was locked.

"Jim, how does a guy like Harden afford a truck like this? You've seen the house they live in. What does he do?" asked Williams.

"I don't know. He's been unemployed for a while. I know he's worked with concrete in the past. How he can afford this truck, I just don't know. However he's paying for it, I doubt that it is legal," responded Dawson.

242

Dawson stood there for several seconds before he asked his officers to remain with the truck. He then turned to the county deputies and asked if they would like to ride with Mills and him to locate the hog feeder.

"Absolutely," the chief deputy replied.

The four of them got into the Chevy Tahoe, the deputies in the back.

"Drive really slowly, OK?" Dawson cautioned his counterpart.

"Sure," Mills responded.

The team closely surveyed the surrounding landscape as they made their way down the bumpy trail consisting of only dual tire tracks. Dust spewed in the air behind them despite the vehicle's slow speed. The SUV had gone a little less than a mile before the tracks came to an end. They got out of the Tahoe then spread out and walked along the ridge that continually narrowed. About a quarter mile away, they could see a clearing below them as the land began to sink into the earth.

"That has to be where the feeder is," Dawson assumed.

"I can get the SUV down there, don't you think, Jim?" asked Mills.

"Probably; just follow that line right there. Looks like it has been done before," Dawson said, pointing to a small route that barely had tracks. "Looks like you may have to veer far to the right and then cut back."

"I see it. I'll go back and get the SUV," Mills told the crew.

"All right, we'll see you in a minute," Dawson responded as he and the two deputies from Armstrong County weaved their way through the brush and juniper trees down to the feeder.

Even before they reached the edge of the thicket, the men caught the stench of the rotting pigs. Once in the clearing, the smell alone would have stopped them in their tracks, but it was what they saw that caused a moment of hesitation. Strewn around the feeder, mutilated boars ravaged by coyotes awaited them. A few remained flat on their backs with their stiff legs stretched upwards. The majority had tumbled onto their sides as the coyotes had ripped into their tough skins, scavenging their meat. The scene was surreal as the men witnessed the largest congregation of turkey vultures any of them had ever seen prancing around the clearing.

"My god! Look at all of 'em! Must be over a hundred!" Dawson claimed. They were about thirty yards from the feeder, and not one bird took flight. Several hissed at them; others spread their wings trying to intimidate the intruders.

"Oh, my god! The smell!" protested one deputy as he quickly covered his mouth and nose with his hand.

Dawson took a few steps toward the birds; the closest ones hopped away, squawking and flapping their wings but not fleeing into the safety of the skies.

The men heard the SUV approaching to their right. Detective Mills stopped well short of the nearest boar. Dawson motioned for his partner to honk the horn and approach the feeder. Mills crept toward the line of decaying beasts and repeatedly blared his horn. The birds only hopped away, refusing to retreat to the air. The three men walked over to the Tahoe, and Mills rolled down the window. He could now smell the stink of rotting boars and the bird droppings that littered the area.

Growing impatient, Dawson said, "This'll clear 'em."

He pulled out his Glock pistol and fired a shot into the air. The reaction of the flock was unlike anything the men had ever seen or heard before. Most of the birds took off, their wings beating the air like the whump of helicopter blades. Several continued to hiss and strut about, expanding their massive wings. Dawson aggressively moved toward the feeder and fired two more times. Within seconds not a bird remained on the ground as they filled the sky forming a dark mass circling above.

Hearing the faint sound of gunfire, Officer Williams immediately radioed Detective Mills. "Sorry about that, we're OK. Jim had to fire a few shots to clear a bunch of buzzards," reported the detective.

The vultures impatiently hovered above the law enforcement agents standing among the half-eaten boars. Already a menacing-looking beast, the boar carcasses were grotesque. Their small eye sockets were gaping holes as every eyeball had been picked clean. Maggots burrowed into their hardened skins, slowly eating what the coyotes had yet to consume and the buzzards had yet to pick.

Dawson tried to look past the carnage at his feet. His eyes deviated toward the feeder where he noticed two rifles lying on the ground just beneath the feed dispenser, the barrel of one rifle on top of the stock of the second one. Immediately he knew something wasn't right. He motioned for his colleagues to approach.

When the other three officers reached the rifles, it was evident to all of them this was a crime scene. Both rifles were daubed with multiple dried blood stains.

"You better call Amarillo Special Crimes Unit," Dawson said to the chief deputy of Armstrong County.

I'm a Fucking Jew

Amarillo; Saturday, November 17, 2012; 9:45 P.M.

The unlikeliest of friends, Rafi and Mitch had developed a friendship far beyond their wildest imaginations. They met three years ago (September 2009) at the open house that was held the second week of school. Their sons were two of twenty-two students taught by Mrs. Gilchrist, one of four third-grade teachers at the public school.

That evening, Mitch Shiller was the first parent to arrive at his son's classroom. He promptly sat in the front row, second seat from the end near the door. Entering the room right behind him, a couple walked past Shiller, proceeded down the center, and sat in two of the four seats that made up the last of four rows. As guests drifted into the room, parent after parent passed by Shiller, ignoring his attempts to make eye contact.

Within moments, the room buzzed as mothers and fathers greeted one another, discussed summer vacations, and caught up on family matters. People congregated closer to the back of the room as they occupied all four seats in the last row, five of the six in the third row and four of the six in the second row. Listening in on the chatter, Mr. Shiller turned and looked back at the friendly handshakes and backslaps between neighbors and the hugs between the wives. He sighed, "My friends back east were right. I don't fit in or belong here."

Seconds later, Rafi entered the room and introduced himself to Mrs. Gilchrist, who was standing just inside the door greeting her students' parents. As they exchanged extended pleasantries, the room's chatter dulled to a murmur. When Rafi turned to face the classroom, the electricity resumed. Surveying the crowd, Rafi smiled confidently to no one in particular. At that moment, another couple entered the room, quickly brushed past Rafi, and took the two far-left seats in the front row. As they sat down, they turned and eagerly began gossiping with the two couples directly behind them.

As with Shiller, no one made eye contact with Rafi, the man whose skin didn't mirror their own. Accustomed to being shunned, Rafi had a choice; sit in the front row next to the husband of the couple talking with the people behind them or next to the man sitting alone. To isolate himself, he could have chosen the chair on the end of the second row behind Mitch, but he was tired of that. Rafi looked directly at the man sitting alone and took a seat right next to him in the third chair of the first row.

"Good evening! Rafi Kadir," he introduced himself as he reached out to shake Mitch's hand.

"Hi . . . I'm Mitch," Shiller responded with a grin on his face, thinking, "Just my luck, a Muslim? Are you kidding me? The one person who wants to talk with me is most likely Muslim?"

"What's so amusing?" Rafi asked smiling back at Mitch.

Distracted by a woman who took the end seat in the row directly behind him, Mitch stuttered, "Nothing . . . nothing at all. It's just . . ."

"Well, you've said more to me than the rest of the town combined," laughed Rafi. "People look at me, and the first thing that goes through their mind is, 'Shouldn't he be wearing a turban?' and 'I wonder if he's been taking flying lessons.'"

He started up again, "I know not many people would consider that humorous. It's just that socially, it really couldn't get much worse for my family and me."

"How's that?" asked Mitch, surprised that his new acquaintance was being so forthcoming.

"Well, first of all, being Pakistani, of course we don't look like everyone else. Second, yes, we're Muslim. Yeah, think about that; a Muslim living in Amarillo, Texas? To make matters worse; guess what city we're from?" Rafi answered Mitch with a question of his own.

"City? Umm . . . Lahore?" Mitch guessed.

"Ah, reasonable answer, impressive! Not the largest, but the second-largest city in Pakistan. A few years ago, I'd bet you would've been the only person in this room who could even name a city in Pakistan," Rafi surmised.

"I know Karachi is the largest city. So where *are* you from?" asked Shiller.

"The only city anyone seems to know, Abbottabad. I'm cursed again," Rafi joked.

"You're from Abbottabad? You do have it worse than me!" laughed Mitch, beginning to loosen up.

"How's that?" Rafi asked.

Mitch leaned forward and discreetly mouthed to the Muslim, "My last name is Shiller. I'm a fucking Jew!"

With that, both men burst out laughing, shook hands, placed their other hand on each other's shoulder and laughed some more.

Their outburst silenced the room. The two proceeded to flippantly mock and then sympathize with each other. Both asked about the other's wife. They laughed again; Mitch's wife, Dena, was attending their daughter's first grade open house down the hall, while Rafi's wife, Aasia, was doing the same for their twin daughters. Many parents looked on mystified, watching the hearty conversation taking place between two men no one knew. The school bell rang, and Mrs. Gilchrist began her presentation. In one of the most improbable scenarios, a potential friendship had taken root.

Outcasts, Mitch's and Rafi's sons had not even spoken to one another during the first two weeks of school. While their other classmates daydreamed, drew pictures, and threw paper wads at one another instead of working, the two loners promptly completed their tasks then busied themselves with enrichment activities the teacher provided them.

They were easily the two brightest children in the room. Other than their high intelligence and strong work ethics, they had little in common. Jeffrey was short, fair-skinned, had a round shape, and was clumsy. Mohamed was tall, lean, dark-skinned, extremely agile, and the fastest kid in third or fourth grade. It wasn't until the beginning of the third week, a full week after their fathers had met, that the boys befriended one another.

Mohamed defended Jeffrey, who sat two desks away, as another boy bullied him, "You fatty, can't even play soccer. Give me your pencil!" the tyrant sitting behind Jeffrey demanded.

When Jeffrey ignored him, the boy rose from his desk and snatched the pencil off Jeffrey's desk. The aggressor taunted him, smashing the pencil into Jeffrey's desk, breaking the lead.

Mohamed stood up and said, "Hey, don't do that!"

"Do what? My dad said you're a damn 'towel-head Musim'. He doesn't like 'Musims'. Said you're all 'terrors', and you don't believe in God. And I don't like 'Musims' either!" sneered the boy.

Mohamed remained silent as he sat back down in his chair. Even with the act of friendship, each boy kept to himself until another unlikely occurrence took place later that week.

Mitch desperately wanted Jeffrey to be involved in activities with his peers, so again he enlisted his son to play on one of the community's soccer teams, despite his son being the worst player in the entire league. On the other hand, the Kadirs were soccer fanatics and eagerly awaited Mo's opportunity to continue the sport he had begun in London.

The league consisted of ten teams, each made up of fourteen to fifteen players, and by coincidence, Jeffrey and Mo ended up teammates. Actually, the first season was not so much by chance but by default. The six subsequent seasons, though, the two remained teammates through under-the-table negotiations.

The league promoted competiveness and conducted a draft by each team's coach prior to the season. The coaches tended to be the same season after season, so they knew most of the players. Unfortunately for Jeffrey, he had played the spring before. Only one of the ten coaches was new, but he wasn't naïve. Being counseled by the father of his first draft pick, the coach systematically followed his assistant's advice. Having the last pick of the fourteenth round, only four players remained.

"Take the Shiller kid!" the father advised the coach. "Worst player in the league but won't give you any problems. The kid with the strange name, I don't know; he must be new. The other two kids are holy terrors, and their parents are worse. They will definitely be thorns in your side, to say the least."

With the last pick of the fourteenth round, Jeffrey Shiller became a member of the Blue Flames, coached by Will Kinkaid. Having the last pick of the prior round meant the Blue Flames had the first pick of the next and final round.

"I don't want any problem kids," stated Kinkaid.

So with the third to last pick in the fall soccer league for nine and under, he selected Mo Kadir, a new kid with a funny name whom no one had ever seen, let alone watched play. Mo Kadir was the fifteenth player for the team.

Two additional teams had fifteen as well while the remaining seven teams played with fourteen. No coach wanted the extra player; they are usually the weakest in the league, and every team member must play a minimum number of minutes per game. In this instance though, the Blue Flames had found a match, a match that ignited them all the way to the championship.

Thursday night of the third week of school brought dread for Jeffrey. He was fully aware his first soccer practice was the next day at four o'clock.

"Ugh! Why do they make me go? Everybody's going to hate me 'cause I'm no good," he thought.

Yet his parents had inevitably signed him up for more embarrassment. He didn't sleep well that night and struggled with anxiety the next day, aware of what he would face less than an hour after school.

He arrived for practice ten minutes early, and to his surprise, there was Mo on the field, dribbling, running, and passing the ball with his father. Unsure of their friendship, Jeffrey remained on the sideline.

Mo spotted Jeffrey and yelled for him to join them. Mo's father looked up, curious to see who his son invited over, and was surprised to see Mitch standing on the sideline with Jeffrey.

He kicked the ball back to his son and said, "Play with your friend now. You've worn me out."

Rafi made his way over to Mitch, and they warmly greeted one another.

"Your son on the Blue Flames too?" Rafi asked.

251

"Yes, as a matter of fact, he is," replied Mitch.

The two glanced over at their sons passing the ball to each other.

"What's your son's name?" asked Mitch.

"Mohamed. He goes by Mo," Rafi smiled.

"Wow, he looks pretty darn good! Has he been playing for a while?" Mitch inquired.

"Growing up in London, he's been kicking a ball since he could walk," answered Rafi.

The whistle blew, and the boys formed a circle around the head coach and his assistant. A new season had officially begun; a new enduring friendship as well.

As dusk approached, Rafi realized the Jewish Sabbath had just begun.

"Do you practice Shabbat?" asked Rafi.

"We're not fanatic about it," Mitch replied. "If we get home thirty, sixty minutes late, so be it. We believe in balance. We'll attend all the Saturday afternoon games and then head home until Shabbat is over. We try and respect the general principles and are comfortable we live a righteous life."

"We do the same. Every day we teach our children to be humble, open-minded, and respectful of different views, but stay within our core guidelines. I said my prayers at mid-day today," Rafi replied.

"I guess our next practice is Tuesday?" asked Mitch.

"That's what I've been told, Tuesdays and Fridays at four o'clock. Our first game is next Saturday at one o'clock. I guess there are a few weekends we play both Saturday and Sunday. Should be a great season! I look forward to watching our boys play!" Rafi expressed as practice ended and everyone headed to their cars.

The ice had been broken, and by the time Monday rolled around, Jeffrey and Mo were immediately best friends. A few times in the past, Mrs. Gilchrist had gently encouraged the two to interact with one another but had hoped it would happen naturally. Even *she* smiled at the irony of the boys who were shunned by the rest of the kids now completing every assignment together.

Tuesday, both fathers were again on the sidelines watching far more closely than the first practice. Mitch realized Mo was a star, head and shoulders better than any other player.

"Your son can play!" Mitch commented to Rafi.

"He works really hard at it, always practicing in the backyard," Rafi confirmed.

"What do you do, Rafi?" asked Mitch.

Now it was Rafi's turn to grin. "Remember how I told you the demographics couldn't be any worse for me? Get this! Not only am I Pakistani, Muslim, dark-skinned, and from Abbottabad, but I work in the nuclear disarmament industry. That *really* freaks people out! I kind of get a kick out of it."

Mitch laughed, "I've never heard anyone from the Middle East, India, anywhere in that region talk like you, use the words you do, and have such an ease about yourself here in America, let alone Amarillo. Did you just say 'freaks people out?' That's too funny!"

"I have to be able to communicate with everyone I work with—on their level. It's one of the reasons I have security clearance from the highest levels of the Pakistani and U.S. governments; clearance that most of these men and women out here would never receive in a million years. Yet, besides you, I haven't been able to break that ice in the community," Rafi admitted.

"What's your role?" Mitch asked.

"To learn from the best. Every process, procedure, technical requirement, precaution, security, and management techniques utilized to oversee nuclear stockpiles, so we can apply the same principles in Pakistan. That's about all I can say," Rafi claimed.

"You came to the right country," countered Mitch.

"Yes, I did," Rafi agreed chuckling with Mitch on his sarcasm.

"I wonder which Jew living here represents Israel?" asked Mitch.

"I don't know. Most of you look alike; I can't tell with certainty who's Jewish or not. And besides, Rafi Kadir isn't even my real name, so I'm sure they changed their Jewish last name to something like Smith or Jones," teased Rafi.

"Israel doesn't even have nuclear weapons, so I guess there is no need for a Jew here anyway," Mitch said.

Rafi looked at Mitch, and they both burst out laughing.

"And you?" asked Rafi.

"I'm in the 'Jew'-elry business, specializing in diamonds," responded Mitch which brought more howls from the two.

Friday's practice was the third for the Blue Flames. Both coaches and Mitch knew the league was in for a rude awakening. Mo was that good. The young Pakistani completely dominated practices from start to finish.

At the end of practice, a few parents grumbled about Mo 'hogging' the ball. But the coaches and Mitch knew otherwise. Mo was a great passer and a team player. He was so much better than the other boys; the ball just always ended up at his feet.

The next day, minutes after one o'clock, the nine-and-under soccer league caught the first glimpse of a tall, wiry, and extremely fast Pakistani kid. He went on to dominate the league in ways coaches and parents alike had never seen.

In his first game, a 9-1 thrashing, Mo scored six goals and assisted on the other three. On two of the three assists, Mo had juked, spun, and weaved between defenders to have point-blank shots only to purposely hesitate, look for a wide-open teammate, and pass them the ball to score the goal. He would have had at least three more assists if his teammates hadn't missed golden opportunities after receiving perfect passes from Mo. Yet, it did not deter him from involving his teammates at the next opportunity. The kid was simply a wizard with the ball. After the second game where Mo prevailed again, leading his team to a 7-2 victory, rumors about Mo's birth certificate began circulating. Parents talked about it during games in which Mo did not even play.

"Did you see the statistics on the web page?" one mother griped. "Come on, he has ten goals and four assists in two games? He has to be at least twelve years old. I heard he's tall and really fast. I thought people from India were short," she protested.

The team went 9-0 in league play before claiming the one-game championship playoff. Mo scored 47 goals and had 18 assists in the ten games for the season, far outpacing the second leading goal scorer with 19.

Playing both fall and spring seasons each school year, the boys teamed up to prevail in 68 out of 70 games over the three-year period. In one of the losses, Mo suffered from a horrendous flu but played anyway. The other loss occurred just two weeks before when the opponents continuously roughed Mo up, eventually spraining his ankle on a dirty and illegal tackle. Mo's team came back to win the following weekend's game and retaliate the bitter loss from the few weeks earlier with a 5-4 victory to take the championship. For the first time, in more than three years of playing, Jeffrey was instrumental in the success when he outwitted the opponent with his unselfish play.

Since the families first met, their boys had secured the fall championship in 2009 and the spring and fall championships of 2010, 2011, and 2012—seven titles in all. It didn't matter who the coach was, Mo's was the victorious team in both league play and championship games.

On draft night prior to each season, the ten coaches rubbed their rabbit foots, paced the floor, and prayed they would obtain the number-one pick. A collective moan was heard from the other nine coaches after it was announced who had just won the drawing and the upcoming championship. Being an open draft, no one questioned until the fourth consecutive season, how one of the worst players in the league—a pudgy, slow, unskilled Jew had earned four titles in a row. In the fall of 2011, one of the coaches who had once been bribed sought to put an end to it. Both parties compromised, and Jeffrey went on to join Mo and celebrate three more titles.

During the incredible run, the families had become close friends. Every Saturday evening after Shabbat, one family entertained the other. Periodically, another family—the Davises joined them.

Whenever the Shillers or Kadirs made a comment about being lonely or feeling ostracized, the Davises joked, "You have no idea how good you have it! At least you believe in something! Try being an atheist! Talk about being shunned!"

Neither of the families ever gave that much consideration, but immediately gained an appreciation for their plight. The dynamics worked. Three families, each distinctive from the rest of the community, found a common thread and an appreciation for one another that enabled them to tease each other, ridicule themselves, yet have intelligent worldly conversations.

The Saturday evenings the families spent together were festive. After dinner the boys invariably ran off and played video games, while Mo's twin sisters played with Jeffrey's younger sister. The twins were eighteen months younger than Mo and only a few months older than Jeffrey's sister. The adults almost always worked in concert to clean and tidy up the kitchen, but more than a few times, the men took complete control.

Once the task was complete, they would sip their after-dinner coffee and discuss current local and world events, usually with the Middle East taking center stage. The conversations were always stimulating. On Saturday evening following the team's seventh straight championship victory, Rafi introduced a new thought process for the Palestinian-Israel peace solution that elicited discourse, yet intrigue.

"Dena, Aasia, Mitch, what do you think about utilizing game theory to resolve the long-standing violence throughout the region?"

"I'm not sure what you mean," Dena replied.

"Is it a one-state or a two-state solution?" asked Mitch.

"It could be a two-state solution, but I think a one-state solution would be more effective," Rafi responded.

"Muammar Qaddafi proposed a one-state solution, and we know his fate. A one-state solution is doomed from the start; why are you proposing something different than one of the few things both sides have agreed to for years? It has to be a two-state solution," declared Mitch.

"Because different variations of the two-state plan have been discussed for decades, and it's never worked. Support for two-states has been eroding anyway. I just reviewed a book I read a few years ago by Bruce Bueno de Mesquita, *The Predictioneer's Game*. He suggests land-for-peace or peace-for-land deals always end in failure due to time inconsistency. [17] Looking back over the past sixty-something years of Israel's existence, that sure seems to be the case. Israel gives land in promise for peace. One group or another takes the land then demands more or continues to systematically attack Israel. Sound familiar?" asked Rafi.

"Of course, that's happened often," agreed Dena.

Rafi continued, "But then how many times has a terrorist group ceased assaults against Israel only to see the Israeli government drag its feet, stall on finalizing a two-state region, then build new settlements on disputed lands when they promised they wouldn't?"

"It has happened for years," granted Dena and Mitch.

"There is no trust. There are two keys for success: timing and self-enforcement. There has to be rationale where neither side has an incentive to deviate," reasoned Rafi.

"How do you do that?" asked Aasia.

"The author knows it's not perfect, and the devil is in the details, but he thinks they should create a verifiable mechanism to share tourism tax dollars throughout the region," explained Rafi.

"And how does that work?" Dena wanted to know.

"Ah, the details. Let me see if I can explain," replied Rafi.

After he rehashed more of the past and a few of the current obstacles, he said, "We know we've been stuck in the never-ending cycle of attacks and counterattacks. Hamas lobs bombs into Israel; Israel launches ground attacks. The last major one in Gaza four years ago killed over fourteen hundred Palestinians. They bulldozed their homes and businesses, causing unbearable suffering for the Palestinians. Israel then created a blockade of Gaza, devastating Palestine's economy, so then Gaza fires more rockets into Israel. It never ends; it's a vicious cycle. Whereas in the past, there was periodically some give and take, there isn't any today. It's like the Israeli government, run by Binyamin Netanyahu, is the equivalent of Tea Party here in America. There is no more compromise, and for every action there is an equal or even more devastating reaction. That's why we need an economic solution where both parties have an incentive to abide by the agreement."

"Equivalent of the Tea Party? Come on," objected Mitch.

"I believe so. Their tactics are only becoming more adamant in nature. They are literally squeezing the economic life out of the Palestinians. Eventually it is going to end badly. Is that the end game we want?" asked Rafi.

"Of course not," said Dena.

"But honey, when is enough, enough? How many rockets can one endure?" asked Aasia.

"We know there will always be an ardent religious group that will never agree, but the solution needs to mitigate them. They are the minority! We need to organize and rally the majority. What's so frustrating is that, prior to the World Wars, the Jews lived in peace with the Muslims, perhaps more so than any other peoples," claimed Rafi.

"Rafi, seriously! That was before the creation of Israel. It's like night and day compared to then. The radicals aren't going to give up until Israel is wiped off the map, which isn't going to happen," countered Mitch.

"You're right Mitch. It is like night and day. Back when the Jews and Muslims lived in relative tranquility, it was the equivalent of a one-state solution, not two," Rafi shot back.

His voice rising, Mitch claimed, "Jews lived all over the world, including several Middle East countries. That makes it more like a two-state solution."

"It's a religion; there was no Jewish state! There's one world; there should be one state," Rafi refuted equally as forceful.

"That's outrageous," Mitch started to say.

"Stop it!" interjected Dena. "You two sometimes don't know when to stop."

Both men cooled it for just a moment before Rafi renewed the debate. "We are closer than ever to the tipping point! Don't you see? The radicals are getting desperate because they realize they are being

259

marginalized. With the Arab spring, for the first time people are rising up seeking democratic principles, principles that align with Israel. After centuries of neglecting science and modern practices, the Muslim world is finally trying to revisit its past; a past when they were world leaders in science, education, medicine, and philosophy. Except for Iran, Turkey, and previously Egypt, the majority of the Muslim world is driven by theocracy, not commerce; nothing like it was in the eighth through the thirteenth, fourteenth centuries. But I think that is slowly changing," argued Rafi.

"Rafi, granted Iran and Turkey are much more business-oriented than the rest of the Muslim world, but the Mullahs still dictate rule of law in Iran and Turkey is far from perfect in creating a secular state. Both are still theocracies. Where is the tipping point you suggest?" Dena wanted to know.

"It takes time. A few are trying to change that; for instance, Saudi King Abdullah. A couple years ago he created a Science and Technology University with over $20 billion in capital. Isn't that a sign the Muslim world is on the cusp of significant change? What about Dubai? Could anyone have imagined the incredible modernization of that city twenty years ago? Don't you think it's time for more of a twenty-first century, free-market solution where trust and reliance on the other guy is obsolete? For more than sixty years, it has been one broken promise after another by both sides. Instead of falling back on ideas that have failed time and again, why don't we explore something new, something that is truly based on free-market and democratic principles?" Rafi challenged.

"Honey, we know better than anyone that the majority of the Muslim world doesn't want American-style capitalism," Aasia said challenging her husband.

"They don't have to implement pure American capitalism. Tourism is tourism, no matter where you are. In order to stimulate tourism, it's in both parties' interests to curb the violence. It's a proven fact less violence equals more tourism resulting in more revenues, while more violence results in less tourism, less revenue. If the tourism dollars are shared in some fashion—and it doesn't have to be equal, and in fact the majority of it should go to the Palestinians, both parties win," explained Rafi. "Author Bueno de Mesquita shows a graph of how tourism revenues correlated with violence. [18] If you curtail the violence, tax dollars increase. No lands change. Israel achieves peace, and it costs them very little, while Palestine generates billions in desperately needed revenues to allocate as they see fit. If they really incorporate free-market mechanisms, it could become extremely beneficial for both sides."

"Rafi, I doubt it's that simple, but I applaud the basic concept," Dena surmised.

Mitch scoffed, "It's pretty ironic, a Muslim telling a Jew there is a business solution to the Palestinian-Israeli problem."

"Something has to change," Aasia said.

Mitch then added, "Well, I do admit that during our entire lives, there has been minimal progress. But this insistence on a one-state solution is totally unrealistic. What happens in twenty, thirty years when the population shifts, and Jews are no longer the majority? Israel will never allow for a non-Jewish state, and the Palestinians won't tolerate apartheid."

"Again you've proved my point that the Israeli government is just like the Tea Party. Never allow for a non-Jewish state? Why not? Where is the compromise?" wondered Rafi.

"It's been settled now for decades. We're not going back, Rafi; the Jews deserve their own state and the Palestinians have theirs," argued Mitch.

"It's not even close to being equal. The Palestinians in Gaza are trapped like rats. They can't succeed economically as currently structured. Agh, I don't know. We have to start somewhere. I still say there is an economic solution that will benefit the majority. And increasing tourism will benefit everyone! Until then, the fervent radicals will continue to exert a disproportionate amount of influence," argued Rafi.

"I think one thing we can all agree on is the root of unrest is typically economics, not religion," suggested Dena.

"No argument there," concurred Mitch.

"If it's all economics and not religion, then why does there have to be a separate Jewish state?" Rafi demanded to know. "Tell me why?"

"Rafi, please!" Aasia pleaded to her husband before she stated the obvious, "So I guess we didn't solve the Middle East tonight?"

Frustrated, Rafi solemnly said, "I'm afraid not."

"But you know what we *are* doing? We're talking rationally, Jews and Muslims, trying to explore a logical solution. If it can happen in Amarillo, Texas, why can't it happen there?" Dena wondered aloud trying to renew the earlier optimism.

The conversation ended without solving the Middle East, but it did create hope. It refreshed their memory that only seventy, eighty, ninety years ago, Muslims and Jews were not threatening each other's existence. The thought that Europe was in flames at that time and now has been at peace for decades brought more optimism. The Arab spring, the slow rise in the Muslim middle class, and the reemerging emphasis of technology, science, medicine, and philosophy in the Islamic world all raised their spirits.

Before the Kadirs left for the evening, Mitch brought up one more topic; "Thank God Obama won. Can you imagine having a hard right-wing in Israel being whipped up and encouraged by the GOP here? We'd be at war within weeks. The Republicans haven't moderated one bit since losing power. It's amazing!"

"So you do agree the Israeli government is channeling the Tea Party, forbidding compromise and hell-bent to impose their will?" Rafi asked.

"I didn't say that!" cried Mitch. "Many in the Tea Party are actually isolationists."

"They may be isolationists, but that wouldn't stop them from encouraging Israel to go it alone," Rafi declared before he stood up from his chair.

"You're impossible," claimed Mitch.

"I know," was all Rafi could say laughing, knowing he had Mitch in a pickle.

Their disagreement behind them, the four made small talk as the Kadirs prepared to leave. Walking out the door, Rafi asked Mitch, "Have you ever been to Palo Duro Canyon?"

"No, I haven't," Mitch answered.

"It's beautiful. Let's go on a hike tomorrow. I've driven through, but never hiked it. What do you say? Pick you up around 1:30 or so?" Rafi asked.

"Sure. Why not," said Mitch.

"Great," Rafi said as they rounded up the kids. The families hugged one another, and seconds later the Kadirs headed for home.

Beer Run, Beer Run

Palo Duro Canyon State Park; Saturday, November 17, 2012; 10:30 P.M.

"Dude, I fuckin' told you we needed more beer! We're gonna run out soon, and we won't have any in the morning!" Erick complained.

Rummaging through the cooler, Dustin counted nine beers.

"Damn it!" he cursed.

"Beer run! Beer run!" yelled Amy.

The eight freshmen from Texas Tech University had arrived earlier in the day to visit the canyon for the first time. The five guys and three girls proudly attended the university based in Lubbock, two hours south of the canyon. They drove in three separate vehicles and were the only campers in the 'tents only' Fortress Cliff Camp Area. Country music blared as they laughed, caroused, and carried on into the night. Disappointed they couldn't have an open fire due to the burn ban, the group kept close to the portable lantern Trey had brought. All of them reveled in the freedom college provided to come and go as they choose, stay out all night, and to flee town on a road trip to a state park for the weekend with no repercussions. No more lectures, no more curfews, no more parental bullshit.

264

"Erick, just chill, man. We're not at the ass-end of the world. We'll just get more. I'll drive. You coming with me, babe?" Zach asked his girlfriend, Amy.

"You betcha, sweetie pie. I'll be your co-pilot anytime," she said.

Zach crossed his eyes at her and grinned then turned to his best friend, "Trey, you're in, right?"

"Hell yeah! Y'all can't do it without me, bro," he replied.

The gofers passed the collection cap to the rest of the group. "We'll be back in about forty-five minutes," Zach told them as he grabbed three beers to go.

Erick immediately protested, "Hey! That only leaves four beers for five of us!"

"We're making the run!" countered Trey. "Plus your drunk ass can't even count. That leaves y'all six, ya moron."

"Hell, y'all will have beer sooner than us," Erick continued to bicker.

Willing to compromise, Zach obliged, "All right, what the hell. Amy and I will share one until we get to Canyon." He put one beer back in the cooler and said, "Adios!" to the gang before the three of them hopped into his Nissan Pathfinder.

Gravel flew and dust filled the air as they sped out on their mission to the nearest convenience store. Trey recounted the money and figured they could afford at least two cases of the cheapest beer and a couple of bags of Doritos.

Zach straddled both lanes as he raced through the canyon and up the steep grade before exiting the state park. It took him only eight minutes to drive the five and a half miles to the top. It was another twelve miles to the city of Canyon. The back country road was wide open, and Zach let it rip, hitting speeds of more than ninety miles per hour on the flat, smooth surface. He slowed down only once when he cruised through the flashing red lights of a four-way stop. Once through the intersection, he was at full throttle until he saw the small-town lights straight ahead. Then he carefully maintained the speed limit as they passed under the highway.

"There's one on the right just ahead," Amy said as she spotted a convenience store a quarter mile up the road.

"Yeah buddy, we're in business now," Trey gleefully boasted before he took the last swig of beer from his can.

Zach parked two spaces away from the next vehicle. Trey boldly walked into the store and purchased two cases of Old Milwaukee with his fake ID. His arms loaded as he bounded out of the store, Zach jumped out of the driver's seat and opened the tailgate. The two secured the beer between the interior wall and a duffle bag and started to get back into the car.

"Where's the Doritos?" Amy asked.

"Fuck! Forgot 'em! I was focused on priorities," Trey laughed.

He went back into the store and bought two bags of Nacho Cheese and one Cool Ranch Doritos. Amy tore into the first bag of Nacho Cheese before Zach was even out of the parking lot.

Wanting to keep a low profile, Zach stayed under the speed limit while crossing under the highway. Once he could no longer see the town's lights in his rear-view mirror, he hit the gas pedal, and the three of them were rocketing back to the canyon.

Life couldn't have been better for the college students with the windows down and the sound of George Strait at maximum volume. It had to be the fourth or fifth time that night Amy insisted they listen to the song, "Amarillo by Morning." She knew all the lyrics and bellowed her favorite verse along with the famous country singer, "When that sun is high in that Texas sky . . ."

Hitting speeds near a hundred miles per hour, papers and trash flew around the car and out the windows.

"Whoa, speed racer!" Trey cautioned.

Zach eased up on his lead foot and slowed to about eighty-five miles per hour and rolled up the windows. Within minutes, they were at the entrance to the park. They had barely been gone half an hour. Remembering what the park officer had told him when they checked in that day, he veered to the left of the building and pulled up to the locked gate. Zach looked up to read the combination numbers written on the park permit he'd taped to the front windshield. It wasn't there.

"Oh shit!" he yelled.

"What's up, man?" asked Trey.

"The permit is gone, dude! Help me find it! We need the permit!" Zach panicked as he began searching the front driver's and passenger sides, the floor, and between the seats and the console.

"Fuck the permit, they know we paid," Trey told him as he stuffed more Doritos into his mouth. "No one will bother us, dude. Quit being so paranoid."

"No, you don't understand! The combination number to the gate was written on it! I can't open the lock on the gate. Fu . . . ck!" Zach said in aggravation.

Confused, Amy asked, "What happened to the permit?"

"It must have flown out the window. Shit!" Zach said, pounding his fist against the dashboard.

"Why is the gate locked?" Amy wondered.

"The park closed at eight," Zach explained. "There's no other way to get in."

"What do you mean there is no other way into the park?" Amy asked.

"Weren't you listening when we checked in today?" Zach wondered in disbelief.

Amy replied, "Not really. I was looking at the maps and brochures."

"Since the park office closes at eight, they wrote the combination code for the gate on the permit to tape to the windshield," Zach explained. "It allows campers to get back into the park if they leave and don't return before eight."

"You're right, this does suck," Trey agreed as he searched the backseat and floorboard with no luck.

Amy couldn't find it either, so she suggested, "Just call the park rangers. They'll let us in."

"Can't you see the office is dark?" Zach pointed out. "I don't have a number to call. Plus we've got all this beer, and all of us are drunk! You want me to get a DUI? I don't think so."

"OK, then just call Erick. He's got a permit that should have the combination written on it, and he can give it to you over the phone," Amy suggested.

"Well, darlin', that would be a grand idea if they could get cell phone service down there," Zach disputed.

"Can't you at least try?" Amy pleaded.

Zach picked up his phone just to appease her. He knew they easily had service at the top of the canyon, but at the bottom there was no connection. He tried Erick first. The call went straight to voicemail. The three of them tried calling their friends who remained at the campsite. Each time, the calls went straight to voicemail, or they received a message that the phone was unavailable. After the third try, Zach left Dustin a message explaining their predicament.

"Oh, my god," groaned Amy. "I cannot believe this!"

"What do y'all think the chances are of retracin' our path and findin' it?" Zach asked without thinking it through.

Amy just rolled her eyes. "Seriously? Are ya kidding?" she said then sighed.

"Fuck it! It is what it is," Trey shrugged. "Just park the car over there, and we'll walk."

"Are you kidding me?" Amy protested. "Walk? Hello! Do I look like a track star? That'll take all night!"

"No, it won't," Trey lightly punched her arm. "Come on, it's a beautiful night. The second mile is all downhill. We can do it in probably an hour and a half."

"Hopefully those guys will come looking for us since it's taking so long, and I'm sure they'll be missin' this beer," said Zach.

"I'd sure be missin' it, that's for sure," Trey added. "We probably won't have to walk more than a couple miles before they pick us up."

"Agh!" Amy objected.

Zach parked the SUV on the side of the road, and the three got out.

"You really think this is a good idea?" Amy asked Zach. "I mean, there are wild animals like coyotes and stuff."

"Hell yeah. It's all good," Zach promised as he opened the tailgate. Among the three of them, they had already eaten one bag of Doritos. "Those animals are more afraid of us than we are of them. They're not going to mess with us. And if they do, I'll protect you, Amy."

"Yeah right, with all your super powers," Amy sneered.

"Should we bring the beer now or just take a few with us then drive back and get the rest?" Trey asked Zach.

"We'll carry 'em. I don't want to have to drive all the way back up here tonight," Zach decided.

Zach grabbed the two remaining bags of Doritos and handed them to Amy. Then he passed two of the twelve-packs to Trey. He lifted the other two and placed them on the ground behind the vehicle. Once he double-checked the SUV to make sure they had everything, he locked the doors with the key fob. Zach bent down, picked up a twelve-pack with each hand, looked at his best friend, and said, "OK, bro, let's do it! And Amy, trust me sweetie, one day we'll look back and laugh about this. I promise."

"Forward march!" declared Trey as he led the way toward the entrance. They climbed over the short stone wall bordering the park's entrance and began their long hike back to the campground. Within moments their dread turned to laughter, and they made light of the situation. Before they knew it, they had already traveled down a quarter of the mile-long, steep decline.

"I think the only way we can make it down this fuckin' road is to shoot a beer. Give us a little fuel," Trey insisted.

"Sounds like a plan," Zach replied.

"Zach, you are going to carry me the last couple miles, right?" Amy wondered.

"I'd do anything for you, babe," Zach replied. Setting down the twelve-packs, he put his arm around her to pull her close and then kissed the end of her nose.

Trey put down the twelve-packs he was toting, pulled out his pocket knife, and with his right hand punctured the bottom of a beer can with the knife's blade then quickly turned it sideways with the hole facing up, barely spilling a drop. The expert beer blaster transferred the small knife to his left hand that held the beer; then using his middle, ring, and pinkie fingers to pin the knife against the bottom of the can and the back of his index finger to grip the top of the can, in one fluid motion he placed his mouth over the hole, tilted his head backwards then pulled the tab with his right hand. The beer whooshed down his throat.

"Ya . . . hoo! Yeah buddy! That's what I call high octane!" he yelled before smashing the empty can on the roadside with his foot.

Holding Amy, Zach said in awe, "You're the king of blasts; poetry in motion, bro!"

"Practice makes perfect, my friend; practice makes perfect," Trey responded confidently.

Trey punctured the second can, bowed to Amy and said, "Ladies second!"

Amy downed the beer and passed the empty can to Zach as she tried to keep beer from fizzing out of her nose. He launched it over the cliff, letting it fall among the brush and trees that scaled the canyon walls. Zach slammed down his shot, crushed the empty can against the rock wall that towered above the roadside, and let out a loud, "Hell yeah! That's what I'm talkin' about!" then howled like a coyote.

Obtaining the jolt they were seeking, they picked up their goods and continued on, zigzagging their way down the steep roadway laughing, joking, and belting out a periodic, "Red Raiders, Red Raiders! Shoot 'em up, Tech! Shoot 'em up, Tech! Fuck Oklahoma State!"

"Y'all see? We're more than halfway there!" claimed Trey soon after they had walked over the first marked river crossing, which at this time was dry.

Unfortunately, they had forgotten that the next four river crossings were not.

"Where the hell are those guys?" grumbled Zach.

"Hell, I know I'd go searching for *them* if they weren't back after this long," agreed Trey.

271

Meanwhile, at the campsite, Sarah became concerned that one of her best friends was not back yet. "Aren't y'all getting a little worried? I am."

"I don't know what's taking 'em so long. We've been out of beer for a while now. This shit's pissing me off!" Erick griped.

"I think Sarah's right," Mary said, nodding. "You know, I saw a news report one time that maniacs roam these parks looking for people and attack them with chainsaws and things. Maybe we should go look for them."

The three boys looked at her as if she had lost the other half of her mind, their mouths hanging open. "Are you talking about *The Texas Chainsaw Massacre*?" Curt finally asked. "That's a movie, blondie. It never happened."

"I heard it was based on a true story," Mary answered with the sageness of the inebriated. "It is *The TEXAS Chainsaw Massacre,* and we *are* in Texas. You don't know. It could possibly happen. There are definitely crazy freaks out there. So do we want to just leave our friends out there in the dark for something like that to happen?"

"Shit. What the hell makes you think I want to go rescuin' anyone from a damn chainsaw maniac?" Dustin scoffed, wondering privately why Amy and Sarah always insisted on including Mary in everything they did, knowing she was such a ditz. "They're fine. Just chill."

"Well, I sure hope so; they should have been back almost an hour ago. But what if they're not? What if there's something wrong and they need help?" Sarah asked.

"What time did they leave?" asked Curt.

"Umm . . . ten thirty, ten forty-five maybe? And it's already twelve fifteen" answered Sarah.

"Shit, Trey probably got 'em all arrested, trying to buy beer with that stupid-ass fake ID," Erick said.

"And who keeps drinking the beer he buys with that *stupid-ass* fake ID, I ask you?" Sarah questioned.

"Hell, we all do," Erick countered. "Includin' you, girly. And I'm not gettin' in my car all fucked up and drivin' into Canyon to look for 'em. What do y'all want? For me to join 'em in the pen?"

"He's right," Dustin agreed. "If anything happened to them, there's not a damn thing we can do about it right now. Drivin' around looking for 'em is just askin' for more trouble."

"They'll be here soon," Erick reassured everyone.

The walk was starting to wear thin on the hikers. Their enthusiasm and laughter began to wane as they grew tired. Their attitudes dipped even further when they approached the second river crossing.

"Oh man! Shit, I forgot we had to cross the water," remarked Zach, dismayed.

"Damn, these are the only shoes I have!" said Trey.

"Same here," Zach added.

"You're carrying me across, aren't you, Zachary Hamilton?" Amy told him firmly. "I'm not ruining my UGGs!"

"All right, woman, but I'm taking my shoes off first," Zach declared.

"Damn it!" Trey complained as they sat down on the pavement to take off their tennis shoes and socks.

The water was ankle deep, so the guys rolled up their pants. Zach carried Amy while Trey lugged two of the twelve-packs and both pairs of shoes stuffed with socks across the gently flowing, icy-cold water. The stream was about thirty- feet wide, and the weight of carrying Amy while walking barefoot on the slick pavement littered with stones under the cold water tested Zach's toughness. Fortunately, the alcohol he had been drinking most of the day had numbed his whole body.

"I'll go back and get the rest of the beer, and you can get 'em the next time, is that cool?" Trey volunteered.

"That's fair," Zach agreed.

The situation wasn't so funny anymore since they knew the routine had to be performed two more times before they reached the campground. As they sat on the road, Trey and Zach used their socks to dry their feet before they put on their shoes without them. The temperatures now in the mid-forties, Zach started to complain again because the crew had not come looking for them yet, but Trey would have none of it.

"We're almost there! It has to be less than a mile. I remember looking at the map. After the first crossing where there was no water, it looked like it was pretty far before the next four water crossings. But those last crossings are real close to each other. The campground is right between the fourth and fifth crossing, and the third and fourth crossings are just ahead. I promise y'all, fifteen, twenty minutes max," Trey tried to encourage Zach and Amy.

The three college students, all with hopes and dreams of bright futures, would never reach the campground, let alone cross another river. Only fifty yards beyond the water's edge where they had stopped to put their shoes back on, hidden in the brush by the darkness of night, a horde of fifteen wild boars waited patiently. Eight in front and seven more just behind, the pack had moved within a few feet of the roadway. Amy sensed the danger, but didn't understand it.

"This canyon's kinda creepy at night," she said nervously as she scoped the area, waiting on Trey to tie his shoes.

"The coyotes are so big here, they've been known to eat people," Zach teased.

"Stop it!" Amy cried as both Zach and Trey started howling like coyotes. Scared and wanting to get back to the campground, Amy told Trey to hurry up.

"Go on, I'll be right behind ya' guys," suggested Trey.

Zach and Amy had barely walked ten yards when Trey rose from his crouched position and let out another howl that ricocheted throughout the canyon. Zach and Amy stopped and turned to look at him.

"In honor of the coyotes, I suggest we have another blast of beer!" Trey proposed.

"Naw, that's all right. We'll celebrate when we finally reach the damn campground. I'll shoot one then, probably two," Zach replied.

Trey laughed, "Y'all can wait, but this coyote can't!"

"Turn the music down! Did y'all hear that?" Mary asked the other four. "Maybe it's them!"

Erick rolled his eyes at her, "Is it your chainsaw maniac coming to get us?"

"Shut up, Erick! I thought I heard something too," Sarah said, playing the peacemaker. "Turn it down a minute. OK, Erick?" He turned the music down.

"What did you hear?" asked Curt.

"Well," Mary paused, "it sounded like a howl or something. Listen!"

"I didn't hear shit," Erick scoffed at her.

Sarah shot him a look, so they stopped what they were doing; the guys sarcastically cupped their hand to their ear, and listened for noises. Erick waited only a few seconds before he mocked Mary.

"We're in a fuckin' canyon! What did you think? There are wild animals, coyotes, whatever. If you want to be safe, you need to make some noise. Scare off those mofos. " And he turned the music up again.

Zach and Amy, trying to stay warm, stood arm-in-arm and impatiently waited for Trey to dig out his pocket knife and go through his ritual. He held the can up and pulled the tab; the beer instantly drained down his throat. Then with his right hand, he reached for the can in his left hand, and clenched it; like a star football player, he wound his arm above his head and spiked the can to the pavement. No one could blast a beer with the fluidity of Trey. The entire process was the envy of all his friends. Amy just rolled her eyes, shook her head, and sighed as she watched Trey standing there with his arms raised to the sky, his right hand balled into a fist, and his left hand holding a pocket knife with a small blade opened pointing to the sliver of moon.

"OMG! Unbelievable! Come on, Zach, let that freak catch up. I really want to get back to the tent," Amy begged.

"I'm paying homage to the coyotes," Trey laughed. "They deserve the respect."

Zach and Amy started down the roadway ahead of Trey. With his blood alcohol level over .20, Trey fumbled with his pocket knife as he tried to close the blade. He took the knife out of his left hand and put the knife's handle into his right hand. His vision impaired, it took him several seconds to grasp what had just transpired only twenty-five paces ahead of him.

Leaving one full and another half-empty twelve-pack of Old Milwaukee lying in the road, he began running back toward the river crossing. The sight of a gang of creatures darting from the brush, plowing over his best friend and his best friend's girlfriend was incomprehensible.

As he ran, his mind tried to process the scene. "Oh, my god! Holy shit! What are those fucking things? Shit! They have to be wild fucking boars with those fucking tusks! Oh, my god! Those tusks goring Zach and Amy!" Feeling a knot in his throat and tears of horror fill his eyes, he tried to run faster. The grunts, the snorting terrified him as he splashed through the water trying to get to the other side. Adrenaline pumped through his entire body. It didn't matter; gravity worked against him as he ran up the small incline on the other side of the river crossing. He dared to look behind him as four animals sprayed water in every direction charging through the water in pursuit of his human blood.

Trey dashed into the brush to his right. He zigzagged in and out of mesquite, cottonwood, and juniper trees as if he were a running back on a football field trying to avoid would-be tacklers. Branches ripped him liked a cat's claw, slashing his face, neck, and arms. He could hardly feel the sting as he tried to run harder, faster, panting, as he saw his life flash before him. Trey veered back to his left to run parallel with the roadway and could hear the boars gaining on him. He looked back in horror as he sensed his imminent demise, took two more steps, and tripped over the trunk of a dead tree. He fell on his stomach with his face planted on the ground. He looked up to see four wild boars surrounding him.

His entire body shaking, he tried not to hyperventilate as the swine, preparing to attack, glared at him, snorting and growling. Desperate to escape, Trey awkwardly kicked out his right foot several times before he scrambled to his hands and knees. The movement prompted the nearest boar to charge. Its tusk sank into Trey's left shoulder and forced him onto his back. Trey attempted to stab the boar with his pocket knife only for it to bounce off the animal's calloused hide, barely scraping the shield that protected the beast's vital organs; the knife tumbled harmlessly to the hard ground.

Trey's shoulder went limp, and he could feel his ankle in a vise as another boar clamped down and ripped at his lower right leg. He screamed while his inoperable left arm was being ripped from his body. Savagely biting and tearing, it was only seconds before the beast severed it just above the elbow and greedily made off with this tasty extremity.

Seeing the open wound and smelling its sweetness, a second boar gnawed at the muscles and tendons of his remaining upper left arm before the heinous creature suddenly clenched onto his face and tore away part of his nose and cheek area. Barely alive, Trey prayed for mercy as most of his left arm and his entire right foot and ankle were no longer intact.

The beasts were merciless. They ripped a strip of flesh from his body, gorged it down, and came back for another slice. By the time Trey took his last breath, he had lost all of his left arm, his right foot and ankle, part of his nose and mouth, and had been gored repeatedly in his torso. Once his chest cavity and belly were exposed, the boars clashed over the human heart and liver. Similar to the previous victims, nothing remained as the boars scuffled for the last scraps of Trey's flesh.

Zach and Amy's deaths had been equally gruesome. Upon initial impact, both were blasted to the pavement, sending both bags of Doritos to the side of the road. The twelve-pack of Old Milwaukee Zach held in his left hand absorbed part of the blow when the boar struck him, rupturing one of the cans. Both cartons plunged to the ground. Without hesitation, the animals immediately clamped their jaws onto the lovers' arms and legs, pulling and violently shaking their heads as they ripped at the two bodies.

A wound to his chest, his left leg shredded at the ankle, and both arms badly bitten, Zach lay helplessly on the pavement as the six boars that had been seizing his body abruptly abandoned him. He tried to scream, but his punctured lung sucked the energy from his body.

For the next several minutes, the beasts tortured him as he witnessed them rip apart his girlfriend, piece by piece and aggressively defend their position to taste the preferred female flesh. When he tried to move, the pain was unbearable as the rawness of his skin scraped the pavement. He tried not to look at the grisly dismemberment of his girlfriend, but when he finally did, only the lower half of her body remained.

Seconds later a boar, then another, then a third and a fourth turned toward Zach. His agony lasted another minute while the boars gnawed on his upper arms and right calf. As his head tilted his head away from Amy, a boar bit him on the side of the head and clenched his ear. With one twist of its neck, the boar effortlessly ripped it off. Additional boars converged on Zach as only remnants of Amy remained. He lived only seconds longer until a boar bit and tore at his neck, fatally wounding the eighteen-year-old business major.

The four boars that had chased down Trey returned, seeking to finish off Zach's remains. As they licked up the pools of blood and the remaining fragments of flesh, they got a taste of the slightly bitter juice that puddled near the torn carton. Realizing what lay inside, a boar began furiously pushing the carton with its snout, flipping it over and over. A second boar ripped at the half-empty carton Trey had dropped in the street. The cans tumbled in every direction as the wild beasts pushed them with their snouts; finally a boar bit into one, spraying beer everywhere. They ripped apart the other three cartons. Beer cans spun on their sides and rolled to one side of the road or the other. Having learned to puncture the cans with their jaws, the boars celebrated with the carbonated liquid. The manmade concoction proved to be the perfect after-dinner drink as they sopped up every ounce of alcohol. The chips were next as the plastic-laminated aluminum bags couldn't mask the aroma of the Doritos. The creatures devoured those too. By the time the boars were finished, forty-two punctured beer cans lay scattered off the roadside. And in a matter of minutes, three more humans had vanished from the face of the earth.

"It's almost one a.m., y'all," Sarah urged. "We need to go look for them."

"Fuck!" grunted Erick.

"I agree someone really needs to go," Curt said. "Come on, Erick, I'll go with you."

"I'm not driving into town. Fuck that!" Erick contested. "I'm not going to get arrested like they probably did. There's not a damn thing y'all can do tonight."

"Fine, then I'll go by myself," Curt decided. "You and Dustin stay here with the girls. All right if I use your car, Mary?"

"That's fine, but I'm going with you," Mary answered. "I don't want to stay here with these jerks. They don't even care that something bad could've happened."

"I'm going too," added Sarah.

"Sarah, you don't need to go. Stay here with me," Dustin commanded.

"I want to go! We need to find them!" Sarah insisted.

"Whatever, do whatever the hell you want," Dustin replied dismissively.

Mary handed Curt the keys to her Ford Focus. The two of them sat in front and Sarah in the backseat. The pitch blackness of the new-moon sky and their concern about driving through the river crossing distracted them; they never noticed the beer cans cast alongside the brush-line less than a mile from camp. They just drove right past them. The concerned friends wound through the canyon and impatiently ascended the steep grade, anxiously watching for their phones to receive service.

Curt heard his phone "ping" and noticed there were several missed calls from Zach and Trey. He redialed Zach, then Trey, but both calls went directly to voicemail. As he proceeded to the top of the canyon, Mary called Amy's phone, and it also went straight to voicemail. Mary and Sarah then noticed they too had numerous missed calls from Amy. Finally at the top, they drove over the tire spikes that protected the park's exit way and were clear of the entrance building when Sarah looked to her left and saw Zach's SUV.

"There's his car!" she shouted.

Curt immediately steered over and parked next to the black Pathfinder. They all jumped out, checked the doors, and peered into the windows. They looked around and found nothing suspicious.

"Why would they just leave the car here?" asked Sarah, puzzled.

"I don't know. Doesn't make any sense," Curt replied.

The three of them began shouting out Zach, Trey, and Amy's names. The only sounds they heard, other than each other, were the cadence of crickets and periodic calls and screeches from a pair of Eastern screech owls; a slight breeze blowing through the trees.

"Maybe they picked up a hitchhiker and ended up going to the motel with that plastic-coated room," Mary imagined.

"You really need to watch a better class of movies," Curt told her. "I doubt that happened to them, either."

"Then I bet they did get arrested," Mary said. "Like those people in the paper who got locked up, and then they disappeared because they didn't have any money to bribe the prison guards."

"That happened in Mexico," Curt informed her. "But it's possible they did get arrested. The way the car is parked, I doubt he ran out of gas."

"Try calling Zach again, Curt," said Sarah. "I don't understand why they didn't leave messages."

"I don't know, either," Curt responded as he redialed Zach's number. "What do y'all suggest we do?"

"I don't know what else we *can* do," Sarah said. "Since their car is here, it doesn't make any sense to look for them in town. I doubt we could bail 'em out tonight, anyway. As much beer as we've had, they'd just lock us up too. At least they're all together." Mary nodded in agreement.

Again Zach's phone went straight to voicemail. "I guess we should just head back to camp. We'll drive into Canyon first thing in the morning if they don't show up before then," Curt decided.

They all agreed and got back into the car. Curt drove up to the entrance gate and noticed that a large, silver metal gate blocked the road. Confused, he asked, "Shit, how do we get back in?"

"Isn't there some kind of combination lock?" Mary recalled a portion of the conversation when they checked in.

"I remember," said Sarah. "We need to go to the other side of the building and open the gate on that side."

"All right, let's try that," said Curt. He drove to the left side of the building and pulled up to the short gate.

"The combination is written on the park permit that should be taped to the windshield," instructed Sarah. Curt turned on the interior lights.

"Fourteen, thirty-six, twenty-three," Curt read out loud.

He got out of the car, turned the dial on the combination lock, and it opened. After removing the chain, Curt opened the gate, got back into the car, and drove to the other side then got back out to close the gate. He swung the gate back across the road, wrapped the chain around the gate and post, and snapped the lock in place turning the dial. Back in the vehicle, Curt and the girls headed back to the campsite.

Dustin and Erick stood near the lantern. "If Trey and Zach would have just bought what I told them to buy in the first place," Erick said, justifying his lack of action.

"It's their own damn fault!" agreed Dustin.

"I gotta take a piss," said Erick.

"I might as well too before Sarah gets back," replied Dustin.

They walked away from the tent area and stood along the edge of the clearing. What they didn't know was that only forty yards away, a group of man-eating boars was silently creeping toward them.

"It sucks not getting service down here! I wonder if we won today." Dustin speculated.

"Fucking Cowboys! We better have beaten Oklahoma State," Erick stated forcefully.

"OSU sucks. You know what I'm going to miss? Beatin' the god-damn Aggies all the time. All they do is flaunt their cult traditions. Only tradition they have is cheating every year, a tradition I'm sure they'll carry on with every other team in the SEC," Dustin laughed.

The two guys finished their business and headed back to the campsite. The hogs were now only twenty yards away; the blaring radio drowned out the whisper-snapping and crackling of the leaves and twigs as they inched closer. Erick and Dustin walked over to the metal picnic table and sat on top of it, resting their feet on the bench. Aligning themselves in strategic formation, the rogue boars were poised to rush the unsuspecting boys.

"We should smoke that shit now, before the girls get back," suggested Erick.

"Never thought you'd ask. Hell yeah, fire it up," encouraged Dustin.

Erick promptly removed a joint from his cigarette pack and lit it, taking a deep draw before handing it to Dustin.

"Man that smells good," Dustin commented taking the potent blunt.

"Tastes even better. God I love this shit," Erick proclaimed.

The strange smell quickly filled the surrounding air as the boys finished smoking the illegal weed. The unfamiliar scent gave pause to the boars, unsure of its meaning. Seconds later, the headlights and noise of Curt driving Mary's car on the gravel road with music blaring startled the wild hogs. The pack turned and bolted deeper into the brush, retreating for the moment.

Oblivious to their surroundings, Dustin and Erick never knew how close they came to suffering the same shocking fate as their college friends.

"So where are they?" Dustin asked, as Curt and the girls were getting out of the car.

"We don't know," Curt replied. "Zach's car was parked just outside the entrance, but we couldn't find them."

"What do you mean his car is parked outside the entrance?" Erick questioned.

"Dustin, have you guys been smoking pot? My god, it reeks! I told you I hate it when you do that!" screamed Sarah.

"We smoked one joint, relax, damn it," Dustin yelled back.

The strange fragrance, the music, the yelling, the roar of the car and sound of its tires kicking up stones, plus five humans in all combined to unnerve the boars; the pack grudgingly raced off.

"His Pathfinder is parked right near the entrance," Sarah said bewildered. "Everything looked OK; the car was locked. We think maybe they got arrested or something. We all have missed calls from them but no messages."

"Those dumbasses!" said Erick. "I'm not wasting party time huntin' down their asses!"

Curt interrupted, "I guess if they're not back in the morning, we'll have to drive into Canyon and possibly bail them out."

"Sure sucks for them," Dustin said shaking his head.

"Sucks for us too! We don't have any more fucking beer!" Erick snarled.

The group stayed awake speculating how the three had possibly been arrested. They all surmised that Zach made himself a likely target by speeding as he likes to do. A little past three a.m., Sarah finally said she was going to bed and asked Dustin to please come soon; she didn't want to be alone in the tent.

Just friends, Mary and Curt had already agreed to share a tent, so they headed off to pass out for what was left of the night. Erick had planned to stay up all night drinking, but now with supposedly nothing to drink, he stomped off to his tent. By three fifteen, all were zipped in, and the campground fell silent.

The Canyon Can Be Unforgiving for All Living Things

Palo Duro Canyon State Park; Sunday, November 18, 2012; 7:05 A.M.

"Idiots!" mumbled the cleanup crew member to his co-worker.

It was just before dawn when the part-time minimum-wage employee with no healthcare got out of the vehicle and walked a few feet to pick up an Old Milwaukee beer can in the middle of the road. Both of them failed to see the second can several feet away, next to the canyon wall. The worker got back into the state-owned truck, and the driver pulled away.

The men proceeded down the steep road with little to say until they reached the bottom of the canyon. Just beyond the Trading Post, they spotted three more dented Old Milwaukee beer cans. The driver sighed before he put the truck in park. His subordinate—a diminutive man with several missing teeth—again stepped out of the truck, picked up the three cans, and threw them into the truck bed.

When he got back into the vehicle, the driver said, "I guess that anti-littering campaign 'Don't Mess with Texas' had no effect on that guy. Just a typical Sunday morning, I suppose."

"Ya shoulda seen Houston," responded the assistant.

"It's a city," replied the driver.

"Yeah, but when I lived there, the highways was full of trash. I passed washer machines, ladders, paint cans, tables and couches, dead dogs—even a porta-potty just layin' in the middle of the highway. Can you imagine hitting one of those doin' sixty-five miles an hour? Talk 'bout holy shit! Ugh. At least you'd live. Hell, one time, at five in the mornin', I dodged a whole buncha long boards and ended up running over one. On down the road, I reckon about a mile or have ya, we seen a big truck hauling lumber. Two-b'-fours was just flying off't th' the back of 'at truck. Them boards wasn't tied down or nothin'. Damn near kill't us! Boards flyin' off th' truck from ten, twelve feet in th' air! If a two-b'-four smashed your windshield cruising down the road, you was as good as dead," claimed the park employee.

"You're right, a lot of it is from people putting things in the back of pickup trucks and not tying the cargo down. This state probably has more pickup trucks than the rest of the country combined," the driver confirmed.

The truck splashed through the water for the first time that morning, and, when it leveled out after reaching the crest beyond the waterway, the men were aghast. They had seen and picked up their share of litter before, but nothing as disrespectful as what spoiled the park that morning. Over a fifty-foot stretch, on both sides of the road near the brush-line, were three to four dozen beer cans.

"Looks like even the vultures like beer," the driver laughed, noting the multiple birds that flocked in two clusters just ahead. The driver stopped in the middle of the Texas mess.

"I'll get the ones behind us; you get the ones up ahead," said the driver, chuckling at his partner.

"Gee-whiz, thanks, make me hafta mess with 'em buzzards," the passenger muttered.

The driver laughed again. Each grabbed a plastic trash bag from the back of the truck to assist with the clean-up task.

"Eighteen cans! That's how many I found," the driver claimed after both of them made it back to the truck moments later.

"Twenty-four, and two tored-up Doritos bags. Some folks 's just perdy white trash," the hourly worker expressed.

"Funny, every can I saw had been punctured. Never seen anything like it," the driver commented.

"Eah, I seen 'at too," said the co-worker.

"Why are people so stupid? I just don't understand it," questioned the driver.

The men tossed the bags of empty cans into the back of the pickup and proceeded down the road to their destination, the Mesquite Campground, where they would then clean the bathrooms.

"Ya see 'em buzzards back 'ere? Didn't even scare off, an' meaner 'an cat-shit. 'At just ain't what I call normal," stated the passenger.

"I saw 'em. They seemed pretty determined to stand their ground," the driver replied.

"Whatever it was 'em coyotes kilt last night, looks like they got 'em a couple of 'em 'cause I seen blood in two spots," the passenger concluded.

"The canyon can be unforgiving for all living things," said the driver as they made their way to the farthest campground in the park.

Sick, I Can See Blood

Fortress Cliff Campground; Palo Duro Canyon State Park
Sunday November 18, 2012; 9:04 A.M.

"Dustin, it's past nine. We need to get up and find Amy and the guys," Sarah said as she nudged him.

"In a minute," Dustin grumbled as he smothered himself inside the sleeping bag. After ignoring her several more times, by nine-thirty Sarah had had enough.

"Get your ass up right now, Dustin!" she shouted, hitting him with her pillow.

Her voice stirred the others and prompted Mary to begin changing out of her sweatpants and top she wore to bed. Curt stayed under the sleeping bag until she finished dressing and had crawled out of the tent. Once everyone was up and dressed, the five contemplated what to do next.

Three times Curt suggested, "We need to drive up to the entrance and ask the rangers if they got arrested."

Aggravated, Erick finally relented, "OK! Shit, Dustin and I'll go in a minute. It's not our fault they got arrested."

Sarah argued they all needed to stick together.

"If we all go, we need to clean this place up first," Dustin told her. "We just can't leave all these beer cans; we need to dump them somewhere."

"Fine, all right, we'll all go in my car," Erick said to appease Sarah.

The five bickering students hastily cleaned up their two sites, put the empty beer cans in the trunk, and got into Erick's Impala. Curt sat in back with Sarah and Mary; Dustin rode shotgun. Erick rolled down his window and lit a cigarette as he pulled out of the campground located only yards away from the fifth river crossing.

Unlike Zach, who was a precarious driver, Erick drove his four-door sedan cautiously as he crossed the fourth then the third water crossing. As he neared the second crossing, the car rolled to a stop.

"Look at those giant buzzards!" he pointed out as he flicked his ashes out the window.

"Damn, they're ugly as hell," Dustin commented.

They all sat in the car for a moment, mesmerized as a half-dozen vultures slowly strutted in circles, periodically pecking at the road. When Erick eased off the brake and began to creep toward the birds, a couple spread their massive wings.

"Those things are really creepy," Sarah said, shrugging her shoulders and grimacing.

"They're fuckin' scavengers," Dustin explained. "They eat dead animals and shit! They're the cleanup crew."

"Yeah, speaking of cleaning up, make sure we dump that shit out of my trunk the first place we see," Erick demanded. "I don't want my car smelling like nasty-ass stale beer!"

He proceeded to move forward and repeatedly banged on his horn, but the stubborn birds refused to surrender.

"I'll run the fuckin' things over if I have to!" Erick threatened. "It would be awesome to see them scavenge one of their own." Not one bird flew away as they all hopped off to the side of the road and into the brush.

"Oh! Sick! I can see blood stains on the road!" cried Mary.

Dustin was ready to mock her when he looked the direction she pointed and noticed what did indeed look like blood.

"Eww! I wonder what happened here," Sarah said.

"Probably somebody ran over an armadillo or a raccoon or something; maybe the coyotes you heard last night killed a small deer," Erick said as he passed the defiant mob of birds. He flicked his cigarette at them.

"There's a damn drought, Erick!" Curt scolded him. "You're gonna catch the whole canyon on fire!"

"Hell, it's just a cigarette! It's not going to start a damn fire!" Erick replied, resenting the lecture.

He continued to slowly roll through the ten inches of water that flowed across the road at the second river crossing. Shortly afterwards, Dustin saw a sign for the Chinaberry Day Use Area. "That looks like a good place to dump all the trash. Turn in there," he advised Erick. Following his suggestion, Erick pulled into the designated area and parked next to a trashcan located near the first picnic table.

"Make sure you get all of it out," Erick requested while pushing the button to unlatch the trunk. Dustin got out of the car, lifted up the trunk lid, picked up the two foul-smelling plastic bags of beer cans, and shoved them into a large brown container.

"All right, let's go find those stupid asses," Erick said as Dustin got back into the car. He turned the car around and headed toward the park's headquarters. Just before they reached the canyon's rim, all but Dustin, whose phone was dead, got phone service within seconds of each other. The girls tried calling Amy while Curt and Erick tried reaching Zach and Trey. Every call went straight to voicemail.

"I can't believe all of their phones are dead. How stupid is that," commented Mary.

Upon their arrival at the park's entrance, all five of them walked into the small office and approached the counter where a young lady sat on a tall stool on the opposite side. "Good morning," Curt greeted her.

"Good morning! How can I help you?" asked the park service employee.

"A bunch of us camped last night at the Fortress Cliff Campground. We all got hungry, so a few of our friends drove into town to pick up some food but they never came back. We got worried, so we drove up here late last night and found their SUV parked right over there," Curt explained as he pointed to the road just outside the entrance.

"Yeah, we noticed that this morning," said the clerk, glancing through the window in the direction of the SUV. "We checked the plates and confirmed that it had been registered at the campground. We wondered why it was parked there."

A door leading to a back room of the office opened, and another park employee, who had overheard bits and pieces, entered the room and stood behind the front desk. Just then Dustin asked, "Do you happen to know if they were arrested or anything?"

"Does this have to do with the black SUV parked out front?" the second employee interrupted.

"Yes, it's our friend's car," Curt explained. "They never came back to the campground last night. We have no idea why they would park it there."

"We're not aware of any arrests last night," replied the senior employee. "You might want to drive into Canyon and check with the police station."

"Can you tell us how to get there?" asked Sarah.

"Sure, it's real easy. Just take 217, and go under the highway. It turns into Fourth Avenue as you get into town. Follow it all the way to Sixteenth Street and turn right. The station is one block down on the corner of Third and Sixteenth," the park employee told them.

"Thanks," said Sarah, as they all walked out of the cramped room.

"Fuckin' great! I'm gonna let them know they owe me gas money for all this bullshit!" Erick complained as they pulled out of the park.

The next thirteen miles to the police station seemed like an eternity.

While Erick complained, Mary worried, "Oh, my god, if my parents find out, they're going to be so pissed!"

"You didn't get arrested, so why the hell would you get in trouble?" asked Dustin.

"You obviously don't know my parents," claimed Mary.

Erick pulled into the police station, and they debated if everyone should go in. Sarah said she was going regardless, and Mary wanted to stick with Sarah. Eventually all five walked into the police station and made their way to the protected window.

"Hello," Mary said.

"Good morning," responded the female dispatch officer.

"We need to get our friends out of this jail right now." Mary ordered.

Sarah quickly intervened. "We're wondering if there were any arrests last night. Our friends never made it back to our campsite at Palo Duro."

"Yes, there were a couple of arrests last night," the officer explained. "This is a college town; we have arrests practically every weekend. I'll check for you. What are your friends' names?"

"Zach Hamilton, Amy Smith, and Trey Dillon," Mary informed her.

The officer told them she needed a minute to look at the list of inmates.

Erick then made a snide remark to Dustin, "They have a college in this piss-ass little town? What's its name, Bottom of The Canyon College?"

Dustin laughed and told him, "I think West Texas A&M, the Mighty Bison." He then remembered about yesterday's football game. "Oh shit! Who won the game last night? My phone is dead; I can't check the score."

Erick pulled up the sports app on his phone and angrily roared, "Fuck! We got slaughtered, dude! Slaughtered like a fuckin' pig!"

"What was the score?" Dustin asked.

"Fifty-nine, twenty-one!" replied Erick.

"God dammit! We lost to Oklahoma State?" Dustin asked in disbelief.

The officer, overhearing them cursing, disapprovingly looked over the frame of her glasses, frowned at Sarah and Mary and said, "No, I'm sorry, I don't see any of their names. Looks like they weren't arrested."

"What? How can that be? Then where are they?" Sarah asked.

"I don't see them on the list," the officer repeated. "They're not in jail—at least not here."

"Well, have you had any reports of hitchhikers in the area?" Mary asked her.

As the officer looked quizzically at Mary, Sarah redirected her attention, "We're very concerned. Do you have any suggestions about what we should do next? I mean it's obvious that something is wrong."

"You can check with some of the other nearby police departments like Amarillo," suggested the officer.

"Huh? Why would they be there if their car is parked at the park's entrance? Do you understand? Our friends have been missing for almost twelve hours, we were camping at Palo Duro," Sarah told her.

"I beg your pardon," the officer said. "I thought you said they had been arrested. Explain to me what happened again."

Realizing both girls were becoming frustrated, Curt interceded. "We were all camping down in the canyon last night. About ten-thirty, eleven o'clock, three of our friends drove into town to get something to eat. They never came back. We were worried, so we drove up the canyon to look for them. We know they didn't have an accident. Their car is parked right outside the state park's entrance. We found it there about one o'clock last night—or this morning, I mean. But they are nowhere to be found. It's weird. It's like they just vanished."

Busy bellyaching about yesterday's loss, Erick and Dustin didn't see it, but Curt, Mary, and Sarah did. As soon as Curt said, "It's like they just vanished," the officer's mouth partially opened; for a second she just stood there staring at them, the color draining from her face, her hands began to tremble.

She looked at the two young girls and Curt and stuttered, "Sta . . . sta . . . stay right here. I'll be . . . right back."

GOP

Texas Panhandle; Sunday, November 18, 2012

Within hours of the mountain bikers' deaths, the entire animal kingdom was aware. After the seven additional acts of retribution, every creature understood the balance between species had now spun out of control. The uncertainty of man's reactions created widespread fear as each species considered the potential aftershocks of the boars' attacks on humans.

While the boars ran roughshod over all other wildlife, every other creature knew it was *man* who ruled the earth. They understood the boar was not man's equal and any attempt to assert otherwise would surely be crushed. The dominant purebred Russian males of the most powerful sounders understood this as well, yet they were unable to reign in the radical fringe that sought new order.

The upheaval started only months after the drought began in late 2010. Nearly half the country's wild-boar population lived in Texas—the Panhandle, in particular—became the epicenter of unrest, where several of the state's most powerful sounders resided.

Extensions of sounders living there had been ruled, for decades, by a pure Russian breed. No interbred animal had dared challenge the purebred's supremacy. But the continued encroachment by man coupled with drought sparked levels of disorder never encountered before. The majority of the boars considered the drought manmade and sought some form of justice. As internal strife intensified, the ability of the pure Russian breed to maintain control eroded as they grappled with two fatal trends.

First, the Russian boar no longer possessed vastly superior physical and mental capabilities relative to the hybrid. The interbred hogs had eliminated those gaps via sheer numbers. With populations growing over twenty percent per year, the Russians were unable to mate with all the available female hybrids. This allowed many of the fiercest male hybrids to mate with the healthiest available females.

Secondly, while the pure Russian variety had always been a minority, the explosive growth dramatically widened the ratio of feral swine to pure Russian. Combined, the two trends of their physical and mental capacities being equalized, and the fact that eight hybrids now existed for every one pure Russian variety signaled an end to what the hybrids considered tyranny by a soulless minority.

The nation of boars knew that despite the drought, their species was thriving, multiplying like no other species. But it didn't matter. A small faction of the super majority desperately sought to instill their philosophies and to end the rule of an immigrated regime, a breed that had been shipped to the continent as prey for the pleasure of man.

Their central argument was, "How could the pawn of man represent the best interests of the boar?"

Tensions mounted as a more moderate branch of interbreeds advised caution; attacking man would lead not only to the decimation of their kind, but to a cascading series of unintended consequences.

Besides, they argued, "We are all immigrants to an extent; many of us have Russian blood. And haven't we always been a pawn of man?"

The intense minority of hybrids thought otherwise. "It is the purebloods who have failed us. Any boar with fifty percent or more of Russian blood lacked the courage and moral conviction to lead the pigs to their destiny as the equals of man. It is man who destroys the environment, who has brought us such hardship. And it is man who should pay."

When the moderates tried to reason, "We, ourselves, are much to blame. Look at the destruction we mount as we uproot man's crops and prey on their livestock. We trample their lands, foul the streams with our wastes, and spread disease. There must be compromise so we can all thrive."

But the small faction only reminded them of the Infamous Six, the latest injustice man had perpetrated on boars after centuries of other outrages. Proof, they alleged, that man would not cease in driving them to extinction, further evidence that they must defend themselves and prove to mankind that it could no longer determine the boar nation's destiny.

The unrelenting faction further argued, "This is not man's land. As hybrids, we are the righteous. Our refusal to compromise in any fashion will be the key to end man's reign of terror. Bestowed by the power of a democracy that upholds the will of the ruling majority, we declare war on man. We are the new face of the Government of Pigs. We are the 'GOP'."

Those Kids are not Incarcerated

Canyon City Police Department; Sunday, November 18, 2012; 10:55 A.M.

"Dawson," he answered the phone.

"Jim, hey, it's Tyson. I think you need to get down to the station."

"Something break on Harden and Mahoney?" the detective asked.

"No sir. Julie at the front desk just took an inquiry from a group of college kids. They said their friends left the campground at Palo Duro late last night and never returned. For some reason, their friend's car is outside the park's entrance, but they are nowhere to be found. They've been missing since around midnight last night," Tyson informed the detective.

"They found their car?" Dawson wanted to clarify.

"Yes sir," explained the officer. "They claim the car their friends drove into town to get some food is parked at the entrance of Palo Duro."

"OK, keep them there. I'll be there in fifteen minutes," requested Dawson.

Exhausted, the detective headed out the door. Driving to the station, he replayed the events of the day before. A K9 team had been brought to the location near Happy immediately after Harden's truck was found. They spent the entire day searching a five-mile radius. Along the road, about a third of a mile from the hog feeder just inside the brush, they found an unregistered handgun, a buck knife and an odd strip of rubber from what appeared to be from the sole of a boot. The handgun and knife both had speckles of blood on them similar to the rifles. Besides the two rifles lying one on top of the other, there were no further clues as the impounded truck provided no insight. Until they checked fingerprints, he wasn't absolutely certain the rifles, pistol, and the knife belonged to either of the men.

When the investigative team met with Karen after the K9 search was complete, she thought one of the rifles could be her husband's but wasn't certain. Watching her inspect the two rifles, pistol, and buck knife drove Dawson insane.

"Well, now I just don't know," Karen said hesitantly, pointing to one of the rifles. "This one might be. Do y'all think it looks old? Because he was fixin' to get a new one." (The rifle she pointed to eventually proved to be Mahoney's rifle, not her husband's.)

Dawson thought, "If she was my wife, we would know everything about each other."

At that moment, all Dawson knew for sure was the two men were gone without a trace; more than likely, four others as well. Hoping clues elsewhere might help put pieces together, he requested a K9 search team from the Special Crimes Unit to comb the area near the late-arrival campground where the two frightened Hispanic boys were found, but Thompson denied it for the second time.

"Budget constraints," he claimed moments after they completed the search near Happy.

"We summoned a helicopter to sweep half the Panhandle, and a canine unit worked the entire day searching for Harden and Mahoney, and we can't . . . ," Dawson contended before the chief interrupted him.

"Exactly why it's not approved," the chief responded before hanging up on Dawson.

Dawson's frustration grew as it became apparent his boss lacked concern for the parents of the two small boys and the men in the motorhome. The sole focus was on Harden and Mahoney. It wasn't until late Saturday afternoon the chief agreed to request a search warrant for the motorhome. It had taken several pleas from the detective, "Chief, there has to be some link between all these cases. A handful of people don't just vanish. You know they're *all* missing. It's not just Harden and Mahoney. We need to thoroughly search that motorhome."

On his way home from the gut-wrenching meeting where Karen was unable to identify her husband's gun, the detective answered his phone, "Detective Dawson."

"Detective, Ranger Jack Wilson," the park employee responded.

"Good evening, Jack," Dawson replied.

"Just wanted to let you know there's been no activity whatsoever at the motorhome. Those men are still missing. What's goin' to be done about it? What's the next step?"

"Chief Thompson requested a search warrant. I should have it first thing in the morning," Dawson informed him.

"OK, both Irving and I are off tomorrow. You have our numbers; call us if you need to."

"Will do, I appreciate it," the detective told him before hanging up.

Only a few minutes away from the station on his way to meet the worried college kids, the detective already knew from earlier calls that morning the search warrant remained unissued. Making matters worse, he still had not heard back from Victor regarding any other aspects of the investigations, in particular if they had matched the fingerprints on the guns and knife to Harden and or Mahoney. Dawson entered the back entrance of the station and went straight to his desk. He picked up a pen and his personal notebook before he sought out Tyson.

"Mornin', Rick. What's going on with the college kids?" the detective asked.

"They're in the lobby," Tyson explained. "They said their friends drove into Canyon last night to pick up some food but never returned."

"But they found their car at the park's entrance?" the detective reiterated.

"That's correct, just like I told you on the phone. It's the strangest thing, Jim; people are just vanishing into thin air. When are we going to alert the public? What more is it going to take?"

"I understand. My whole body feels queasy," Dawson agreed. "In a matter of a couple days, five, six people are missing, now possibly three more? I'm going to go out and take their statements."

Dawson walked to the front of the building where Julie sat. Looking into the lobby through the thick, bulletproof window, he asked her if those were the college kids from Tech.

"Yes, they thought their friends must have been arrested, which is why they came here. But the names are not on any inmate lists. I've already checked with all the other local jurisdictions. They're not in jail, Jim."

"And you're positive about that?" the detective asked.

"Jim, this is my job. Those kids are not incarcerated in any of the surrounding counties," she replied, concerned.

"I know you're thorough. I'm sorry. I'm just tired," Dawson apologized.

"It's OK, Jim, we're all on edge. This is getting pretty scary. There could be nine people missing in just a few days. They've just vanished. People in the department are talking."

"Have you heard from Chief Thompson today?" he asked her.

"No. No one has seen or heard from him."

"All right, let me see what I can find out," the detective said. Julie pushed the button to unlock the secured door, and the detective entered the lobby.

Dawson introduced himself to the students and requested they follow him to a room where they could talk. As he approached the door, Julie again pushed the button, and the detective led the way to a conference room. They all sat at a long, wooden table as he prepared to take notes.

"If you would, please, I need your names and phone numbers," he requested. "Then I will need your friends' information as well."

After he jotted down the specifics, he asked, "What can you tell me?" He focused on Mary since she seemed ready to speak.

"Well, Erick made a big to-do about not having enough b . . . , uh, food, so Zach, Amy, and Trey volunteered to go get something to eat. We all chipped in, and they drove into Canyon to pick it up and bring it back," Mary explained.

"What time was that?" asked the detective.

"I think it was around ten forty-five or so," she tried to recall.

"It was, around ten forty-five, maybe a few minutes earlier," confirmed Curt.

"Then what?" the detective probed.

"We don't know. They never came back," said Sarah.

Mary leaned forward and stared at the detective intently. "We got worried because we heard these noises like animals or something. But Erick said, 'Of course there's animals', and . . ."

Sarah interrupted, "Mary, Curt, and I drove up to the entrance looking for them last night."

"And that's when you saw their car?" asked the detective.

"Yes," said Sarah.

"What kind of car is it?" the detective inquired.

"Umm . . . well, it's black," Mary ventured. "And it's not a car. It's one of those—you know—truck thingies."

"It's a black Nissan Pathfinder SUV," Curt interjected attempting to make this as painless as possible.

"You know what year?" Dawson asked.

"It's a few years old, 2007, 2008 maybe," Curt guessed.

"And you're sure it's their car?" asked the detective.

"It's his car for sure," Curt insisted. "It has a Tech parking sticker on the back window, and we could see some of his stuff inside."

"So about what time did you find the car?" the detective asked.

"Maybe a little after one a.m. or so," said Sarah. "But before we even saw the car, all our phones got service, and we saw we had a bunch of missed calls from all of them. But they didn't leave a message. We all tried calling them back, but the calls went straight to voicemail."

"What time were those missed calls?" asked Dawson.

"About 11:15 or so," replied Sarah.

Checking his phone, Curt confirmed, "I have a missed call from Zach at 11:21 and another from Trey at 11:24 last night. And I tried calling both of them at 1:07 a.m., but both calls went straight to voicemail."

Erick butted in, "Are you sure they didn't get their asses locked up in one of the other jails around here?" he asked impatiently.

Dawson looked at him coolly. "Yes, we are. We verified they're not in any jails anywhere near here." The detective remained composed, but his mind was swirling trying to connect the dots. "Let's go take a look. I'll follow you to the park," the detective said before they all stood and exited the station.

"Oh, my god! Where are they, what could've happened to them?" Sarah cried the moment they all got into the car.

Curt was stunned, "Man! It's weird! It's like they just disappeared into thin air!

"May . . . be they . . . got abducted by . . . aliens," Erick taunted. "Shit! Y'all are so freakin' dramatic! I bet those assholes are back at the campsite right now. Quit exaggerating this whole damn thing!"

"I have no doubt something off-the-wall happened! It is Trey, you know," added Dustin.

"We are not exaggerating, Erick," Sarah sneered. "You're such a jerk!"

"Oh, fuck off! Always such damn drama queens!" he shot back.

Erick stayed within the speed limit before the detective grew impatient; he passed the kids and waved his hand for them to follow him to the park's entrance. Dawson saw the SUV off to his right and pulled up next to it. Erick parked his Impala next to the detectives.

Dawson remained in his cruiser for a minute and radioed dispatch to immediately run the tags. He got out and walked around the vehicle.

"You said the vehicle belongs to Zach Hamilton?" the detective asked the group.

"Yes," said Curt.

Detective Dawson peered through the windows, looked underneath the SUV, and then stepped into the brushy area just off the side of the road. He found nothing.

"Was this vehicle registered with the park?" asked Dawson.

"Yes, we all went in and paid," said Sarah.

"Well, there is no permit sticker in the window," Detective Dawson noted.

"I don't know why," Sarah said. "All three vehicles had permits. The park service said this morning the car had been registered."

"Did y'all check over in the late-arrival camp area?" the detective asked.

"We don't know where that is," Curt answered. "We're in the Fortress Cliff Camp Area."

"There is a late-arrival camp area over there." The detective pointed across the landscape to his right. "Let's check it out. If we don't find anything, I'll follow you to your campsite."

Slamming his door, Erick grumbled, "This is bullshit!"

"What is your problem, Erick?" Sarah confronted him. "Aren't you worried about them?"

"Hell no! I'm drivin' all over to hell and back because those dumbasses got lost, arrested, abducted by aliens, whatever," Erick shouted.

The cars slowly crept down the gravel road. As they approached the loop, Dawson could immediately see the campground was empty. He continued on anyway looking for any signs of the missing students.

Annoyed, Erick used his knee to steer, so he could quickly light a cigarette.

"Why the fuck would they be here?" asked Dustin.

"Dustin, seriously, you're getting more like Erick all the time. Aren't you at least one bit worried?" Sarah asked him sharply.

Dustin turned around and raised his voice, "Quit being such a bitch! You're all so paranoid!"

"What did you say, jerk?" yelled Sarah.

"That's enough! Shut up! All of you!" Curt shouted, attempting to stop the verbal confrontation before it escalated any further.

Completing the short loop, Detective Dawson pulled out of the late-arrival camping area, drove directly to the building at the main entrance, and parked his car.

"What's he doing?" asked Erick.

The detective raised his index finger to the college students and mouthed the words, "Just a minute," as he walked into the building.

"Shit, I hope he's not getting the rangers!" Dustin implored.

The detective showed his badge to the park employee at the counter and asked her to have the rangers meet him at the Fortress Cliff Campground. She said she would.

The detective left the building and walked up to Erick's window, "I'll follow you, OK?"

"Sure," said Erick. He proceeded to lead as they descended into the canyon.

"Thank God you guys listened to me, and we cleaned up the campsite!" Dustin bragged.

"It won't matter. Like I said earlier, be just our luck those guys will be at the campsite when we get there with the detective, drunk off their asses," Erick laughed. "Then what?"

They had already passed the dry river crossing and were now approaching the first crossing with water, the one which had freaked Erick out the first time he drove across it. "I better not get any water in my car!" he warned the previous day.

"Look at the marker; it's not even a foot deep! Relax!" Dustin responded at the time trying to calm his friend.

After slowly crossing the water, they started up the small incline and had reached the crest when they saw the vultures again. There were only three now. This time, Erick maintained his speed, and the birds hastily hopped off to the side of the road.

"Man, those son-of-a-bitches have been here all day," noted Dustin.

Seconds earlier, dispatch radioed the detective with information on the SUV. It was registered to Zach's father, Isaac Hamilton of Fort Worth. There were no outstanding warrants or tickets. Distracted with the call, Dawson only caught a glimpse of one of the vultures as he drove by, and he did not see the blood stains on the road—stains that were quickly fading in the bright sunshine. The detective parked in the loop behind Erick. Exiting his vehicle, he approached the students. Immediately he noticed a pair of Old Milwaukee beer cans sitting underneath the picnic table at the site next to theirs. Erick realized the detective saw them.

"Anyone else in the campground last night?" was the first thing the detective wanted to know.

Erick started to speak when Mary quickly answered, "No, just us."

"Just y'all?" the detective wanted to reaffirm.

"It was just the eight of us," said Sarah.

All six turned towards the campground's entrance as two Texas park ranger trucks pulled up next to Dawson's car. As the detective went to greet the rangers, Erick tried to get Dustin's attention. When he did, he nodded towards the Old Milwaukee cans under the bench.

"Oh shit!" Dustin whispered.

Having never met the two rangers filling in for Wilson and Irving, Detective Dawson calmly explained the latest disappearance. The rangers were fully aware of the six missing people and tried to appear nonchalant, but they were astonished by the news. The students could see the concern on their faces.

The detective turned back to the students and asked, "Mind if I have a look in the tents?"

"You can look in the green one," Mary offered. "It's kind of messy though."

The detective walked over, opened the flap of the tent and briefly glanced inside. "How about the others?" he asked.

"Yeah, sure," Dustin said, which prompted Erick to say, "OK."

Sweat began to form on Erick's face. He couldn't remember if he had thrown out the can he had confiscated and hid in his tent when the beers started running low—the beer he drank after everyone else went to bed. The detective checked the tents, then pulled the empty Old Milwaukee beer can out of Erick's tent, and set it down on the picnic table.

He turned around and asked, "How old are all of you?"

The girls responded, "Eighteen."

"Nineteen, sir," answered Curt.

The officer looked at Erick and Dustin, and they both meekly said, "Eighteen."

"Do you know how to get a hold of your friends' parents?" Dawson asked.

"I can get you Amy's parents' information once I get out of the canyon and can call someone," replied Sarah.

"I don't know about Zach and Trey, but they're both from Fort Worth and have been best friends for years," said Curt.

Dustin and Erick both told the detective they didn't know.

"That's all right. I can reach the Hamiltons from the car registration. When you get out of the canyon, call me and give me Amy's parents' contact information, would you please?" the detective asked looking at Sarah.

"I will," she promised.

Dawson then inquired, "You said Zach and Trey are best friends?"

"Yes sir," Curt responded.

"Then I'm sure I'll be able to reach Mr. Dillon's parents through the Hamiltons," the detective surmised.

Dawson then took out five business cards and gave one to each of the college students. "I need to go check on something. I suggest y'all pack up and head on home. I'm about to have the vehicle impounded so we can thoroughly inspect it," the detective explained. "I'll call you if I have any questions."

"Oh, my god! We can't leave without them!" Mary cried.

"What are we going to do?" Erick argued. "Wait all day for them to show up? And what if they don't? We have classes tomorrow!"

"He's right. There's nothing you can do right now," the detective agreed. "I need to go. I promise we'll do all we can to find your friends."

Dawson motioned to the rangers, and they got into their respective vehicles and drove off. The students stood there, shocked, as they watched the detective and the two rangers turn to the right leaving the campground instead of back towards the park's entrance.

"Holy shit, I thought we were busted when he pulled that beer can out of your tent, Erick!" exclaimed Dustin.

"I was freaking out too!" Erick responded.

"I don't understand why they didn't arrest us. Did you notice the looks on those rangers' faces when the detective was talking to them?" asked Sarah.

"Their faces went almost as white as the police officer's this morning," Curt affirmed.

Mary solemnly added, "I just think they know something really bad happened."

"More of your chainsaw maniacs and hitchhikers?" Erick derided her. "You guys are always overreacting!"

"Overreacting? Where did you get that beer from anyway? I thought we had run out long before we went to bed," Sarah wanted to know.

"I left it in there earlier. I forgot about it," explained Erick.

Sarah knew better. "You're such a liar!"

"Shut the fuck up, Sarah! I'm not a liar!" Erick shot back.

"Let's just pack up and go," Curt suggested. "The sooner we're out of the canyon, the sooner Sarah will be able to get that number to the detective."

"I've *been* ready to get the hell out of here!" Erick yelled as he stomped off to pack up his tent.

It took less than thirty minutes for the students to be packed and ready to go. They were all hungry and agreed to go directly into town and grab something to eat before heading back to campus. Dustin got into Erick's car and had expected Sarah to do the same; just as they had ridden on the way to the canyon. When Sarah started to get into Mary's car, another argument broke out.

"Sarah, what the hell are you doing?" Dustin yelled out his window.

"I'm riding with Mary and Curt. Erick's an asshole!" she responded.

"I take that as a compliment," boasted Erick as he started the car.

"Sarah, that's bullshit! Get in this car!" Dustin demanded.

"Come on, let's just go," Sarah said to Curt and Mary as she sat next to a large duffle bag and Zach's tent Curt had packed up and set in the backseat of Mary's tiny Ford Focus.

Mary pulled out of the campsite with Erick tailing her. As they approached the second river crossing, the vultures were gone.

A few minutes later, Dustin said, "Honestly, I just want to get the hell out of here."

"We're close," Erick said. He lit another cigarette just as they began the steep climb out of the canyon.

Looking at the vertical wall to his left, he noticed a can and laughed, "There's an Old Milwaukee can against the wall!"

"Shit, without Trey, we can't even get any beer now," Dustin complained.

Minutes later, watching Mary cross under the highway and continue past the frontage road, Dustin said, "To hell with Sarah! Let's just get back to Lubbock!"

Taking Dustin's cue, Erick veered left onto the feeder road at the last second and entered the ramp for southbound I-27 back to Lubbock.

Noticing their split decision in her rearview mirror, Mary shook her head and said, "Oh well, I guess they didn't want to eat with us."

Sarah spun around and caught a glimpse of the white Impala heading for the highway and said, "They're both jerks!"

Warmth of His Hug

Canyon City Police Station; Sunday, November 18, 2012; 1:26 P.M.

The two rangers followed the detective to the Mesquite Campground. The moment Dawson turned in, he realized nothing had changed except a second motorhome and two additional campers had joined the older couple's trailer and the mysterious motorhome.

They turned right and proceeded past the first open lot, site number ninety-six, and then number ninety-five where the second motorhome was parked. They continued on before they stopped dead center of the back curve where the motorhome with New Jersey plates remained. Although it was apparent site number ninety was still undisturbed, Dawson and the two rangers exited their vehicles and proceeded toward the motorhome.

The detective asked the rangers to announce themselves and knock on the door while he scoured the site. There was no answer.

They walked over to the detective standing under the wooden shelter next to the site and one of them asked, "Don't you think it's time to get a search warrant, Detective Dawson? For all we know, they could be injured or, heaven forbid, dead inside."

"I've already requested one. It should be waiting at my desk as soon as I get back to the station," the detective replied, relieved that rangers Wilson and Irving had not mentioned the fact they had already been inside the motorhome.

The series of events started to consume the detective. He wanted resolution.

"We're just wastin' our time here, nothing's changed," Dawson said. "Will y'all please talk to the other campers and verify they've seen no activity here. I need to get back to Canyon, get the chief's approval, and have the Special Crime Scene Unit out here to search for those college students. Here's my card. Call me immediately if you learn anything, and I mean anything of interest."

The two rangers then pulled out their own cards, so the detective would be able to reach them as well.

It was already well past one p.m. when the detective continued around the small loop and passed one of the last of the twenty sites in the campground, site number seventy-nine where the older couple camped. Aggravated, the detective shook his head over the fact he still had not spoken to the chief.

"What the hell is Thompson thinking?" he wondered. "And where the hell is he? I have no idea why he's suppressing information, and he won't even try to find the parents of those two little boys."

Mentally torn, Dawson planned on calling Karen as soon as he reached the top of the canyon. Despite her distress, he just wanted to hear her voice. Then he would try contacting the chief again, he decided. As he began the ascent out of the canyon, the detective's heart rate rose nearly as fast as the incline he climbed. As soon as he had service, he touched the name Karen in his phone's contact list.

"Hello," she answered.

"Hello, Mrs. Harden, it's Jim, Detective Dawson," he said warmly.

"Oh, Jim!" she responded. His pulse surged to a new high.

"I'm just callin' to check up on you. To see how you're holdin' up," he said. "I know how difficult this must be."

"Jim, it's all over the news!" she complained. "Do you have any idea how hard it is to watch TV and hear about the mysterious disappearance of your husband?"

"I have no doubt it's very tough," he empathized.

"I don't know where these reporters are getting their outrageous information," she said in disbelief.

"Yes, I've heard several rumors," replied the detective.

"One report said Tom and Len possibly staged this whole thing," she cried indignantly. "That they were in such financial trouble, they faked their own disappearance. Do ya know how difficult it is to hear that? It's even worse than reports that they up and passed away somehow. They're saying Tom has gone and just abandoned me and Emma. You don't think it's true, do you?"

"Karen, I know you're hurting right now. But at this point, we can't rule out any scenario. People do inexplicable things when they have financial problems." Just then the detective received an incoming call from the chief. He ignored it.

"Then there was another rumor that they had a side bid'ness and borrowed a lot of money they didn't pay back. So they killed 'em and buried their bodies. It's awful! I can't take this anymore! Where is he?" she began to cry.

"I'm going to stop by and check on you. Is that all right?" the detective asked.

"Yes, of course you're welcome to stop by," she encouraged.

"OK, I'll be there in twenty minutes," he promised before he hung up.

No matter what the chief had to say, Dawson was not going to let it destroy his excitement over seeing Karen in a few minutes.

"Dammit, Dawson! Why didn't you pick up?" the chief barked when he answered the phone.

"I was on my way out of the canyon," the detective offered, twisting the truth.

"Why the hell are ya wastin' time down there? Forget about that god-damn motorhome and those illegal wetbacks! We have to find Harden and Mahoney, now!" he snapped.

"Chief, three college students were reported missing this morning. Their car is abandoned at the entrance of the park. They'd been camping at the bottom of the canyon," Dawson informed the chief.

"What the hell are ya talkin' about, now?" Thompson grumbled.

"Two males and a female, all freshmen at Tech, are missing. It's like they've just vanished," explained the detective.

"Christ almighty! Seriously?" Thompson replied.

"Chief, we really do need to alert the public," Dawson advised. "Reporters are all over the Harden and Mahoney case, and it's just a matter of time before this information gets leaked. There are all kinds of rumors floating around."

"We will, detective, but I have to look into somethin' first." Then Thompson asked, "Heard anything else from Amarillo?"

"No sir. But if I hadn't gotten a hold of you as soon as I was out of the canyon, I was going to give them a call." The detective then redirected the conversation back to the disappearances in the canyon. "We need the Special Crimes Unit out here immediately. Three college students are missin' along with all the others, and we need to get on top of this before it spins out of control. We need to start a search."

"God dammit, Dawson! Canyon City does not have the budget for this crap. Focus on Harden and Mahoney! Is that clear?"

"What is it you need to look into that's more urgent than this?" Detective Dawson asked tersely.

"There's just some other business I need to tend to. Keep Mills in the loop. I should be available this evening. Meet me at the station around six."

"Detective Mills and I'll be there. I'm also going to contact the parents of the missin' college students," replied Detective Dawson.

"Hold off on that for now. Let's discuss how we want to handle that when we meet," instructed the chief.

"Chief, time's a wasting. Those parents have a right to know their children are missin'. Every minute is valuable, could be a matter of life and death," protested the detective.

"I said wait!" Thompson commanded. "Once it goes public that we have all these people missin', the media is going to descend on us like fucking vultures. I want to have an answer for every god-damn monkey wrench they throw my way."

Dawson was incredulous. "Chief, one more . . ."

But the chief had already hung up.

When Dawson pulled into Karen's driveway, he expected the door to open and for her to soon be on the front porch like all the other times he had visited, but she wasn't. The idea of possibly sitting down and talking with her in the living room excited him. Just as he was about to ring the doorbell, the front door swung open, and Karen asked him to please come inside.

318

"Hello, Mrs. Harden," he said as he stepped forward. He looked across the cramped living room and greeted her parents, who sat on a faded worn couch next to a plastic end table.

"I'm sorry, but I don't have any other news for y'all," he said to the family. "We're workin' diligently in conjunction with the Amarillo Special Crimes Unit. You can rest assured; we have the best people in the Panhandle involved in this case."

"Detective, we understand. I'm sure you're considerin' 'bout everything," said Karen's father.

"It's just all these awful rumors," her mother complained. "It only makes it harder for Karen. For all of us, Mr. Dawson."

"I'm sure it's very trying. I'm sorry y'all have to go through this," replied the detective.

"We should sue sumbody," threatened Karen's sister, who was listening from the kitchen.

"I can assure you, we're doin' absolutely all we can," Dawson said supportively. "I will let you know the moment we learn more. If I don't hear anything today, I will check back with you tomorrow. And remember, I'm just a phone call away."

"Thank you, Detective," Karen said as she gave him a hug.

Dawson tried to be professional, but he was confident she could sense the warmth of his hug, the reassuring pats on her back.

"Once again, call me immediately if anything, anything at all comes up," the detective said before he opened the door to leave.

Halfway out the door he was sure he heard Karen's mother say, "He seems like such a fine man."

"It's the Economy, Stupid"

Lighthouse Trail; Sunday, November 18, 2012; 1:27 P.M.

Rafi picked up Mitch around one-thirty. Noticing his friend was carrying a cooler, Rafi popped open the trunk and got out to greet him.

"As always, you're prepared. What's in the cooler?" Rafi asked.

"Water, lots of it. Dena wouldn't let me out the door without it," Mitch responded as he grabbed a couple of bottles for the road.

Rafi waved to Jeffrey, who was standing outside the front door. He felt bad about not asking the boys to come, but he figured with Jeffrey's injury from the soccer game the day before, the last thing the boy could have done was hike six miles on a rugged canyon trail.

The drive to Palo Duro was simple. South down Interstate 27, east onto Texas Highway 217, a dozen more miles to the entrance.

"And to think that the second largest canyon in the country exists only a few miles away, right in the middle of this giant pancake we live on," Mitch commented in wonderment.

"Yeah, pretty amazing, huh? We need to take the entire family someday," Rafi suggested.

"Uh, we'll see," Mitch said.

It was Rafi's treat, so he paid the entry fee and continued through the gate. About a mile down the narrow road, they began their descent into the canyon.

"Wow, this is incredible! Are you kidding me? I never gave this place a thought!" said Mitch.

"Yeah, I think the hike will be great. I'm sure you'll really enjoy it," replied Rafi.

"How long is the trail?" asked Mitch.

"The Lighthouse Trail is about six miles round-trip. Should take us about three hours or so. Our timing is perfect. We'll easily be back at the car by dusk," Rafi predicted.

He carefully steered the Audi A-6 down the mile-long steep grade as he and Mitch took in the sights. Once they got to the canyon floor, the road wound along the bottom, taking them past the Trading Post and a few campgrounds and picnic areas. After the second designated river crossing, Rafi drove by the parking area for the Lighthouse Trail.

"I think you just passed it," Mitch informed his friend.

"No, it's OK. All the trails are interconnected. We're going to start at the Capital Peak Trail. The parking area should be just ahead," Rafi explained.

Seconds later he turned right, drove a few hundred yards, and pulled into a gravel lot that abutted the road. He parked next to another vehicle, just left of the Capital Peak Mountain Bike Trailhead sign.

Reading the thermometer prominently displayed next to the trail map, Rafi said, "What a fabulous day for a hike. The weather is perfect, seventy degrees, bright sunshine, gentle breezes."

Rafi popped opened the trunk, Mitch grabbed two water bottles from the cooler, and they were quickly on their way.

"Great idea, Rafi! Really, really nice! Look at the canyon walls. I can't believe we've lived this close and have never been here. It's only forty minutes away," Mitch commented.

At this juncture, the trail was mostly level as it snaked its way around the bottom of the canyon. The men had walked nearly half a mile, hardly speaking, taking in the canyon's beauty. They stopped for a quick breather. While taking a photo with his phone, Rafi explained his earlier visit. "We've only been here and Caprock Canyon once ourselves. We didn't hike any trails. Occasionally, we would get out and walk up to the viewing areas to get a better look and take pictures. But that is nothing like this. This is fantastic, being right in the thick of it. We really need to bring the wives and kids, especially now that soccer's over. I've been told there are some rustic stone cabins you can rent. We should check it out before we leave if we have enough time."

Taking a sip from his water bottle, Mitch agreed, and a moment later they were meandering around another sweeping bend in the trail that offered a new perspective of the canyon.

They approached a man and a woman coming back down the trail. Staying near the right edge of the path, Rafi nodded to the couple and said, "Good afternoon."

"Hello," said Mitch.

The couple only mumbled, "Hello," and walked on past them, making little eye contact.

Mitch laughed, "They were real friendly, huh? I was going to ask them to take a picture of us, but . . ."

"Ah, forget it," said Rafi.

But Mitch didn't want to forget what he noticed: the couple's apprehension once they saw Rafi's medium brown skin. "Rafi, look at this world we live in! This place is beautiful! God created it, and He made it for everyone. All of us. And you know what, I don't believe this nonsense that Islam is a religion of hate, war, and intolerance. It didn't become the second largest religion in the world by espousing violence against those who won't convert. Good gracious, there are over one and a half billion Muslims in the world and less than fourteen million Jews!"

"It's amazing. I bet few people realize that. Think about it, for every Jew, there are over a hundred Muslims in the world. And this whole notion that the majority of Muslims support violence against other religious sects is absolute nonsense," Rafi added.

Wanting to emphasize that economic opportunity was the key to peace, Rafi asked Mitch, "Have you ever heard of the Blue Mosque?"

"It's in Istanbul, right?" Mitch clarified.

"Yes, it has over 20,000 cobalt-blue Iznik handmade ceramic tiles forming more than fifty different tulip designs. That's how it got its name. Mosques don't have paintings and art depicting saints and prophets. Everything is geometric motifs and calligraphy. The patterns and motifs are spellbinding. And the calligraphy is usually excerpts from the Koran or quotes from Muhammad. Did you know that one of the last scrawls visitors see when they leave the Blue Mosque are words from the Prophet? 'A merchant is the beloved of God,'" [19] Rafi explained.

"For the majority, it's all about economics, just like we discussed last night," said Mitch.

"Yes, it is, even in Islam; and regardless of cultures, the same problem exists around the world," answered Rafi as he glanced back at the trail behind him.

Mitch noticed Rafi's instinctive uneasy peek behind them before he asked, "And what problem is that?"

"An intense minority dictating to an unorganized majority. Remember last night, how I referred to Binyamin Netanyahu's Likud party basically being the equivalent of the Tea Party here? All autocrats, never willing to compromise," Rafi stated.

"Uh, huh," responded Mitch.

Rafi continued, "I agree with what you said earlier. God created this world for everyone. You understand like I do, the vast majority of Muslims, just like Jews and Christians, are moderates, not zealots of the hard right. It's the same problem across the world where an intense minority is dictating to the masses. Look at the Saud family. Despite King Abdullah donating $20 billion to start a science and technology university, they are arguably one of the most corrupt regimes in existence. Depending upon who you believe, there are approximately 5,000 Saudi Princes along with as many as twenty to thirty thousand members within the families—all claiming royalty and getting huge monthly stipends for nothing. That number will only continue to explode. Fifteen of the nineteen hijackers from 9/11 were from Saudi Arabia, not to mention their mastermind, Osama bin Laden. The dominant faith in the kingdom is Wahhabi, an ultra-conservative branch of the Sunni faith."

"You're Sunni, correct?" asked Mitch.

"Yes, I am. And I promise you, the vast majority are moderates. It's the overzealous factions of the Wahhabis from Saudi Arabia who should be feared, not the majority of Shia and Sunnis throughout the rest of the world. Not to say there are not radicals amongst them as well, because there are, but the Wahhabis are the equivalent of the ultra-orthodox Jews. And the Tea Party here is the caffeine- and calorie-free version of those two sects, derived from the same origin—extremism. They are one and the same, just camouflaged in different cloaks," asserted Rafi.

"Rafi, that's insane! You can't compare the Haredim living in Israel and the U.S. to the most radical factions of Islam! You don't constantly hear the leaders of the ultra-conservative Jews screaming, 'Death to all Muslims,'" snapped Mitch.

"Well, I didn't quite . . . ," Rafi tried to say.

"And comparing them to the Tea Party is just despicable!" claimed Mitch.

"I did say they were the caffeine- and calorie-free version," Rafi said, trying to lighten his stance. He attempted to continue, but Mitch cut him off again.

"Look, neither group is nearly as extreme as the most radical factions of Islam. Yet, the truth is, as the Haredim slowly integrate back into mainstream society, the tension between the common citizen and the ultras only intensifies. And with their much higher birthrates, I think the Haredim will only continue to aggressively pursue their agenda of instituting more stringent religious observances on everyone," stated Mitch.

"The world is getting stranger and stranger. Who could have predicted after the Arab Spring Egypt would elect the Muslim Brotherhood? Even Turkey is now growing more conservative, while Saudi Arabia is actually beginning to moderate," expressed Rafi.

"Well, America is definitely moving back to the center," declared Mitch.

"How can you say that? Four years ago, the United States almost had the equivalent of Mahmoud Ahmadinejad for Vice President," argued Rafi.

"Whoa! Whoa, Rafi! You're doing it again! You're comparing Sarah Palin to Ahmadinejad? Are you trying to get yourself deported?" wondered Mitch.

"I'm not backing down this time, Mitch. Hear me out," said Rafi.

"Well?" Mitch asked.

Rafi went on to defend his comment, "Both were former mayors."

"You can't even call that an analogy! That's asinine, Rafi," retorted Mitch.

Rafi grumbled, "Can we agree both are populists?"

"Go on," as Mitch listened.

"Ahmadinejad routinely taunts the wealthy clerics and opposition politicians. Palin does the same thing. She taunts Obama and the Democrats—belittles them with her rhetoric as if they are not as saintly as the Republicans and she. Maybe the Democrats are corrupt, but are they worse than her own party? Both Palin's and Ahmadinejad's spiels are routinely nothing more than circular arguments about good and evil, with little to no facts. Each tends to answer questions with questions, and then mock the blue-blooded and those with higher education. Most importantly, both cater to their core constituencies with little regard for other philosophies. For instance, Ahmadinejad enacted numerous redistribution policies to placate the poor, and then rolled back many reforms previously implemented by the moderates. The simple people, often the most religious, loved it, while the majority hated it!" Rafi explained.

"What did he roll back? What did he do that was so bad?" asked Mitch.

"Even before he was president, while he was mayor of Tehran, he did several things. In municipal buildings, the lunatic segregated elevators for men and women and forced all male city employees to grow beards and wear long sleeve shirts. [20] But what really caused extreme resentment was what he did after he won the presidency. First, he banned western music and closed most western fast-food restaurants. Then he allowed the Basij to roam the streets to crack down on dress codes. With the mullahs' support, the volunteer militia harassed, detained, and arrested well over a hundred thousand people. The government then confiscated satellite dishes to prevent access to the western media. [21] What appeared to be the final straw was when he began to suppress opposition and intimidate rivals, often using the Basij as his henchmen. That's when the mass public became irate. That's why there was so much revolt during the 2009 election. Now do you know why the majority, the moderates, hate him?" Rafi instructed.

Their pace began to slow as the path began a modest but steady incline. The added exertion only increased Mitch's anger about the current situation right here in the Panhandle, in fact, the entire state of Texas.

"I understand why the majority hate Ahmadinejad. It's like Iran is going back in time. And I see an analogy right here in Texas. At least relative to many other states," revealed Mitch.

"How's that?" asked Rafi.

Mitch then lambasted Texas state officials. "Instead of easing drug laws, in particular marijuana, some jurisdictions are increasing the fines and jail terms. It's ludicrous! The war on drugs has been an adjunct failure. Of all people, Rick Perry should know that. He has a damn war raging on his border that has resulted in tens of thousands of deaths! Hell, a few years ago a consulting firm that advises large corporations on international travel rated Mexico more dangerous to travel than Iraq or Afghanistan. Why? Because supplying drugs to the U.S. is so lucrative. The Mexican drug cartels will stop at nothing. They've become some of the most ruthless organizations in the world, and yet the American people continue to turn their heads. Remember the outrage when the four American captives were beheaded and their torsos were hung from a bridge in Iraq? We labeled the Iraqi people savage dogs. Yet this type of violence occurs routinely in Mexico, a nation over 80 percent Roman Catholic. Where's the outrage when it's right on the American border?" asked Mitch

"Because the people dying are Mexicans, not Americans," suggested Rafi in a cynical tone.

"That's not entirely true! Several hundred Americans involved in the drug trade have been tortured and brutally killed. Maybe people think they got what they deserved. But several U.S. officials working to stop the traffickers have been tortured and killed, plus numerous innocent bystanders have died as well," claimed Mitch.

"What can you do when there are tens of billions of dollars to be made selling drugs, and people are willing to do anything, including die, for a slice of that?" asked Rafi.

"For one thing, reform our drug laws and solve two issues at once. We need to start with marijuana. Make it legal, regulate it, and take the market away from the bad guys. That right there should put a dent in the violence. Plus, it will solve one of our biggest issues at home as well," argued Mitch.

"They'll just kill each other over the next new drug. Then what, continue legalizing more and more drugs? Why don't we just put twenty different brands of crack behind the counter at every local convenience store? That will do the country a lot of good," challenged Rafi.

"Agh, I don't know. But the current policies have failed all the way around," offered Mitch.

"Well, what will legalizing marijuana solve here in the U.S.?" asked Rafi.

"It will at least end the needless arrests and convictions of so many people over a victimless crime, that's what. It's not crack, let alone alcohol. Do you know what the typical penalty for one marijuana cigarette is for a juvenile in Texas? A year probation, monthly drug tests, dozens of hours of community service, and a thousand dollar fine. And don't forget about all the attorney fees. Between the fines and the criminal records, these kids get so far behind the eight-ball over something so minor, they just go into a shell. The whole process is demoralizing the lower and middle class youth of today while the rich kids often get off with no jail time or record. It's another form of class warfare. It's crazy! And it's all supported by Rick Perry and the radical right, trying to impose their ideals on society. It's not 1980 anymore. Views have changed. I'll bet if you took a vote, the majority of people would be outraged by that penalty and, in fact, would support out-and-out legalization of marijuana. Again, like you've mentioned before, it's a radical minority swaying enough moderates to dictate to the majority. They have to be stopped!" Mitch answered, nostrils flaring.

"You're downright angry about this," replied Rafi.

"You're damn right I am. My god, America has 5 percent of the world's population, yet nearly 25 percent of world's prisoners. [22] And we're the land of the free? Since the mid '80s, when America was in line with rest of the world with percentage of people in prison relative to total population, we've increased the percentage of people incarcerated sevenfold. Mostly due to the war on drugs! Sevenfold! That makes no social sense and is killing us economically," declared Mitch.

"Was it Reagan who declared the war on drugs?" asked Rafi.

"No, but it's Reagan's philosophy of severely punishing users, a policy still in effect. That's the main reason we have this mess today. The drug problem has been going on for over a century. Nixon coined the term 'war on drugs' and implemented measures to combat both supply and demand. It failed miserably. Then Reagan came to the conclusion that fighting the supply side was useless, so he enacted a 'zero tolerance' policy, severely punishing those convicted, believing tough laws would intimidate potential users. That's why our prison population is so large. It's a travesty, especially for the minorities who have been jailed at an alarming rate. It was great to see a state like Colorado lead the way toward legalization. If it had been California, everyone would have said, 'Typical California liberals with no morals'. With new leadership, maybe Texas could lead the south out of the 1950s, but it won't be in my lifetime," Mitch complained.

"You know there are rumors of a new movement to turn Texas from red to blue, don't you?" asked Rafi.

"What? That's crazy. That will never happen, impossible," responded Mitch.

"A source told me a grassroots effort called 'Battleground Texas' will soon be formed and that Jeremy Bird, founder of the consulting firm 270 Strategies, will play a pivotal role. He was Obama's National Field Director. You know, it wasn't that long ago Texas voted Democrat," Rafi informed Mitch.

"I don't care how long ago it was. Texas voting Democrat is light years away," predicted Mitch.

"Mitch, you're pretty jaded. I don't think you've thought this through. The demographic swing and current lack of voter turnout in Texas is strongly favoring the Democrats. Crazier things have happened," advised Rafi.

They continued their journey to the Lighthouse Rock Formation. The path had leveled off again, and the walk was relatively easy when Rafi turned the discussion back to how Palin was like Ahmadinejad.

"You know, while Ahmadinejad was mayor of Tehran, he lived in his family's modest house, a small house in a middle-class neighborhood. When leaders visited, they would sit on the floor and eat. Even world leaders he treated like common men, not the powers that they were. His constituency loved that! When elected president, he wanted to remain there, but security forced him to move because they knew so many despised him. [23] In multiple instances, he cut back or eliminated many of the amenities of the presidency, so he and his family could live a very ordinary life, void of greed and selfishness," Rafi explained.

"I still don't see the comparison to Palin," countered Mitch.

"Palin does, or did, the same type of thing before she cashed in on her popularity. She represented herself as the grizzly mom who managed a dual-income household, attended hockey games, hunted, and prayed every day. She represented the white middle and lower classes who sensed their way of life was slowly eroding away, especially in the south. She kept portraying that she was just like them. And in many cases, she was," Rafi claimed.

"And how's that?" asked Mitch.

"She speaks in simple metaphors and seeks the lowest common denominator. Her educational background is a joke! Her knowledge, or lack thereof, of history, geography, world leaders, and policy is pitiful. She carries on about freedom, following the constitution according to her interpretation, glamorizing guns, and brazenly tries to intimidate those who oppose her. Remember her tweet, 'Commonsense Conservatives & lovers of America: "Don't retreat, Instead – RELOAD!" Pls see my Facebook page.' [24] Or during a campaign rally, she whipped up the crowd, telling them 'Obama launched his political career in the living room of a domestic terrorist . . . He is palling around with terrorists . . . Obama is not a man who sees America the way you and I see America.' [25] You don't consider that highly inflammatory rhetoric? After she and McCain lost the election, she posted on her sarahpac website a list of Democrats who voted for Obamacare. She didn't just post their name and districts; she superimposed crosshairs over their names like they were target practice. [26] One of the congresswomen on the list, Gabrielle Giffords, was eventually shot. Without a doubt, Palin was the most polarizing, unqualified candidate in history. McCain's selection was reckless. He really did this country a disservice," contended Rafi.

"When Bush ran for president and couldn't name several world leaders, he stated it was only important they knew *his* name," added Mitch.

"Again, the height of American arrogance; however, Bush was distinctively more qualified than Palin," countered Rafi.

"Well, I definitely don't agree with you regarding Palin being our Ahmadinejad. You're way off target, Rafi, and in fact way out of line," argued Mitch.

Not willing to give in, Rafi continued to make his case. "You have to admit both are more than a little frightening. Ahmadinejad calls for the annihilation of Israel. Palin has been quoted, '. . . that our leaders, our national leaders, are sending [U.S. soldiers] out on a task from God. That's what we have to make sure that we're praying for, that there is a plan and that that plan is God's plan.' [27] She has been associated with some pretty fringe religious leaders, focused on training a young army to become an Armageddon-ready military with a divine mandate to physically impose Christian 'dominion' on non-believers of the United States and the world. [28] That's scary, like she was praying for the end of the time. You don't think that's intimidating to the Muslim world, especially the radicals looking for any argument to stir up the disenfranchised for jihad?"

Starting to understand a little better Rafi's rational why the Muslim world would be alarmed by the hard right wing, Mitch tried to soften Rafi's perception. "Seriously, I think you've taken Palin out of context. I think maybe it's just her snarky tone."

"It's a matter of perspective, Mitch. Hell, the liberals and moderates fear Palin right here in America. You don't think the rhetoric of Palin and the hard right doesn't concern the moderate Muslims around the world?" Rafi said before he made one last point. "I truly believe that the majority of people, regardless of religion, believe if they live a good life, their success on earth will lead to their vision of heaven later. It's radicals on the fringes we must contain. I'm not sure if Ahmadinejad is blustering or not when he calls for Israel to be wiped off the face of the earth. Yet, I'm not sure about Palin or Michelle Bachmann, either, when they use the rhetoric they use. The problem is all three believe in their own country's exceptionalism, predicated on religion. And that leads to conflict."

"Palin's rhetoric is super-aggressive and, no doubt, offensive to many, especially to the president," Mitch agreed.

"It's the year 2012. We have enough economic problems to resolve. Adding inflammatory religious and cultural rhetoric only adds fuel to the fire. And her lack of respect toward the president is a disgrace. Case closed. She is no different from Ahmadinejad—a polarizing, antagonistic, and dangerous public figure," argued Rafi.

"All right, all right, maybe she is Ahmadinejad-lite," conceded Mitch, acknowledging Rafi's earlier analogy of the Tea Party being the caffeine- and calorie-free version of the hard right in Saudi Arabia and Israel.

A moment later, Rafi and Mitch reached the landing that marked the final ascent to the Lighthouse Rock Formation. A bike stand stood before them, and a picnic table sat about fifteen feet to their right. There appeared to be a lightly traveled trail just beyond the picnic table. Between that and the bicycle stand, a wide rut carved into the landscape lay in front of them. Uncertain if it was the right track, the two looked around for a sign or indicator of which path to follow. There was none. The assortment of stones that had once lain in the form of two arrows pointing to the rugged channel were now scattered around the bike stand. The trail on the far right of the picnic table didn't seem right, so they walked back to the bike stand and studied the crude trail. A third trail that was off the beaten path was visible on their left, but it didn't seem right either. Compared to the other two options, the jagged rut was, by far, the most worn route, so they walked straight ahead.

Carefully, they advanced their way up the carved path. About thirty yards around a bend, the path's slope steepened dramatically. Rafi followed the footsteps of Mitch, making sure he didn't slip. The incline had several areas with loose stones, ruts, tree roots, and boulders to navigate. Without too much difficulty, the men reached the Palo Duro Canyon's most infamous setting.

"Rafi, we absolutely must bring the children here! This is magnificent!" proclaimed Mitch.

"Incredible! Sometimes we don't even see what's right in front of us, and it's flat! Forty-five minutes away! What have we been thinking?" asked Rafi.

"I guess we *haven't* been thinking," replied Mitch.

The gentlemen sat on a small wooden bench that was strategically located on a crest about a-hundred and fifty yards from the actual rock tower. The location provided visitors unobstructed views of both the formation and the canyon's beautiful colors below.

"I read in the pamphlet, the hike's elevation gain is 940 feet," Rafi informed his friend.

"That's a good hike! Look at the tower, how the wind and rain have shaped it. You said it's about three hundred feet tall?" asked Mitch.

"That's what it says in the brochure," answered Rafi.

"It's pretty imposing, like it is standing vigilant, keeping the canyon safe," suggested Mitch.

Content, they watched birds zip from tree to tree as they playfully chased one another. Off in the distance, they spotted a couple of vultures gliding over the canyon base. The scene was just what the men needed; something to awe them and relieve them from their daily burdens and worries of the future. Nearly thirty minutes passed with little discussion before Rafi looked at his watch. He knew it was time to go.

"Mitch, we better get moving, so we can make it back to the car by dusk," he said.

"I'm ready. This was perfect!" said Mitch.

The two of them carefully worked their way down the trail. Rafi led this time, stopping periodically to make sure Mitch kept his footing. They successfully made their way down the three-tenths of a mile slope and were again at the clearing where the bicycle stand and picnic table sat. They took in one last sweeping view before they began their two and a half mile trek back to the car. It wasn't long before they continued their conversation.

"You know what I admire most about you, Rafi?" asked Mitch.

"What's that, Mitch?" Rafi replied.

"Your confidence, your ability to speak and feel like you're an American citizen, even though you're not. I think you're much more in the spirit of what the founding fathers envisioned than many of the politicians are," complimented Mitch.

"Thanks, Mitch! I love the United States! While I'm not, I like to consider myself a citizen. The same as with Germany, Britain, Israel, China, India, Russia, Cuba . . . ," Rafi began to reply.

Perplexed, Mitch interrupted him. "What? What do you mean you're a citizen of China, Russia, and Cuba . . . Cuba?"

"Mitch, I've been fortunate to travel and live all over the world. I've seen a lot. I don't consider myself Pakistani. I consider myself a citizen of the world. That means Cuba too," Rafi explained.

"Why in the world would you want to be a citizen of Cuba? The Castro regime is a disgrace to human dignity. As far as I'm concerned, Cuba doesn't even exist," complained Mitch.

"So you turn your back on eleven million people residing right on your doorstep, ninety miles off your coast? What do you do, close your eyes and pretend they don't exist? What has fifty, sixty years of embargo accomplished?" Rafi wanted to know.

"We've kept them secluded, in poverty, so they can't spread communism," proclaimed Mitch.

"Little ol' Cuba spreading communism, sugar, and cigars around the world! Isolating them has benefited whom? Has it stopped the Castros from imposing their will on the country? It's the people who've suffered. The policies enacted decades ago are fruitless. Maybe it's those policies that have actually enabled the Castros to remain in power! The travel ban to Cuba? It's lunacy. The U.S. should lift the travel ban for everyone, with no restrictions, immediately. Can you imagine what the ripple effects could be if hundreds of thousands, possibly millions of Americans began traveling to Cuba? It might be like Facebook: instantly connecting everyone and letting the people decide. The monies spent there and the interaction between people would do more to promote capitalism and freedom than any policy employed, or I should say, not employed to date. It's time to move on. Cuba is not a threat to America!" Rafi reasoned.

"Are you crazy? If we let people travel freely to Cuba, they'll spend a bunch of money there, only further empowering the communist regime," argued Mitch.

"You mean instead of spending the money here? That's what this is all about. The tourism industry in Florida doesn't want any additional competition. Mitch, you can't have it both ways. Cuba already has a burgeoning tourism industry. It's our northern neighbors and European allies that account for the majority of two million-plus tourists that go to Cuba every year! Haven't sixty years been long enough to prove isolation doesn't work?

"It does work," Mitch voraciously replied.

"It's so hypocritical. The U.S. allows specific export products but outlaws any imports; thereby, keeping Cubans from competing against U.S. interests. Americans can travel to Iran and North Korea, two countries with far more oppressive policies and true threats to America, but not Cuba? That doesn't make any sense," Rafi argued.

Mitch shook his head in disagreement before saying, "We need to stay the course. It's only a matter of time before the Castros fall. Once they do, the remaining communist bastards won't be able to keep the people from overthrowing their dictatorship."

"How much longer are you going to wait? You're starting to sound like you belong to the Tea Party yourself. The policy is being dictated by a bunch of angry, old Cubans now protecting their interests in Florida. It's time to move on," Rafi declared again.

Frustrated with each other, the two stopped to look at a cactus plant near the edge of the trail. The contrasts of the plant were striking. Purplish in color, the cactus grew low to the ground. The plant's two small palms resembled the hands of a man once in prayer who had opened his hands and kept his wrists joined together. The palms were circular; the plant's flesh wrinkled, yet, smooth to the touch. Protruding from the pocked-marked flesh, thorns as sharp as a boar's tusk protected the plant.

Observing the plant for only a few seconds, they continued walking. Mitch tried to bolster his argument. "Technology, smart phones, the instantaneous transfer of information has and will continue to change the world. We keep seeing these uprisings; the ebbs and flows of a burgeoning democracy only to peter out or be squashed by a tyrant. The day is coming when regimes like Cuba and North Korea will no longer be able to withhold information from their people."

"The technology is already there. It's going to take interaction. Lay the groundwork. Make it a grassroots effort. That's how campaigns are won, Mitch. This is no different. We need to do the same thing around the world. Open up; promote hyper-interaction, cultural, and educational exchanges far more than we do now. That's how we can stimulate change. Why can't you see that?"

"You're wrong, Rafi. We need to continue to reward countries that promote democratic and free enterprise principles. To hell with the dictators and communists," Mitch continued to argue.

"Mitch! Agh! I don't understand you. You realize the drug war has been a complete failure for decades. So you support a new tact. Yet, with Cuba, you want to continue supporting the same failed policies. How can you support change in one but not the other?" asked Rafi.

"It's apples to oranges, Rafi. They're not the same. It's our drug culture that has sparked so much of the violence in Mexico. Cuba on the other hand is a self-imposed communist regime that needs to be isolated," argued Mitch.

"I guess the only thing we've agreed on is the majority of problems revolve around economics," Rafi stated, trying to find a common ground.

"Outside of the few radicals, yes, it's all about economics. Something you apparently know little about," cracked Mitch.

The two noticed a bench around the corner.

"You want to take a quick break at the bench ahead before we finish strong, my Tea Party friend?" asked Rafi.

"Sounds good to me. You know, Rafi, Bill Clinton still has two of the greatest catch-phrases in our generation," declared Mitch.

"And what are those?" asked Rafi.

Mitch replied, "Bill Clinton said, 'It's the economy, stupid.' [29] And it is. It's all about the economy."

"So, what's the second one?" asked Rafi.

Mitch proclaimed his favorite one was "People are more impressed by the power of our example rather than the example of our power." [30]

"Thanks for making my point, Mitch; I mean thank you, President Clinton. Yes, it's all about the power of example. Maybe we should be setting a few more," Rafi urged his Jewish friend.

"And what do you suggest, Rafi?" Mitch asked.

"How about ending Obama's drone reign of terror? His continued military activities inside a sovereign nation without the knowledge and consent of the ruling government are just one mishap away from an international crisis. I don't care if he got bin Laden or not. It's reckless," Rafi advocated.

Mitch could only clear his throat.

Sitting leisurely on the bench, both sipped from their water bottles. Mitch commented on the new appearances the canyon created as the light began to fade.

"It's beautiful. And coming back down the trail gives a whole new perspective. Look at that view of *Santana's Face*! You can really see the profile in the rock formation much better from this angle," added Rafi.

The two sat quietly for another moment. A break in the relentless bantering was needed.

Wanting to lighten things up, Mitch began to reminisce about their friendship. "Remember when we met at that open house three years ago?"

Rafi laughed, "Yeah, I was complaining about being ostracized when you told me, 'Well, I'm a fucking Jew, not much better.' I still laugh about that moment. And then the luck of the boys being drafted on the same team. What were they called? The Blue Diamonds?" asked Rafi.

Now, Mitch laughed. "The Blue Flames is what they were called. God that was fun!"

"It started a pretty incredible run! Seven straight championships!" added Rafi.

"Remember the only goal Jeffrey scored his entire career?" inquired Mitch.

"I think so. I do remember how excited he was," replied Rafi.

"You don't remember how he scored?" Mitch asked.

"No, I don't think so," responded Rafi.

"Mo had already scored a bunch of goals. Whenever a game was in hand, he never stopped trying to pass to teammates, even if he had wide open shots. Yet, more often than not, they would miss. But he never stopped passing, so others could feel the joy of scoring. He was so unselfish. I think he got more pleasure out of watching a teammate score than scoring himself," praised Mitch.

"I have to admit, he's a pretty good player and a great teammate. I'm very proud of him," confided Rafi.

"A great teammate? You really *don't* remember how Jeffrey scored that one time?" Mitch asked more excitedly.

"No, what happened?" asked Rafi.

"Mo had tried to pass to Jeffrey numerous times during the year, and Jeffrey could never control the ball to shoot and score. One time, out of pure luck, Jeffrey was standing dead center about five feet from the goal. Mo gained control of the ball and weaved through a couple players along the goal line, giving him a clear shot to the goal. He just had to tap it in the corner. Instead of kicking it into the open net, he kicked it right at Jeffrey who wasn't ready. Mo did it on purpose. The ball ricocheted off Jeffrey's shin and went right into the goal. Jeffrey never even knew what hit him!" Mitch broke out in laughter.

Cracking a smile, Rafi said, "I remember Mo running over to Jeffrey and lifting him up as Jeffrey raised his arms. I do remember now! That was something special."

"Your son is very special," added Mitch.

While Mitch took another drink of water, Rafi asked, "Is Jeffrey's ankle better?"

"Huh? I'm not sure what you're talking about," Mitch stated.

"He had to come out of the game yesterday," Rafi replied, a little curious why Mitch had forgotten his son's injury.

Mitch again burst out in laughter and shook his head. "He wasn't even hurt! Can you believe that?" laughed Mitch.

"What do you mean? Now that I think about it, I don't remember him limping last night at dinner, yet, he could hardly walk after the game. I feel bad. If I would've known, I would've invited the boys to join us," responded Rafi.

"It's OK, I considered it too. I thought it was best I came first, see what it was like," replied Mitch.

"Well, I'm confused. What happened to Jeffrey's ankle?" Rafi wanted to know.

"You know how each kid has to play at least twenty minutes per game?" asked Mitch.

"Yeah," responded Rafi.

"Well, Jeffrey wanted to win so badly, he faked his injury, so he wouldn't have to play. He thought he might cost them the game. That the team would have a better chance if he was hurt," explained Mitch.

"What! Are you kidding me?" asked Rafi.

"No, I'm not. I had no clue. I thought he was really hurt, Dena did too. Then to think he was smart enough to do it, literally in the very first minute of his playing time is just hilarious!" shouted Mitch nearly in tears from laughter.

"So, the whole time he was crying, holding his ankle, he was OK?" Rafi asked in disbelief.

"Yes, the whole time on the sidelines when he acted like he was dying. It really became somewhat embarrassing. Dena and I about went over to the bench to tell him to quit whining and toughen up. He even faked the injury during the celebration and the entire way home. We had even started questioning ourselves, maybe he was truly hurt badly, and we should take him to the hospital for x-rays. We didn't know until a half-hour later when he rumbled down the stairs like nothing had happened. Dena and I asked him what was going on; he could barely walk up the stairs thirty minutes earlier. That's when he confessed. Dena and I didn't even know what to say," answered Mitch.

"What *did* you say?" asked Rafi.

"We're glad you're ok," answered Mitch before he continued, "Dena and I still don't know what to say. I mean it's true. The team was much better without him on the field. It probably made all the difference in the game. Probably why we won," finished Mitch.

"Those two are so different, yet, so much alike. What a great kid!" Rafi complimented.

"He is. I'm very proud of him as well. He basically humiliated himself, crying so much just so the team could win," replied Mitch.

The discussion continued when Rafi mentioned something that had been on his mind for nearly two years, "Aasia and I have always wondered but didn't want to ask."

"What's that?" responded Mitch.

"The league conducts a draft every season. How in the world did they wind up on the same team seven straight seasons?" inquired Rafi.

The question drew even more laughter from Mitch. "Remember, I'm in the *'Jew'*-elry business. After the initial season, I bribed the coach who drafted your son to take my son in the second to last round," responded Mitch.

"Wait! How did you know which coach selected Mo?" asked Rafi.

"The league's director has purchased several items from me in the past. Each draft he would call me and provide me the name and number of the coach who drafted your son. After the third season, it became common knowledge amongst the coaches that whoever won the draft, not only won the title but would be a recipient of a nice set of earrings for drafting my son. Hell, one coach who drafted Mo twice asked for a necklace the second time," laughed Mitch.

Rafi just laughed and laughed and laughed. "I guess that's proof you value our friendship," stated Rafi.

"No, not really, I just wanted Jeffrey to win," teased Mitch.

"I can't believe you pulled that off seven straight seasons!" said Rafi.

"Well, there was a hitch. It ended up costing me several other items as well," Mitch claimed.

"What do you mean?" asked Rafi.

"Remember that one coach I told you I didn't like?" asked Mitch.

"Yeah," responded Rafi.

"The bastard was our coach in the third season. In our fifth season, the fall of 2011, the jerk called me in the sixth round and told me he was going to draft Jeffrey the next round. I was like, 'What? Why would you do that? He stinks!' And then he said, 'Unless . . . um,' and the phone went quite for a second. Then the son of a bitch demanded a necklace, not to draft Jeffrey. I had to bribe him the next season as well. So, not only was I giving nice jewelry to coaches to draft my son, I had to start paying off Joe Delaney not to draft my son!" exhorted Mitch.

"Damn, they're not even teenagers yet!" howled Rafi.

"Well, I got the bastard back, sort of. The coach who drafted Mo the last time received a call from me immediately. I made it worth his while to draft Jeffrey in the second round before Joe could extort from me again. Of course, it almost cost the team the championship, losing the caliber of a player you can get in the second round, but I guess Jeffrey faking his injury was poetic justice," explained Mitch.

"Especially since we just beat Delaney in the championship game! That is poetic justice!" Rafi exclaimed, astounded by the whole story. "That's hysterical!"

The two had been chatting for fifteen minutes and lost track of time. The sun was quickly setting, and they knew they had better be on their way.

Mitch looked at Rafi and said, "Let's move, partner!" Seconds later the men were on their way back to Rafi's car.

Life and Death are One; Right and Wrong are the Same

Armstrong County; a Few Miles North of Historical Marker on Texas Highway 207; Sunday November 18, 2012; 4:30 PM

Mr. Lin and two of his colleagues were waiting for the chief when he arrived at the favored location. The Houston businessman had tried calling him a few times on Saturday, but Thompson ignored his attempts. With the $60,000 truck impounded, the chief attempted to stall as long as possible. Thompson realized he could no longer avoid the inevitable tongue-lashing when he answered his mobile phone earlier that morning. The call was from an unknown number, but no doubt from one of Lin's cohorts. The message was clear.

"Mr. Thompson, four thirty this afternoon. The boar expects you to be prompt."

The chief bristled; he despised being subservient to anyone, let alone a damn Asian. "If he's so heated about me being in debt nearly 150 head of hog over the past few months, how infuriated will he be about a $60,000 truck he'll never see again?"

With no defined road leading to the clearing, Thompson hesitantly coasted over the cracked dirt and weaved between the native trees and brush, then past a simple windmill. He continued on until he entered an oval clearing approximately 250 yards off Texas Highway 207, just south of Claude, Texas. Thompson recognized the clearing had a thick border of trees surrounding it, making it fairly isolated. But he still wondered why Lin had selected this obscure site for his sporadic rendezvous. This would be their fifth or sixth meeting since operations commenced less than two years ago. Yet, the chief was still trying to interpret Lin's body language and use of words.

Thompson proceeded across the clearing and angled right toward the Lincoln Town Car. Two men abruptly exited the front doors of the vehicle and moved in opposite directions. He watched as the driver gravely planted himself a few feet in front of the driver's side headlight while the second man stepped toward the rear of the vehicle on the passenger side.

In typical fashion, using intimidation to overcome his fears, Thompson brazenly rolled to a stop just a few feet short of the driver's knees, leaving the cars parked nose to nose as if they were on a collision course. While the chief switched off his ignition, the other associate opened the door for Mr. Lin, and Lin stood outside the Lincoln glaring at the chief. Feeling the piercing look, Thompson immediately regretted he had irked the scrawny, slope-eyed tyrant.

Despite the fact he was the chief of police, Lin intimidated him, and they both knew it. Thompson wasn't sure if it was Lin's presence or the aura of menace surrounding the car that was unsettling, or both. Bathed in black, the Town Car Signature Limited Edition radiated a wickedness he had never encountered before. Thompson took a deep breath then opened his door and warily acknowledged the three.

Lin mentioned nothing to Thompson regarding the audacity he displayed blocking the Town Car as they convened in a small nook of the clearing. He just chuckled to himself, knowing all would be resolved by meeting's end.

Patiently waiting as Thompson slowly made his way to the front of his car, Lin welcomed the chief, "Ah, Mr. Thompson, good afternoon."

"Gentlemen, what brings you to the canyon on such short notice?" Thompson responded as he nodded to the three men. Neither of Lin's colleagues acknowledged the chief's greeting.

"You didn't return my calls yesterday, Mr. Thompson. I was concerned," replied the Houstonian.

"It's been unusually busy the past few days. We've had a number of unexplained occurrences in and around the canyon," claimed the chief.

"Yes, Mr. Thompson, I am aware. I have been informed that a couple of hunters are missing. Strange, strange indeed," commented Lin.

"It's unfortunate," Chief Thompson stated.

"And my truck?" asked Lin.

"Pardon me?" Thompson responded acting naïve.

"The $60,000 truck that is now impounded?" Lin calmly asked.

"Oh, I'm not sure what we're going to do about that, yet. I did as you told me back in January when we purchased it. I paid cash and put it in my most trusted associate's name. But unfortunately, he is one of the two who are missing," the chief explained.

"One of the two?" asked Mr. Lin.

"Yes, I don't know the second man," replied the chief. Lin's accomplices exchanged glances as they knew the businessman didn't appreciate being lied to.

"Tell me, Mr. Thompson. What has prompted the rumors in the media about these men you speak of possibly staging their disappearances?" Lin asked sternly. "Worse yet, that they might have been killed due to a business deal gone sour?"

"I'm not sure what you want me to do," the chief blustered. "I have no control over the media." He had expected Lin to become agitated.

"I see, you cannot control the media or locate the men," Lin calmly replied. He put both hands behind his back and said, "Follow me, Mr. Thompson."

The two henchmen waited for the chief to move before they followed. Thompson reluctantly trailed Lin to the rear of his Town Car.

"Mr. Thompson, do you drink alcohol?" asked Lin.

Surprised by the question, Thompson hesitated before he pointed to himself and restated the question, "Do *I* drink alcohol?"

Now irritated, Lin asked, "Why do you only repeat my question, Mr. Thompson?"

"I did when I was younger but have not in many, many years," answered the chief.

"And why is that, Mr. Thompson?" his boss asked.

Not sure where Lin was going with this line of questioning, the chief stated, "I'm an Evangelical."

"What does that really mean?" asked Lin.

"Through God's mercy, I'm a born-again Christian. I no longer need alcohol. It's my Lord and Savior Jesus Christ who provides me eternal strength," Thompson professed.

"I see," Lin acknowledged. "I am pleased you are of good health," Lin commended, "That your body is pure."

The chief was confused. "I appreciate your concern, Mr. Lin, but I'm not sure what this has to do with business." Thompson could now sense a storm brewing inside of Lin.

"Should alcohol be legal? What about marijuana or selling wild boar meat?" Lin probed.

Getting perturbed himself, Thompson stated, "Of course, alcohol should be legal. Selling wild boar is, and should be as well. But marijuana, never!"

"Never?" Lin confirmed.

"It's the gateway drug! If we eliminate pot, we could win the war on drugs. I attempt to make an example out of every drug arrest I make, Mr. Lin. I push for the maximum sentence!"

"Interesting!" replied Lin.

Lin stood silent for a minute as he rubbed his chin between his thumb and index finger. He was a slender man, five feet ten inches tall with a few days of stubble on top of his head. He contemplated his next line of reasoning.

"Here is my concern, Mr. Thompson," he began, "to sell wild boar meat legally, you must trap the animal alive; transport it to a government-regulated swine-holding facility for it to be inspected, which takes days; then, if healthy, ship the god-damn thing to one of only two facilities in the state with the licenses to process the meat. How fucking inefficient is that?" Lin asked.

"The animals *are* known to spread many diseases," the chief stated.

"I have committed to deliver large quantities of meat each month all over Asia, Mr. Thompson. Every time you short me what I have contracted for, every fucking time, I have to purchase it from the god-damn regulated facilities at a cost multiple times what I can achieve through our operations. I must have Texas hogs; it is my contractual obligation. So every time you short me, you are robbing me of my profit margin. Is that clear, Mr. Thompson?" asked Lin.

"Yes, I understand," the chief replied derisively.

The adopted Houstonian wanted to make sure the native Texan knew how much he had loathed him for nearly two years now.

"Do you recall our last conversation?" asked Lin.

"Yes, I do," replied Thompson.

"What did I call you, Mr. Thompson? What did I say you were?" asked Lin.

"I reckon I don't remember," said the chief.

Lin muttered to himself, "Motherfucker!"

"I called you a wild fucking pig!" Lin reminded the chief.

"Um, yes, I remember now."

"You know what else? You are a hypocrite too! I think I need to make an example out of you," claimed Lin as his voice grew louder.

"Excuse me?" Chief Thompson asked again.

"I 'reckon' I need to make an example out of you! Just like you and all your god-damn redneck kin do each and every day. You aggressively enforce drug laws, in particular marijuana, when the user knows the risks. Yet, you assist me in selling potentially tainted meat to unsuspecting consumers in my homeland!" Lin snapped.

Thompson interrupted, "But you said . . ."

"Shut the fuck up! You disgust me, Mr. Thompson! Even though you say you are sober, you advocate alcohol then harass and inflict your morality on those who smoke a weed far less dangerous than alcohol. It is a statistical fact, Mr. Thompson, drunk driving and the resultant fatalities drop significantly with the legalization of marijuana. [31] So your morality is responsible for thousands of deaths each year, you fucking pig! I am going to make an example out of you, like you try to do with the harmless pot smokers of the world, like me!"

"What does marijuana have to do with anything? I don't understand. You told me the meat we deliver to Asia is far better than the domestic food they have access to," claimed Thompson.

"You're the chief of police, and yet, you're such a fool, Mr. Thompson. Weed is illegal, yet, Serenity and all the synthetic spices that are far more dangerous are sold at convenience stores across the nation. As you poison your youth because of your ignorance and corruption protecting entrenched interests, you purposely do the same with my homeland—selling uninspected wild boar meat, knowing full well we do not have the rules and regulations to protect the masses like Americans do," declared Lin.

"What do ya mean, you're goin' to make an example out of me?" the chief nervously asked Lin.

"Come with me," Lin said as he began walking toward the tree line. Stunned, Thompson hadn't budged when Lin turned and said, "I suggest you follow me, Mr. Thompson."

The chief apprehensively moved toward Lin. The two took another few steps when Lin stopped, commanded the chief to take five more steps past him, then stop and face him. Trembling, the Canyon, Texas, chief of police staggered six, seven paces before Lin warned him, "Do not try to run, Mr. Thompson."

The chief stopped and turned toward the men. He tried to breathe, but the sight of Lin's two assistants holding semi-automatic pistols compressed his lungs.

"Your car keys, Mr. Thompson, where are your car keys?" asked the man who only gave orders.

"In my car," the chief lied again.

Doubting him, Lin asked, "You are sure, Mr. Thompson?"

"Yes, they're in the ignition," Chief Thompson stuttered.

In reality, Lin didn't care. He wanted the car to be visible.

"Fine, Mr. Thompson," said the Asian.

"You can't kill me! I'm the chief of police!" threatened the vulnerable chief.

It was Lin's turn to ask sarcastically, "Pardon me?" knowing the chief had no chance to successfully draw his firearm.

"You can't kill me! The Texas Rangers will go to the depths of Hell to find you," asserted Thompson.

All three men from Houston snickered.

"Mr. Thompson, not only can I kill you, but I must, and I will. Put your hands behind your head and get down on your knees. Now!" snarled Lin.

"They'll get you, Mr. Lin!" the chief said as he put his hands behind his head then slowly bent into a crouched position. He tentatively placed his left knee on the unforgiving ground and then his right.

Lin glared at the pathetic wild pig on his knees; hands behind his head, eyes glazed and said, "Mr. Thompson, you will be another fine example for the rest of my organization."

"What do ya mean another example for your organization? Did you already kill Harden and Mahoney?" cried the chief.

"A few minutes ago, you claimed you did not know the second man, yet he did work for you, for me. But I already knew that. Like I said, you are such a fool, Mr. Thompson."

"There are none like the Texas Rangers! They will hunt you down and enjoy bringing a chink to justice!" threatened Thompson.

Lin laughed, "The Texas Rangers? Six of them work for me, plus several sheriffs, and two other police chiefs. There are as many corrupt officials here as there are anywhere else in the world, especially during a recession. I can assure you, Mr. Thompson, your sacrifice will not be in vain. Once your body is found, your fellow immoral lackeys will learn a valuable lesson—that I, Mr. Lin, hold everyone accountable. You have broken the eighth commandment. You are a sinner, Mr. Thompson."

"I don't want to die! Please! Please give me another chance. I can meet the quota!" begged the chief of police.

"Ah, I believe in second chances, Mr. Thompson, but not third. Now, you must die," Mr. Lin informed him.

"What did I do? I don't even know the eighth commandment!" claimed Thompson.

"I thought you said you were an Evangelical? And you do not even know the Ten Commandments? Would you like me to list them for you, Mr. Thompson?" asked Mr. Lin.

"I am! I am an Evangelical! I've been born again!" pleaded the devout Christian who had only read the first and last books of the Bible, Genesis and Revelations.

"Then I do not understand," claimed the Taoist.

"Please, don't kill me!" pleaded the chief again.

"As I said, you are a hypocrite, Mr. Thompson. You should be begging me to kill you, not spare your life. I just attended the funeral of an ex-business partner who died an untimely, but necessary death. The pastor repeatedly romanticized the notion of death, that the afterlife was much better than life here on earth. In fact, the pastor told the children of the deceased that if their father was given the choice, he would not choose to come back, even to see them. Strange. Strange indeed, this Christian philosophy of relishing death," lectured the man who neither feared nor desired death.

"I don't want to die! One of the Ten Commandments is 'Thou shalt not kill'," cried the man on his knees.

"Ah, the sixth commandment, my favorite. Taoism has its own proverb, Mr. Thompson. 'Life and death are one; right and wrong are the same.' [32] You truly are not born again," argued Mr. Lin.

Chief Thompson's hands never lost contact with his head as he gently inched them from the back to the side of his head, over his ears, then cheeks, finally melding into the prayer position, resting under his chin. Mr. Lin smirked at the pig who knelt before him, eyes closed.

Seconds passed; the chief's hands were now tightly clasped together, trembling at his chest, when the man who saw things from a different perspective said, "Mr. Thompson, I do appreciate that you have lived a clean life for so many years. It will, no doubt, help recoup some of my losses from the truck."

In horror, Chief Thompson opened his eyes and peered into Lin's cold black eyes before he screamed his last words, "No! No! Not my liver!"

Chief of Police's Nephew

Canyon City Police Department; Sunday, November 18, 2012; 4:55 P.M.

Dawson stood at his desk with Mills, writing on a whiteboard, desperately trying to determine a common theme, any clue to tie all the missing people together. The Plymouth van was stolen from Houston sixteen months ago. The Oklahoma plates and vehicle's state emissions safety check that Justo requested when they entered the country had both expired three months earlier. Nothing was found inside the van or the trailer with a name, number, or any type of identification. They did find the original owner of the trailer via the serial number, but the man had sold the twenty-year-old trailer five years after purchasing to a man in Norman, Oklahoma. The trailer's expired plates were then traced to a third owner in Tulsa who had been dead for several months.

The two young Mexican boys, known only as Juan and Carlos, had finally revealed their last name of Vasquez a few hours earlier, but six-year-old Juan insisted that their name was actually going to be Jiminez in a few weeks. Carlos, only five, didn't know who Jiminez was. For the detectives, it was a minor breakthrough, but they wanted far more. Child Protective Services, however, continued to urge caution and insisted on a methodical approach with the two young boys.

The detective and the head of CPS clashed late Saturday afternoon when she refused to let him speak with the boys, arguing, "Detective, I have a Ph.D. in cognitive psychology from the University of Texas, considered one of the finest programs in the country. I'll be damned if I'm going to let *you* tell me what is in the best interest of those children! You push them now, and you might, and let me emphasize *might*, get a few more nuggets of information, but at what cost? Trust me, give us some time to earn their trust and confidence. Let them adapt, and you will be rewarded with far more pertinent information that will not psychologically harm the boys but will actually benefit in their recovery."

A search was in the works for the boys' school. Investigators were obtaining enrollment information from every public school in Oklahoma. Considering it was early Sunday evening, he knew that it would probably be at least another twenty-four to forty-eight hours before he heard the results.

Earlier, Dawson had been relieved to see a search warrant for the motorhome on his desk. Although he knew it probably held little value, the opportunity to legally examine every inch of the vacant motorhome was better than nothing. Mills joined him on the assignment. It at least provided the second man's name, Lance A. Hart, also of Morristown, New Jersey. The detectives found a prescription bottle of Xanax in Kenneth McDonald's name and another for Lexapro in Lance Hart's name but little else. Both bottles did have the same prescribing doctor from the neighboring town of Basking Ridge, New Jersey. After thirty minutes of investigating, both detectives concluded the men had intended on returning to the motorhome, considering Dawson found a note near the prescription bottles to order refills of both medications on Wednesday, November fourteenth.

Dawson grew impatient as they had to wait for the same company who impounded the minivan and trailer two days earlier to send a wrecker capable of towing the motorhome back to Canyon. Standing outside the motorhome, the two discussed what little evidence they had besides a $60,000 truck with no lien, a Nissan Pathfinder driven by some college students, and a stolen Plymouth Van with a cargo trailer. On the way back to the station, the senior detective suggested the most intriguing clue was no lien on the truck.

"How could that be? How does someone like Harden have an extravagant truck and not have a lien?" Dawson pondered out loud.

"I'm wondering that too, Jim. The sad part is I'm quite confident Mrs. Harden has no idea either. It's certainly an area where we need to start diggin'. That was one of the finest trucks I've ever seen: rear dual wheels, a built in tool case, the fancy coolers, and water tank," responded Mills.

"They're up to no good. It had to be them who killed all those wild pigs. But they can't sell that meat, can they? Those hogs have to be inspected before they're slaughtered. Who would buy it without it being certified?" wondered Dawson. "Yet, you know what?"

"What's that?" asked Mills.

"Whatever they were up to, I don't think it had anything to do with their disappearance," Dawson speculated.

"I know. If it was just those two, it would have *everything* to do with their vanishing. But in this case, with seven others missin', I don't think it does either. Those two were undoubtedly up to no good at all, and that in itself is a whole 'nother crime," suggested Detective Mills.

During the drive back to town, Dawson received a phone call from Sarah, notifying him that she thought she had reached Amy's parents but wasn't sure. The phone had gone straight to voicemail that only provided the number she had dialed. She was an emotional wreck, and it took him five minutes to calm her down.

"I didn't want to leave a message, but I called two different numbers a whole bunch of times. I didn't know what to do," she cried.

"Sarah, it's OK. What are the numbers, and I'll try calling them," the detective asked her, not bringing up the fact she was never supposed to call them in the first place, but only provide him their number, so he could notify them.

Once off the phone with Sarah, the detective immediately called both numbers she gave him.

When each phone's voicemail greetings was the generic, "You have reached the Sprint voicemail box of . . ." and only provided the cell phone number and not the person's name, the detective understood Sarah's frustration.

"Why the hell do people do that? You can't leave a name? How do I know this is even the right number?" Seconds later, he left a brief message to the unidentified recipients to call him immediately.

The detective had called Victor earlier, but there was still little to no results back. When he began to vent, Victor went into the same old routine. "Between the budget cuts and it being a weekend, we are short-staffed. I am doing the best I can, detective," before abruptly terminating the call.

Dawson looked at his watch; it was 5:15 p.m. when he began another rant, this time against the chief. "You know what, Dan? I'm not sure this is even worth it anymore. We have a chief who, for some reason, is draggin' his feet in the biggest crisis this town has ever seen. He hired his racist, unprofessional asshole cousin, Barron. The whole force is talkin' nonstop among themselves with rumors flyin' every which way. And where in tarnation is he? Nowhere to be found! Won't pick up his phone or radio. I don't know if I want to be around when this whole thing blows up!"

Mills started to reply when Dawson's phone rang.

"Detective Dawson," he answered.

Panic-stricken on the other end of the line, a man said, "This is Charles Smith, Amy's father. Where is my daughter? What the hell is going on? I have all these crazy messages from some bumbling girl named Sarah."

"Mr. Smith, we're not sure at this time," Dawson answered before he briefed the father on everything they knew at this point.

The detective's explanation of the actions that had taken place so far outraged the father as he screamed into the phone, "Where the hell is the damn search and rescue team? What about helicopters? Has an Amber Alert been issued?"

The detective tried to calm the man to no avail.

"I will get results!" screamed the father as he promised to have his lawyer involved immediately. "The mayor of Canyon will be hearing about this the moment I get off the phone with my attorney!" he screamed some more before hanging up on Dawson.

The detective shook his head. The mayor was the chief of police's nephew.

Unclean

Lighthouse Trail; Sunday, November 18, 2012; 5:22 P.M.

As the season progressed and the weather moderated, the boars increased their daytime activity. Twenty minutes to sunset, the pack waited patiently for the men to begin moving again. The group had been stalking the humans since they had descended from the vantage point of the Lighthouse Rock Formation.

The men's extended rest, reminiscing about old times, allowed the predators to carefully survey the surrounding landscape. Positioned at the top of a gradual incline on the far side of the creek bed, the boars held every advantage. They had a direct line of sight to the men as they descended into the gully. The slight decline into the ravine would help build their momentum when they charged. And if the humans tried to run, the clearing of the dry creek bed would provide the boars ample opportunity to make a beeline for their victims. Finally, the low-lying area of the channel would mute their victims' cries.

Standing silently less than twenty yards on the other side of the drain, the creatures waited in two groups. Four beasts stood abreast on the side of the trail where the men were seated while the remaining three lined the far side. The attack was coordinated to transpire the moment the second man set foot in the gulch.

Rafi led the way and immediately picked up the pace. He knew they were a little behind schedule, and he wanted to be back at the car headed home by dusk. Little did he or Mitch know, less than a mile from where two mountain bikers had met their brutal demise, they too would become victims of a species seeking equality.

The unsuspecting men, a Muslim and a Jew, didn't stand a chance. The moment Mitch set foot into the dry creek bed, just a step behind Rafi, the boars stormed down the small impression and converged on the startled pair. On impulse, Rafi quickly turned and grabbed Mitch. The two began running to their left down the creek bed several feet before they stopped and turned back toward the beasts.

Having missed their initial opportunity to plow into the men as they rushed toward them on the trail, the boars instinctively maneuvered and encircled the two. Grunting and growling, the seven boars inched closer. Panicked, the men quickly scanned the area for an escape route. They were surrounded; there was none. Mitch, slightly behind Rafi and to his right, took a step back. They were now about three feet apart. Suddenly Rafi balled his fists, spread his arms, flexed his muscles, and began screaming, waving his arms at the animals and stomping his feet toward them. Mitch followed suit, and together they tried to frighten the creatures. Their acts of intimidation proved futile. The largest of the boars attacked first, striking the side of Rafi's left knee, thigh, and hip just as he started to turn his body. The animal's tusks grazed his thigh, but the blow thrust him forward. There he lay on his stomach, crumpled on the creek's bed, directly in front of his friend.

Mitch was in shock and only flinched when a second boar struck him from behind, below his right knee. The low angle and brunt of the hit forced his legs out from under him, hurling him into the air and over the beast's back. Mitch helplessly landed on the rocks that lined the creek bed only a foot and a half away from Rafi, sprawled out on his back, his feet beside Rafi's head. Once Mitch was down, the animals were again systematic and ruthless. Instantly, tusks from a third boar plunged into Mitch's abdomen as he gazed up into the fading sun. As the beast violently shook its head, its tusks sliced Mitch's liver, sending a pool of blood trickling into the dry river bed.

Using his arms and elbows to lift his upper body, Rafi exposed his back for a clean strike by another boar from behind. Upon impact, the boar's lower right tusk pierced Rafi's left kidney. His ensuing shriek caused the canyon's birds to flutter into the air, deer to bound away, and cottontail rabbits to scurry into their holes. Striking a second, third, and fourth time, the boar spearing Mitch plunged even deeper into his belly. With its tusks probing the inside of Mitch's mangled stomach; the boar violently jerked its head away, extracting portions of Mitch's small intestines. Mitch could see only a faint white light in the sky.

The largest boar that had originally thrashed Rafi now took aim for his torso and punctured his lower left lung. His face smashed to the ground; he could feel and smell the putrid breath of a boar draped over him. His eyes shut, Rafi desperately reached for his friend. It was the last thing he would remember. The boar sank its teeth into the back of the man's neck. As blood streamed down its mouth and snout, the animal let out a horrific squeal, then backed away from the nearly-lifeless body.

Seconds later, another boar began gnawing on Mitch's internal organs and began to violently shake its head and produce a series of blood-curdling squeals, choking out the tainted fluid. Both men, faintly alive, lay next to one another; Mitch on his back, gazed skyward. The last thing he vaguely saw were two vultures circling above. The boars squealed, grunted, and growled furiously as they circled the bodies. The largest boar approached Mitch and reluctantly placed his snout in the open belly. The animal instantly wrenched his head the other away, began squealing in distress and then bolted into the canyon's thicket. Promptly the other six creatures took off following their leader. The pigs' unrecognizable squeals could be heard throughout the canyon as they rampaged through the brush. The animals never stopped until they reached the river's stream. Once at the Prairie Dog Town Fork tributary, the wild beasts floundered in the stream, squealing, growling, flopping back and forth, and cleansing themselves of the unclean blood.

The entire night, the whole animal kingdom of the Palo Duro Canyon remained on edge, except a pack of coyotes and the pair of vultures, joined by dozens of others that descended from the skies to begin cleansing the canyon floor.

High Alert

Texas Panhandle; Sunday, November 18, 2012; Dusk

Within moments of the pre-dusk slaughter, word spread throughout the animal kingdom. The two humans left lying in a dry river bed were the tenth and eleventh slayings of the week, the fourth and fifth in the past eighteen hours.

The boars understood man would not remain idle much longer. Upon the first declaration of equality last Monday evening, the heads of the region's sounders remained in constant communication.

The moment the two innocent men were left to rot, the leaders put the network on high alert as the boars prepared to move. They knew war was imminent, and every hour was critical.

WTF

Canyon City Police Department; Sunday, November 18, 2012; 6:30 P.M.

"What the fuck!" Dawson screamed.

The entire staff was rattled. The only communication with the chief of police since late Saturday night was Dawson's brief conversation with him a few minutes earlier that afternoon. The chief had requested the six o'clock p.m. meeting with the detectives, yet had failed to appear and did not respond to his cell phone or car radio dispatch.

Barron, the chief's cousin, heard Dawson's outburst and sneered in the direction of the two detectives. They needed to move forward with the information they had received from Victor of the Amarillo Special Crimes Unit; Dawson and Mills were no longer willing to wait.

"If you had any concern for your cousin, maybe you'd swing by his house and check on him again!" snapped the lead detective to Barron.

"I checked earlier, he wasn't there. He can take care of himself," Barron responded. "He *is* the chief you know."

The two detectives began a full communication blitz with relatives of the missing people. Dawson contacted Zach's parents, Isaac and Caroline Hamilton of Fort Worth. Distraught with the news, they planned to leave immediately for Canyon and expected to be at the station before midnight. The Hamiltons were friends of Trey's parents, Jerry and Deborah Dillon, also from Fort Worth, and provided the detective their contact information. Moments after speaking with Trey's mother, Mr. Dillon called the detective right back and told him they would be following the Hamiltons.

While Dawson was on the phone with Mr. Dillon, Amy's father left a message. He, his wife, and attorney were already in route from San Antonio, and he expected the chief of police and the mayor to be at the station upon their arrival sometime between 1:00 and 2:00 a.m.

In the meantime, Detective Mills had reached out to the police department in Morristown, New Jersey, regarding the two missing men from the motorhome, Kenneth X. McDonald and Lance A. Hart. As for the other four missing people, there was no further action the detectives could take. They still had no information whatsoever on the young Mexican boys' parents or any further leads on Harden and Mahoney.

For years, Len Mahoney had been a loner with no official first of kin. And as much as Dawson wanted to hear Karen's voice, he did not want to bring her more distressing news, news that would only create more doubt about her husband's fate but provide no lead to his whereabouts. Bewildered, the detective sat at his desk only to become more distressed when he finally remembered what he had kept trying to remind himself to do.

"Damn it!" he muttered as he picked up the phone and informed Animal Protection Services about Mahoney's savage dog.

Detective Dawson hung up and asked himself again, "What the fuck? Where is Chief of Police Floyd Thompson?"

One to Many

Texas Panhandle; Sunday, November 18, 2012; 7:20 P.M.

The twelve female and five male boars were on the move. They understood time was of the essence. Similar to the several hundred other herds in the region, upheaval splintered sounders that had thrived for years, often decades. A group of thirty-five other boars sought to join the seventeen that were headed west but were staunchly opposed by the new faction's leaders. Similar disputes and negotiations among members of each sounder took place across the Panhandle and then spread throughout Texas and surrounding states.

News of mayhem spread throughout the animal kingdom as every species carefully took mental note of who aligned with whom in the nation of the boars. Sounders seventy, eighty, one hundred twenty strong, which had been united only twelve months ago, now broke off into three, four, five separate groups and instantly became rivals for the precious resources of a drought-stricken region.

While the times called for greater cooperation and compromise and more sacrifice for the long-term good of the species, intolerance and lust for power by an overzealous minority overwhelmed the common sense and will power of the majority. It would be years, even decades, if ever, before the boar nation would again thrive similar to their current standing in the animal kingdom.

Equals? Equals of man? The rest of the animal kingdom shuddered to think about the retribution man was about to exact on the entire boar nation due to a rogue minority. A minority that was hell-bent on fighting to the death and willing to sacrifice every soul to impose its values. Sunday, November 18, 2012, marked the coming of the boars' day of reckoning.

The World is Now a Better Place

Fire at Will Ranch; Sunday, November 18, 2012; 7:36 P.M.

"Ted, this has been one of the greatest weekends I've had in a long time!" Derek commented.

"Yes, it has, pardner," agreed Ted as they made their way down the canyon.

Reliving the last couple of days, Derek said, "Friday mornin' I killed one of the most beautiful sheep I've ever seen, a real trophy. What a thrill!"

"I couldn't agree more. Between your marksmanship and my bullet, you nailed that sucker! It certainly *is* one of the most beautiful sheep we've seen."

"Then dinner Friday night with all those true Americans, just great, great people. Did ya get the guys' names and numbers?" asked Derek.

"Yes, I did," Ted replied. "I'm gonna invite 'em to the ranch next spring."

"Then yesterday, the weather was perfect! Just relaxin', target shootin'. It's good to be alive!" Derek added.

"Ah, yes, it is! Ted agreed. "And now we get to do what we really came here to do, kill as many fuckin' pigs as possible!"

On the canyon floor thirty minutes later, Ted and Derek sat in a hunting blind thirty yards from a feeder dispensing the lodge's infamous slop. In anticipation of Ted's arrival, Gilbert's experts had transferred the setup to a spot swathed in sideoats grama and big bluestem native grasses mixed with star thistle. Strategically placed in a cavity, void of any scrub, cedar, or mesquite trees, the location was ideal for attracting and ambushing large numbers of hogs.

To help attract the pigs, Gilbert's crew had sprinkled the area with raccoon urine. By the sixth day of dispensing slop every half hour between ten o'clock p.m. and four o'clock a.m., his guides had estimated over 100 head had begun to mingle nightly near the feeder.

The hunters sat dead silent for over two hours before the first hogs appeared. Ted and Derek were quite content sitting on metal stools in the classic four-by-six, dark green blind. Built by Dillon Manufacturing, the rugged fiberglass blind had one small flip-up window in the door approximately ten by twelve inches in size, one large flip-up window on the back wall, and two large flip-up windows on either side; each of the side windows were about twenty-eight inches wide by ten inches tall and shoulder-high from the floor. The blind had window and door drip rails along with two gun rests and a shelf that ran along the backside.

The men waited patiently as the area surrounding the feeder now showcased a multitude of hogs of all sizes and colors. Soon after the night's second feed dispensing, promptly at 10:30, the number of hogs predicted by the guides proved true. Well over a hundred wild boars feasted on the region's greatest slop. Ted knew his partner was getting an itchy trigger finger, so he waited only a few minutes longer before he gave Derek the signal.

The well-known rocker caught Derek's eye, nodded, and began a silent count from five. The countdown gave Ted plenty of time to aim before unloading a barrage of ammunition. The gunfire exploded throughout the canyon. Each man unloaded their first clip and most of a second. Dust and smoke clouded the air while the shrieks and squeals of the hogs scampering off warned every creature of man's dastardly methods.

Several boars seriously wounded and lying on their sides let out ear-piercing cries for help as they frantically tried to regain their feet. The men again took dead aim at the helpless pigs and began riveting their bodies with bullets.

"Die, fuckin' pigs! Die!" screamed Ted.

Approximately fifteen seconds later, the canyon fell silent. One last boar twitched and let out a whimper that was barely audible. Derek promptly fired back-to-back shots into its neck area. In all, eleven boars lay dead around the feeder, the lure that always worked.

"Whooo-hoo!" Ted yelled.

The confinement of the fiberglass blind amplified Derek's screaming. "Now, that was an ambush! Look how many fuckin' pigs we killed!"

The two exchanged their brotherhood handshake before Derek pumped his balled right fist in victory. They were still congratulating each other when their world was turned on edge.

"Bam!"

The nearly indestructible four-by-six blind was rocked by a boar that had escaped during the rampage. The shock wave knocked over both stools the men had been sitting on. A second blast from the backside literally shoved the entire structure a foot.

"What the fuck!" yelled Ted as he tried to regain his balance.

Derek attempted but failed to place the barrel of his rifle through one of the windows when another boar struck the fiberglass compound from the side nearest the feeder. The blow was so forceful it lifted the side of the blind six inches off the ground.

"Shiiit!" yelled Derek.

Repeated blasts from all sides began without challenge.

"Get your pistol! Get your fucking pistol!" yelled Ted.

Both men dropped their rifles and drew their semi-automatic pistols. Firing shot after shot from point-blank range, the men were able to slow the onslaught.

"You can't get me, you fucking pigs!" Ted screamed provokingly as scores of boars fell attempting to pummel the sturdy structure.

Adrenaline pumped through the men's bodies as they manically fired as many rounds as possible before reloading and emptying their clips again.

Prior to this evening, the boars who had attacked man were only a fringe group—boars that never ate from the human trough, the manmade machine that sucked pigs in with free handouts. They recognized the machines were traps, and nothing came for free. The boars now attacking Ted and Derek were "takers," part of the majority that had hours earlier sided with the fringe, those who fervently advocated that it was man who had brought drought and hardship to their sounders, a fringe who sought nothing less than equality with man.

Their societies in anarchy, the converted pigs placed blame squarely on humans and resented their current predicament that squared fellow pig against fellow pig. Seeing their own enticed by man only to be ambushed, whipped the previously moderate boars into a frenzy. Filled with hatred and need for revenge, they continued their assault, unable to penetrate the shelter that protected their most hated enemy.

"They can't get us, Ted! Fuck you, pigs!" hollered Derek.

"Kill 'em! Kill 'em!" responded Ted as both men took aim from each side of the blind, splattering pig brains all around it. Despite the boars' strength, anger, and determination, their repeated blows against the sides of the blind were no match for the manmade structure. The men continued to fire away as boar after boar took turns ramming the blind while suffering heavy casualties.

Boars are smart, considered the most cunning beast in the animal kingdom. They have the capacity to analyze and learn, and learn they did. Ted and Derek began to grow cocky and implored the boars to continue to attack, so they could fire from point-blank range.

"Come closer, you fuckin' pigs!" Ted taunted them. They willfully obliged.

Realizing the blind had slightly tipped several times when struck by the most powerful blows, the boars determined their next line of attack. In tandem, three hogs raced toward the backside of the blind and began rooting and digging, trying to create space between the dirt and the structure's foundation.

Ted raced to the backside, opened the window, and began firing.

Watching their fellow comrades, several boars followed suit and rushed to all sides of the structure, furiously pushing against it, rooting with their tusks and extraordinarily powerful snouts.

Derek continued to fire toward the opposite side of the feeder. It took multiple shots to down an animal despite the close range. Scoring a lethal head or neck shot from their angle was almost impossible.

"Fuuuck!" screamed Ted as he now ran to the door, opened the window, and tried to deter another gang of beasts.

"I have enough ammo to kill all you fuckin' pigs!" he screamed.

Unfortunately for Ted and Derek, all the ammo in Texas was not going to be enough.

Seeing a handful of hogs turn and run, Derek screamed victoriously, "Fuckin' pigs are retreating! They're retreating!"

He celebrated too quickly. The pigs weren't retreating; they were just getting out of the way. Unbeknownst to the men, a half-dozen enraged beasts had been rooting furiously on the side of the blind nearest the feeder and finally gained enough leverage. Their tusks firmly entrenched underneath the blind's foundation; six boars in coordination thrust and toppled the blind onto its side.

Ted fell awkwardly, slamming his head against the fiberglass shell. Derek screamed in agony. His arm from the elbow down was outside the window while he tried to defend his side of the blind. The structure tumbled so quickly, Derek was unable to get his arm back inside. When the blind overturned and hit the ground, it literally snapped his forearm in two.

Lying on his stomach with his face plastered against the inside of the fiberglass, his forearm pinned between the outside wall and the ground, Derek screamed, "My arm! My arm! Agh!" in a way Ted had never heard any man scream before.

The pain in his arm was so intense, Derek never felt the metal stools fall on top of him, gouging the back of his head.

Delirious, Ted tried to stand up, but hit his head on the ceiling that was now only four feet tall since the blind was on its side.

"Fuck!" he screamed while Derek began wailing, "Fuck! Oh God! Oh God! Fuck! My arm! I can't move my arm!"

Ted crawled on his hands and knees to get to the middle of the blind. When upright, the windows were shoulder-high, but with the blind now lying on its side, the window in the door was less than two feet from the ground. The door which used to swing outwards now opened like a window flap in reverse.

The boars sensed blood and began plowing their snouts into the window in the door and the large back window that now ran vertically. The boars gripped at the windows' edges and violently shook their heads as they desperately tried to tear the fiberglass apart.

Ted fired toward both openings again and again, repelling animal after animal that stuck its snout into the hole. But in all the mayhem, he missed the holes several times as he frantically kept firing away. Each misfire tore through the fiberglass and compromised the structure's integrity.

"Fuck you, pigs!" Ted screamed as the enlarged opening enabled a boar's entire head to thrust through the window.

Derek looked on in shock, helpless to assist defending their shelter. He realized the tables had turned, and now he and Ted were as vulnerable as the pigs had been previously against the hunters' tactics.

Boars are very smart.

"Crack!" The instant the boar hit the blind's flat side which was once the building floor, it knew the contact didn't have the same feeling or sound as before. Made of three-quarter-inch thick, treated plywood, the floor had no fiberglass.

A second boar rammed into it again. "Crack!"

A third blow splintered the side. It took a half-dozen more strikes before the plywood floor completely fractured. Ted scooted as far back into the crown of what used to be the roof and fired as often as he could. It wasn't enough.

Despite killing twenty-eight boars and wounding dozens more, there were another hundred or so that hungered for human flesh. Boars plowed through the splintered plywood floor and clenched the legs of both men. Violently shaking their heads as they ripped at the men's legs brought more screams from Derek. Gripping and pulling, the boars dragged the pair across the fiberglass and out to the canyon floor. Derek's right forearm caught between the blind and the ground was severed from the weight of the men and the 1600 pounds of animals inside the tiny structure. Ted's right cheek suffered a deep gash as his face was dragged across the screws that attached the flip-up windows to the side of the blind. Blood streamed down his cheek and into the infamous one-inch vertical strip of hair that adorned his chin.

Screams of, "Fuck you, pigs!" turned to screams of help and despair.

Twenty-eight boars in one ambush was Ted's greatest hunting coup. It would be his last. Boar after boar ripped at the Motor City Madman's body, sparing him a slow death. Derek also died in a heartbeat as pigs simultaneously gnawed on every part of his body. Nearly a hundred boars fought and forced their way to get a taste of the self-professed greatest boar slayer of all. It took only three minutes for both bodies to be entirely consumed.

Only later, as the boars recounted the victory and recalled the smells, sights, and sounds, they fully understood what they had accomplished. In the smells the men left behind in the blind, in the recollections of sounds, smells, and sights from slaughters of the past, the boars came to realize they had not only eliminated threats that came against them that day, but they had indeed eliminated two threats that had come against them countless times in the past—times that had horrified the entire boar nation. The men's legendary accounts had become a warning and a watchword for boars everywhere. For the two who died in that tiny blind under the cover of a dark Texas night were none other than two of the boar nation's most wanted—two of the Infamous six.

The animal kingdom did not approve of the boars challenging man. Tonight, however, the entire kingdom quietly celebrated the death of two men who relentlessly terrorized them. They did not know if Ted and Derek went to a more honorable place, but their keen senses told them the world was now a far, far better place.

One is Your Daughter

Canyon City Police Department; Monday, November 19, 2012; 12:59 A.M.

Mr. Hamilton tried numerous times to comfort his wife as she sobbed uncontrollably. Mrs. Dillon regained her composure then again succumbed to perhaps the most gruesome news imaginable. Both fathers were stunned. Detectives Dawson and Mills continued to express optimism, emphasizing nothing was definitive except their children were missing; their last known whereabouts was around 11:30 p.m. Saturday night when Zach left Dustin a message about their predicament, a fact Dawson had only learned a few hours earlier when Dustin called him. When asked why it took him so long to relay the information, Dustin could only respond, "I forgot to check my messages after I recharged my phone."

Dawson and Mills avowed that soon after dawn, the Amarillo Special Crimes Unit would begin an extensive search effort in the canyon. Just when the detectives thought the Hamiltons and Dillons were beginning to calm, the parents had to hear the entire story all over again which only deepened their grief.

"My name is Charles Smith. Where's the chief of police?" Amy's father demanded as he burst into the lobby.

The dispatch officer had been waiting for the Smiths and their attorney to arrive from San Antonio. He asked them to move toward the electronically controlled door as the desk officer hit the buzzer. Mr. Smith opened the door and barged in, followed by his wife and attorney. The dispatch officer calmly led them to the meeting room where the detectives were meeting with the boys' parents. Seeing them approach, Dawson stood up and waved them in. Mrs. Hamilton immediately hugged Amy's mother, Mrs. Smith.

"What the hell is going on, Detective?" demanded Mr. Smith.

Dawson directed the Smiths and their attorney to empty chairs. "Please be seated so I can fill you in on everything we know."

Before Dawson could even begin to explain, Mrs. Hamilton broke down again.

Although the room was designed to seat ten, the nine occupants were cramped. The detectives sat at the far end of the room, while the parents of the boys sat to their right. Mr. Smith took the end of the table opposite Detective Dawson, and his wife sat next to him. Their attorney took the third seat to the left of the detectives.

"Where are the mayor and chief?" Amy's father demanded.

His attorney shot him a stern look.

"Mayor Jeffries will be available later this morning around seven o'clock," answered the detective.

"And the chief?" Mr. Smith asked.

"We have been unable to reach him," stated Detective Dawson.

"Are you serious? What kind of two-bit operation are you running in this podunk town?" Mr. Smith wanted to know.

Mrs. Hamilton began sobbing so hard the whole room froze.

Amy's mother pleaded with her husband, "Charles, please let the detective talk. We need to listen. Just once, please shut up!"

Mr. Smith was far from speechless when he heard that the forensics team had found fragments of human bone and hair in wild boar feces surrounding the Late Arrival Campground.

"What do you mean?" Smith interrupted. "You found those traces before Amy was even missing! How does that have anything to do with her? Just what are you saying happened to my daughter, Detective?"

The detective tried to explain, "All we know is that a number of people are missing without reason. We've been working with the Amarillo Special Crimes Unit and are trying to identify if there's a connection with the cases, but at this point have found none. The bottom line is there are nine people presumed missing with no trace of their whereabouts. All nine vanished, and one is your daughter."

"And who are you?" Mr. Smith turned his attention to the other four parents.

The Dillons introduced themselves first, and then Mr. Hamilton answered, "I'm Isaac Hamilton, and this is my wife, Caroline."

Trembling, Mrs. Hamilton could hardly speak when she stammered, "Amy is our son Zach's girlfriend. We met her last month."

"Amy didn't have a boyfriend!" Mr. Smith responded angrily.

"Yes, she did!" Mrs. Smith contradicted her husband. "She met him at school."

"If anything happened to my daughter, be assured you and your son will be held accountable!" threatened Mr. Smith.

The threat caused Mr. Dillon and Mr. Hamilton to exchange glances.

"Please," interjected Dawson. "We need to focus on finding your children."

"That's your responsibility! I will be here at seven a.m. sharp to meet with the mayor! I expect to see a detailed report of all the current findings and the proposed efforts to locate my daughter!" Mr. Smith declared without any mention or concern for the two missing boys.

Mrs. Hamilton again began howling uncontrollably.

Still not satisfied, Mr. Smith pressed on, "What are your suspicions, Detective? That somebody has murdered several people, and wild hogs ate their corpses?"

"Boars eat carrion, Mr. Smith. Other than that, I'm not suggesting anything. We just don't know," responded Dawson.

"What is carrion?" asked Mrs. Dillon.

"Carrion is dead, decaying matter, flesh," answered Detective Dawson.

Hearing the scenario phrased that way was too much for Mrs. Hamilton. She tried to make it to the waste basket, but didn't. Vomit spewed down the wall and in and around the wastepaper basket near the office door.

Mrs. Dillon immediately went to Zach's mother and escorted her to the women's restroom.

Having seen and heard enough, Mr. Smith made it perfectly clear his expectations as he stood up, glared at the detectives and ordered, "Do your damn jobs and find my daughter, now!"

Sidestepping the bile, Amy's father then stormed out of the station in the same manner in which he had arrived, leaving his wife and attorney trailing behind. Mills then exited the room in search of maintenance.

Still shocked, Mr. Hamilton and Mr. Dillon remained seated, unable to move despite the foul smell. Dawson could only look at them with regret, wishing he could provide them with more details on the whereabouts of their sons.

"All you have is a few wild boar hairs from the chrome stripping of a van, an undisturbed motorhome, an idle minivan with a trailer, an abandoned truck in the southern part of the canyon, my son's SUV and nothing else?" Mr. Hamilton asked.

"Actually, we received missing person's reports a few hours before your arrival. Two men from Amarillo hiked the canyon trail yesterday afternoon but never returned. We found their car parked at the trailhead. The vehicle appears undisturbed. We will be searching for them as well, at first light," Dawson explained. "All of the vehicles appear normal. The only evidence of possible foul play is about a third of a mile from where we found the truck. But I can't go into details about that right now. Of course, we have the two young Mexican boys, but they won't speak Spanish or English."

"And the blood you found where all the wild hogs had been slaughtered; is that of two of the missing men from Canyon?" Mr. Dillon wanted to confirm.

"Yes, that came back in the report we received from forensics shortly after six o'clock tonight. We confirmed it was from the two local hunters," replied the detective.

"My God!" cried Mr. Dillon.

Many to One

Twenty Miles West of Palo Duro Canyon
Monday; November 19, 2012; 1:05 A.M.

Moving westward, members from other sounders had converged on the trail. The pack of seventeen boars had now grown to sixty-one. Comprised of forty females and twenty-one males, the emerging sounder encompassed all ages and had one urgent goal in mind: to escape the Texas Panhandle immediately! They knew man would respond swiftly and unconditionally. Months ago, a safety zone had been established. The boars knew that if they failed to reach it expeditiously, their existence was at severe risk.

The most cunning of the entire boar population traveled a route that had been trekked numerous times in preparation for a day they had hoped would never come. The farther they traveled, the larger the sounder grew. Since the rules and landscape had changed, statutes of a herd's maximum size no longer applied.

Twenty miles farther west, the sounder topped a hundred head. Soon afterward, it began to expand exponentially. Unlike man, this federation of boar realized when change was necessary; cooperation and compromise were essential for all to have an equal chance to thrive. These select boars had only one interest in mind: balance in the animal kingdom. They knew that was the key to long-term survival of their species.

Twenty Clicks Later

Fringe of Palo Duro Canyon; Monday, November 19, 2012; 1:09 A.M.

Sunday night's hunt was to be the climax of the men's excursion. During breakfast Saturday, Jimmy's brother Carl bragged that the site he had carefully selected over a week ago was going to rewrite the Richters' legend of slaughtering wild hogs. "Jimmy, wait 'til you see it!" he had told his brother after he had visited the site on Thursday. "It works better than the four of us going out for a night of two-stepping."

Jimmy laughed at Carl's reference, remembering the nights he and his brothers would take Amarillo by storm, often bringing home more than one girl each.

Jimmy then commented, "We've never installed two feeders before."

"The camera I installed to monitor the feeder worked perfectly. When I saw the photos from Monday night, I about fell over. I thought, hell, why not put up a second one and see how many more of the damn things show up for free handouts? The pigs have always been greedy, wanting to eat the slop, but many were always leery. Now when the dispensers go off, you should see 'em fight for every last bit. The numbers that depend on the machines to survive are staggering," stated Carl.

384

"Maybe it's the drought," suggested Mark.

"Sounds like the food-stamp line to me. Gimme, gimme, gimme," Jimmy decided. "Just a bunch of fuckin' takers lookin' for a free lunch. Makes me sick! Serves 'em right if we kill every last one of 'em. Once they get a taste of the slop, they become too lazy to find their own food," Jimmy ranted.

Mark could barely stomach the analogy. While he stewed in his room trying to sleep after the flight, he thought, "Maybe it will be good killing a bunch of pigs. Give me a chance to get it all out." Now eating bacon and eggs, listening to Jimmy compare all the pigs to Obama supporters like him, the thought of randomly gunning down a slew of pigs was no longer appealing.

Jimmy had told the gang they would be hunting near the canyon, and they were, just not until Sunday evening. Carl convinced his brother that the boars in Cottle County were still the biggest in the region. "Jimmy, remember the two boars ya killed in Cottle County that we had mounted? Well, they just keep gettin' bigger. I stopped off at the Walters' ranch last Saturday. Butch showed me pictures of two boars they killed the week before, and both topped five hundred pounds. He told me there's plenty for the takin', especially farther south into Cottle County. So let's hunt that territory today and tomorrow. It's open range. The guys will have a blast on the ATVs, and we'll stalk 'em. Chase the bastards down on the ATVs. Then tomorrow night we'll ambush 'em at the feeder. That'll be the topper to the whole weekend. Just like last Christmas, what do ya think?"

"I was thinkin' we should stay a little closer to the canyon, but now that I think more about it, I like your plan. Haulin' ass after hogs on the ATVs will be somethin' they won't forget. Near the canyon you cain't hit top speeds like ya can in Cottle."

As he was finishing breakfast, Jimmy told Carl, "I want to see the pictures from the field camera and Google Earth before we leave this morning.

"Sure," Carl replied.

The talk of all the killing had Kevin fired up.

"How fast can we go on the ATVs?" Kevin asked.

"Fast, real fast. But trust me, it doesn't matter; you won't be able to keep up," Carl said. "No one keeps up with Jimmy once he's on the ass of a pack of wild boar."

A few minutes later, Carl and Jimmy viewed the feeder site on Google Earth, then the photos from the motion detection camera. Jimmy was pleased with the location and excited about the number of hogs appearing each night. His thoughts turning toward the hunt later that day using the ATV's, Jimmy reminded his younger brother, "I haven't shot a pig in months. If those guys can't keep up, to hell with 'em! Nothin's gonna stop me today from chasin' down a bunch of fuckin' pigs and killin' every last one of them."

Carl laughed, "I'll be right behind you."

As with the gun collection, everything at the ranch seemed to come in fives. When the crew left the ranch that Saturday morning, they rode in a convoy of excess. Five GMC Sierra 3500 HD Denali pickup trucks stormed out of the ranch's gates, each loaded with Yamaha 2013 Grizzly 700 ATVs in the trucks' beds and rifles affixed to the gun racks.

Within thirty minutes of unloading the ATVs, the five were in pursuit of a pack of seven hogs. The hogs split; four ran one way, and three another. Jimmy and Carl veered left to follow the group of four while Mark, followed by Steve, maintained his bearings on the other three. Kevin tried in vain to keep up with his boss, but by the time Jimmy and Carl had run down the vermin, took aim and fired, he was over a hundred yards behind.

The brothers had executed all four and were hooting and hollering before Kevin even pulled up. Mark and Steve killed the three they pursued with Mark taking the largest first. He let Steve fire five times before he downed the second boar. Instinct prompted Mark to yell, "Come on!" as he spurred Steve to continue after the last boar.

They crisscrossed the rolling terrain for another mile before Steve could line up the last wild pig and gun him down with multiple blasts. Steve never felt more alive.

"Whoa! Holy shit, those things can run!" Steve exclaimed. "That was incredible! My heart was pounding like a freakin' jackhammer!"

Mark did not experience the same exhilaration. The thrill was long gone.

After the hunters carefully inspected the dead pigs, they determined Mark had killed the largest of the seven. The recognition did little to boost Mark's enthusiasm.

Especially after Jimmy stated, "Don't get too big for your britches, Mark! Not one is trophy worthy."

Late that afternoon, the five men tracked down a female and four piglets. Jimmy being Jimmy, he insisted Kevin be allowed to shoot the last remaining piglet as it tried to escape.

"Just the right size and ferociousness for ya, Kevin!" Jimmy badgered his beleaguered employee.

On the third shot, Kevin took the piglet down.

That evening, on the way back home, they stopped by the Walters' ranch. There, they sat quietly in a number of blinds set up by Butch. They spotted no hogs. After three hours, Jimmy had had enough.

"Let's go!" he called out, making sure everyone heard before he strayed from his blind.

They began the mile-long walk back to the already loaded trucks for the drive back toward Amarillo.

"Boys, don't let it get ya down! Tomorrow night, we'll shoot so many fuckin' hogs, they'll be piled on top of one another, I swear!" Carl boasted.

Jimmy backed his brother up, "I saw the pictures this mornin'. So many fuckin' hogs, even Kevin cain't miss."

Steve laughed the hardest, never letting a chance go by to wear down his competitor.

Jimmy continued, "So here's what we're gonna do since we'll be slayin' boars by the truckloads this time tomorrow night. We're gonna spend the last few hours of the day in Caprock Canyon takin' it easy, sightseein'. Then we'll head back to the blinds for an early evenin' hunt. It's on the way back to Palo Duro. Give us another shot at a trophy hog. Then we'll head on over to the feeder for the mass slaughter.

"Accordin' to the film, we want to get to the feeder b'tween midnight and one o'clock," Carl recommended.

"That's fine. Then we can spend the mornin' in Palo Duro and hike the Lighthouse Trail before y'all fly out Tuesday," Jimmy added.

"Are there pigs in Caprock Canyon?" asked Kevin.

"Yeah, but chances of seein' one are slim. Too many people," Jimmy said.

"I'm fine with the plan. I've seen enough pigs in my life," Mark stated sarcastically.

Driving back to the Richter ranch, Mark could barely stay awake. Thursday evening he had too many drinks, no sex, and not enough sleep. On Friday, the worst day of his life, he didn't sleep at all. The only thing that kept him going was his growing hatred of Jimmy. By the hour, the bar chart trended higher. It revolted him to think that his wife, the woman he loved and cherished, found Jimmy's arrogance and slick persona appealing.

"Now, I'm driving one of his trucks, sleeping at his ranch, and acting as if nothing is wrong after he slept with my wife the other night?" Mark thought.

The normally mild-mannered Mark felt like it was the first time in his life he could snap at any moment.

He kept telling himself, "I'm halfway home; just two more days. Just get to Tuesday morning and start anew. It's no different than trading. If it's not working, get out, reanalyze, and find the next trade that is moving in a direction that is logical."

Thinking of Jimmy in terms of a trade, he knew that was one market he would never go long again.

"And Elaine?" his heart ached at the thought he would have to sell the most bullish market he had ever ridden. No market, no amount of money had brought him as much euphoria as her being by his side. When he returned, he knew he had to let her go. A split was in order. Facts were facts, his reasoning justified. Yet he wondered, "Will I be able to forgive, buy her back, and go long Elaine again someday?"

Then he considered, "She's been sleeping with Jimmy! No telling what STDs she's picked up."

He intentionally fell back from the caravan heading north to the Richter ranch. The distance between him and the truck ahead brought a sense of relief. It enabled him to regain control of his emotions, so he could use reason like always. By the time he pulled into the ranch, Mark had come to terms with his decisions. He slept well and was the last to breakfast the next morning.

Sunday morning brought more beautiful, clear blue skies.

"Told ya the weather here is great! Highs again in the low seventies. Perfect sleepin' weather, don't ya think, Mark? Lows in the high thirties or so, no moanin', groanin', or squeals keepin' ya awake?" Jimmy laughed, driving the stake deeper and deeper.

Mark ignored Jimmy's comments. He didn't want to get sucked into Jimmy's mind games. Someday, he was confident he would get his revenge, hopefully economically, where it would hurt Jimmy most.

Mark purposely didn't look the first time they were all introduced, but his quick glances during breakfast couldn't stop his thinking how attractive the "live in" maid was. She was probably in her mid-forties, only ten to fifteen years older than the five she catered to. He considered how James Sr. never remarried.

"Maid, yeah right! How convenient, her living quarters are adjacent to the master bedroom."

As she served up a huge breakfast that resembled something you would see for brunch at the finest establishments, he had no doubt she understood her position.

The small chat taking place was abruptly interrupted when James Sr. burst into the room and looked at his eldest son, "I want you in my office, immediately!"

For Mark, Mr. Richter's tone confirmed his suspicion; everyone in the Richter family had a defined role. It was clear; there was a king and certainly no queen.

But what he wondered most, "Is there no royal line at all? No rooks, knights, or bishops? Is everyone just a pawn?"

Two and a half hours later, Kevin and Steve were poolside basking in the luxury that surrounded them. Mark remained in his room reviewing the settlement prices of each option position from Friday's close. He estimated the losses totaled 11 percent of their capital since the election, a devastating amount. Carl was nowhere to be found.

"Where's Mark?" snapped Jimmy as he stepped onto the elaborate flagstone deck.

"In his room, said he had some work to do," replied Steve.

"Tell 'em there has been a change in plans," Jimmy commanded. "Y'all enjoy the day here. Swim, hang out, watch football, I don't give a fuck. Adriana will make whatever ya want. We leave 11:00 p.m. sharp, and I mean fuckin' sharp! We're gonna kill every fuckin' boar in the god-damn county!"

"Sure, Jimmy!" Kevin said.

"Make sure ya shower around ten with the scent-free soap. Adriana will have all your gear cleaned and ready to go. I'm gonna kill every fuckin' pig b'tween here and Lubbock!" vowed Jimmy.

"What the fuck was that all about?" Kevin asked Steve as Jimmy walked off as abruptly as he arrived.

"Who the hell knows? At least we can watch football all day, except the damn Giants have a bye this week," replied Steve.

Mark wasn't surprised when he heard the news just before noon. He realized James Sr. probably knew to the penny the debacle of the past two weeks. He hadn't accumulated these riches being a fool.

"Five of everything? It is sheer narcissism from the father to each son. Jimmy is probably in his father's office receiving an old-fashioned beat down as Mr. Richter tunes every string of Jimmy's guitar," thought Mark.

Mark returned to his room and stared out the window overlooking the sparkling pool and surrounding gardens. Despite the contrasts of the open plains to the skyscrapers of the city, the serene setting reminded him of his beloved garden back home. Knowing the two annoyances were watching a game, he opened his door, walked outside, and strolled through the lush landscape of the pool area.

A couple of sculptures caught his eye, and he assured himself, "I'm half-way home. More than half if Jimmy stays occupied all day," until he reconsidered. "Half-way home? I have no home."

The entire day, Kevin and Steve entertained themselves watching football. The two were in heaven, switching between games. As expected, the Richters had access to every game. Being in Texas, they had to monitor both teams. They weren't disappointed; the Cowboys and Texans each won in overtime. They kept a close eye on the Jets as they thrashed the Rams. The late-afternoon games pitted Denver against San Diego and the hated Patriots versus the Colts.

When Mark came out of his room, he could only stand a few minutes of the venom Kevin and Steve spewed toward the Patriots and Tom Brady.

"My god, how much football can someone watch in one day?" Mark wondered.

"You going to watch the Ravens-Steelers game with us?" Kevin asked Mark as he helped himself to an extraordinary dinner which was kept warm in the finest buffet warmers.

"I don't think so. I need to make sure the house is in order tomorrow morning. I'm still writing a few memos to Elliot and Robert," responded Mark before he retreated back to his room.

Ignorant of the seriousness of the losses suffered by AAC, Kevin questioned, "How long can someone hole themselves into a room?"

"Let him be. Who cares? In four hours, we'll be on our way to kill some fucking boars!" shrugged Steve.

The next three hours, Mark stayed busy reading report after report on every market, focusing particularly on gold. He was a strong believer in reading as many different viewpoints as possible; in particular, ones that countered his philosophy. Shortly before ten, he found himself reading articles that he had found on the Internet about forgiving a cheating spouse. He shook his head and closed the browser. His mind was made up.

He had to shower and get ready for the first and last hunt he would ever participate in with Jimmy. Mark left his room precisely at 10:30. Carl, Kevin, and Steve were waiting in the massive kitchen. It was the first time he had seen Carl since breakfast. Jimmy's brother informed Mark everything was ready; all they needed was Jimmy. Mark could tell Carl was jacked, ready to slaughter a host of pigs.

"Mark, you ride with me. Kevin and Steve will go with Jimmy," Carl said. "We should be there in about forty-five minutes. We'll park the trucks and walk about a mile. We have to be as stealth as possible. No noise, no talkin'– nothin'. The damn things can hear and smell like no other creature. We want to rewrite the Richter record books. With the five of us, we could kill at least eighteen to twenty boars! Ya ready to kill some fuckin' boars?"

"Hell yeah!" yelled Kevin as Steve nodded in the affirmative.

Eleven o'clock had come and gone.

Concerned, Kevin asked, "Where's Jimmy?"

"He'll be here, don't worry," Carl told him.

Soon enough, Jimmy came blasting through the front door.

"All right, I need fifteen minutes to shower and dress. Then we're off to kill every god-damn boar we see!" Jimmy exclaimed.

Mark shook his head in bewilderment over how Jimmy and his brother used the Lord's name in vain so often. Kevin's excitement continued to blossom as he listened to Carl boast on and on about previous exploits and how this hunt will be the best ever.

"Not only more boars than ever, but bigger too!" claimed Carl.

A few minutes later, Jimmy burst into the kitchen full of vigor.

"T'night nothin' matters but pigs! I want to see dead pigs, pig blood everywhere! We will raise the bar on how many fuckin' pigs we can kill at once. I'm gonna take down a dozen myself!" he promised as he headed for the door.

Jimmy took the lead as the two trucks raced to the east edge of the Palo Duro Canyon.

After about thirty-five minutes, the two trucks turned left off of Texas Highway 207. They barreled down the first two miles of a flat dirt road that ran parallel to the canyon's edge. Jimmy slowed as the road crept closer to the canyon walls on their right. Carl pulled up next to him and waved him on. The two trucks traveled another quarter-mile before reaching a peninsula of flatland that penetrated the canyon. Slowly coming to a halt, they quietly exited the trucks, and Carl put his finger to his mouth.

The men quietly gathered their gear, sprayed each other in scent blocker before Jimmy spoke in a whisper, "From this point on, follow me. Don't speak, walk lightly, and carry a damn big stick when we get there. When I give ya the signal, Mark will flank to my right by seven yards. Kevin, you will then space yourself another seven yards wide of Mark. Carl, you'll be to my left, and Steve, you will flank Carl. Understood?" Jimmy asked.

They all nodded.

"Let's kill some fuckin' pigs, a lot of fuckin' pigs!" Jimmy exclaimed.

Jimmy and Carl were always pumped, no matter what they were doing. Their intensity had rubbed off on Kevin. The unproven trader and even less-experienced hunter worried Mark. He let Kevin walk ahead of him. The five slithered along, hugging the canyon wall to their right, making their way deep into a pocket of flatland that continually narrowed.

The feeder was located at the far end of the peninsula where a tight ridge formed with drop-offs on each side. The location was perfect. There was no quick escape for the hogs. If 150 gathered as expected, one of three things would occur: The pigs would create a log jam as they funneled down the narrow ridge. The steep slopes on either side would hinder their ability to make a quick escape. Even better, if they tried to flee on the flatland, the hogs would have to run right past the men, providing point-blank range to fire. In any scenario, they would have ample time to slay the beasts en masse.

When Carl had shown Jimmy the location on Google Earth, Jimmy agreed this was a prime opportunity to kill twenty, maybe two dozen boars.

The eager hunters slowly moved toward the kill zone. Approximately two hundred yards away, Carl signaled to Jimmy it was just on the other side of the next cranny of canyon that pierced the flatland. Jimmy stopped and turned to his four compatriots. His rifle in his left hand, he pumped his right fist, gritted his teeth, and implored his flank to be ready to kill, kill, and kill some more. They inched forward, one step at a time, to the edge of the nook dotted with brush and small scrub trees, exposing the last small opening of flatland. The second they passed the periphery, the gang expected to see a vast army of pigs primed to be slaughtered.

Kevin's hands trembled. Mark fell back another step and noticeably lagged behind. Looking back to make sure his troops were properly aligned, Jimmy gave Mark a piercing look before he took the next two steps that would provide ample view of the despised pigs, pigs he was determined to kill to the very last one.

Jimmy couldn't believe his eyes. Carl stared in silence, shocked at what he saw. Steve, then Kevin, and finally Mark, all made the turn to see what had stunned their pig-killing mentors. Nothing! Jimmy put his finger to his mouth and took another few steps forward. Carl held his hand up and motioned the three to wait while he followed his brother. In tandem, the two moved forward ever so slightly to see the second feeder. Nothing! Bewildered, they kept moving forward until they started a fast walk toward the end of the flatland. Nothing! Without saying anything to the three left behind, Jimmy and Carl started jogging to the feeders now 120 yards away.

Worried, Kevin starting running, and Steve followed. Mark stood and chuckled for a second before he started half-heartedly making his way to the feeders thirty feet apart.

Jimmy was livid. "What the fuck? No fuckin' pigs? Fuck, Carl, what the fuck?" he screamed.

Click.

Mark, still fifty yards away, could hear every word of Jimmy's tantrum. "Where are the boars?" Kevin asked innocently.

Click.

"Shut the fuck up, you dumbass, Kevin! You're fuckin' worthless! I'm damn tired of carryin' your damn jock!" screamed Jimmy.

Click.

"I don't understand!" said Carl.

"Somebody probably saw your god-damn feeder earlier and scared them off!" screamed Jimmy.

Click.

Jimmy was wrong. Very, very wrong.

Click.

There were a lot of boars, over 200, in fact. On the opposite side of the peninsula from where the traders had hiked, less than a hundred yards away, a throng of revengeful boars watched from the brush. Now, it was the five humans who were trapped.

Click.

The disintegration of the sounders into several blocs Sunday evening meant new decrees were in force. One faction chose to flee to new territories and establish hundreds of larger, more powerful sounders within the domain of one super class. Small minorities broke off, sounder by sounder, to form new coalitions based on one key law: isolation and avoidance of man at all costs. It was the two remaining parties, however, that made up the bulk of the boar nation. One consisted of moderates who sought compromise with man and opposed violence to impose equality.

Unfortunately for the five hunters, it was the last and the largest contingency that was willfully approaching the feeders. The radicals, once a fringe, now comprised nearly 40 percent of the population. Irrefutably the largest faction, the extremists claimed they had secured a clear mandate and determined a policy called "austerity" would take effect at midnight that fateful November evening.

There were four key proclamations of the new decree. First, they planned to use intimidation and force to segregate the two dominant parties. Second, the plan required all members to fight to the death for the favored territorial ranges. Third, the organizers deftly persuaded the rank and file; it was due to their leadership, their efforts that the party prospered. And because of this, sacrifice by the masses to benefit the strongest was in everyone's best interest. Finally, the leaders maintained no boar could eat from the hand of man. No longer would the notion of handouts be tolerated. Man had tricked them time and time again, the superiors argued. It was the evil operators of the manmade feeding machines that tried to make the boars dependent on man. Thus, the operators would die first. Moments into the second hour of the first of day, the radicals eagerly sought to enforce the new statute to the fullest extent of the law.

While Jimmy ranted and raved, thirty of the more than two hundred vengeful beasts had quietly edged within fifty yards of the distracted hunters.

Click.

The men's meager sense of smell didn't detect the beasts' repulsive odor as dozens more positioned themselves to corner the arrogant men.

Click.

Surprisingly, Kevin noticed them first.

"Fucking boars! Look at them all!" Kevin screamed excitedly.

The five of them quickly scanned what seemed like a tiny island to them and realized there was nowhere to run.

"Fuck!" Jimmy mumbled.

Impulsively, Kevin fired the first shot toward the flatland.

Click.

The gunshot triggered the boars to charge.

Ten yards away, a small cottonwood tree grew with a second one just beyond it.

A few yards farther, and neither of them would have ever made it.

Click.

Steve, not to be outdone by Kevin, fired three successive shots and then a fourth. In the scramble to get to the trees, Carl fell and never got up.

Click.

Desperately clawing to get up the first tree, Jimmy dropped his rifle. Mark had already thrown his to the ground as he leapt, latching onto the nearest branch of the second tree to pull himself up.

Click.

The trees were barely twenty feet tall, and the highest branches either man could scale were no more than eight feet off the ground. In what seemed like a heartbeat, dozens of boars circled below them.

Click.

In their mad dash to safety, neither heard any of the initial screams. Defending his turf, Kevin never even hit one boar. Struck at full speed, he went flailing to the ground before a second hog immediately ripped his neck open, killing him instantly.

Click.

Steve realized at the last second the impending danger but couldn't escape. His four rapid shots failed to down even one charging boar.

Click.

Pummeled, Steve sprawled to the hard barren dirt and was instantly in the jaws of several boars. He lasted only seconds as boars fought to get at any portion of the human flesh. Carl scrambled to his hands and knees, only to be knocked onto his back with a ferocious blow to his side that cracked several ribs.

Click.

The boar's tusks penetrated his rib cage, collapsed his right lung, and ripped cartilage as the tusk withdrew from his chest. Unable to scream, Carl looked up in horror as a boar clenched and tore at his left bicep. He lived another twenty seconds as swarms of the beasts skirmished and pounded their way to rip at his body.

Click.

"Oh, my god! Oh, my god!" screamed Jimmy. "Carl! Carl! Oh fuck!"

Mark shook so hard, he struggled to retain his perch only seven feet off the ground.

Click.

Boars circling under the tree, dashed over to one of the fallen victims, fought their way to the rapidly disappearing bodies, took a pound of flesh, and then circled back under the feet of Jimmy and Mark, chewing on the body parts of their hated enemy.

Click.

Jimmy and Mark looked all around. There were easily two hundred boars in a frenzy; grunting, growling, seeking more human flesh. Before Jimmy and Mark could process what to do, the hogs had consumed all three bodies. Guts, bone, clothes, blood, everything gone.

Click.

Sweat poured down Mark's face. The whole tree shook as he desperately hugged the tree's trunk, cutting his right hand on a branch in the process. In a panic, Jimmy pulled out his massive Smith and Wesson 500 4" barrel and fired a direct hit in the eye of a boar below. The animal dropped immediately.

"Fuck you, boars!" he screamed as he dropped a second and third hog.

Click.

"Kill the fuckin' things!" screamed Jimmy.

Without thinking, Mark pulled out his matching monster hand gun and fired once, twice, thrice, and then a fourth time. All direct hits to an eye or ear instantly killed the ruthless beasts.

Click.

It was at that moment that something clicked for the boars, the intelligent species with the superior brains, capable of learning, of adapting, capable of never forgetting. At that moment, one of the older boars remembered a day similar to this one when the sounder had been feeding peacefully before surprise and noise felled a dozen of their members in rapid succession. He remembered that, and he remembered the condescending tone. The human laugh, cruel and triumphant, near maniacal.

The laugh of one of the "Infamous Ones."

The message passed from swine to swine. He was not dead. He was not gone. He was here before them now. Here once again with noise and surprise. Only this time, the boars did not flee in terror.

Panicked, Jimmy lost count as he fired again, again, and again. The fourth and fifth shots dropped two more boars. Jimmy's sixth aim was futile.

Click.

"Fuck, I'm out of ammo! Fuck!" Jimmy screamed.

Nine boars lay dead just below their feet. Yet, boar after boar aggressively rubbed their thick hides against the trees, shredding bark off the trunks while shaking the trees more than the men did themselves. Still over two hundred boars grunted and growled at the men just above them. Several pigs squealed and raced one after another as they fought to lick any remaining drops of blood.

"Oh, my god!" cried Jimmy.

Click.

It had been only six minutes since the unthinkable had occurred. The two were numb. While Mark clutched one drought-stricken cottonwood tree and Jimmy another, the boars continued to antagonistically scrape their hides against the trunks. They circled, growled, and grunted some more at the humans. And slowly, imperceptibly, they began to focus on one tree in particular. One tree holding one particular human.

"What the fuck are we gonna do?" cried Jimmy.

Another minute passed.

Twelve more clicks.

Mark asked, "Why did you do it, Jimmy?"

"What the fuck are you talkin' about?" Jimmy focused his attention on the boars below, not bothering to look at Mark.

"I know what you did," Mark confronted him.

"It was the way we were raised!" screamed Jimmy.

"Then you were raised like pigs," Mark stated flatly.

"God damn it, Mark! It's kill or be killed," Jimmy said. "Carl woulda done the same thing. Only one of us was gonna make it to the tree. I made sure it was me."

Not quite sure what Jimmy was talking about, Mark said, "The same thing Jimmy? He would have done the same thing?"

"He was in my way!" Jimmy screamed. "He didn't react fast enough. I pushed him out of the way, and he fell."

"Jesus, Mary, 'n Joseph. You even betray your own flesh and blood," Mark said, amazed and disgusted.

"He fell, god dammit! It wasn't my fault!" screamed Jimmy.

"It's no wonder no one wants to do business with us; we've earned our reputation," declared Mark.

"It doesn't matter, Mark! It's over! It's done! What do ya think Dad and I were doin' all day? AAC is done, Mark, you stupid fuck!"

"I figured your father knew to the penny," Mark surmised.

"You're a fuckin' idiot, Mark! There are no pennies! None! Don't cha get it? Our share of the equity is gone, has been for a while, plus hundreds of millions more of investors' capital. Dad couldn't believe it lasted this long. Some of those investors were his best friends."

"So there's nothin' left at all?" Mark asked.

"Hell, if a trip around the world cost a dollar, I couldn't make it to Oklahoma. We got nothin'; our family is bankrupt. Why didn't cha catch on? You think I'd buy all those options for no reason? Dad ordered me to. I was just his fuckin' pawn, always have been. We put on the airport trade, Mark. The fuckin' airport trade!" Jimmy cried.

Twenty-four more clicks and two hundred boars still mingled below, chomping at the bit to devour both of them. The numbness Mark felt now turned to disgust, outrage, and vengeance.

"If the world economy doesn't collapse by six a.m. Tuesday, we're fixin' to be long gone. Dad made all the final arrangements. He and I will be on a plane to a destination I don't even know," stated Jimmy.

"I know other things, too, Jimmy!" Mark said.

"What? What the fuck do ya know, Mark? That half my trades were bullshit? That I had multiple accounts that offset one another to make it look like I was a genius because I only bragged about the winnin' trades? Is that what ya know, Mark, huh?" demanded Jimmy.

"You slept with my wife, Jimmy!" Mark abruptly accused him.

There was silence.

"You fucked Elaine, Jimmy! She bucked you off like a rocket ship! Is that true, Jimmy? She about took your whole earlobe off?"

Jimmy didn't respond.

"I should kill you," Mark stated sternly. "You make wild boars look civilized!"

"Really? Look around, Mr. Reason who has to analyze everything. There are a couple hundred boars waitin' to tear us to pieces! You can't kill me! I can wait up here all night if I have to! When the boars disappear, I'm gettin' down from this tree! You will too, and we'll drive back in those trucks! I'm catchin' that plane on Tuesday! What you decide to do, I don't give a fuck!" responded Jimmy.

"I'm going to kill you, Jimmy," Mark told him again.

Jimmy laughed and then mocked his friend. "I have to admit, Mark, Elaine is one fine piece of ass—probably the best I've ever had! She liked it rough!"

Mark reached into his holster and drew the Smith and Wesson.

"It only holds five rounds, asshole! You're out of bullets!" Jimmy told him.

Mark looked down and started counting out loud, "One, two, three, four, five, six, seven, eight, nine?" as he emphasized the last number. "*Nine* dead boars, not ten. Lordy, lordy, how could that be? Ya prick!"

Jimmy stared him down, "Who gives a shit if it's nine, not ten? You can't kill me. They'll find the bullet. You ain't man enough to go to jail."

"You know, if they ever find that bullet, Jimmy, where it will be?" asked Mark.

Jimmy refused to respond.

"In a pile of shit, Jimmy!" Mark answered for him as he raised the gun.

"You won't kill me! You're a liberal fuck! You don't have the guts! You don't even believe in the death penalty!" Jimmy continued to mock his old friend.

"You're wrong, Jimmy," Mark said as he coolly lined up his friend.

Just then a boar slammed into Jimmy's tree. Then a second and soon afterwards a third boar rocked the tree Jimmy clung to.

As they stared each other down. It wasn't Jimmy that Mark saw. Mark saw the biggest wild pig he had ever seen, and it was clinging to a tree.

Mark had one last revelation for the pig. "You know, Jimmy, as we chased those boars down yesterday? I thought I had lost the thrill of the hunt. I guess I was wrong. Like you always say, 'It's kill or be killed'."

Realizing Mark was dead serious; Jimmy began maneuvering between branches, trying to make his body a smaller target, trying to put as much of the tree's narrow trunk between his body and Mark's bullet. Before he could firmly plant his right foot, one of the biggest of the boars slammed into the tree with all the force his 500 pounds could muster, causing Jimmy's foot to slip. He lost hold of the branch he gripped with his left hand. As he started to fall, he barely caught hold of a new limb with his right hand. Dangling above the animals thrashing and maneuvering for position below, he knew his grip was weak.

In a panic, he screamed, "Help me! Help!" as he tried in vain to replant even one foot on a sturdy branch.

Mark lowered the revolver and stared at Jimmy. "Help you? Not this time, you heartless shyster."

"I can pay you," Jimmy offered desperately when he felt his grip slip further as the hogs, one after another, continued slamming into the cottonwood tree. "I can fuckin' pay you!"

Mark snorted at the pig. "You're gonna die just like you lived, lying. I'll remember you to Elaine. I'll tell her you died squealing like a cornered pig."

"Fuck you!" Jimmy screamed. Whether it was directed at Mark or at the boars was not readily apparent. "Fuck you!"

One final slam and his grip gave way.

Thud.

Click.

Mark was surprised to discover Jimmy did have a heart after all. The hogs proved it to him when they ripped it from Jimmy's chest and devoured it while Mark watched.

Twenty clicks later, Jimmy was gone.

Finders Weepers

Lighthouse Trail; Monday, November 19, 2012; 6:40 A.M.

Their routine was the same as always. The passenger that week was responsible for unlocking and opening the gate, waiting for the car to drive through, then closing the gate and putting the chain and lock back in place before jumping back into the car and descending into the canyon.

"Damn near 2013, and they still use a padlock!" Gary complained.

Stuart laughed, "It's the state, what do you expect? At least they give us the combination!"

Other than the one strange occurrence last week—finding the demolished bike frames and helmets, almost every weekday morning was machine-like for the men. They arrived at the park's entrance well before sunrise, let themselves in, and then drove to the trailhead. After stretching, they had just enough light to begin their run. Typically, they were back at the car well before any visitors arrived. For the second time in a week, their daily regiment would be far from typical.

Unbeknownst to them, only twenty minutes behind was a convoy of Canyon City and Amarillo police officers plus search and rescue teams prepared to begin an exhaustive search of the state park, aided by

406

helicopters that would fill the canyon with their unmistakable rumbling sounds. Their lives would never be the same.

"How long do you think we should wait 'til we put those frames on eBay?" Stuart asked as they wound their way through the canyon to the Lighthouse Trailhead.

"As badly as I need the money, I want to do it now, for the holidays. But I think we should play it safe and wait until spring," answered Gary.

"The longer we wait, the less we'll get for 'em," countered Stuart, the one who didn't want to take the bikes in the first place.

"Good point. They're still this year's model," added Gary.

"I'm game right now," suggested Stuart who needed the money even more than Gary.

"All right, what about the helmets? Should we list those too? I bet we can get seventy-five for each," Gary guessed as he pulled up to the trailhead.

"Absolutely, I really need the cash," Stuart answered.

The runners had it down to seconds. By the time they reached the trailhead, it was 6:56 a.m., thirty minutes before sunrise. They spent the next ten minutes stretching before they began their daily jaunt.

Maintaining their usual pace, Stuart began the inevitable conversation, "I'm not even sure how much longer I can afford the gas to get here."

Gary understood. "I'm not much better off. Hell, I have no idea how I'm gonna pay child support in December. And I have to get the kids somethin' for Christmas."

"They doing OK?" asked Stuart.

"It's tough, man. All their mother and I do is fight," Gary confided. "It's so hard on the kids. I guess I shouldn't be surprised. We separated because all we did was argue. Thought it was best for the kids if we divorced.

You know what? Marriage, divorce didn't matter. Nothin' was ever best for the kids."

"Sorry, man. Our generation has really screwed up. Hopefully our kids will learn from it," replied Stuart.

"It's sad. I'm thirty-five, and these runs are all I have to look forward to; they keep me sane," admitted Gary.

Stuart agreed, "I know. Runnin' here in this beautiful canyon helps me chill, burns off all the bitterness and bullshit."

It would be the last time either of them would run the Lighthouse Trail.

Rounding a sweeping bend, the runners approached a dry riverbed. Alarmed, Stuart reached out and grabbed Gary's sweatshirt bringing him to a dead stop. Both stood frozen in the middle of the trail as two coyotes stared them down thirty feet ahead.

"Don't run, just stay still," Stuart advised Gary.

Ten, fifteen seconds went by before the coyotes bolted off into the brush. The men didn't budge.

"Wow! Never seen coyotes so bold. Normally they just run off," said Stuart.

"That was strange," Gary agreed.

The two hesitantly took a couple steps forward.

"Do you think we should turn back?" asked Gary.

"No, I think we're OK," Stuart said. "Let's walk until we get across that riverbed."

"OK," Gary replied.

Both felt something wasn't right, just as Amy had two nights ago, but neither understood the vibe the canyon radiated that morning.

Slowly walking down the modest slope that led to the riverbed, they were taken aback again. A large turkey vulture launched itself to the sky from a little ways down the gulch to their left.

"Something's dead in that gulch. That's why the coyotes and buzzards are there," Stuart said.

Apprehensively, they tried to decide which way to focus, left where the vulture took to the air and the coyotes came from, or the direction to which the coyotes ran. Their senses told them left as they warily moved down the grade.

A few steps further as they reached the river bed, Stuart screamed "Oh shit!" as he again gripped Gary's sweatshirt.

Death can be peaceful, the aftermath respectful. But being killed by wild boars and then left to decompose in a dry riverbed to be feasted on by a host of scavengers is downright grotesque. The sight of Rafi and Mitch side by side, rigor mortis set in, their bodies ravaged from the attack then shredded by coyotes, only to be picked at by a host of vultures overwhelmed the pair. Frozen, similar to the bodies that lay in front of them, the two looked on in horror. The coyotes gone, several turkey vultures hopped toward the dead bodies to peck at the open wounds.

"What the fuck!" Stuart yelled.

Both turned to run only to see the coyotes staring them down again. Neither animal flinched as they lurked in the riverbed on the other side of the trail. The men inched a few steps forward before both took off running back to the trailhead.

Stuart quickly glanced back. The look slowed him just enough for Gary's toe to hit the back of his shoe. The contact sent both men sprawling. Bloodied hands, elbows, and knees, Stuart and Gary were up as fast as they fell.

"Go! Go! Go!" screamed Gary.

The two kept running, periodically looking back to make sure no one or no thing chased them. As they approached the trailhead, they saw several police cars in the lot and lining the park's road.

"Two people are dead! Two dead bodies! On the trail!" Fighting to breathe from his mad dash and panic, Stuart screamed to the horde of police officers.

Gary gulped in air and told them, pointing back the way they had come, "Two dead men. In a gulch about a mile up the trail! There are two dead men lying in the gulch."

Within seconds, four police officers on mountain bikes raced up the path. Bent over, hands on their thighs, Stuart and Gary tried to catch their breath so they could tell the officers what they had seen. Teams scurried to prepare a team of dogs from the K9 unit. A few minutes later, the first helicopter buzzed the canyon before hovering over the dead bodies.

Never before had Stuart and Gary seen such a grisly sight. Never again would they run the trails of Palo Duro Canyon.

Bedlam

Texas Panhandle; Monday, November 19, 2012; 9:49 A.M.

Less than two hours after the runners had hysterically informed police of the two dead bodies along the trail, bedlam engulfed the entire Panhandle. Search dogs quickly found the site where Zach and Amy had been devoured. A few minutes later, the dogs signaled another area where Trey's pocket knife was found.

A K9 unit continued to circle and sniff the area around the shaded bench where Kenny and Lance had become the boars' first victims, but nothing definitive was found. What rocked the entire state, however, were the reports of finding Canyon, Texas, Chief of Police Floyd Thompson dead in a clearing a few hundred yards off Highway 207.

Spotted from the air, authorities found his unmarked car in the recess of a small, oval-shaped clearing bordered by a thick ring of mesquite, cottonwood, and juniper trees. Armstrong County sheriff deputies were the first to arrive at the scene. The chief of police had been fatally shot with a single bullet to his forehead, his left forearm crushed. Officers speculated his arm had been run over twice by a vehicle, possibly when the car backed up and then again when it moved forward. But the most disturbing aspect of the murder was the crude removal of Thompson's liver. Combined with the fact that coyotes and turkey vultures had already begun scavenging the body only intensified the appalling scene. The murder of a police official prompted both the Amarillo Special Crimes Unit and the Texas Rangers to investigate.

Moments later, the news grew more sensational. The helicopter pilot who had spotted the chief of police excitedly radioed headquarters, urging units to respond. He claimed he had just dispersed the largest pack of wild boars he had ever seen. As he descended to get a closer look, pigs of all colors and sizes fled in every direction.

To his astonishment, he found a lone man signaling him from a cottonwood tree. Being in a flat area on the edge of the canyon, the pilot was able to land the helicopter. The moment he touched down, the man jumped from the tree and chaotically ran for the helicopter. Panic stricken, the man said he was from New York. He had such a thick New England accent and was speaking so fast about his friends being eaten by a bunch of pigs, the pilot could hardly understand him.

New information rushed in so fast, law enforcement agencies had a difficult time distinguishing fact from fiction. With the public monitoring police radio channels on their handheld devices, word spread like wildfire. Before noon, every flight into Amarillo was booked by media personnel. No story could top a mass murderer terrorizing the Palo Duro Canyon region where wild pigs, sometimes referred to as feral hogs, had been eating corpses, eliminating evidence of crimes. Adding fuel to the fire, another report disputed the mass murderer speculation and claimed it was actually wild pigs, better known as wild boars that were responsible for the deaths.

Back in Canyon City, Amy's father, Charles Smith, was so livid he had his attorney start drafting the initial lawsuit. The astute furniture retailer from San Antonio still had not seen or talked with anyone of authority. Mayor Jeffries, who was supposed to meet the Smiths and their attorney at seven o'clock that morning, never showed. With the chief of police dead and the detectives at the scene, the three from San Antonio finally met with an officer named Barron. The businessman and his attorney immediately recognized they were dealing with a complete idiot, regardless of the fact he was distraught about his cousin being murdered. It would only become more surreal when the next rumor went viral.

CNN and *The New York Times* both reported that anonymous sources indicated that photos existed of wild boars attacking a group of hunters, killing them before savagely consuming their bodies. Fox News disputed the report and ran a breaking news story titled "Hogwash," mocking CNN, *The New York Times*, and the liberal media for fear mongering. The notion that climate change had caused harmless pigs to kill people was ludicrous and demonstrated how desperate the left wanted to keep environmental issues on the front page. The news agency claimed they had reliable sources stating that a now-unemployed illicit marijuana dealer from Colorado, who tried to establish new territory in the Texas Panhandle, went crazy and killed more than a dozen innocent people who then were eaten by the pigs. The report blamed the irresponsible legalization of marijuana in Colorado for the deaths. Fox News suggested the country should expect more of this type of violence as drug dealers battled over dwindling territories where marijuana remained illegal. No matter what news organization people watched or who they believed, the world's eyes turned to Texas, in particular, the Texas Panhandle.

With elections come and gone, the media was ecstatic about the shock value of the story. Just when they thought the buzz couldn't get any more captivating, it went nuclear. Fox News announced that rocker and frequent network guest Ted Nugent was identified as a potential victim. A man named Gilbert, who stated he was the majority owner of a ranch that comprised several thousand acres of the canyon, found a hunting blind overturned, its floor caved in, and the fiberglass around the windows shredded from dozens of bullet holes. Two hunting rifles and two pistols were found at the scene—guns believed to be owned by Ted Nugent and his hunting partner, Derek Fine, both of Waco, Texas. Gilbert tearfully acknowledged he found blood stains inside the structure but completely broke down when he attempted to explain the most haunting aspect at the site; a severed forearm he found underneath the blind when it was turned right-side up.

The reporting of Ted Nugent's apparent demise put a face on the tragedy.

Whether people loved him, hated him, or were indifferent, the man's unique personality and distinct facial attributes prompted people to decide, "If it could happen to a master hunter like Ted Nugent, it could happen to me!"

Fox News didn't help when it plastered a photo of Nugent holding a semi-automatic, military-style rifle with the caption, "Are You Next?" followed by footage of wild boars running through the streets of Amarillo from a few weeks earlier. The public's response was predictable. Walmarts throughout Texas proclaimed there was another run on firearms and ammo, even larger than when Barack Obama had first been elected then reelected. Governor Rick Perry of Texas called for calm and ordered a statewide media ban for all government and law-enforcement personnel.

Despite the directive, all hell broke loose when Fox News alarmed the public at 5:57 p.m. (CST) via email, smartphone alerts, and Twitter of shocking photographs they had obtained and would broadcast at the top of the hour. Warning the public, Shepard Smith explained that a series of photographs taken from a camera found at one of the scenes, designed to snap every five seconds if motion was detected, revealed the most stunning pictures he had ever seen. Smith went on to describe the setting where five hunters were standing near a feeder to attract wild boars when an enormous horde of deranged beasts attacked, killed, and then ate three of the men. Two men miraculously made it to a pair of trees that were within proximity of each other. Later it appeared one of the men fell and was also eaten alive by the man-eating creatures.

The first photograph unveiled showed the moment of impact of one of the hunters when he was struck by a boar. The snapshot clearly demonstrated the brute force of the animal as his body was badly contorted. Two photographs later captured the horde of animals surrounding the man. Photo after photo depicted dozens of wild pigs fighting to get at the body as they ripped the hunter into pieces. Smith went on to say the photographs were the most gruesome images he had ever seen and that Rupert Murdoch and Roger Ailes were personally reviewing every picture to determine what could be aired. The photographs stunned the world, prompting several web sites featuring wild boars to crash as people around the world frantically searched for additional information about a beast few knew about.

In the wake of the pigs' savagery, most of the south followed Texas's lead as gun retailers reported shelves of ammunition were being bought in whole, leading to claims of price gouging at hundreds of shops. The cascading events forced Texas Governor Rick Perry to call for a special press conference at nine o'clock the next morning. The governor's address would further entrench the worldwide brand name of "Texas."

Price Willing to Pay

Twenty Miles East of the New Mexico Border; Tuesday, November 20, 2012; 7:00 A.M.

Three thousand strong and growing exponentially by the mile, the select bloc of boars continued their westward migration. It was days, often weeks, before all of the privileged boars reached their final destination; the eastern and central counties of New Mexico.

The trip took its toll on the community as nearly 10 percent of the population died en route to perceived safety. Between disease, excessive exertion for the extreme old and young, automobiles, and the hands of man, the death totals eventually exceeded twenty thousand boars. It was a price the leaders deemed warranted for their long-term survival.

The Press Conference

Austin, Texas; Tuesday, November 20, 2012; 9:05 A.M.

"My fellow Texans, I'm here to announce that the great state of Texas is unequivocally at war," Governor Perry opened his address. He stood in the glare of television lights, in front of reporters, staff members, and general hangers-on, talking in somber tones.

"We all know that wild hogs have been a nuisance in Texas for years. It's been estimated that nearly half of the several million vermin nationwide cohabitate right here in our great state. With the ruthless killings that have taken place in the Panhandle the last few days, I promise I will utilize every resource at my disposal—and I mean every resource—to root out these vicious creatures and annihilate every last one of them. Except of course the ones we need for sport. Over the years, I've done my part. I will continue to do so with a heavy heart as I seek revenge like several others who have lost relatives and friends. To the pig nation, let it be known the reprisal will be disproportionate for the apparent demise of my great friend and hunting partner. I pray Mr. Nugent is alive and safe, but if he is not, I have faith that he is in a much, much better place. It appears he and sixteen others—Texans—lost their lives. These attacks were unwarranted. It is my responsibility as governor of the Great State of Texas that the boars suffer consequences so unequal that another attack would be unthinkable. A human life is a precious thing. You can be sure the toll on the boar nation will be nothing less than devastating."

Taking a cue from a staff member, the governor corrected an earlier statement. "Excuse me, I meant to say fifteen people died; two of the presumed dead, we believe, were illegal aliens. We won't count them among the totals."

He inclined his ear to another aide urgently whispering to him, and then returned to the microphone. "And, well, not all of the legal dead were in fact Texans. They also include two from New Jersey and one from Pakistan. Fellow Texans, I assure you I have top people looking into that death to see if there is any connection to the Al-Qaeda network and its attempts to bring shame on this great state of ours. His wife and children are already being held for questioning."

The governor continued, "Of course fighting this war will be costly. As promised over the years, I will not spend one dime of the good people of Texas's money that is not accounted for. Estimates to exterminate these wild pigs are in the hundreds of millions of dollars. I'll be working with my staff to determine the allocation of the monies. But again, I vow to my fellow Texans, I will not now, or ever, raise taxes to pay for a war."

"Questions?"

The horde of media from across the globe implored to ask questions. The governor pointed to a reporter in the third row.

"Governor, how many people are presumed missing and dead?" asked the first reporter.

Looking at his staff member, the governor said, "Fifteen."

"But don't the two illegal aliens who are presumed dead count?" quizzed the reporter.

"No, they were here illegally," he said.

"What about the two boys?" the reporter persisted. "What's going to happen to them?"

"We'll be working with the Mexican consulate to repatriate them to their native country as soon as possible," the governor answered. "It's not the Texas taxpayers who should be supporting those who came illegally."

"Governor, if the illegal aliens don't count, what about the two presumed dead from New Jersey? They are not Texans or promote Texas values," noted the reporter.

"I will have to confer with my staff," answered the governor. He then pointed to a reporter to his right.

"Governor, what about the chief of police?" asked the reporter from Mississippi. "Wasn't he murdered?"

"I can't comment on that right now. It is an ongoing criminal investigation at this time."

"But Governor, do you think the boars may somehow be involved?" she asked.

"We have not ruled out anything," declared the governor taking the next question.

"Governor, some are claiming drought caused by climate change led the wild boars to turn on man. Do you believe that?" asked a reporter from Seattle.

"I can't speculate what provoked the wild boars to attack humans. I do know climate change is a hoax perpetuated by the liberal media. If there was such a thing, it wouldn't cause droughts. Droughts are caused by acts of God," stressed Perry.

A reporter yelled without being called on, "Governor, how do you plan on eradicating the millions of wild boar roaming the state?"

"Again, I'll be working with my staff on that plan," the governor answered. "Between the Texas Rangers, the Texas National Guard, local law enforcement agencies, and the over one million registered hunters in our great state, we plan to hunt down and kill every one of these varmints; except, again, the ones we'll keep for game. The boars have run roughshod over this state too long. I plan putting an end to that as of today."

"But Governor, won't that create a dangerous situation having all these people roaming the land trying to kill the boars?"

"Absolutely not! Gun owners are notoriously the most rational and cautious people. We don't expect that to be a problem."

The governor then pointed to a local reporter who asked, "Governor, you mentioned there would be no new taxes levied to pay for this. Do you know where the monies will come from?"

"Again, I will work with my staff on that one. But I would expect the usual suspects."

"Governor, Governor, will you be more specific?" demanded another reporter.

"Folks, I don't know yet," he answered.

"But Governor, when you say 'usual suspects' doesn't that mean education, arts, Medicaid, and an assortment of social services?" the reporter continued to pry.

"Most likely," said the governor.

"Governor, how can you do that?" the reporter persisted. "Haven't you already slashed education by several billion dollars? [33] The last published report claimed Texas now has 65,000 more students this year, yet fewer teachers. The document estimated the shortage of teachers is between 15,000 and 20,000. Don't we need to increase education spending?" [34]

"We have those extra students because under my leadership, the great state of Texas is the country's first and foremost job creator," bragged the governor, ignoring the question.

Another reporter jumped in, "Governor Perry, many of those jobs created pay minimum wage. Isn't Texas tied with Mississippi with the highest percentage of the workforce making minimum wage?" [35]

"True, but if the Obama administration gets their way, that rate will go up. Besides, what's wrong with having the highest percentage making the minimum wage? Texas is the state of equal opportunity where we give people a chance to succeed," the governor proudly boasted.

A reporter shot back, "Maybe because so many working for minimum wage don't have healthcare. Doesn't Texas have the highest percentage of uninsured at over 25 percent, far higher than the national average, Governor?" [36]

"Statistics don't always tell the true story. The fact is we create jobs here. Healthcare is not a government issue. It is an individual responsibility," the governor stated before he tried to end the question and answer session.

"But Governor, what about mental health? Will you be cutting those services too?" asked another concerned reporter.

"Mental health is nothing more than a state of mind," the governor nodded sagely. "My message is come to Texas, a state of freedom. If people can't find it on a map, it's just south of heaven."

"Governor Perry, including the District of Columbia, Texas ranks dead last, fifty-first in mental-health spending. It's not even close to the national average, and you've already cut the budget in half again this year. [37] Don't you think this travesty only increases the need for mental-health services?" debated the reporter from CNN.

"Not at all," claimed the governor. "In fact, spending hundreds of millions decimating the boars is the best method to improve mental health."

"But, Governor—" the CNN reporter tried to ask another question before being cut off.

"I think all you liberals should think about that. Freedom and keeping Texans safe is the best prescription for mental health. As Governor, I pledge to do just that," added the staunch freedom fighter.

The governor looked around the stunned room for the next question.

"Governor, how did these wild boars get here in the first place?" a new reporter asked.

"My understanding is they were shipped to America decades, even hundreds of years ago, for sport."

"Governor Perry, if that is the case, shouldn't the hunters pay increased license fees to help offset some of the costs?" reasoned the reporter.

"No, I've already said I will not raise taxes in any fashion," Perry answered sternly.

Another reporter shouted out, "How long do you think it will take to kill all the pigs?"

"I don't expect it to take long. We have the finest state guard and law-enforcement agencies in the country plus an army of rabid hunters like me. To show my patriotism, I plan on heading up to the Panhandle early Saturday to personally kill as many wild hogs as possible. I pray it will be a good example for all the other fine Texans who are outraged by these travesties."

Even the beat reporters were stunned, unable to ask the next question.

"Thanks, and God bless Texas!" the governor said before he walked away from the podium.

Win-Win-Win

Houston, Texas; Wednesday, November 21, 2012; 1:00 A.M.

Word of the unfathomable tragedy swept the globe. Journalists from every corner of the world descended upon Amarillo and the surrounding Panhandle. Hotel rooms as far as Dallas, Oklahoma City, and Albuquerque were booked to fill the insatiable demand for real news. Governor Perry, after his initial news conference, proudly welcomed all and boldly proclaimed Texas was still and will always be the land of the Wild West.

It was one in the morning when Lin, still awake, answered the phone. On the other end, the man spoke in Mandarin.

"Mr. Lin, I want to make sure you fulfill your quotas each and every month until the contract expires at the end of December 2013," the man said.

"Yes, yes indeed. I understand," Lin replied in his native tongue.

"You are in a very enviable position, Mr. Lin," advised the man from Shanghai.

"Indeed, I am, Mr. Chen," he responded in a confident manner.

"I would like to increase our agreed-upon contract, Mr. Lin," requested the man from seventy-six hundred miles away.

"I see," responded Lin.

"Is that possible, my dear friend?" asked the businessman.

"By how much?" questioned Lin.

"I would like to double my order starting in December," suggested the eager buyer.

"Interesting, interesting, I just . . ." replied Lin.

"What will it take, Mr. Lin?" he asked bluntly before Lin could fully respond. "I have some very excited buyers for such exotic meat."

To guarantee the suggested amounts, Lin demanded triple the current contract's price. Chen was unhappy with the offer but didn't bicker.

"You are a very greedy man, Mr. Lin, but I will do that. They must come from Texas of course," he emphasized.

"Yes, of course, they'll be from Texas. And if I certify they are from the Panhandle?"

"Interesting thought. And the premium?" an intrigued Chen asked.

"Seven times the original seems reasonable," Lin offered. "And just for you, I will increase the volumes delivered fourfold instead of doubled at the same increased prices."

"Consider it done," a pleased Chen said before he hung up.

Over the course of the next few days, Lin secured a very state-friendly contract with the governor's office to collect the remains of the slaughtered wild hogs. It was a win-win-win scenario for the state, buyer, and the seller.

POS

Texas; Wednesday, November 21, 2012 - Easter 2013

Stuck in the Texas Panhandle for the Thanksgiving holiday weekend, the media grew bored. Just one day after the press conference, without any new attacks to report, they understood the photographs revealed all that needed to be known: the boars had stalked, killed, and consumed seventeen humans.

By mid-day Friday, the day after Thanksgiving, the media had abandoned Amarillo, Lubbock, Albuquerque, and Oklahoma City. Most, who used Dallas-Fort Worth as a base, remained there on Friday night to party before heading home on Saturday. A few journalists with no family ties remained in the area in hopes of new attacks but were disappointed as the boars were already in retreat.

The Sunday morning talk shows made brief mention of the incident before the panelists returned to a more conventional issue they knew even less about: the fiscal cliff. With no traditional burials, less than a week later, the names of sixteen of the seventeen victims were long forgotten.

Despite a temporary spike in sales of Ted Nugent paraphernalia, most had even disregarded Nugent's death until a blip regarding the case was announced on November 28, 2012, eight days after Governor Rick

Perry's press conference. In the aftermath of the attacks, forensics had collected hundreds of piles of fecal matter. In one pile of dung, searchers found an intact plastic guitar pick with the drawing of a hand giving "the finger." The guitar pick was one of Ted's infamous designs. Tests confirmed the feces contained DNA of the man who glamorized guns and intolerance. The definitive evidence proved it was Ted Nugent who literally was a piece of shit, not President Barack Obama.

Sales of the guitar pick surged as liberals bought the entire inventory. Soon afterwards, sales faded again, and in reality, the discovery of the soulless shit only hastened the decline of the Motor City Madman's popularity. For weeks, however, wild boar paraphernalia flew off the shelves. Spurred on by periodic hoaxes and the public's fascination with a beast that had the gall to challenge man as equals, sales of "anything and everything" wild boar continued unabated.

Later, despite a temporary injunction awarded the Nugent estate, the city of Canyon auctioned on eBay the guitar pick found in the pile of shit, the profit used to offset budget deficits created by the unprecedented investigations. A bidding war between an Arab sheik living in Dubai and a prominent NRA member resulted in the pick selling for $1,325,000, easily offsetting the deficits incurred. Conservatives cried foul as another historic piece of Americana left its shores.

The enchantment with wild boars only heightened the resolve of Governor Rick Perry. A man of his word, the Governor used every tool available to eradicate the boars. By Easter of 2013, Texas had culled the state population of wild boars by nearly seven-hundred fifty thousand, approximately a third of the total. Radicals, moderates, and even independent sounders that attempted to avoid man at all costs incurred devastating losses.

One class of boar, however, cleverly escaped the wrath of the Texas governor. Over two hundred thousand boars safely crossed state lines into New Mexico and formed a new federation made up of thousands of new sounders. Together they compromised, cooperated, and put the species' long-term best-interests front and center. Their lone guiding principle was simple: the pure Russian variety would remain pure.

But the animal kingdom knew stability was the key for all species' survival; that if one species or faction of species had no checks and balances, the world would spin out of control, and the cascading events would prove dire for all. As the mass genocide of feral hogs left dead carcasses littering the state, coyotes and vultures moved into Texas from all borders, while the rat and raccoon population surged.

The scavengers knew their place; they were there to help clean up man's mess.

Domesticated

Mark & Elaine's Condominium; Upper East Side Manhattan
Wednesday, November 21, 2012; Early Evening

"Oh, my god! Honey, honey, I never thought you'd make it home. I've been worried sick!" Elaine wept, tightening her embrace of Mark despite the slight discomfort. He stood emotionless in the doorway, one hand at his side, the other a firm grip on his luggage.

Quickly breaking from her grasp, he left his suitcase at the front door, removed his hat, and hung it on the luggage's pullout handle. Walking toward the main living area, Mark responded, "After everything that transpired, there were a lot of questions. Local police, Texas Rangers, Special Crimes Unit, media, even Texas Wildlife officers."

"I'm so happy you're OK. It's horrible, just horrible," she sobbed.

"It's all over," responded Mark.

"I can't believe this happened. Oh, my god! And Jimmy. His poor family," cried Elaine as she trailed him into the formal study.

"What a way to go," was all he could say.

Elaine was shocked. "I never knew wild pigs were so dangerous. I just can't imagine. How could this happen?" she asked.

428

"When a species is threatened, they become unpredictable. I guess the hogs reached their breaking point," Mark suggested.

"Are you OK? Are you hurt at all?" she wondered as she tried to gain his attention.

"I'm fine. It's over," he said again, refusing to make eye contact as he rifled through his files.

"What's going to happen with AAC? . . . What are you looking for?" Elaine asked.

"The regulators will freeze any remaining assets then liquidate the open positions as soon as possible. That's over too," Mark stated indifferently, ignoring her second question.

Finding what he was looking for, he placed a sealed envelope into the front inner pocket of his jacket.

Elaine remained in a daze.

Their eyes meeting for the first time, Mark humorously told her, "AAC is completely gone, nothing's left. Just like Jimmy."

"What are you going to do? And Jimmy. I can't believe he's gone. They can't even properly bury him," cried Elaine, attempting to embrace her husband again.

Ignoring her gesture, Mark turned and walked out of the study, Elaine cautiously following him. He quickly made his way to the refrigerator at the far end of the kitchen, grabbed a cold beer and a bottle opener, popped off the cap, and took a long gulp. The coldness ran down Elaine's spine.

Expressionless, looking at nothing in particular, Mark said again, "It's over."

Elaine stood at the opposite end of the kitchen island. "What's over? Why do you keep saying it's over?" she asked.

"We're over, Elaine, us," Mark calmly informed her.

Stunned, Elaine asked, "What? What do you mean?"

"It's over. We're over. I don't want to see another pig the rest of my life," Mark replied.

"What are you talking about?" Elaine asked, desperately trying to figure out what her husband was saying.

"Selfish pigs—that's what I'm talking about," Mark answered without changing his demeanor.

"I don't understand," Elaine said coyly.

Not surprised by her deceitfulness, Mark took another long swig of beer.

Chewing on her thumbnail, Elaine's mind desperately began trying to justify her actions. "Mark, please, please, I love you. What is wrong?"

Staring at her, his lust completely gone, Mark explained, "You and Jimmy, sharing a pigpen. That's what's wrong."

Mark instinctively tugged on his ear a few times.

"Mark, Jimmy was just . . ." Elaine tried to reason.

"He was a friggin' pig, eaten by his own kind. And you were his slop!" Mark abruptly interrupted her before finishing his beer.

"Mark. Please, Mark, please listen," she pleaded, taking a few steps toward her husband.

"You were raised like Jimmy; you did what you needed to do to satisfy your own self-interest. Since we've met, it's evident you've come full circle, Elaine. I'm sure your parents will be relieved," Mark carefully explained, letting her know he understood her actions, but the market had turned and he was fully prepared to sell, to sell *her*.

"I don't know what I was thinking. Mark, please!" she again tried to reason with her husband.

"Perched in a tree just a few feet above a couple hundred wild boars clamoring to shred my body to bits, I had a revelation, Elaine. Now when I relive the terror, when I look at or even think of you, all I see is you and Jimmy wallowing in a bed of mud. You two have become the pigs trying to devour me," Mark informed her.

"Jimmy's not a pig! How can you say that? He was a good man. He created jobs. He hired you. Look at all he accomplished," Elaine said, defending Jimmy while not mentioning herself.

"A good man? He had names for all his women. The Growler, the Grunter, the Wallower. You know what your name was? The Squealer! You, my wife, he named the Squealer! Real classy, huh? Is that what you consider a good man? He accomplished nothing except making it to the tree safely. And he did that by pushing his own brother down to get there first. Carl died because of Jimmy," Mark explained.

"Jimmy wouldn't do that. He loved his brothers. I saw their pictures!" protested Elaine.

Disgusted, Mark proclaimed, "Poor Jimmy. He existed for his own sake, even at the expense of his own brother. He deserved to die!"

"I can't believe you're relishing in his death! Damn you, Mark!" Elaine cried, confronting her husband.

"He died squealing like a pig. Let me hear you squeal, Elaine. Don't all pigs sound alike?" Mark challenged her, wanting to know as they now stood face to face.

"How dare you!" Elaine roared, slapping Mark hard across his left cheek.

He took the blow like a man, rubbed his cheekbone, and looked directly into her eyes.

"You're jealous! You're being spiteful!" Elaine shouted, trying to deflect the blame.

Knowing his cool was getting under her skin, he dug deeper. "Maybe if he hadn't been protecting himself from me, the bastard never would have fallen," Mark chuckled, mocking her.

"What are you talking about?" Elaine demanded to know.

Eager to confess, Mark explained, "We were in separate trees, just feet apart. I had one bullet left, Jimmy had none. I threatened to kill him and was intent on doing it. As he was trying to move to another branch, making it harder for me to take aim at him, a boar slammed into the tree, and Jimmy lost his balance."

"Oh, my god!" Elaine gasped.

As Mark continued, she could no longer withstand his condescending look. Watching her turn away, his voice rose to make sure she heard him as he enjoyed sharing the details of Jimmy's demise.

"He dangled from that branch, desperately trying to hang on, begging me to help him, bribing me, squealing like a cornered pig. What could I do? I couldn't help him. The boars kept ramming the tree until he fell. I guess the enraged beasts got their revenge. He didn't suffer much. It didn't take long, Elaine, as they tore him to pieces. Just like that; right before my own eyes, he was gone."

Thinking about the highs Jimmy provided her, Elaine blurted, "You bastard! You'll never be like Jimmy!" before she quickly bit her tongue.

Mark shook his head in pity. Elaine glared at him, her anger escalating. Mark walked back to the refrigerator, grabbed another beer, opened it, and took a healthy chug. He wasn't done tormenting Elaine.

"You know, I've hunted my whole life. Thought I knew the beast. But those boars near Palo Duro Canyon were a whole different animal. They would have loved to have eaten me too if I had fallen, but they didn't even attempt to knock me out of the tree. But Jimmy? They were relentless, repeatedly pummeling the tree he clung to. They were determined to get him. And they did. It was eerie," Mark told her.

Desperately trying to unnerve him, Elaine tried again to belittle her husband. "You weren't worthy, Mark. The boars obviously sensed Jimmy's greatness!"

"Greatness? Jimmy? Yeah, right. They killed Ted Nugent and his hunting partner too. In a matter of hours, they killed four of the most prolific pig hunters perhaps in history. Is that what you call greatness? Friggin' hog hunters who ambushed a bunch pigs they led to slaughter? Yet, since their demise no one else has been attacked. Hmm . . ." wondered Mark.

"Jimmy was special, Mark. Something you'll never be or understand," declared Elaine.

"Understand? Are you kidding?" Mark fired back.

"There's something special about the elite, Mark. My father was right. You weren't when we married nor will you ever be one of us," claimed Elaine, lowering her tone, trying to portray she was now in control and had no regrets.

Mark walked to the far side of the room, set his beer on the window ledge, and stared out the posh condominium located in the exquisite Upper East Side of Manhattan. Reminiscing about the two-bedroom bungalow where he grew up in Boston, sharing a bedroom with his two brothers, the Miller Lite his father drank, he smiled knowing how far he'd come, then smiled again knowing how far away he was from whom he didn't want to be.

Not satisfied, Elaine continued to deflect the blame. "America rose to prominence because we rewarded the difference makers, people like my grandfather. Today, we ridicule and punish them. There are no more incentives to be great like Jimmy's family or mine. We keep diluting the wealth, giving to the *takers* like you, Mark. We gave you—the unsophisticated, the unrefined—an equal opportunity. *We* paid for your schooling, allowed you in our inner circle. And this is how you pay your respects? God help us."

"I remember the days when you'd tell me how proud you were of me. Now I'm a leech who's sucking you, the elite, dry?" he asked. Reaching for his beer he noticed the crevice of the windowsill overflowed in dust.

"Over the past few years you've changed, Mark. What hope do you have now? You have nothing!" threatened Elaine.

Mark turned and grinned before he spoke. "I've changed; I'll be more than fine."

"You worked for Jimmy. Without him you're nothing," Elaine continued, disparaging her husband.

"I may have worked for Jimmy, but I was the head trader who mentored the entire office. Jimmy was oblivious to the facts and blinded by hatred. He couldn't reason. He was nothing but a pawn of his father who was a fraud. Jimmy was no great trader, except of women, Elaine," explained Mark.

"You'll never be Jimmy. He was a wild boar. You're nothing but a domesticated pig, eating from the public trough," she claimed.

"And like everyone else, always forced to eat the slop you served, but not anymore—at least not me," replied Mark.

Elaine stared him down as Mark confidently strode by her, making his way toward the door. Pausing, Mark asked, "Just curious, Elaine, what is your legacy? I mean Jimmy was a hedge fund trader, just like me—a friggin' joke. And you? What have you done that's trickled down to the masses that made their lives so much better?"

"You're an asshole!" spewed Elaine.

"Find someone else to feed your slop to, Elaine," Mark told her.

After opening the front door, Mark, with his index finger swiped the exquisite imported table that sat near the entrance, and then turned toward

Elaine and said, "Haven't you noticed? The entire apartment is coated in a blanket of dust. I swear I can taste it in my mouth."

Elaine could only stare at him in disbelief.

Standing in the doorway, he raised his Samuel Adams and quickly drained it, removing any hints of grit from his lips and tongue. Studying the words "Boston Lager," he smiled again, knowing how far he'd come as he set the bottle down on the small table. Reaching for his suitcase planted next to the door, Mark eyed Carl's hat he had hung on the pullout handle of the luggage. He picked it up, appreciating the irony of it all; one pig killing another. Closely examining each of the tusks protruding from the band that held them in place against the hat's crown, he plucked the largest tusk from the hat and slipped it into the pocket of his jacket where it nestled against the envelope he had so desperately sought. He set the hat back down on the edge of the dust-coated table; the hat fell to the floor. Smiling one last time, knowing how far away he was from whom he didn't want to be, he turned and dragged his suitcase behind him.

"Mark!" Elaine cried.

Mark didn't look back as he closed the door.

Click.

Author's Notes – The 80-20 Rule

October 2013

"You never let a serious crisis go to waste. And what I mean by that it's an opportunity to do things you think you could not do before." [38]
 – Rahm Emanuel, 2009 White House Chief of Staff

"My being there (South Africa) isn't going to affect any political structure. Besides, apartheid isn't that cut-and-dry. All men are not created equal."

"The preponderance of South Africa is a different breed of man. . .They still put bones in their noses, they still walk around naked, they wipe their butts with their hands. And when I kill an antelope for 'em, their preference is the gut pile. That's what they fucking want to eat, the intestines. These are different people. You give them toothpaste, they fucking eat it." [39]
 – Ted Nugent, *Detroit Free Press Magazine, July 15, 1990*

"There is not an action that I take that you don't have some folks in Congress who say that I'm usurping my authority. Some of those same folks think I usurp my authority by having the gall to win the Presidency." [40]
 – President Obama, in an interview with The New York Times, August 2013

Man left the world with quite a mess in 2008—debilitating individual, corporate, and governmental debt; economies severely contracting; massive job losses; unchecked fraud in the financial system; the largest income disparity in decades; a tax code favoring capital over labor; a never-ending state of war; unknown ramifications of climate change; an abundance of social injustices; abuses of privacy; and more—all less than twenty years after the collapse of communism. Unfortunately, all the scavengers from the animal kingdom combined weren't capable of fully cleansing the earth. Only man could do that. Only man could foster a healthy environment where balance reigned for all to thrive. Yet five years later, the autumn of 2013, the country still suffers from a toxic atmosphere. While racism and social and religious intolerance in particular play a role, the resistance to change is equally responsible for the virulent tone.

It's not 1950 anymore, not even 1980. Those unwilling to evolve, and worse yet, those who want to return to the past, must be soundly defeated by a passionate and engaged middle—a progressive majority who understands and believes in *genuine* respect for all religious beliefs; same-sex marriage; resolving the immigration quandary compassionately; revamping gun control; preventive and basic healthcare for all; fair and balanced financial rules and regulations; draconian improvement in public education; college tuition relief; a short, medium, and long-term climate change strategy; a complete overhaul of drug laws; investment in green technologies; and game-changing infrastructure projects. It's all very attainable.

For those who claim the majority of Democrats are European socialists who are rotting this nation to the core economically and morally, I say hogwash. Today's greatest risks aren't a rabid group seeking equality for all like the wild boars sought equality with man. The true risk today is the

437

polar opposite: It is a minority group I refer to as the Collateralized Right Wing Fringe (CRWF). A marginal faction, the CRWF openly promotes social intolerance, subtly and not so subtly supports religious prejudice, and believes in a holistic Darwinism philosophy that will, no doubt, further restrain upward mobility for all but the privileged.

The Pareto Principle, discovered over a century ago, exists for a reason: not everyone is equal. Like Jimmy in *SLOP*, many believe the 80-20 rule has actually become 90-10 and even 99-1 in some instances. Regardless of the current ratios, there will always be "takers." The question is: how does society empower more people, so the ratio can become 75-25 or even 70-30? Imagine the benefits of that.

Nothing is perfect; society is not equal. Free enterprise and democracy embodies equal opportunities, not equal outcomes. Both are messy. Both can be unjust. Over time, however, people, like markets normally correct themselves, find common ground and stability to flourish again—but not always. While large segments of society are strained economically and socially, the CRWF has employed every means possible to prevent a healthy correction, or "change," and will continue to do so until they convince a large enough contingent of disenfranchised moderates to eat their SLOP. They will seek to establish the current state of income disparity as the "new normal" while stealthy attempting to expand the disparities even further—all under the guise of personal freedom, the end of big government, and of course, individual responsibility regardless of the circumstances.

The decline of the middle class has been over thirty years in the making, culminating in the world-wide 2008 crisis. Obama didn't create the crisis; he inherited it, and he can't solve it. Neither can the moderate right, even if it had not been hijacked by the CRWF. Only the people in the middle can resolve their own plight. And it will take years of demanding and implementing real structural change before tangible results are achieved. But if the middle class remain unorganized, and change is forestalled—beware.

Because somewhere, there is the equivalent of a quarter-million pure Russian boars standing their ground, stirring, brewing, waiting—the skies above them filled with vultures.

More frightening?

Ted Cruz or Rand Paul succeeds where Rick Perry failed.

It can happen.

Click.

Why I wrote *SLOP – The Wild Boar Nation*

Soften the edges of an intense, fervent, and determined hard-right-wing fringe I call the Collateralized Right Wing Fringe (CRWF).

Remind the far left that no, we're not all equal. Equal opportunities, not equal outcomes, are what the majority seek.

Persuade those in the middle that change can be good. That it is up to us to demand and then help implement social and economic ideals that align with the majority and reject extremism and intolerance at all levels—social, religious and economic—so that the Pareto Rule, better known as the 80 – 20 rule, can someday be obliterated and become the 75 – 25 rule, or even the 70 – 30 rule. Can you imagine the benefits of that?

I'm extremely proud of what I wrote. It was the hardest thing I've ever done. And it took a collaborative effort to accomplish it. First and foremost, Ms. Charlotte Clebosky Kelley. Without her complete dedication editing and revising the book for an entire year, including contributing to the storyline, this book never would have been completed. As important was her love for and belief in me; for that, my eternal gratitude. Ms. Averyl Re; her efforts editing and revising the story, including her contributions to the storyline, will always be appreciated. Many thanks. Finally, Adept Word

Management, who advised and assisted me in getting to the finish line. I'll always be grateful.

I tried to write a book that was informative while challenging the reader's viewpoints on a number of social, economic, religious and geopolitical issues. To be effective, both real and fictional characters are used so the reader can empathize with storyline. Hopefully it is entertaining as well so I can accomplish the real objective: empower people to reject extremism and intolerance, to realize rigid, uncompromising personal beliefs often have unintended consequences. Only together can we make the world a better place for everyone.

Keith

Bibliography

http://www.huffingtonpost.com/2012/11/08/ted-nugent-on-obama-election-twitter-rant-economic-spiritual-suicide_n_2094490.html (1), page 64

http://www.huffingtonpost.com/2012/11/08/ted-nugent-on-obama-election-twitter-rant-economic-spiritual-suicide_n_2094490.html (2) page 65

http://www.huffingtonpost.com/2012/11/08/ted-nugent-on-obama-election-twitter-rant-economic-spiritual-suicide_n_2094490.html (3) page 65

http://abcnews.go.com/blogs/politics/2012/04/ted-nugent-rebuffs-democratic-attacks-im-a-black-jew-at-a-nazi-klan-rally/ (4) page 71

http://www.wnd.com/2012/04/ted-nugent-fires-back-at-secret-service-probe/ (5) page 71

http://www.huffingtonpost.com/2012/11/08/ted-nugent-on-obama-election-twitter-rant-economic-spiritual-suicide_n_2094490.html (6) page 71

http://www.cnn.com/2010/WORLD/americas/12/15/mexico.juarez.homicides/index.html (7) page 91

http://www.nytimes.com/2012/01/12/world/americas/mexico-updates-drug-war-death-toll-but-critics-dispute-data.html (8) page 91

http://www.nytimes.com/2011/02/09/world/americas/09juarez.html?pagewanted=all (9) page 91

http://www.huffingtonpost.com/2012/10/29/one-marijuana-arrest-occu_n_2041236.html (10) page 92

http://www.theatlantic.com/politics/archive/2012/04/quote-of-the-day-ted-nugent-threatens-barack-obama/256025/ (11) page 180

http://www.theatlantic.com/politics/archive/2012/04/quote-of-the-day-ted-nugent-threatens-barack-obama/256025/ (12) page 180 http://lybio.net/tag/nugent-compared-obama-and-democrats-to-a-coyote-that-needs-to-be-shot/ (13) page 180

https://www.sportsmansguide.com/Outdoors/Subject/SubjectRead.aspx?sid=0&aid=168256&type=A (14) page 182

https://www.sportsmansguide.com/Outdoors/Subject/SubjectRead.aspx?sid=0&aid=168256&type=A (15) page 183

http://www.washingtontimes.com/news/2010/aug/19/muslim-mosque-teers/?page=all (16) page 184

The Predictioneer's Game Bruce Bueno de Mesquita copyright 2009 page 104 (17) page 202

The Predictioneer's Game Bruce Bueno de Mesquita copyright 2009 page 107 (18) page 204

Forces of Fortune Vali Nasr Copyright 2009 page 11 (19) page 255

http://www.biography.com/people/mahmoud-ahmadinejad-38656?page=2 (20) page 258

http://www.biography.com/people/mahmoud-ahmadinejad-38656?page=2 (21) page 258

http://www.nytimes.com/2008/04/23/world/americas/23iht-23prison.12253738.html?pagewanted=all&_r=1& (22) page 260

http://www.biography.com/people/mahmoud-ahmadinejad-38656?page=3 (23) page 261

https://twitter.com/SarahPalinUSA/status/10935548053 (24) page 261

http://www.nytimes.com/2008/10/12/opinion/12rich.html?_r=0 (25) page 261

http://www.huffingtonpost.com/2010/03/24/sarah-palins-pac-puts-gun_n_511433.html (26) page 261

http://thinkprogress.org/politics/2008/09/02/28464/palin-iraq-god/?mobile=nc (27) page 262

http://open.salon.com/blog/tazlmo/2008/09/12/sarah_palins_church_tied_t
o_jesus_camp_armageddon_dogma (28) page 262

http://www.thedailybeast.com/articles/2011/06/20/bill-clinton-s-ideas-to-
get-america-back-to-work-and-revive-the-economy.html (29) page 267

http://www.goodreads.com/quotes/94502-from-bill-clinton-speech--people-
are-more-impressed-by-the (30) page 267

http://healthland.time.com/2011/12/02/why-medical-marijuana-laws-
reduce-traffic-deaths/ (31) page 276

http://www.christiananswersforthenewage.org/Articles_YinYang.html   (32)
(from the Chuang Tzu as quoted in World Religions, Geoffrey Parrinder, p.
333 page 278

http://www.huffingtonpost.com/jim-moore/rick-perry-
education_b_2421776.html (33) page 331

http://www.dallasnews.com/news/education/headlines/20120528-texas-
schools-short-by-15000-teachers-this-year-analysis-shows.ece (34) page 331

http://thinkprogress.org/economy/2011/06/16/246892/perry-minumum-
wage-jobs/ (35) page 332

http://www.nytimes.com/2013/09/05/opinion/uninsured-in-texas-and-
florida.html (36) page 332

http://www.dentonrc.com/local-news/local-news-headlines/20130816-
report-shows-mental-health-needs-unmet.ece (37) page 332

http://www.brainyquote.com/quotes/authors/r/rahm_emanuel.html   (38)
page 344

http://www.campusprogress.org/articles/ted_nugent (39) page 344

http://www.nytimes.com/2013/07/28/us/politics/interview-with-president-
obama.html?pagewanted=all (40) page 344